To Gertrude
From
Ethel .1927

THE ARISTOCRATIC MISS BREWSTER

THE ARISTOCRATIC MISS BREWSTER

By JOSEPH C. LINCOLN

AUTHOR *of*

"The Big Mogul," "Rugged Water," "Dr. Nye," "Fair Harbor," "Galusha the Magnificent," "Mary 'Gusta," "Queer Judson," "Shavings," "Extricating Obadiah," etc.

A. L. BURT COMPANY

Publishers New York

Published by arrangement with D. Appleton & Company

Printed in U. S. A.

THE ARISTOCRATIC MISS BREWSTER

CHAPTER I

ALL day it had rained and all day the wind had blown savagely from the northeast. The last yellow, desperately clinging leaf had been whipped from the silver-leaf poplar by the front gate and the two tall elms in the yard were naked skeletons of limbs and twigs, which rasped and scraped against each other as the gusts twisted them. All day the gutters had roared and the windowpanes streamed. Now, at five o'clock of this afternoon in November, 1904, the rain had ceased, but the wind blew almost as hard as ever.

Mary Brewster stood by the west window of the sitting room looking out. It was a sodden, dreary scene upon which she looked. The old house, square, white, green-shuttered and red-chimneyed, stood at the top of a little hill. From its paneled and fan-lighted front door the red brick walk, bordered by the inevitable box hedges, sloped down to the just as inevitable white fence and gate which separated the Brewster property from the main road of Wapatomac. Along that road the houses were scattered, shapeless, gloomy blotches against the slaty sky of that dark afternoon, with but the infrequent gleam of a kitchen lamp as evidence that they were inhabited. Not a soul was in sight on the puddle-sprinkled road or sidewalks. The only sounds were the snarling of the wind, the drip from the eaves, or the occasional rattle of a falling branch. A cold, wet, miserable, lonely, depressing outlook. Mary Brewster pulled down the window shade and turned her back upon it. Her spirits needed no external weight to force them lower. They were depressed sufficiently as it was.

She lighted the hanging lamp above the black walnut center table and sat down in the black walnut rocker. From between the leaves of a book upon that table she took an envelope which bore in its upper left-hand corner the name and address of a Boston firm of stockbrokers. From this envelope she drew a letter. She did not read it immediately, however. Instead she sat with the letter in her lap, looking absently across the room at the portrait of great-grandfather Captain Benjamin Brewster, which hung over the mantel. From its frame the portrait frowned back at her with a frozen, if slightly cross-eyed, stare, the uncompromising, disapproving stare which, when she was a little girl, made her hate it. It had hung just in that spot, frowning at her in exactly that same way, ever since she could remember. She looked about the room. That room, and practically everything in it, were as they always had been during her lifetime. They were older, that was all, and they looked it. She, too, was growing old; thirty-five years was her age, according to the entry in the big Bible on the parlor table. Just now she felt at least seventy.

She had been born in that house. Her father was born in it; and her father's father. *His* father was the Captain Benjamin Brewster of the portrait. He it was who, in 1790, built the home in which a Brewster had lived ever since; in which she—one of the two members of the family left alive—was living now. There had been a Benjamin Brewster in Wapatomac since 1710. There was none there now, but that was because her half brother

Benjamin, ten years older than she, had gone out West when he was a young man and was living there yet. At least she supposed he was; she had not heard from him since her mother's death. The Brewsters were the flower of Wapatomac's aristocracy and Wapatomac prided itself upon being an aristocratic town. True, of later years, as the arrogant old sea captains and well-to-do shipowners died and their descendants moved to the cities, so many of the fine old houses were closed during the winter and opened only for a short summer season; but nevertheless Wapatomac was still irreverently termed "Snob Town" by the inhabitants of Wellmouth and Harniss and other communities less regardful of social distinctions.

The old Brewster house was the purest of "pure Colonial." So were all the Brewsters who had lived in it. She, Mary Brewster, was pure Colonial. Just now she devoutly wished she were not. To be the flower of an aristocracy which was slowly but surely going to seed had distinct disadvantages. She was—for she and her half brother did not even correspond—alone in the world. She was thirty-five, single, and, even had there been no other complications—which there most emphatically were—the brightest prospect to which she might reasonably look forward was a life spent in that house, as one more forlorn item in Wapatomac's collection of "old maid" antiques.

Azure Crisp entered the sitting room. Mrs. Crisp was another fixture in that house. Like the portrait of great-grandfather Brewster, Mary could remember her as long as she could remember anything. Azure had not been born a pure Colonial, but years of association with the genuine article had embellished her hit-or-miss architecture with aristocratic trimmings. She was going out that evening, to a supper and meeting of the Ladies of Honor Lodge in its rooms over Gallup's store. Consequently she was arrayed in her purple silk and wore her gold breastpin and jet earrings—also her hair. During morning hours, when at work about the house, Azure's hair was thin, gray, and twisted into a knob at the back of her head. Evenings or Sundays or on special occasions like the present it was thick, elaborately "frizzed," and of ebon blackness. She bustled into the sitting room and sat down with emphasis upon the haircloth sofa.

"There!" she exclaimed with a sigh of relief. "I believe I'm ready, finally. Such a time as I've had this afternoon! Glory's land! I set down to do a little sewin'. I was cal'latin' to see if I couldn't fix up that gray dress of yours, the one you wore to meetin' Sunday. Now of course—"

Miss Brewster interrupted. "Azure," she said, a little sharply, "I have told you that I would attend to that dress myself. I know it is shabby."

Mrs. Crisp's back straightened.

"*I* never said 'twas shabby," she declared, with dignity. "And if anybody else said it they wouldn't but once, while I was around. When a Brewster gets to wearin' shabby clothes then things in this town *will* have come pretty nigh to the finish, I guess. I said it needed a little fixin', that's all. The neck and where the cuffs are let in—and here and there up and around. I saw a real lovely pattern in the Bazar last week and I—"

Once more Mary cut in on the flow of speech. "Azure," she said, firmly. "I don't want you to touch that dress. Put it back in the closet with the others until I see fit to attend to it, myself. Now please."

Azure's gold breastpin quivered with the stir of emotion beneath it.

"The others!" she repeated, tartly. "What others? There's hardly a dress in that closet that isn't as much as five year old. What your mother would say if she could see 'em *I* don't know. She prided herself on havin' you dress accordin' to your station, and always did. The very last words—that is, almost about the last she said to me—on her deathbed, 'twas—says she to me: 'Azure,' she says, 'you'll look after my poor girl, won't you?' Says I to her, 'Annabelle,' I says, ' "This world is all a fleetin' show, for man's profusion given," ' and woman's, too, I guess, but— Eh? What was you goin' to say?"

Mary was smiling faintly. "I was wondering why you said that," she explained, and added, hastily: "Not that it matters."

"That? What? Oh, about man's profusion and the rest of it? Well, I'd been readin' some lovely poetry in a book I got out of the library. Thomas Moore's poems 'twas. You know how poetry gets aholt of me sometimes. I said it 'cause my head was full of it and it fitted, that's why. . . . Mary Brewster, why don't you march yourself right straight down to Emma Holway's and have some new dresses made? I do wish you cared more about such things."

Mary's smile faded. "I care about them, Azure," she said, quietly. "And I shall have the dresses made when I can—when I get around to it. . . . You'll be late at your lodge meeting, won't you?"

"No. Or if I am it won't make much difference. They never do anything the first half hour but sit and chirp and chipper all at the same time, like a passel of swallows strung along a telegraph wire. Mary, now that I'm talkin' to you I might as well cruise right ahead and say what's on my mind. Have you told Frank Simmons to come here and do the carpenterin', same as you said you would? He ain't come, anyway. And every time it rains, same as it did last night and to-day, there's a new set of leaks up garret. I've been droppin' my sewin' and runnin' 'round settin' pans and kettles under them leaks till it seems as if I should die. It ain't a question of patchin' any more. The whole all roof ought to be shingled."

"I know it, Azure."

"Yes. Well, that's only the beginnin'. There's four more pickets blowed off the front fence."

"Really? Oh dear! I'm sorry."

"Yes, there is. And if the henhouse isn't whitewashed pretty soon the hens won't be able to find it on a dark day."

Mary sighed. "I suppose *I* could whitewash that henhouse," she observed. "I like to paint, you know."

Mrs. Crisp was horrified. "My glory's land!" she exclaimed. "*You*—a Brewster—startin' in to whitewash a henhouse! Oh, now, Mary, *don't* set there and make fun. *You* know the shinglin' and whitewashin' and all the rest ought to be done, just same as I know it. Now don't you?"

"Yes," wearily. "Yes, Azure, I know it well enough."

"Then why don't you see to it? 'Tain't as if you couldn't afford it. You've got money enough to do anything."

"Have I?"

"*Have* you? Why, how you talk! What ails you this afternoon—yes, and all day yesterday, too? You've been mopin' around like—like Galahad after he ate that last rat he caught out in the barn. Rats always make him sick; but he's possessed to eat 'em just the same. I give that cat dinner enough to—to—well, so's he's so fat he can hardly waddle and yet, this very day, he waddled straight out in the rain and came back with a great big rat in his mouth. Lugged it into my kitchen, too, and I never noticed it till I was hurryin' over to the sink with a kettle full of bilin' water in my hand. Then I pretty nigh scalded myself to death and him, too. I screeched right out, and he yowled and the kettle lid went a-flyin' and—Well, there! I must go, I suppose, and I haven't said half I meant to. Mary, you will see about gettin' those new dresses and about the carpenterin' and all the rest of it? You won't just set right down and forget, will you?"

Miss Brewster drew a long breath. "I won't forget, Azure," she announced. "I promise you that."

"I hope you mean it; but you're *so* absent-minded lately. This family's got a position to keep up in the town and there's only you and me left to keep it up."

"All right, all right, Azure. Good night. Have a good time."

"I'll have as good a one as I can. If they'd only talk about somethin' worth while down at that lodge I'd have a better. *I* suggested takin' up Shakespeare and talkin' about his writin's; either him or Brownin' or somebody. Ever since that Boston woman gave that elocution readin' from Brownin' down to the First Church vestry I've just been brimmin' full of him, as you might say. I got his poems out of the library and I read 'em and read 'em. So I says: 'Why not discuss Brownin' at *our* meetin's?' But that Marietta Beasley woman—you know what *she* is—she spoke up and says: 'Maybe *you* know what Brownin's all about, but I declare *I* don't.' 'Well,' says I, 'maybe I don't, either, but what of it? Any numbskull can talk about somethin' they know all about.' Well, there now; let me see. Your supper's all laid out on the dinin'-room table, Mary, and the teapot's on the back of the stove. . . . I hope you won't be lonesome. I hate to leave you alone."

"I shall be all right. I expect a caller pretty soon. Captain Cummings is coming to see me, or he sent word he would."

Azure was at the door, on her way to the hall closet where she kept her bonnet and cape. Now she turned.

"Who?" she asked, in surprise. "Dave Cummings? Comin' here to see you? What for?"

"I asked him to come. Something about one of my investments."

"Oh! . . . Humph! . . . Well, Dave Cummings is a smart business man, I suppose likely. Though why they ever made him president of the Wapatomac bank is more than I can make out, with a half dozen *real* fine men to pick from, men that used to sail all over the world in command of their own ships—not just little mackerel boats, which was all Dave Cummings ever skippered. I guess he's smart enough about money and all that, but he's as common as dishwater. Why wouldn't he be? His father was only a clam digger. As for old Barney Cummings, his grandfather—well, if there's anybody who can get on my nerves it's that old critter. I just can't *stand* him, that's all. Why, when—"

Mary Brewster rose from the rocker. The feud between Mrs. Crisp and old Captain Barnabas Cummings was of long standing. When the housekeeper got on that subject it required desperate measures to stop her.

"I know, I know, Azure," she put in, hastily. "Now run along, please. Captain Cummings may be here any moment now. You'll be awfully late if you don't hurry. Good night."

Mrs. Crisp went out, as far as the hall, but a moment later, arrayed in her sealskin cape and bonnet—the cape an inheritance from the late Mrs. Brewster, Mary's mother—she looked in at the sitting-room door to fire a final shot.

"I'm thankful it's pretty nigh dark already," she declared with fervor. "Melissa Knowles won't be able to make out who 'tis comin' here, that's some comfort. What your father, or your mother—to say nothin' of your grandmother—would think of a Cummings comin' to this house—except to peddle clams at the back door—*I* don't know. Mary Brewster, don't you let him stay a minute longer than it's needful, will you? I—I almost wish I wasn't goin' to lodge meetin'."

She went, however, and Mary, closing the front door behind her, breathed a sigh of relief. Then she returned to her chair by the table and again opened and read the letter from Bolles and Snell, the Boston brokers. It was a long letter and every word was like a ton weight upon her spirits and—yes, her conscience. If only she had heeded Captain Cummings' advice and had not bought the Boroda stock. If only she had not gone to see Mr. Snell in the beginning. But she was desperate. Snell, Senior, had been a friend of her father's; he had handled the latter's investments during his lifetime. The present Snell, his son, of course knew nothing as to the amount of the Brewster fortune. Like every one else—except Mary herself—he accounted Mary Brewster a rich woman. But she was far from that. When her mother's estate was settled by the executor, Judge Baxter of Ostable, since dead, the income from it netted scarcely three thousand a year. The old house and all the real property were left to Mary, but brother Benjamin, in Denver, shared equally with her in money and securities. Consequently Mary's annual income from her share of these was less than fifteen hundred. The Brewster house was old, it needed constant repair; so did the barn and outbuildings. The upkeep of the place was considerable. And, as Azure had reminded her that very evening, a Brewster had a position to maintain. She did her best to maintain it, economizing in every way she could contrive, postponing the needful repairs until the very last minute, scrimping herself in the matter of clothes, of little personal comforts, everything but the barest necessities. And always, of course, hiding from every one her reasons for so doing. Even Azure's modest wage had become a burden, but Azure Crisp was as much a part of that house as its rooftree. It is doubtful if she would have given up her situation even if ordered to do so. And Mary could never have given the order. If the proud old Brewster ship must sink it might as well go down with all hands. Azure should—she would anyway—stay in that house as long as its mistress.

But something had to be done, it must be done. She went to Boston and called upon Mr. Snell. She did not tell him how poor she was. She had meant to, but the Brewster pride was too strong. Instead she told him merely that she felt she should have more money than she was receiving from her investments and asked him how that money might be provided. "Other people make money, a lot of money, in the stock market," she said. "I know they do. Why can't I? I want to make some money, Mr. Snell. Tell me how to make it."

Snell gave her the customary caution against speculation. "Of course I might suggest certain stocks which I believe are almost sure to increase largely in value," he said, "but with the chance of profit there is always a corresponding chance of loss. If I were you—"

But Mary insisted. Still protesting, she laughingly declared that she was determined to make money somehow and did not see why she should not succeed in the stock market as well as others. Snell, after reflection, suggested several stocks in the future of which he believed. Among them, and offering perhaps, the most glittering possibility, were the shares of the Boroda Copper Company.

"The Boroda people have a fine prospect out there," he said. "From what I hear from reliable sources the property they own is in the richest section of copper production. They have only just begun to mine, of course, but the ore already taken out is very good indeed. I believe in the thing myself and I have personally bought several thousand shares. Of course, as I say, it is a risk. You never can tell."

He was so reluctant to have her act immediately upon the suggestion that she promised to give the matter a few days' consideration. But her mind was really made up before she took the train to Wapatomac. The day after her arrival there she dropped in at the local bank, and the little room at the rear where, between the hours of eleven and one, Captain David Cummings, the bank's president, was sure to be found.

She had known Dave Cummings since she was a little girl. He was older than she, a big boy in the "upstairs" grade at school when she attended "downstairs," in the primary department. Later on, he and she had met often, never at her house or his, but at public functions, amateur dramatic entertainments at the town hall, or during her short period of attendance at Mr. Hathaway's dancing school, a period which her mother had ended abruptly the night when young Cummings had "seen her home" after the evening lesson was over. In Annabelle Brewster's eyes for a Cummings to act as escort for her daughter was presumption unparalleled.

"I am sorry, Mr. Hathaway," she said, when the dancing master called timidly seeking an explanation of his pupil's absence, "but I have decided to have Mary take private lessons with Miss Danby in Ostable. Oh no, I have no fault to find with your teaching. This seems best to me, that is all."

And Hathaway, quite aware of the sharp line of social distinction in "Snob Town," understood and argued no further. Between the families of the aristocracy and the common herd was a great gulf fixed. To be of the former one must have, not only money, but fathers and grandfathers who had commanded, perhaps owned, square-rigged deep-sea merchantmen; one must reside in one of the fine old houses like the Brewster house; must attend, control and support the old First Church, founded in 1698. Others—poor relations, or family retainers like Mrs. Crisp, or occasional vouched-for newcomers like Doctor Hamilton and his wife, or Peter Hall, the bank cashier—were permitted to attend services or "socials" or other functions of that church, but they were neither encouraged nor expected to offer opinions concerning its management or the kind of religion preached from its pulpit. The remainder of Wapatomac's churchgoing residents attended the "New Meetinghouse" on the lower road. The First Church had its own cemetery, neat, select and enclosed within a granite and iron fence. The "New Church burying ground" was on the outskirts of the village and its fence was of wood.

The Cummings family was, so far as term of residence in Wapatomac was concerned, as old as the Brewsters. But there resemblance ended. The Cummingses had been fishermen and longshoremen from the beginning. Captain Barnabas, David's grandfather, had for forty years owned and commanded the mackerel schooner *Sophia*. His son, David's father, had sailed and fished with him until the *Sophia* was wrecked in the great gale of 1898. His ambition seemed to have been wrecked with the schooner and, after the catastrophe, he was content to do "odd jobs" and, as Mrs. Crisp said, to peddle clams and fish in the village. He was dead now. During the last few years of his life his son, David, supported him.

For David *was* ambitious. Even as a boy he had been a hard worker, shrewd, saving and capable. He worked and planned and prospered. Now, at middle age, he was the head of D. Cummings & Co., wholesale dealers in oysters and shellfish, with buildings at the Narrows where Scallop River joins the South Harbor. Always, except in the brief season when the river was frozen, sloops, scows and an occasional fore and aft schooner were moored at or near the Cummings wharves, and a dozen dories and as many men were busy. David had commanded his own schooner at one time, hence his title of Captain. Later, as his business grew, he gave his attention to that. He dabbled a little in local politics, was a member of the Board of Selectmen and, for the past few years, had been president of the Wapatomac bank. It was the first time in the institution's history that one other than an ancient, dignified, retired captain of a square-rigger had filled its presidential chair. The fact that David Cummings had been chosen to fill it was a testimonial to his honesty and business ability. The commoners among the townspeople respected and trusted him and looked up to him. The aristocracy shared the trust, but, socially speaking, continued to look condescendingly down upon him. After all, he was only a Cummings and the Cummingses did not attend the First Church, nor, when they died, were they buried inside the granite and iron fence.

Nevertheless, in spite of all this, the members of Wapatomac's inner circle felt perfectly safe in entrusting their bank accounts to his care. And it was to him that Mary Brewster had gone, the day following her return from Boston, to ask his opinion of Boroda Copper.

Captain David had listened intently to her questions. He took some time to reflect before he answered. Then he said:

"Why, yes, I do know somethin' about the Boroda stock, as it happens. Last week, when I was up to Boston, seein' about some loans and other bank matters, the Boston bank fellow I was talkin' with had a good deal to say about it. He seemed to think it was more or less of a sure thing. Anybody who went into it, he said, and could afford to hang on long enough, would make money—probably. He gave me the company's statement and a whole lot of printed stuff and I took it back here with me and read it, careful. You see, I—well," with evident fear that she might consider him as boasting, "once in a while—a great while—I have a little extra money to put by and sometimes I take a little flyer in a stock that looks liable to make a good turnover. And this Boroda Copper, I give in, does look a good deal that way."

Mary's eyes sparkled. "Oh!" she cried. "Then you think I should buy it. I'm so glad. I wanted to very much."

He shook his head. "No," he said, firmly. "No. I don't think you should. I think you'd better stay out of it."

She leaned back in her chair. "Why?" she demanded, surprise and disappointment in her tone. "Why do you say that? This banker—you just said so—thought it was almost a sure thing. And you said yourself you thought it might be."

"Yes, so I did. But 'might' is the word that counts there. It might—and then again it might not. Any minin' property, any new one anyhow, is risky at the best."

"Captain Cummings, tell me the truth. Did *you* buy any of that Boroda stock? For yourself, I mean. . . . I believe you did."

He was a little embarrassed at first. Then he smiled, a smile which broadened and ended in a laugh.

"Well—yes," he admitted. "Yes, I did. I bought a pretty fair-sized block of it, if you must know. Whether I was a fool or not remains to be seen."

She nodded triumphantly. "I thought so," she declared. "I don't know why, unless it was because you looked so—

so guilty. You bought that very stock, a lot of it, and yet you sit there and tell me not to. If you can explain *that* I shall be obliged."

He shrugged his broad shoulders. "I bought it," he said, "as a chance that looked to be worth takin'. I had a little extra money, some I wasn't expectin', and I took a risk with it, that's all. If I win—first rate. If I lose I shan't be very much worse off than I was before that extra money dropped in. *But,*" he added, very earnestly, "I never would have let this bank buy any of it. No, and I wouldn't advise you, or any one else to buy it. It isn't an investment really, not a sure, safe one. It looks good now; that's the best I can say for it."

She persisted, feminine fashion.

"But you did buy it," she asserted. "And if you did, why shouldn't I?"

He ran a big, sunburned hand through his thick hair.

"It's—it's kind of hard for me to say just what I'm thinkin'," he replied, hesitatingly. "I haven't got any right to say it, really. I don't know—naturally, I don't—how you—er—well, how much you can afford to risk in a thing like this. Your investments now, and your income, they—well, they are your own business, you see."

"Certainly they are," with dignity.

"Yes. Yes, of course. Don't think I'm tryin' to pry into 'em. But if I had a mother, or a sister, or even a friend, whose money was invested in sound securities that brought in a fair income, I'd surely tell 'em to be satisfied with that and not go playin' with a minin' stock. You see," he added, with a smile, "this buyin' a fog bank cheap with the idea that it may turn out to be a rain cloud by and by has got two sides to it. Just as likely as not the wind comes up no'thwest and blows everything clear. If you've got a few spare thousand that's troublin' you and you feel you can afford to go fishin' with it—that's one thing. But if it's goin' to hurt to lose the bait then—well then, I should say don't touch Boroda Copper."

This was his advice, the opinion she had come there to ask. But, nevertheless, on the afternoon mail of the very day of this interview she wrote to Bolles and Snell ordering them to sell certain bonds which were hers and invest the proceeds in shares of the Boroda Copper Company.

And since then, for a period of two months, she had been an eager searcher of the financial columns of the *Boston Advertiser*. During the first six weeks what she found there was pleasant. Nothing to cause undue excitement, but distinctly pleasant. Boroda shares had risen slightly in value day by day. And then they began to drop —drop. Now they were selling at a figure much below that which she had paid for them. Her anxious letter to Mr. Snell had brought the reply which she was now reading for the fourth time. Snell had written that news from the Boroda development was not as reassuring as it might be, as he had confidently expected it to be. The vein of ore which the new company had been working was far less rich than at first. Apparently the main copper deposit was deeper down than they had expected. Consequently they must go after it. New machinery would be needed, and soon.

"It is nothing to worry about, I feel sure," he wrote. "It means delay, of course, perhaps a delay of a year or even more, but every one on the inside is as confident as ever; I am, myself. I did my best to make clear to you that Boroda was a speculation, not a certain investment, and, as you bought with that understanding, why, although the temporary shrinkage in price is a disappointment, I take it that it is not of great importance to you. Hold on, and in the end, I feel certain you will make money."

"Hold on"— "A year or more!" And meanwhile her income, instead of being greater, was smaller by the interest on the bonds she had sold. She had been barely able to make both ends meet before. Now it seemed impossible to do even that. And the repairs, and clothes, and all the rest! After two dreadful days and two sleepless nights she had so far resolved: First, that calling herself wicked and a fool for buying the copper stock in spite of Snell's and Captain Cummings' advice was, although she continued to do it, of no practical use. Second, that she must do something which was useful and practical and do it at once. Her ideas of what that something was to be were of the vaguest. She had dropped in at the bank that morning and left a note asking Captain David to call and see her on a matter of business. He had sent word that he would do so "just before supper time." It was Wapatomac's supper time now.

And, as she sat there, the letter drooping despairingly from her fingers, she heard his step upon the walk.

CHAPTER II

SHE hastily replaced the letter between the pages of the book on the table and hurried to the hall. Her hand was upon the knob of the massive front door and she was about to open it, before she realized that she was not allowing him time even to knock. For her, a Brewster, to appear so eager to admit a caller as all that was to say the least undignified. What would Azure say if she were present? And that caller a Cummings! Azure would have allowed him to knock three times before deigning to open. Mary's dignity was far below the high plane of Mrs. Crisp's, but she waited, nevertheless. She must be careful—very careful. She had determined to make perfectly plain to Captain David that she was in earnest in what she should say to him, but she was just as determined that even he should not guess the desperate need behind her appeal for advice. No one should guess that, no one in Wapatomac.

She stood there, waiting, until the knocker on the other side of the door squeaked upward and fell with a clang. Then, after another brief wait, she opened the door.

"Oh, good evening, Captain Cummings," she said. "I imagined it might be you. Azure is out; she has gone down to the lodge supper. Won't you come in?"

He entered. He was a big man and wore a heavy and shaggy overcoat and a blue cloth yachting cap with a leather visor, the usual headgear of most Wapatomac men, those not members of the aristocracy, at that period. He removed the cap and stood there looking down at her. His florid cheeks were even redder than usual, for he had walked fast and faced the wind all the way up the hill.

"Good evenin', good evenin'," he said. "I've kept you waitin', I'm afraid. Weren't just in the middle of supper, were you?"

"Oh, no, indeed! I didn't expect you before. I am glad to see you. Thank you very much for coming. Won't you throw off your coat?"

"Eh? No, no, I guess not. My own supper's about ready, I suppose, and the Skipper and Kohath will give me an overhaulin' if I'm too late."

"The Skipper" was his pet name for old Captain Barnabas Cummings, his grandfather. Kohath Briggs was the Cummings "help," a veteran who had worked at many trades during his lifetime, but had succeeded in making a living only at the one he hated, namely that of cook. He had cooked for Captain Barney aboard the *Sophia,* and it was on the old gentleman's recommendation that Captain David had hired him in that capacity six years before. Mary knew them both, of course, and they were favorite subjects of Azure Crisp's conversation—particularly when she was "out of sorts" and seeking a vent for her feelings.

Miss Brewster led the way to the sitting room and her caller followed her. At her invitation he sat down upon the sofa. She took the rocker. Captain Dave, bolt upright beneath the portrait of great-grandfather Brewster, appeared distinctly ill at ease. She had suggested that he leave his cap on the hall table, but he had brought it with him and did not seem to know exactly what to do with it. He laid it upon the sofa beside him and it slid from the shiny haircloth to the floor. He picked it up and again it slid to the carpet. This time he laid it on his knee and held it there with his hand.

Mary noticed his obvious embarrassment with some surprise. In his office at the bank, where day after day he was, as she knew, accustomed to meet all sorts of people, he never seemed awkward or embarrassed. Why he should appear so uncomfortable just now she could not understand. And yet Azure would have understood. During David Cummings' forty-two years of life he had crossed the threshold of the Brewster house but twice before. He had attended Captain Ben Brewster's funeral and that of his wife, but most of Wapatomac kept him company on those occasions. His visit this time was quite a different matter. Every tradition of Wapatomac was broken by a member of his family calling upon one of hers. Captain Dave Cummings was by no means the possessor of what, in these psychologic days, would be termed an "inferiority complex"; he was self-respecting and bowed the knee to no one. But custom is custom and Wapatomac was Wapatomac.

He clutched the cap tightly and made a remark concerning the weather. It was still blowing a living gale of wind, he observed. Mary said it sounded as if it were. Then she thanked him again for taking the trouble to climb the hill in such a gale.

"Oh, that's all right, that's all right," he said, hastily. "Not a mite of trouble. Does me good to stretch my legs after keepin' 'em folded up astern of a desk most of the afternoon. Sorry I wasn't in when you traveled way down to the bank in the rain," he added. "I was a little mite late this mornin'."

"No, I was early. . . . But you got my note? Yes, of

course you did. You answered it and you are here now. That was a ridiculous question, wasn't it?"

She was beginning to share his embarrassment. What she had to say to him was so—so personal and so hard to say! If he would only ask her what she wanted. But he did not. He sat there and waited, that was all.

"I—I haven't asked about your family," she said, in desperation. "They are well, I hope?"

This remark was more inane than the other. He was a bachelor.

"I mean your grandfather," she explained, reddening. "How is he?"

This seemed to amuse him. He chuckled.

"Oh, he is lively as a June bug in May," he replied. "The Skipper will be eighty-two in January, but you would never guess it. He's talkin' already about what he's goin' to plant in the garden next spring. He is the youngest one in our house and Kohath is next. Kohath is over sixty himself. They are a pair, those two. Compared to them I'm all of a hundred and twenty."

He chuckled again at the thought. Mary did not find it amusing. "Oh, don't talk about ages," she said, impulsively. "It's a hateful subject, *I* think."

He nodded. "That's because you are young," he observed. "I'm not so old myself that my birthdays don't keep addin' on in the regular way. The Skipper and Kohath now, theirs subtract, seems so. The Skipper had whoopin' cough last summer. I told him I'd been expectin' he might. 'By the time you're a hundred,' I said to him, 'you'll be young enough to have the croup.' Ho, ho!"

She made no comment. He went on.

"The Skipper reads every word of the 'Wapatomac Jottin's' in the *Item* the minute the paper comes to hand," he continued. "Reads 'em and has an opinion ready to spring on me soon's I get home. And before that he's tried 'em out on Kohath. Course Kohath's opinions are always just the opposite. If the Skipper says 'Port' Kohath says 'Starboard,' and they're off. They never agree on anything while they are by themselves, but you let an outsider come aboard and they agree on everything —everything the outsider doesn't, I mean. I don't know what I should do," he added, "if I didn't have that pair around to keep me stirred up and interested. Be pretty lonesome, I guess."

He looked up at her with a smile. She managed to smile also, but it was with an effort.

"It must be wonderful," she said, "to have things which interest you and keep you busy. I don't think you should talk about being lonely, Captain David. You have your oyster business and the bank—and, oh, a thousand things. All your life long you have done what you wanted to do. No one has told you you mustn't do this or you shouldn't do that. And now look at you! You are comfortable and prosperous and respected and—oh, everything! You have done it all yourself, too. . . . Lonely!" with a sudden catch in her voice. "Oh, how can you! You don't know what the word means."

She had not intended to say so much, certainly not to permit the way she felt from expressing itself so obviously. She had intended to be dignified and casual at first; then gradually to lead up to the important subject of their interview. If only he had not mentioned ages and loneliness! She was provoked at him for mentioning them and more provoked with herself for permitting them to trap her into such a premature revelation of her state of mind. Now it was too late. He was regarding her with astonishment and some concern.

"Why—why, what's all this?" he asked, quickly, and before she could continue. "Why do you say—"

"Oh, never mind!" she put in, hastily. "I beg your pardon for saying it. I shouldn't have, of course. I am—I am nervous to-night and I—well, I scarcely know what I am saying, I'm afraid. I want to talk with you, Captain Cummings, about—about ever so many things."

He was still looking at her intently.

"Hum," he observed, after a moment. "You're nervous, you say. Why?"

"Oh—because I am. I have enough to make me so."

"I'm sorry to hear that. Trouble of some sort, eh? I hope nothing serious."

"Serious enough. I am—I am perfectly wretched. Yes, and desperate. That is why I asked you to come here. I must talk to some one. Captain Cummings, will you let me talk to you? Yes, and will you help me, if you can? Try to help me? Somebody *must.*"

The dignity and calm had again fled. There was no attempt at pretense now. The cap slid from his knee to the floor and he did not pick it up. He leaned forward on the sofa.

"Why—why, sure I will, Mary," he said, earnestly. "I'll help any way I can, of course. Only I don't see—You are desperate, you say? What does that mean? What's gone wrong?"

She shook her head. "Everything!" she declared. "Just everything. Nothing is right."

He absently ran his hand through his hair. He had combed it very carefully before leaving the office, but he forgot that now. He rumpled it until it bristled. He was thinking hard.

"Humph!" he mused. "So nothin's right, eh? Humph! . . . Mary, in your note you wrote that you wanted to see me on a matter of business. I took it for granted that it was some—well, some money business, like—like that Boroda Copper matter you came to see me about a couple of months ago. I'm thankful I said for you not to buy that copper stock. That company's sort of run aground from what I hear, and it may be some time before they get it afloat again—if they do. If you'd bought that stock . . . but, thank goodness, you didn't."

This last sentence was not precisely a question, but there was a hint of question in it. It forced Mary Brewster to the realization that she must be more careful. The subject of Boroda Copper was the very one she had meant should not be broached during their talk. No one in Wapatomac should know she had bought that stock, least of all this man whose advice she had asked—and disregarded the day it was given. She was prepared to confess a good deal but not that—to him. She must be more guarded, she must be. She fought for composure and regained it, in a measure. Her next speech was calm enough certainly and it had nothing to do with Boroda Copper.

"I don't wonder you think it odd I should break out in this way," she said, trying to smile. "I must have sounded as if I were on the verge of suicide. Well, I am not. It isn't as desperate as all that. It is just that, as I said before, I have reached the point when I must talk to some one and you were the only one I could think of. Captain Cummings, I want to do something in this world, do it on my own account."

He rumpled his hair again. His expression of puzzled bewilderment was funny. She laughed, in spite of herself.

"And you can't guess what I mean by that, can you," she said. "I don't wonder. Well, now listen, and I'll explain. To begin with, no matter whether you are lonely or not, I am. Terribly lonely. I said I was desperate—and that is true, too. If you were shut up in this big house with not a single worth-while thing to occupy your mind from week to week-end you would be as desperate as I am. I can't stand it any longer, Captain David, I want to work."

If the Queen of England had come to him with a similar declaration it could not have sounded more ridiculous. The Brewster men had always been hard workers, during their working years; but the Brewster women—! He stared.

"Work!" he repeated. "You! . . . Oh, come now, what's the joke?"

"There isn't any joke at all. I am very serious. *Don't* look like that—please. I don't mean I want to shovel sand or—or open oysters at your wharf. I mean that I have made up my mind to do something, some sort of work, that will keep me busy and—yes, bring me in a little more money. And I hope you can help me to find that work. . . . Oh, *please!"* impatiently; "don't sit there and stare as if I were asking you to help me commit murder. There's nothing so terrible about it."

One word in this statement had made an impression upon his mind. All the rest he would have dismissed as a "woman's notion." His experience with women had not been extensive, but during his occupancy of the president's chair at the bank he had been consulted by a number of widows and spinsters and they were full of "notions" most of which were impractical. But the word "money" meant something. It might explain what otherwise was quite unexplainable.

"Well, well!" he said, after a moment. "I guess I understand—a little anyhow. So you want more money, eh? Well, lots of folks would keep you company there. Most everybody wants more than they've got. But—Humph! Thinkin' of shiftin' some of your investments, were you? I'll be glad to look over the list with you. It isn't a bad idea to do that every once in a while, anyhow."

She shook her head. "That isn't the point at all," she declared. "I wish I could make you understand. I want to work. And I shall work—somehow and in some way. Now listen and I'll tell you just the situation."

She did tell him. Not the whole but enough to make plain the reasons for her determination. She explained that her income was not nearly as large as people imagined it to be. She wanted money to spend for the house, on herself, for clothes, for all sorts of things. She was obliged to figure closely and it irked her to have to do it.

"Humph!" he observed, when she paused momentarily. "Yes, yes. Well, perhaps that isn't so desperate. Maybe we can find a way to help that state of affairs. We can try anyhow. Suppose you get that list—"

But she broke in. She had no intention of letting him see that list.

"Never mind the securities," she said, hastily. "They are well enough, I guess—what there is of them. But lack of money isn't the whole trouble, although I suppose if I had enough of it the other troubles might settle themselves. I haven't a thing in this world to keep me interested. I am all alone in this house. Day after day I sit here by myself and think until it seems as if I should go crazy. Azure is with me, of course, and she talks and talks and talks, but never of anything except the shingles off the roof and the pickets off the fence, and the new clothes I ought to have and the neighbors and the church squabbles and the cat and the rats and the teakettle and—oh, mercy, I don't know! I can't stand it, Captain Cummings. I *won't* stand it. If I sit here any longer with my hands folded I shall *die*. . . . Now what shall I do?"

She was very close to tears; but even yet it was clear that he did not wholly understand, although he was trying hard to do so.

"Humph!" he mused, reflectively. "Humph! Yes—yes, I suppose maybe it *is* kind of dull for you, although to give in I shouldn't have thought of it that way. With this fine house to look after, and the church work and all, I should have supposed that you'd be kept pretty busy."

"Busy!" scornfully. "Busy fretting and worrying myself into the grave. That is precisely the sort of business I want to get away from."

He was struck with what he evidently considered a bright idea.

"Then *get* away from it," he said. "Do just that very thing. Pack up and go somewhere else for a change. Go off on a trip. Get clear of Wapatomac and Azure Crisp and the front fence and the cat and the teakettle. Go away for a while and forget 'em. That's my prescription."

She sighed wearily. "I am afraid I haven't made it plain enough, after all," she said. "Your prescription isn't exactly new. The last time I had a cold and Azure insisted on sending for Doctor Hamilton he suggested that a sea voyage might be of benefit. Perhaps it would. No doubt a trip around the world would be a wonderful thing for me. Unfortunately it would be expensive. If I can't afford to live here I can scarcely afford to travel. I should think that was fairly obvious, Captain Cummings."

"But I wasn't thinkin' of your goin' around the world. You've got lots of friends—must have. I haven't got so many, of course, but even I can think of a half dozen who would be glad to see me if I dropped in on 'em for a fortni't or so. They've said so lots of times and I guess likely they mean it. With all the friends you must have, and your father and mother had, why—"

"Oh, don't! We are wasting time. Friends? Why yes, I have friends and they often invite me to visit them. But to do that I should need new clothes, and money to spend, and I haven't got it."

"Now, now wait a minute. I've just thought of the very thing. Your brother Ben—out West there—in Denver, ain't he? You could go and see him. He wouldn't care about your clothes. It is you he would want to see. Of course he would!"

She shrugged. "You are taking a good deal for granted," she said. "My half brother and I are far more like strangers than relatives. I have seen him but twice in twenty years and I never hear from him. He would be the last person on earth I should dream of visiting. And I can't visit any one. I can't go anywhere.

And I can't stay here, either—as I am. Captain Cummings, you *must* understand that I mean exactly what I say. I want to do something, something which will keep my mind occupied and for which I shall be paid, even if the pay is small. I'm not clever, but I won't believe I am quite a fool. You know ever so many business people in Boston, or Denboro or Ostable—everywhere. And they know you. Isn't there somebody who could give me a position of some kind? I don't much care—no, I don't really care what sort of position it is, so long as it is respectable and pays a salary. . . . There! that is the exact, plain truth. I mean every word of it. Now do you believe I am in earnest?"

He was obliged to believe. But his astonishment was not lessened by that belief. He picked up the cap from the floor and sat twisting it between his hands.

"Humph! . . . Pshaw!" he muttered. "Mary, I—well, I must say! Then—then the matter of business you sent for me to talk about was this, eh? You want me to help you find a—a job? I mean—"

"'Job' will do perfectly well. Other Wapatomac girls and women have their 'jobs.' Why shouldn't I? I won't believe I am more stupid than they are."

He whistled between his teeth. She persisted.

"Do you think I am?" she demanded.

"Eh? No, no! Course I don't. I've known you all your life. You're the last one I'd call that. And I've known your family. If there ever was a stupid Brewster then he or she never crossed my bows."

"Well, then!"

"That's just it. You *are* a Brewster. If your name

was Oaks or Beasley or—well, Cummings, it would be different."

"Suppose it was. What of it?"

"Eh? Well, then I suppose likely I shouldn't have been sittin' here on this sofa for half an hour, like a pullet on a roost, without makin' a cackle that was worth listenin' to. I'd have understood what you were after in the beginnin'."

"You understand it now. And if you will be good enough to forget my name, or try and think it *is* Beasley or Oaks or—anything but what it is—I shall be very much obliged. If I wished to be reminded of my family name Azure would do it for me. She takes pains, a dozen times a day, to remind me that I am a Brewster. For a month or more I have been wishing I were anything *but* that. If I were a Beasley I should probably have been self-respecting and self-supporting long before this."

"Hum. . . . Have you got any idea as to the kind of—of work you'd like to do?"

"Not definitely—no. I have tried to think, but thinking hasn't helped me at all. I can paint a little—so can a hundred others. The market for hand-painted chocolate sets and velvet panels ornamented with sprays of goldenrod isn't extensive. I embroider fairly well, but there are women in our own sewing circle who are far better at it than I. Those are my accomplishments and I am not proud of them. I *am* fairly accurate at figures. I studied bookkeeping at the academy, when I was away at school, and I used to help father with his money affairs; he was interested in a number of small business ventures after he retired from the sea. He was very particular and, even when I was a girl, he insisted on my keeping a personal expense account. I have kept one ever since, and kept it correctly. Unfortunately I know it is correct now—too discouragingly correct."

He was looking at her with a peculiar expression.

"So you can keep books, eh?" he murmured. "I didn't know that."

"Of course you didn't. And perhaps I can't, really. I don't pretend that I could keep an elaborate set of books."

"No-o. . . . Still you could learn, I suppose."

"I suppose I might, if any one gave me the opportunity —and was patient."

"Humph! . . . Sho!"

Again he was rumpling his hair and the expression upon his face was still peculiar. He looked like a person to whose mind had suddenly flashed a most unexpected idea, an idea which was intriguing but disturbing. After a moment of anxious expectancy she could wait no longer.

"What is it, Captain Cummings?" she begged. "You are thinking of something, I can see that. Have you—oh, *do* you know of a chance for me? Do you?"

He had dropped the cap again, but now he picked it up and sat absently crumpling it between his palms as before.

"Pshaw!" he muttered impatiently. "I'm gettin' into the habit of thinkin' out loud, I guess. It's a bad habit, too, and I don't need any extra ones—of that kind."

"But you do know of something. You have just thought of it. I can see you have. Oh, don't keep me waiting. What is it, please?"

He was evidently loath to reply. And the reply, when it came was noncommittal.

"Why—why, yes, Mary," he admitted. "Yes, I do

know of a place where a sort of assistant bookkeeper is goin' to be needed pretty soon."

"You do? . . . Really?"

"Yes, I do. And so do a dozen others; although it's been agreed, for reasons, not to tell outsiders until a decision is made. I shouldn't have let the cat out of the bag, even to you. I shouldn't have done it. Your sayin' you could keep books caught me asleep on watch."

"I'm glad it did. If there is any hope for me anywhere I must know it. Where is it that a bookkeeper will be needed, Captain Cummings?"

He shook his head. "That I can't tell you—yet," he said. "And you mustn't pin any real hope in it, because —well, because—"

She finished the sentence for him.

"*I* see," she sighed. "You think I wouldn't be competent to fill the place. No doubt you are right. I don't suppose I am competent to do anything worth while."

He raised the hand with the crumpled cap in it in protest.

"Now, now, now," he cautioned, "you mustn't say that. It isn't true and I wasn't thinkin' any such thing. I shouldn't wonder if you could fill the bill. It might be kind of strange and hard for you along at first, but you would pull through. Of course you would!" with absolute conviction. "You could do anything you set your mind to."

"Could I? Thank you. I wish I were as certain as you pretend to be."

"No pretendin' about it. You could do it. The only thing is that—no, there are a lot of things. First, there has never been a woman at that desk. It's always been a man."

"What of that? Women are doing such work more and more. In Boston offices I have seen ever so many women bookkeepers. So have you; you must have."

"Um-hum. I have. But that was Boston, not Wapatomac. Mary, what do you suppose Wapatomac would say if you, Captain Ben Brewster's daughter, went to work at a job—like Georgianna Beasley or Elsie Oaks. say—for so much a week, right here in your own town?"

In spite of her brave resolve this plain presentation of the question staggered her. She was quite aware of the sensation her taking such a step would cause. She had tried to put it from her mind, had called it false pride and fought against it, but here it was—an actuality—a question to be faced and answered.

"Oh, the position is in—in Wapatomac?" she faltered. "I thought, perhaps—"

"That it might be somewhere else? Well, this one isn't. It is right here. Where you would be meetin' about everybody you know, summer folks as well as the rest of us, every day. There would be things said. For instance, what do you think Azure Crisp would say when she found it out? The first hullabaloo would be raised right in this sittin' room, I shouldn't wonder."

There was no doubt of that. Yet Mary was ready this time. She rose from the rocker.

"I don't care what Azure, or any one, may say," she declared, resolutely. "It is my own affair, and no one else's. If you can get that place for me, Captain Cummings, I will take it. And I will do my best not to make you ashamed of me afterward."

He rose also. That he was disturbed was evidenced by his expression. He frowned and shifted his feet uneasily on the Brussels carpet.

"Well," he said, after an interval of deliberation, "you must think it over carefully and so must I. And remember, it is a long way from sure that I could put you in that place if we both were certain you ought to try for it. As a matter of fact there are two others after it already. Oh," with a sudden glance and a smile, "*that* needn't discourage you so much. To be honest, if there had been only one he would most likely have had it before this. When there are two boats runnin' even in a race, and each skipper is dead set on keepin' the other from winnin', it is pretty often the third entry that lifts the cup. It probably won't work that way in this race, but—well, it might. That isn't the whole thing, nor, as I see it, even the main thing.

"Mary," he went on, earnestly, "when I say we must take time to think this over, I mean it. Think! After all, in spite of your lonesomeness and—and the rest of it, you're pretty comfortable here. You are respected and looked up to. Your friends are the best and oldest families in the town. Maybe you've been sittin' here alone too much, broodin' about this and that. We are all liable to get dissatisfied every now and again. You just wait a week or so and consider. If you do I shouldn't be surprised if you changed you mind. Your position here in Wapatomac is—well, you know what it is, as well as I do. Your family have—"

Her foot had been impatiently patting the carpet while he offered this well-intentioned counsel. Now she brought it down with a stamp.

"Oh, stop!" she exclaimed, sharply. "You talk exactly like Azure. My family is—I haven't any family. As for my position, it is impossible. My mind is made up and no amount of thinking can change it. If you don't care to take the responsibility of recommending me for this bookkeeper's place you have hinted at—and I'm sure I don't blame you if you feel that way—then tell me where it is and I will apply myself, without any recommendation. Where is it, Captain Cummings?"

His refusal was just as firm. "I can't tell you," he said. "You'll have to take my word that there are good reasons why I can't. I've got to do a barrel of thinkin' on my own hook first of all, and then, if I do decide to go ahead, I've got to handle the trick the way the boy spread the bread—with butter in each hand. The best I can say now is that I'll think hard and do what seems good—to me and for you. That is all I can promise to-night and, to be right down honest, it is more than I have any right to promise at all. Of course you won't say a word to anybody about our talk."

"Of course not. Is it likely I should?"

"Not a bit. I beg your pardon."

"That's all right. I am very grateful to you for thinking of me at all. It was kind of you to come here and very kind of you to listen to my lamentations. Of course you have been wondering all this time why I selected you to hear them. I knew you were used to advising and helping people. Mrs. Carleton told me how you helped her when she was in trouble about her steamship stock. I—well, I felt that you would be willing to help me, if you could. And—oh, I don't know—it just seemed natural to go to you. You were the first one I thought of when I made up my mind I must ask somebody for advice and help. As father would have said, you were my sheet anchor, Captain Cummings."

His reply to this confession was brief and embarrassed, but it was evident that what she had said pleased him.

"Sho! sho!" he muttered. "No trouble at all. How much real help I'm likely to be is doubtful enough, but I'll try; you needn't have any doubt of that."

"I haven't any. . . . Now I am sure I have made you late for supper."

He protested that the Cummings supper hour was variable.

"The Skipper and Kohath are used to havin' me drift into port 'most any time," he said. "They wait about so long and then have supper by themselves. Lord bless you, *they* don't care. They rather like it, I guess. It gives 'em a chance, while I'm eatin', to tell me everything that's happened while I've been away, and what might have happened if other things hadn't happened to stop 'em happenin'. . . . Well, good night, Mary. I'll let you hear from me in a day or two."

She said good night and thanked him again for the trouble he had taken on her account. He was standing by the door, with his overcoat buttoned, but it seemed to her that he was listening absently, and, when she met his look, that he was regarding her with a questioning expression, as if he were unsatisfied, as if he were seeking an answer to a puzzle which baffled him.

"Well, good night," he said, once more. "Oh, and if you should feel like goin' over those investments of yours at any time, I'll be glad to run through 'em with you. We might raise that income of yours a little, you know."

She nodded. "Yes," she answered, quickly. "Perhaps, by and by. That can wait. It is that bookkeeping—er—'job' which is the important thing just now."

"Yes. Sure. Of course. . . . Humph! Well, just the same, I am mighty glad you didn't buy that Boroda stock. As things are with you just now—as you've told me they are, I mean—your puttin' your money in that copper mine would have been pretty unfortunate. . . . Eh?"

She glanced up, met his eye, and looked down again.

"It surely would," she agreed, trying hard to make her tone casual and her manner unconcerned. "Now you *must* go. I feel guilty about that supper of yours."

The door closed behind him. She turned back to the rocker and sat there for a few minutes lost in a reverie which, although not quite as hopeless as that preceding Captain Cummings' call, was far from pleasant. There was a faint gleam of encouragement in it. She might—she *might* soon be earning sufficient to provide for the needs of her wardrobe, the ell roof, the front fence and the henhouse. But in return for these additional dollars she must face the disapproval and scornful disgust of Wapatomac—the aristocratic section, her section of it. After a time she rose from the rocker and, without daring to glance at the portrait of great-grandfather Brewster, went out to the dining room and sat down to her lonely supper.

And Captain David Farragut Cummings, striding along the rain-washed sidewalks toward his own supper, was lost in reflection. He had noted Mary Brewster's confusion when he referred to the Boroda Copper shares. He guessed—he was almost sure that he had the answer to his puzzle. If that answer were the true one then Miss Brewster's desperate determination to break Wapatomac's rigid code of social ethics was explainable. But she had asked him to assist in the breaking and, knowing his native village as he did, he dreaded to be a partner to such a proceeding. More than all, he was provoked at himself for having, on the spur of the thought as it came to him, mentioned his knowledge of the soon to be vacated desk of assistant bookkeeper. For that desk was in the Wapatomac National Bank, the institution of which he was president. The trust and confidence of his fellow-directors as evidenced by their selecting him to fill that important office had been a gratifying tribute. He had accepted the presidency with reluctance but, having accepted, he had done his best to justify the choice. So far he had steered his way through the shoals of petty jealousies and attempts at undue influence on the part of directors and depositors, with one fixed resolve to mark the course, namely, that nothing whatever—personal considerations, friendships, nothing—should be allowed to interfere with the bank's welfare.

Just now he was in the midst of a battle no less strong for having been fought in secret. His board of directors had split into two factions, and each had a candidate for the position of assistant bookkeeper. So far he had managed to keep the warfare under cover, hoping for and seeking a basis of compromise. When Mary Brewster mentioned the fact that she could keep a set of books it had suddenly occurred to him that here, possibly, was a basis of compromise provided. And, speaking without thinking, or, as he said, thinking aloud, a most unusual indiscretion for him, he had given her encouragement which he had no right to give. A moment later he realized it and ever since the realization had been growing.

The thing was almost an impossibility. First, it was by no means certain that either faction would consent to a compromise. Second, provided he were enough of a diplomat to bring that consent about, there would be strong opposition to the appointment of a woman. Well, that opposition might be overcome. If it were, and Mary made good at the work, criticism would die away. His expressed belief in her ability was sincere, but there was always a possibility of mistake. Suppose she did not make good? Suppose, after a fair trial, she proved incompetent? As it was he who had brought her there, so upon him, and justly, would devolve the unpleasant duty of telling her she could not stay.

He had known and admired Mary Brewster since she was a girl. The fact that she had turned to him when she needed help and advice was a pleasant thought. But there was the bank to be considered, first and always. Pshaw! He had let himself in for a heavy responsibility either way, and the more he reflected upon it the heavier it became.

CHAPTER III

THE Cummings house was not pure Colonial. Captain Dave had built it in 1895 and it bore the architectural stamp of the period. It was white, with green blinds, but it lacked the formal dignity of the Brewster house and aristocratic Wapatomac sniffed at the scroll-sawed ornamentation of its porch pillars and the colored glass windows at each side of its stained oak front door. Its situation, moreover, was not upon the exclusive section of the main road, but at the top of Nickerson's Hill, which rises above Scallop River near the Narrows. No ancient elms shaded its yard or screened it from the curious gaze of passers-by. There was a grove of pitch pine at its right and at the left the hill sloped sharply down to the cove and the buildings and wharves of D. Cummings & Co. House and barn and fences and outbuildings were neat and trim; they bore the stamp of self-respecting prosperity. A stranger, viewing them for the first time, might have guessed that their owner was a person who was comfortably well-to-do, who paid his bills and expected others to pay theirs, who took pride in his business and his home and the town he lived in. So guessing he would have guessed rightly. If he were very discerning he might have supplemented his guess by another, that the said owner, being a self-made man with ideas of his own, had built that house in accordance with those ideas and was perfectly satisfied with the result.

"No, sir," said Captain David to the Ostable architect who had drawn the plans; "I don't want you to copy anybody else's house. If I wanted a two-hundred-year-old house I could have bought one; there's at least one for sale that I know of. I'm buildin' this house to live in and be comfortable in—to be myself in, as you might say. I'm not buildin' it to make believe be a Hathaway or a Carleton or a Brewster in. I like that kind of a front door and I'm goin' to have it. If I liked a blue one better I'd have that."

The gale was still blowing as the captain entered his yard and as he turned the corner of the house a salty gust swept in from the bay and the sea beyond with a force which struck his broad chest like the push of a mighty hand. The clouds were breaking, however, and in the rifts between them a few stars twinkled. The lighthouse at Setuckit Point showed its speck low down in the east, and beyond was a lesser one which marked the lightship at Hog's Back Shoal. The main portion of the Cummings house was dark, but the windows of the rear section glowed brightly. Captain David turned the knob of the door beneath the lattice where, in summer, the Virginia creeper was wont to twine, and stepped directly into the dining room.

The table was set for supper, but the room, save for himself, was devoid of human occupancy. From the kitchen beyond, however, sounded voices, animated masculine voices, their owners too busily preoccupied to hear or heed his entrance. He removed his overcoat and hat and hung them in the closet. Then, as the argument in the kitchen continued without any apparent prospect of cessation, he hailed.

"Ahoy there! you in the galley," he shouted. "It's struck six bells, didn't you know it? Seems to me it is 'most time to stop talkin' and think about eatin'."

The duet in the adjoining room broke off in the middle. There was the sound of a chair upsetting and then of hurrying feet. Captain Barnabas Cummings appeared in the doorway. Captain Barney—no one in Wapatomac, no commoner that is, ever called him anything but that—was a little man, inclined to stoutness, with a round red face surprisingly free from wrinkles considering his age, and a shock of bristling, white hair. He moved quickly, stepped briskly, and when he spoke it was in a voice as strident as the note of a small 'hand-powered' foghorn.

"Why, hello, Dave!" he roared. "What do you mean catfootin' in like this? I never heard you come aboard. . . . You're an hour late; did you know it?"

Captain David nodded. "Sorry, Skipper," he said. "I had some business that kept me. You and Kohath have had your supper, of course."

Before the Skipper could answer Kohath Briggs entered, bearing a steaming platter in one hand and the teapot in the other. Mr. Briggs was tall and thin and moved and spoke with a deliberation which caused a section of Wapatomac to refer to him as "awful moderate." He was dressed in a dark suit, shiny at knees, elbows and shoulder blades, wore a black bow tie, and looked like a seedy book agent, or an undertaker's helper, or a street corner preacher—like almost anything except a man who had spent the greater part of his life at sea in a schooner's galley. He placed the platter at one end of the table, the teapot at the other, and stood mournfully regarding them.

Captain David took the chair at the end where the platter had been placed, Captain Barney that at the opposite end. Mr. Briggs remained standing. So far he had not spoken a word. Captain Barney, fidgeting in his seat, barked at him like a petulant terrier.

"Well, well, well!" he snapped. "What's the matter now, for heaven sakes? You look as if you was goin' to cry. Don't the remains look natural, or what ails you? Sit down. Dave and me are hungry."

Kohath pulled back the chair at the side of the table and, folding his long body in the middle, and his long legs at the knees, slid awkwardly into place.

"I cal'late everything's all right," he drawled, sadly. "I was lookin' to see what I'd forgot."

"Forgot! If you ain't had time enough to remember everything by this time you never will have it. You commenced to set table at five o'clock and that codfish has been fried and settin' on the back of the stove since six. . . . Here! Where you goin'?"

Mr. Briggs had unfolded himself and was rising to his feet.

"I'm goin' to fetch the spiderbread and the potatoes," he drawled. "I had a feelin' I'd forgot somethin'." He meandered as far as the kitchen door and there paused. "There's been so everlastin' much talk goin' on," he added, "it's a wonder I ain't forgot my head."

He vanished into the kitchen. Captain Barney called after him.

"If that was all you forgot nobody'd ever notice the difference," he shouted. The cleverness of this retort pleased him so much that he was still chuckling when the cook reappeared with the hot bread and potatoes.

Captain David served the fish and his grandfather poured the tea. Mr. Briggs sorrowfully passed the plates and cups. Captain Barney, who was seldom silent for long, was the first to resume conversation.

"What do you cal'late that—that ignoramus there has been tryin' to do for the last two hours?" he demanded, pointing an accusing fork at Kohath. "He's been tryin' to stand up for that Azure Crisp woman, that's what. Tryin' to make out that, because she's been livin' up at Ben Brewster's ever since Noah put to sea or thereabouts, that gives her an excuse for behavin' as if the crowd she was brought up with was dirt under her feet. He lets her shove him to one side and hand out orders and all he does is touch his hat and say: 'Thank you, ma'am. Please kick me again, if it ain't too much trouble.' I am ashamed for him, I declare I am."

Mr. Briggs's dignified equanimity was, outwardly at least, quite unaffected by this outburst. He swallowed the section of fried codfish which had been occupying his attention, took a drink of tea, and turned his gaze upon the peppery ancient at the foot of the table.

"I never neither asked her to kick me," he said solemnly. "She never offered to kick nobody. Women folks do about everything they want to nowadays, seems so, but they ain't started in kickin' people around the post office, I guess. If you'd only listen once in a while, instead of bein' so set on doin' all the talkin' yourself, 'twould be smoother sailin' for all hands."

Captain Barnabas bounced in his chair.

"Who do you think you're slingin' out that to?" he demanded, in hot indignation. "You've been cook and roustabout aboard here so long that you seem to figure you're commodore or somethin'. I've stood about all of it I'm goin' to. D'you understand?"

Kohath buttered a fragment of spiderbread.

"You don't have to stand nothin'," he drawled, calmly. "If you don't like the cookin' all you've got to do is say so. There's another job waitin' for me any minute I want to take it. And it won't be a cook job neither."

"*I'll* bet it won't! What you goin' to tackle next? Goin' to try makin' a livin' stuffin' birds, I presume likely. Remember what Hannah Perry said about your stuffin' her poll parrot after it died. She said she didn't know but 'twould have been better if she'd been contented to remember it as it was."

This was a dig in a sore spot. Mr. Briggs had of late been experimenting in taxidermy. He had sent two dollars by mail to a firm which published a book on the subject. He laid down his knife and fork.

Captain David, who had been enjoying the squabble, as he had previously enjoyed hundreds of similar ones, took a hand.

"Here, here!" he ordered. "What's all this about, anyway? Waitin' for supper must have put an edge on your tempers as well as your appetites. Skipper, be still. You too, Kohath. You don't either of you mean what you say. Either one of you would die of lonesomeness without the other to fight with. Behave yourselves. What set you goin', in the first place?"

Both started to explain and, as neither would give way to the other, the result was more noisy than enlightening. David Cummings rapped for order.

"Sshh, shh!" he commanded. "Heave to, Skipper!

Whatever it was seems to have happened to Kohath, so let's let him tell it."

Captain Barney sniffed. "'Twill take him two year and *then* he won't get anywhere," he vowed. . . . "Oh, all right! All—*right!* Never mind me. It's gettin' so nobody pays any attention to me in *this* house."

Mr. Briggs began his story. It seemed a trivial bit of tinder for such a bonfire as had been blazing all the afternoon. Kohath had gone to the post office, after washing the dinner dishes. He was standing at the postmaster's window, awaiting his turn for attention, when Azure Crisp appeared and, without waiting for any one, had coolly pushed him and one or two others aside, asked for and obtained the Brewster mail and made a dignified departure. That was all.

Captain Barney, who had fumed and fidgeted during the cook's deliberate and wandering recital, broke out with a sputter.

"And—and he stood there and let her do it," he cried, furiously. "Stood there and let that—that upstart woman shove him out of line and never opened his mouth. I wish I'd been there. She wouldn't have crowded *me* out of the channel, I tell you that. And here I was, to home, sittin' waitin' and waitin' for my *Item* while he was too meek and mealy-mouthed to stand up for his rights. Tut, tut, tut!"

Kohath finished his cup of tea. "There wasn't no *Item* there," he drawled. "'Tain't due till to-morrow, anyway. I told you to-day was Wednesday and you vowed and declared 'twas Thursday. I offered to fetch you the almanac and prove it and you wouldn't let me."

The Skipper was a trifle taken aback but he stood to his guns.

"Yes," he retorted, with sarcasm, "and you know perfectly well that the only almanac in the house was a last year one. You put this year's in the fire."

" 'Twas the one you handed me to put there. You said you was sick of seein' the old one around. How did I know you'd lost your spectacles for the ninety-fifth time that day and had got hold of the new almanac by mistake? And I could have proved by last year's just as well. If—"

Again Captain David interrupted. "Hush, hush! both of you," he commanded. "You've been squabblin' about that almanac for two months. Forget it. There'll be another ready the first of the year and that isn't so far off. So Azure was at the post office, was she? Humph! And it was rainin' pitchforks, too. She is pretty faithful at her job, I must say. She's queer and cranky and all that, but she does try hard to do her duty by Mary Brewster. I don't know what Mary would do if it wasn't for her."

This remark was a distinct error in judgment. It had an effect which the speaker, from his long experience, should have foreseen. For hours the Skipper had been voicing detestation of Azure Crisp, her manner, habits and general characteristics. And Kohath had just as stoutly defended her and them. Now, when a third party ventured to throw a favorable comment in her direction, Mr. Briggs promptly changed sides and began to criticize.

"She's a stuck-up upstart, just as Cap'n Barney says," he proclaimed. "I presume likely I should have stood up in my boots and when she tried to push by me I'd ought to have shoved her back where she belonged. I would have, too, only I was kind of took by surprise and didn't have time to think. When I did it was too late."

"Ye-es; well, your thinkin' is generally about a week late," was Captain Barney's ungracious comment. "Never mind, though," he added, hastily. "Better late than never. Next time you see her you tell her a few things, Kohath. I'm waitin' for my chance. I'm waitin' to ask her if, as treasurer of the New Church society, I am to consider that she's through with that society for good and all. Ever since Annabelle Brewster's time she's been taggin' to First Church meetin' Sunday mornin's, but for a spell she was pretty reg'lar with us Friday nights and at socials and so on. And she paid in her fifty cents a week same as when she was a professin' Christian. Now she ain't paid a cent since February. What I want to ask her is if I'm to understand that she's hove religion overboard and has turned First Church for keeps. That's what I'm waitin' to ask."

"Suppose she says she has?" drawled Briggs. "What then?"

"Then, by the great and holy, I'll have her in a clove hitch. I'll really begin to *talk* to her then. Sailin' around rigged up in that old sealskin cape of Annabelle Brewster's, and talkin' poetry and gettin' books out of the library and airin' herself all so high and mighty at lodge meetin' don't fool me any. I'm too old a bird and I've been roostin' hereabouts for eighty odd years. Wrappin' a secondhand sealskin 'round a sculpin don't change what's inside of it. Tut, tut, tut! *She* makin' believe she's a big bug just because she washes dishes for those that are! Why, I've known her folks forever, as you might say, and there wan't one of 'em that had more than a quarter to his name at one time—and that one he owed somebody else. Why, her own uncle, on her mother's side, old Zebedee Beasley, I remember him comin' to meetin' Sundays with so many different kind of patches on his britches that they looked like a chart of the South Sea Islands. But he always come, I'll say that for him. He didn't try to cover up the patches with any sealskin capes. And her husband, Obed Crisp, he's been dead a long spell, and never amounted to much when he was alive, but he went to the church where he belonged —when he went anywhere. And he's buried where he belongs, too, and that's in the New Church buryin' ground."

Kohath put in a word. "I was ashore the day Obed was drownded," he mused. "That was of a Sunday. He wan't to church that day. He was off haulin' lobster pots."

"That's because 'twas a couple of days after the Fourth of July and him and Abram Oaks and some of their gang had had a jug come down from Boston. He'd have been to home and to church if he was sober."

Captain David, who had been calmly eating his supper, was now pushing back his chair and rising from the table.

"I'll leave you two to dispose of Obed and his wife," he observed, cheerfully. "You are good for an hour when you start haulin' Azure over the coals. I'm goin' to my desk in the sittin' room. I've got some bank matters I want to look over."

The last sentence seemed to remind Mr. Briggs of something.

"Humph!" he grunted, reflectively. "I heard somethin' down to the post office to-day, somethin' that had to do with the bank. Don't cal'late there was anything in it, but it sounded funny. There's a story goin' around town that Allie Jones is givin' up his job there and is goin' to work in Boston. It ain't so, is it, Cap'n Dave?"

David frowned. So the secret, which had been kept surprisingly well for a Wapatomac secret, was out at last. He passed his hand through his hair. "Who said that?" he asked.

"Olsen Snow was the one that told it. He works for Mrs. Cap'n Eleazir Bradley, you know, and he vows he heard her and her daughter talkin' it over. 'Cordin' to Olsen old Mrs. Eleazir was terrible interested. Seems she's got a nephew over to Bayport who'd like first-rate to have Allie's place when he quits. Olsen, he gathered from what he heard that Mrs. Cap'n Eleazir wan't by no means happy about the prospects. She said somethin' to the effect that Cap'n Donald—"

"Cap'n Fred Donald, the Ostable one?" broke in Captain Barney, eagerly curious.

"Um-hum. That's the one. She said that Cap'n Fred had a cousin he was tryin' to get the job for and 'twas nip and tuck who'd win out. I told 'em I didn't believe there was a word of truth in it because you'd never mentioned it to home here. I was right, wan't I?"

Captain David did not answer the question. "Did Snow say any more?" he inquired.

"Not much. Seems to me he did say Mrs. Eleazir said that she didn't know but that, if she was sartin her nephew couldn't get the place, she'd be willin' to use her influence for almost anybody else provided 'twan't the one Donald wanted. Olsen, he judged that with her 'twas anything to beat Cap'n Fred."

Captain Barney nodded. "The Bradleys and Donalds haven't more than hardly spoke to each other for seven or eight year," he declared. "There was a row betwixt 'em way back afore Cap'n Eleazir died. Somethin' about church conference, seems to me 'twas—or about a vessel they owned shares in together—or about a cow one of 'em sold the other. No, wait a minute. 'Twas on account of the Donalds sittin' on the platform at the Ostable town hall one Cattle Show Day, when the Governor was makin' a speech, and the Bradleys havin' to be down on the floor with the rest of the crowd. That's what started it. I knew 'twas somethin'."

Captain David left his grandfather and Mr. Briggs pulling to pieces the family histories of the aristocratic Bradleys and Donalds and, going into the sitting room, closed the door behind him and sat down at his desk. There were papers on that desk which needed attention, but he did not touch them. Instead he sat there, puffing moodily at a cigar and thinking—thinking. What he had just heard made him regret more than ever the unfortunate slip which had betrayed to Mary Brewster his knowledge of the bank's secret. Now the secret was town property. Every one would be talking of it. A dozen new entries would be in the race. And each additional one made her choice less likely.

He believed he understood the true reason behind her appeal to him for help. She had, in spite of his counsel to the contrary, bought the Boroda stock. How much she had bought, how greatly her income might be depleted, he did not know. But he knew her, and he was certain that the situation must indeed be desperate which forced Captain Benjamin Brewster's daughter to confession of her poverty and a willingness to accept a salaried position in the town where the Brewsters had received homage and ruled in dignity for a hundred and fifty years.

He would have done his utmost to help her, anyway. Now that he had been so rash as to offer her more or less definite encouragement, he must, somehow or other, justify it. She had called him her "sheet anchor." That anchor, it seemed to him, was resting on a muddy bottom. How on earth could he make it hold?

He thought and planned, but each plan presented unsurmountable difficulties. In his thinking, however, he forgot one very important factor, namely, that others also were thinking. And at that moment one of the thinkers knocked at the Cummings door.

He did not hear the knock but Mr. Briggs did and, as Captain David impatiently threw aside the stump of one cigar and reached for a fresh one, Kohath tiptoed into the sitting room.

David looked up. "Well, what is it?" he asked, briskly. "Don't bother me unless it is important."

Mr. Briggs' face was proof of the importance.

"Say," he whispered, bending down to his employer's ear, "who do you cal'late is here, come to see you? They say when you talk about angels you're liable to hear their wings flop. I believe it now."

Before he could say more voices in the dining room became distinctly audible. The voice of Captain Barnabas and another.

"Well, well, well!" Captain Barney vowed; "this is a surprise, sure enough. Didn't expect to see you in these latitudes—not to-night, anyhow. Take off your things, won't you? Blowin' consider'ble, ain't it?"

"Blowing a hurricane," was the brusque reply. "Coming across that open stretch by Goulds' I thought the damned buggy would blow out of the road."

Captain David grinned. "Is that your angel?" he inquired, dryly.

The sarcasm slid by Kohath without touching him. "Uh-hum," he said, solemnly. "That's him. Ain't it queer now that, right while me and the Skipper was talkin' about him out there in the kitchen, he should come knockin' at the door? Ain't it, now? Eh?"

"I can tell you better when I know who it is."

"Eh? I thought I told you. It's Cap'n Fred Donald himself. Drove all the way over from Ostable, he has. I don't cal'late he's been in this house since that time when he come to coax you to be president of the bank. And now, to-night, the very minute when we was talkin' about him, here he shows up. It's enough to make a body believe in signs, I declare if it ain't."

David had risen to his feet. "Cap'n Fred!" he repeated. "What. . . . Humph!"

For the second time that day Kohath was pushed unceremoniously to one side. Cummings strode to the door of the dining room and opened it.

"Why, good evenin', Cap'n," he hailed, heartily. "Glad to see you. Come in, come in."

The visitor accepted the invitation. He was square-shouldered, white-bearded, red-faced and blue-eyed. He walked with dignity and he spoke with authority. Captain

Frederick Donald had "bossed" his crews on the old square-riggers and, after retiring from the sea, had continued to boss his family and a majority of the residents of Ostable. He was a man of wealth, position and influence in the county, and no one knew it better than he did.

"Sit down, sit down, Cap'n," urged David. "That's all, Kohath. Shut the door when you go out."

Mr. Briggs prepared to obey orders though with evident reluctance.

"You won't want the Skipper—Cap'n Barney, I mean —you won't want him neither, will you?" he asked, hopefully.

"I guess not."

Donald settled the question. "No, we won't," he said, with decision. "I've got to talk business with Dave."

Kohath nodded. "All right," he answered, with satisfaction. "I'll tell him you don't want him."

He departed to carry the glad news to the Skipper, who was waiting just at the other side of the door. The powwow which ensued died away in the direction of the kitchen. Captain David turned to his caller. "Make yourself comfortable, Cap'n," he said. "Here! Have a cigar."

Donald accepted the cigar. While he was lighting it Cummings regarded him thoughtfully. The pompous old magnate had driven the twelve miles from Ostable through the gale and at night, to talk business with him. There was but one business they had in common, that pertaining to the bank. And David could conjecture only one phase of that which was of immediate importance. He leaned back in his desk chair, outwardly casual and serene, but inwardly alert and watchful. He did not offer to begin conversation; he waited for his visitor to do that.

Captain Frederick Donald appeared to find it hard to begin. He puffed at the cigar, crossed and uncrossed his sturdy legs, scowled, and then leaned forward.

"See here, Dave," he said, gruffly. "That job down at the bank. Has anybody said anything to you about that to-day, or yesterday?"

Cummings thought it over. "Jones was speakin' of it this noon," he replied. "He says he can't stay more than another week. And Hall was asking about it, too."

An impatient movement of the Donald hand. "I don't mean them; I mean folks outside the bank."

"Well, of course, Mrs. Cap'n Bradley is at me every chance she gets. She's just as set on gettin' her nephew in as she ever was."

"I don't mean her, either. Somehow or other it's getting to be known that Jones is leaving us. It has got as far as Ostable. I heard it there to-day."

"Did you? Pshaw!"

"Yes, I did. And, if they know it there, it is dead sure that all Wapatomac knows it. Of course you realize what that will mean. It means that we shall have a dozen applications by to-morrow night. I'm surprised they haven't come to you already."

"Um-hum. . . . Well, if the news is out, so am I. Lots of young fellows would like to work in the bank. It isn't such a big job, but they figure, I suppose, that, just as it did with young Jones, it may lead to somethin' better."

"Yes, yes," fretfully. "Well, that troubles me a little bit. To tell you the truth, Cummings, getting that place for my wife's cousin had come to be a—a sort of matter of principle with me. It isn't the place itself. He can find another one, or I can find one for him. That isn't it. It is just because—well, just because I *said* he should have it. And," his voice rising, "I have as much right to have my way as anybody else has. . . . Humph! You seem to think that is funny. What are you laughing at?"

Captain David was not laughing, exactly. There was a suspicion of a smile at the corners of his lips, however, and a glint of humor in his eyes. He hastened to smooth his caller's ruffled feathers.

"I'm sorry, Cap'n Fred," he said. "And I understand just how you feel. There is nothin' funny about that. Only, you see, as you were talkin' it came across my mind that you were sayin' almost exactly the same thing that Mrs. Cap'n Bradley said to me yesterday noon. She was in to see me and she said—odd, too, she should say it in almost the same words—that gettin' that bank job for her nephew Jim Henry had come to be almost a matter of principle with her. It wasn't the job itself, she told me; it was because she had told him he should have it."

The Donald chin beard quivered and the Donald eye flashed.

"Oh, did she!" he sneered. "Is that so! Well, I hope you asked her who made it her business to give orders. What has she got to do with that bank, I want to know?"

Cummings shrugged. "She is one of our heaviest depositors," he said, "and she owns a lot of our stock. And her husband, Cap'n Eleazir, was president for eight years; was president when he died."

"Well, what of that? She didn't take his place, did she? You're president now, aren't you?"

"Ye-es. But her influence made me president—hers

and yours, Cap'n. She wouldn't let me forget that, even if I wanted to."

Captain Donald's teeth clenched. He lifted the hand holding the cigar.

"See here, Cummings," he demanded. "Does that mean you're getting ready to take her side against mine? Is that what it means?"

David shook his head. "You know it doesn't, Cap'n Fred," he answered. "All through this rumpus over Jones's place I've tried to play fair. The board has split right in the middle. Three of the directors, Small and Cahoon and yourself, have been with you and your cousin. But the other three, Colton and Baker and Freeman, have stood out for young Henry. You know as well as I do whose influence is behind them."

Donald did know it. "Sam Freeman is her brother-in-law," he growled. "She's worked on him and he's worked on the others. If it hadn't been for that we could have picked a new bookkeeper without the least bit of trouble. A fine state of affairs, when a fifteen-dollar-a-week understrapper's job gets to interfering with the business of an institution like the Wapatomac National Bank. And now the whole county is going to hear about it. A ridiculous mess, I call it."

Cummings nodded agreement. "That's what I've called it all along," he said.

"Humph! Well, you could have ended it any minute you wanted to. All you had to do was cast the deciding vote."

"For you and your wife's cousin, you mean?"

"Certain."

David laughed. "Emma Bradley says I could have

ended it by votin' for her nephew," he observed. "No, thank you, Cap'n Fred. No, sir, I've stood by and kept my hands off. I had the bank to think of. As I see it, that's what you made me president for."

Ostable's great man fidgeted gloomily in his chair.

"Then you won't vote for my man?" he asked.

"Can't. Any more than I can vote for the Bradley nephew."

"Humph! Well, Small and Colton will stick it through with me, I can tell you that."

"Mrs. Cap'n Eleazir says her crowd will stick by her. . . . Now, don't blame me, Cap'n Donald. All I'm tryin' to do is keep the Wapatomac National Bank in the middle of the channel. Might as well be plain about it. While I'm president I won't have a family grudge runnin' it on the rocks. It ain't a question of the fitness of your man or the other one. So far as that goes, either could fill the bill, I don't doubt. But I know—yes, and you know—that neither one would ever satisfy the opposition. And board meetin' every Saturday would be a cat and dog fight. And as for us poor devils *in* the bank—particularly the assistant bookkeeper—we'd have happy days, wouldn't we. Come now, that's sense, isn't it?"

Donald did not attempt denial. He chewed the end of his cigar and muttered something profane behind it.

"Then how long do you think this is likely to go on?" he demanded, angrily.

"Forever, I guess likely. I don't see any end; do you?"

Captain Frederick swore again. He rose and paced back and forth, his hands jammed in his trousers' pockets. Suddenly he stopped and turned.

"Cummings," he said, "it can't go on—it's got to stop somehow. As I told you when I first got here, now that Jones or somebody has let the cat out of the bag, we'll be pestered to death. Every living soul that has two dollars in that bank will be for takin' sides. The row won't be about a bookkeeper any longer; it won't be just a bank row, it will be a town row. Yes, half the county will be in it. People will be withdrawing their accounts and taking 'em over to the Harniss bank, and I don't know what all. We can't have that. It's got to stop, somehow."

"Seems so to me. But then, it's seemed so to me from the beginnin'."

"How can it be stopped? I'll let the bank go plumb to the devil before I'll vote for any relation of Emma Bradley's."

"Sure I understand. Well, the Bradleys say the same thing—or what amounts to it—on the opposite side. And there we are, abreast the same buoy as we started from."

The visitor again crossed from the chair to the window and back again. And once more he paused.

"I know how it *might* be stopped," he growled, after a moment's hesitation. "There's just one who could stop it before any outsiders took a hand. That is you, Dave Cummings. . . . No, no, wait! hear me through. Suppose at next Saturday's meetin', you told the board you had a candidate yourself. Somebody you knew was all right and that hadn't anything to do with either me or that condemned Bradley woman. Somebody whose name had never been mentioned. Maybe—I say maybe—some of us would be willin' to vote for that one. There's a chance in that, isn't there?"

This was what David Cummings had been waiting for. During this dialogue and while Captain Donald had been speaking, he had been wondering, guessing, trying to surmise the real reason for the call. He was sure that the Ostable magnate had not come merely to urge that he vote for his relative. They had discussed that matter over and over again and each time he had pleasantly but flatly refused to take either side in the dispute. He had shown no marked surprise at the condescension of a Donald in coming to the house of a Cummings, instead of peremptorily summoning the latter to his own. He had asked no questions, evinced no curiosity. He had waited and listened. And now that his unspoken question was answered, and answered precisely as he could have wished, he was outwardly just as calm and unmoved. In fact, he received the suggestion with hesitation.

"Hum—why, yes," he murmured, as if in doubtful consideration of a new and novel idea. "Why—er—yes. Yes, I presume likely that might settle it, if it worked out that way. What have you got in mind, Cap'n Fred? Somebody else you are thinkin' of proposin'?"

Donald impatiently shook his head. "Of course I haven't," he snapped. "In the first place I don't publicly back down when I start out to put a thing through, and in the second there would be nothing gained by my changing candidates. All I would have to do was say I was in favor of—well, no matter who—and Freeman and Josh Colton and Eben Baker would vote no so quick your head would swim. It isn't a question with them of getting the right bookkeeper, it's a question of seeing that *I* don't get what I'm after. . . . No, no," bending forward to point a finger at the Cummings nose, "you are the only one who can handle this. *You.* Do you know of some young chap—a decent one, of course—who wants that place and could do the work? If you do I'll—well, by George, I'll cast my vote for him! There!"

Captain David was tilting slowly back and forth in the desk chair. He was, seemingly, lost in thought. The peppery gentleman from Ostable grew tired of waiting.

"Come, come!" he ordered. "You heard me, didn't you? Say something."

"Eh? Oh, yes, Cap'n, I heard you. That's all right; your vote would help—provided I could manage to think of a good party for the place. But one vote—or two—wouldn't do it."

"Four would. Seth Cahoon and Small will vote as I tell 'em to. They, with me, and you—voting for your own nominee, of course—would make a majority. Then Emma Bradley's pet poodle dogs could howl or keep still, just as they liked."

"Ye-es. But we'd have to be careful who that new bookkeeper was or they'd keep on howlin' all winter. If we—you and I, I mean—could only think of *just* the right one."

"That ought to be easy enough. Lord A'mighty!" in huge disgust. "You talk as if I'd asked you to pick out a Senator or something."

"You have asked me to find a bookkeeper that will satisfy all hands. That would have been easy enough before this squabble got goin'. It isn't so easy now. . . . Humph! . . . Well, I declare! . . . I wonder."

"What do you wonder. You've thought of somebody; I can see that. Who is it?"

"It just came to me that— But no, it isn't possible."

"How do you know it isn't? What are you talking about?"

Captain David was regarding him earnestly but doubtfully. He appeared to be on the point of offering a suggestion, but fearful that it might be too ridiculous for consideration.

"Humph!" he mused. "I know you'll think I'm crazy, but— Well, here goes! Cap'n Donald, what would you say to hirin' a girl—a woman—for that job of Allie Jones's?"

Donald said nothing immediately. He stared in incredulous amazement. Cummings did not wait; he hurried on.

"It just came to me," he confided, "that a little while ago—this week, as a matter of fact—a woman right here in this town, a mighty fine, smart able woman from one of the best families in Wapatomac, told me that she had made up her mind to take some sort of position where she could do somethin' to keep her interested—yes, and earn a little extra pin money for herself. She knows somethin' of bookkeepin'; she isn't any relation of Emma Bradley's; she's respected by everybody and I believe she would be a real help to the bank in a lot of ways, provided—provided, of course, she could be coaxed into comin' there. If she wasn't a woman—if she was a man —I should say right off: 'Here's the very one!' But, as she *is* a woman, why—well, I don't how you and the rest of the board might feel. Personally, I haven't any prejudice. Women are workin' everywhere nowadays and just because we've never had one in the bank is no reason why we shouldn't, as I look at it. I—"

But his caller had been quiet long enough. He broke in.

"What the devil is all this?" he demanded. "Who is this woman, for heaven's sake?"

Cummings leaned forward. "Now I am goin' to surprise you," he declared. "She is Mary Brewster. That's who she is."

There was no doubt of the surprise. Captain Frederick Donald stared, opened his mouth, choked, and then fulfilled his host's prophecy.

"Mary Brewster!" he gasped. "Mary *Brewster!* Ben Brewster's girl! Lookin' for a *job?* You're crazy as a loon."

"Um-hum. That's what I expected. Now you listen, Cap'n Fred. Sit down in that chair again and listen. I'll tell you all about it."

He proceeded to tell, by no means all, but as much as he deemed advisable. He said nothing of Mary's "desperation," her actual need of money, he breathed not a word concerning what he was convinced was the cause of that need, the unfortunate speculation in Boroda Copper. He stressed her loneliness, "all alone in that big house with nothing to take up her mind"; he praised her ability, her character, her family and social position. "Her friends are the best people in Wapatomac and Bayport and Ostable and everywhere. She's hand and glove with the summer crowd. I tell you, Cap'n Fred, havin' her in the bank—provided, as I say, we could coax her to work there—would be a fine thing for that bank."

He went on and on. He talked with an earnestness which brought the perspiration to his forehead. But, with it all, he was careful not to express any personal interest. "And," he said, in conclusion, "of course she is a woman. And there's bound to be talk at our pickin' a woman for that job. What do you think, Cap'n?"

Captain Donald slapped his knee.

"I'm for it," he declared. "I don't believe she'll take the place. I believe she was lonesome and blue and discontented and said a whole lot more than she really meant. But if she did mean it and will come to work in the bank I'm for her. Ben Brewster was a good fellow. Havin' a Brewster to help take care of our depositors' accounts won't do us a bit of harm. And," he added, with a triumphant chuckle, "your proposing her for the place will put the Bradley crowd in a hole. The Bradleys and the Brewsters have always been thick as thieves—no thicker, of course, than they were with my family—but close, just the same. It will be fun to watch Sam Freeman's face when you name her. Ho, ho! I wonder what he'll say —and do. If he and Colton and Baker vote against her—why, that will put them and that Bradley woman in bad with some of their best friends. Ho, ho! Heave ahead, Dave! Heave ahead! It will be the best joke in ten years. As for the town talk—well, I shan't let that get in the way. If Mary can stand it I guess the bank can."

They parted at the door. "Then it's settled, is it?" whispered Cummings. "I am to see Mary and do my best to make her promise to come. If she says yes, I'll propose her name at Saturday mornin's meetin' and I can count on you and Small and Cahoon votin' for her?"

"Sure as you live! Look here," rather anxiously, "do you suppose you can make her say yes? Do you think I'd better go and see her myself?"

"No, no," hastily, "I wouldn't do that. She—well, I

was the one she talked to about her affairs and perhaps it might be better if I talked this time. She's proud and—well, sensitive, I imagine. And—you understand?"

"Yes. Certain. Guess you're right, Cummings. I wish you luck. And I *do* want to see Sam Freeman's face Saturday morning. Ho, ho!"

David refused to answer the eager questions of his grandfather and Mr. Briggs. "Just bank affairs, that's all," he told them. He went to his room immediately. After the office of D. Cummings & Co. had closed the following afternoon he walked up the hill and turned the handle of the bell attached to the pure Colonial front door of the Bradley residence. He was admitted to the Bradley parlor where the widow and daughter of the late Captain Eleazir received him with condescending graciousness. And in that parlor he remained for a full hour. He was weary but smiling when he closed the front gate behind him.

And, Sunday morning, just before church time, he called again at the Brewster house. Mary listened in amazement to what he had to tell.

"Of course," he said, when his surprising story ended, "I wasn't certain that you would be willin' to take the place. The wages aren't very large, but they are somethin', and at any rate the work, although it isn't hard, will keep you fairly busy. We all hope you will come to the bank. Will you?"

She drew a long breath. "Of course I will," she said. "Indeed and indeed I will."

"There's bound to be talk, you know. You're a Brewster."

"Oh, please! We went through all that the other evening. If you and—and the others really want me I will take the place and try awfully hard to keep it. I can't tell you, Captain Cummings, how grateful I am. I can't even try—now. . . . But—but it's so—so wonderful I can hardly believe it. You say you just proposed my name and all the directors—every one of them—voted for me. It was unanimous?"

"That's it. Unanimous."

"Well, I don't see why. You just told them I wanted it and they all said yes. It was as simple as that."

David Cummings nodded. She could not see his face, for he had turned to look at the portrait of great-grandfather Brewster, but his tone was convincing. "Yes," he agreed, solemnly. "Just as simple as that."

CHAPTER IV

IT was arranged. Mary was to report at the bank, ready for work, on Wednesday morning. Young Jones, the retiring bookkeeper, had agreed to remain until the end of the week, and, as Captain Cummings said, help her in "learning the ropes." She stood at the window, watching her caller walk briskly away from the Brewster gate and Mrs. Crisp entering the sitting room found her standing there.

Azure was gowned in her "go to meeting" regalia, purple silk, breastpin, sealskin cape, black transformation and all.

"Well there!" she exclaimed, snappishly. "He's gone at last, has he. I was just on the point of marchin' in here to ask if you'd decided not to go to church this mornin'. I thought maybe even Barney Cummings's grandson might catch on to a hint like that. Nice time to make calls, Sunday forenoon! This is the second time in four days that he's been here. *What* in the world is he comin' for?"

Mary hesitated. She realized that Azure must be told the truth, but she could not bear to tell it then. There would be a scene, and she did not feel equal to the crisis. She would wait until later.

"I'll be ready in a jiffy, Azure," she said. "You needn't wait."

"Wait! Course I'll wait. If I've waited all this time

I cal'late another five minutes won't hurt me. But do tell me; what is he pesterin' you about?"

"Oh, just what I said, a business matter."

She hurried to get her coat and hat, leaving Mrs. Crisp to call after her that any one who didn't know better than to come to talk business on a Sunday mornin' just at meetin' time was not fit to be president of a hencoop, let alone a bank.

During the walk to church Mary's conscience was troubling her. She must tell Azure, of course, but, oh dear, how she dreaded it. Twice during their progress she was on the point of breaking the news, but each time her resolution failed. They were a few minutes late and the opening hymn was being sung as they entered the stately portals of the old First Church.

"Why don't you sit with me this morning, Azure?" she whispered at the door. "You might just as well."

But Azure was proud of possessing a sense of fitness.

"Sit with you!" she whispered in return. "Likely, ain't it. I get enough digs already from New Church folks about toadyin' to riches. If I should take to sittin' way up front along with you and right next to Sam Freeman and the Bradleys and all their kind, I'd never hear the last of it. I'll sit in back where I always do."

But this particular morning the rear seats were crowded. Old Mr. Sampson, the minister, had exchanged pulpits for that Sunday with the new divine from Bayport. The latter was reputed to be a "smart preacher," and suspected of certain heresies, and visitors, hoping for sensation, were present from West Wapatomac and Denboro, even as far away as Bayport. Elkanah Bearse, the sexton, who met them at the door, was troubled.

"I declare, Mrs. Crisp," he confided, "I don't know where I can squeeze you in. Every pew that doesn't belong to somebody is chock full."

Mary solved the difficulty. "She must sit with me," she said, firmly. "Come, Azure, don't stop to argue. They are singing the last verse now."

She led the way up the aisle and Bearse, seizing the Crisp arm, towed its owner reluctantly in his wake. The Brewster pew, rented and occupied by Brewsters since the church was built, was in the very front row. It was empty, of course. An uninvited outsider, daring to press its sacred cushions, would indeed have been sitting in the seat of the scornful. The sexton opened its door and Mary entered. She sat at the farther end. Azure, her genteel Sabbath composure for once completely wrecked, sat rigidly upright at the opposite end, staring straight ahead, her black lace mits clutching each other and her cheeks reddening under the stares which she knew were fixed upon her.

Mary, although not for the same reason, was also quite aware of the stares. She felt, rather than saw, Captain Samuel Freeman in the pew at her right, lean forward to look at her. She heard the rustle which accompanied Mrs. Freeman's turning to look. She knew that, behind her, Mrs. Captain Eleazir Bradley and Miss Elvira Bradley were gazing at the back of her neck. When they whispered she was certain they whispered about her. The Coltons and the Cahoons and the Bakers were members of that church and were all present that morning. They all knew of her acceptance of the bookkeeper's position at the bank and, although as directors the men had voted for her, she could easily guess the remarks made at their tables and in their sitting rooms by them and the members of their families. They were all wondering at her "comedown" in the world and guessing at its cause. And, being a woman of imagination, she could picture each one of them as demanding, "*What* would Captain Ben or his wife say if they were alive?" And by Wednesday—oh, yes, sooner than that—all Wapatomac, high and low, would be saying the same thing.

She was not ashamed of her determination to earn a living. She had a right to do so if she wished. It was solely her affair. But all the philosophy in the world, all the scornful disdain of snobbery in the world, were not sufficient to salve the irritation caused by the certainty that she was being talked about, would soon be talked about by everybody; and that those who had hitherto taken the greatest pains to cultivate and maintain her friendship would now be her sharpest critics, would invent the meanest excuses for her action.

By the time the service began, however, her shoulders were as straight as Azure's. Let them talk. Friendships dependent upon such ridiculous distinctions were better lost than kept. As the congregation rose to sing the final hymn she looked calmly about her and when eyes in adjoining pews met hers it was not hers that turned away.

After the benediction her walk through the crowded aisle to the outer door was not in the least hurried. Azure had fled at the moment the minister pronounced the closing amen. Mary's exit was even more deliberate than usual. She bowed here and there and when Mrs. Bradley extended a hand she took it as casually as if she had no inkling of the thoughts beneath its owner's flowered bonnet.

Mrs. Captain Eleazir bent toward her.

"My dear child," murmured Mrs. Bradley, "how do you do? You look tired—and no wonder. We are all so anxious about you."

Mary turned. "Anxious?" she repeated. "About me? Why?"

The lady's black kid glove patted the hand its mate was holding. "You have surprised us all so much," she whispered. "We can't imagine why you do it, but no doubt you have good reasons. Only—only are you *sure* you are not making a mistake?"

"Mistake? . . . Oh, I see! You mean my going to work in the bank. No indeed," with a beaming smile. "If you only knew how gloriously happy it makes me to think that, at last, I am really going to do something worth while, instead of sitting alone and useless there at home, you wouldn't speak of mistakes. I think I am to be congratulated, Mrs. Bradley."

Their hands fell apart. The widow of the late and great Captain Eleazir seemed to be at a loss for words.

"Well!" she gasped. "Well, I—I am sure I am glad to hear that you feel that way. I hope you will always feel so. Of course Elvira and I, being such *old* friends, will call upon you soon and—and perhaps then you can tell us more about how you came to—to do it."

Mary nodded. "Yes, do call," she said, heartily. "Only you must come on an evening or Sunday, because I shall be busy at the bank all the rest of the time. Thank you so much for your interest."

Captain Sam Freeman was pushing his way toward her, but she managed to avoid him, as well as Mrs. Baker, who was edging over from the other direction, and to escape to the outer air. There she found Azure, waiting for her at the foot of the steps.

They walked in silence for a little way. Then, Mrs. Crisp, whose face was a study in crimson, broke out with the protest she had kept to herself so long.

"Mary Brewster," she sputtered, "don't you ever, *ever* coax me into sittin' in that pew with you again. I could choke that dodderin' old Elkanah Bearse for draggin' me up that aisle like a calf on the end of a rope. Couldn't you tell how every soul in that meetin' house was starin' at me all through the service? They never took their eyes off me. I wouldn't turn to see 'em do it—I wouldn't give 'em that satisfaction—but I could *feel* 'em."

Mary shook her head. "Don't be foolish, Azure," she said. "There is no reason in the world why you shouldn't sit with me. Besides," with a half smile, "I don't think they were looking as much at you as at me."

Azure, naturally, misunderstood. "And no wonder," she declared. "They were thinkin' that you must be crazy to let me sit there. I am just as good as any one of 'em and you don't catch me belittlin' myself when I'm where I belong. But I don't belong in a front pew in the First Church of Wapatomac and neither does anybody else except them that has paid rent for those pews for a hundred year or so. There's such a thing as doin' what you're born to do. You and Emma Bradley and the rest was born to one thing, Mary Brewster, and I was born to another. Stay where you do belong, that's my motto."

Mary did not answer. Nor did she reveal to Azure during their homeward walk the startling news which, sooner or later, must be told. She judged the present moment inopportune and once more the revelation was postponed.

Nor was it made that day. All the afternoon Azure was busy in the kitchen or in her room upstairs. Mary could not imagine what she might be doing, but at supper time her question was answered. Azure announced she had been "scrabblin' around" in her trunks in the attic trying to find suitable contributions for the "missionary box" which the Ladies' Society of the New Church were to pack at the church vestry the afternoon of the next day—Monday.

"I don't know how many have asked me if I wasn't goin' to give anything to that box," she said, "and every time I've said I didn't know whether I was or not. You see," she added, sitting down on the haircloth sofa, and looking really embarrassed, a state in which, with the exception of her enforced sojourn in the Brewster pew that very morning, Mary had seldom seen her, "you see," she went on, "I—I'm in a kind of queer place when it comes to anybody's askin' what society I belong to. I was brought up New Church, of course, and Obed—my husband as was—he was New Church, too, when he could spare time to be anything. But while your mother was alive, Mary, long towards her last years she kind of got me into the habit of 'tendin' mornin' meetin' at the First Church. I do like to hear a sermon that satisfies my intellects. If you've got intellects use 'em, *I* say."

She paused, evidently expecting favorable comment on this statement. Mary gratified the desire.

"Certainly, Azure. Yes, of course," she agreed, absently.

"Yes. Well, that's why I go to First Church Sunday

mornin's. But Obed, when he was alive, he was a great New Churcher. He did just love to 'tend Friday night experience meetin's and get himself all worked up and holler 'Amen' and 'Glory' and sing and carry on and—and all like that. He got an awful sight of satisfaction out of it, seemed so, poor soul. So I always used to go with him. And," more reluctantly, "of course all my own folks have been New Meetin'house from the first. That's why I've kept up my subscription down there, paid my fifty cents a week regular. Well, lately I've kind of let that slide and now I'm commencin' to hear about it. Every time I meet that dratted old Cap'n Barney or some of the rest of 'em I get a dig about goin' back on my own crowd. And now, after this mornin', when I was ninny enough to let you and Elkanah Bearse shoo me up that aisle to your pew, it'll be worse than ever. No use my vowin' and declarin' I didn't want to sit there. That won't do any good."

She paused again. Mary was silent. She had heard but little of this long speech of self-justification. Azure fidgeted on the sofa.

"Of course," she went on, "I don't really care a mite about what they say, only—only—you know how 'tis, Mary. It ain't comfortin' to know folks are whisperin' about you behind your back, even if you don't care if they do. You know that, don't you?"

Mary nodded in complete agreement.

"I know, Azure," she said, soberly.

"Um-hum. Well, that's why I thought maybe 'twould be a good idea if I did give somethin' to that missionary box. Yes, and be on hand while 'twas bein' packed. If I'm there," with a toss of the head, "they won't talk about me, for I'll get there so early they won't have a chance. Do you suppose you can get along without me to-morrow afternoon, Mary?"

"Why, of course, Azure. And perhaps I can find some things of my own, or mother's, that will do for the box."

Mrs. Crisp was pleased. She rose from the sofa, once more the complete picture of gentility.

"That'll be just elegant," she gushed. "And," with another relapse into naturalness, "I do want to see what Barney Cummin's fetches for that box. He used to go whalin' when he was a young man and if anybody ever was down on missionaries it's him. He's one of the head New Churchers so he'll have to give somethin', but I bet you 'twill come hard as pullin' teeth."

Mary retired early and the next forenoon she and Azure spent in selecting contributions for the missionary box. Mrs. Crisp, heavily laden, departed shortly after dinner for the New Church vestry in a vehicle which her mistress had insisted upon providing from the local livery stable. Mary, as she heard the door close, felt another pang of conscience. She had not yet told her faithful retainer of the great change which Wednesday morning was to bring to that household.

Azure was in earnest when she announced her determination to arrive at the vestry sufficiently early to head off caustic comment concerning her supposed desertion from the church of her fathers. The dinner dishes, which she insisted upon washing, detained her however, and there were already half a dozen laborers in the vineyard when she entered the door, followed by the youth from the livery stable who was bearing the unwieldy bundle containing her, and Mary's, donations. Upon two pine tables were heaped the articles so far sent in and two more were ready for those to come. Azure, quite conscious of the grandeur attending her entrance with a servitor, pointed to one of these.

"You can put it down there, Enoch," she directed. "That is, unless that table is bein' saved for somethin' special."

Enoch did not wait to learn whether it was or not. He deposited the huge bundle upon the table.

"There!" he grunted, straightening his shoulders. "I *hope* my back ain't broke, but I guess likely 'tis. What in time is in that thing, Azure? Couple of whales?"

Mrs. Crisp did not deign a reply. "You can go now," she said, loftily. "Miss Brewster paid you. I saw her."

Enoch rubbed his right shoulder. "She give me thirty-five cents," he admitted. "You can give me another quarter, if you want to. It'll come in handy for doctors' bills."

Azure scornfully turned her back. Enoch was not in the least abashed.

"It ought to be worth that to you," he observed, with a wink at the assembly. "You don't get a chance to ride in a carriage every day, with a good-lookin' fellow like me to pilot you. . . . Hello there, Elsie!" addressing one of the younger members of the group. "How are you these days? I'm drivin' over to Bayport to-morrow. Want to go along? Get good ice creams over there. Remember them we had the last time? Eh?"

Elsie, judging by her sudden change of color, remembered perfectly. The expression upon the face of Mrs. Noah Oaks, her mother, was quite different. Mrs. Oaks had that moment learned of the Bayport excursion. Take it altogether, Mrs. Crisp's impressive entrance was rather spoiled.

"You needn't come back for me," she said, tartly. "I shan't want you."

"Wasn't cal'latin' to," retorted the unimpressed Enoch. He went out whistling. Azure removed her bonnet and the sealskin cape. When she turned it seemed to her that there was a peculiar air of restraint evidenced by those present. The moment she came in she had been conscious of it. Before opening the door she had heard an animated hum of conversation. The instant she crossed the threshold it had ceased. And even now it was not resumed. They were all looking at her and apparently waiting for her to speak. But when she looked at them they looked away. She voiced her feelings.

"Well!" she exclaimed. "What on earth is the matter? Why doesn't somebody say somethin'? What are you all so fussed up and solemn about? Is somebody dead; somebody I ain't heard about?"

They all spoke then and together. No, indeed! No one was dead. There was nothing the matter. They were *so* glad to have her there with them. Azure believed she understood.

"I see," she said, rather sharply. "You didn't expect me, I suppose. Barney Cummings told you I was through with this society for good and all, I shouldn't wonder. Humph! It's a dreadful thing to get so old that your mind dodders along with the rest of you."

Mrs. Oaks hastened to declare that she, for one, had never believed the Cummings sneers.

"I knew you wouldn't leave the meetin'house you was

brought up in, Azure," she said. "I've said so right along. Of course you have been going to First Church Sunday mornings, but I understood that. Mary Brewster is all alone and she likes to have you go with her for company. That's natural enough, and I told Cap'n Barney so."

Azure did not accept the olive branch. "I guess I can go to meetin' where I want to, *if* I want to," she snapped. "If this meetin'house is the only front door to heaven then I suppose Barney Cummings is Saint Peter and Kohath Briggs carries the keys for him. Well, it'll take more than their word to make me believe it. They better be sure they are goin' to make the right port themselves before they bother about the rest of us. You can tell 'em I said so, if you want to."

Mrs. Oaks was properly squelched and was silent. Azure fired one more broadside.

"I know what the real truth is, of course," she declared. "It is all over town that I set in the Brewster pew yesterday mornin'. Well, I didn't do it on purpose and I shan't do it again. Unless I take a notion to," she added, emphatically. "Then I shall and I don't know who is goin' to stop me."

Mrs. Roxanna Beasley poured oil upon the troubled waters.

"Don't you think we'd better begin lookin' over the missionary things," she suggested. "Let's look at what Mrs. Crisp brought first. I am sure as she brought 'em right from Cap'n Brewster's house they'll be perfectly lovely."

This was gratifying. Azure's temper subsided to its wonted genteel calm. She untied the bundles brought by the livery man. The exclamations which greeted each item were as enthusiastic as even she could have expected.

"Oh, isn't that sweet!" gushed Elsie Oaks, holding up and displaying a black velvet hat, trimmed with black satin ribbon and jet ornaments. "I think that is too nice for—for heathen savages, don't you?"

Most of them did, but Mrs. Crisp was grandly firm.

"*I* put that in," she proclaimed. "Mary didn't want me to. She laughed and seemed to think 'twas funny. 'That's an old hat of mother's,' says she, 'and years and years out of style besides. What in the world will a South Sea Islander do with it?' I had my answer ready. 'Do with it!' says I. 'Wear it and be glad of the chance. Judgin' by the pictures of those South Sea folks I've seen they'll be glad to get *anything* to wear. . . . Don't you think so, Mr. Bacon?"

Bacon was the new, and young, minister of the New Church. He had that moment arrived at the vestry. His expression, as he was shown the velvet hat, was a trifle peculiar, but in the face of the approval he offered no objection. He and Azure shook hands.

"I am very glad to have you with us, Mrs. Crisp," he said. "I hope you are well."

Azure said she was very well indeed.

"And—and Miss Brewster?" he asked, with some hesitation. "She is—er—all right?"

The bustle and stir about the tables had ceased. As he asked this question the silence was absolute. Every one seemed to be awaiting the reply. Mrs. Crisp noticed this, she could not have helped noticing it.

"All right!" she repeated. "Of course she is all right. Why shouldn't she be?"

The minister, too, was now aware of the silence and universal attention. He seemed embarrassed.

"Oh, she should, of course," he stammered. "No doubt—yes. It was only that—that considering the—well, we were all surprised to hear of the change she was about to make, and—and—"

Azure broke in. "Change!" she repeated. "What change? What are you talkin' about, Mr. Bacon?"

The reverend gentleman looked about him at the faces of his parishioners. Mrs. Noah Oaks touched his arm.

"Won't you come back here a minute, Mr. Bacon?" she said. "There's somethin' I want to ask you about."

He followed her to the rear of the room. Mrs. Oaks whispered in his ear.

"I don't believe she knows it yet," she whispered. "Anyhow she don't act as if she did. Perhaps it isn't so. I don't believe we'd better mention it. Let her tell it herself, if she's a mind to."

Azure was gazing after the pair. "What did he mean by a 'change'?" she asked. "Mary Brewster isn't makin' any changes. Who said she was?"

No one seemed to know. The bustle of opening the various packages began once again. When Mr. Bacon and Mrs. Oaks rejoined the group the minister did not resume his conversation with Mrs. Crisp. Like the others his interest was centered upon the contributions for the missionary box.

One by one the donations were revealed and passed upon. Many were fitting and likely to be useful. A number, however, were to say the least, peculiar.

"My heavens and earth!" exclaimed Mrs. Beasley, holding in one hand a mass of wrapping paper and string and in the other an ancient fur cap; "*Who* do you suppose thought *that* would be any use to a South Sea cannibal? With earlaps on it, too! My husband sailed years ago out of San Francisco aboard a tradin' vessel and he's told me more than a hundred times how hot it was in those parts. Who ever figgered those poor sun-baked critters would strut around in furs? Well, I never! And all full of moth holes!"

She should have been more careful, for old Mrs. Simeon Bean, standing almost at her elbow, piped up in high indignation.

"That cap belonged to my own father," she sputtered, "and he paid four dollars and seventy-five cents for it up to Boston—himself he did—and he wore it till he died. He was drownded in it, if you want to know. If it ain't good enough for a heathen naked nigger then I guess nothin' is. You can hand it right straight back to me, Roxanna Beasley. Moth eat! I want to know! I guess if you was as old as that cap is you'd be moth eat, too. And you wouldn't look nigh as harnsome neither."

Mrs. Beasley was profuse in apology, but it was not until the minister took a hand that the old lady was in the least pacified. The cap was by no means the most unsuitable donation to the welfare of the South Sea Islanders. A pair of skates, minus straps, and a coal hod with no handle were awarded the palm in that respect. As these had been sent in by a member not present freedom of comment might be, and was, unrestrained.

"Mercy!" snapped Mrs. Oaks, pettishly throwing the skates under the table. "I should think we were filling up an ash barrel instead of a missionary box. I told Sarah

T. to *give* something, not get rid of stuff she was too lazy to throw outdoors."

On the whole, the contributions brought by Mrs. Crisp were adjudged by far the best and Azure was gratified and her temporarily injured dignity regained.

"Well," she observed, bridling, "I'm glad you like 'em. Of course I don't pretend to have better taste than other folks, but I look at it this way: I said to myself, 'If *I* was a cannibal,' I said, 'what would *I* like to have sent to me?' What was it that elocution woman read that evenin'? 'Twas at the First Church, of course, but some of you were there, because I saw you. 'Twas a piece from Mr. Kipling's poems she read, and it came back to me when Mary and I was pickin' out these very things here.

"The heathen in his blindness,
Bows down to wooden stone.

"That's what 'twas. 'Well,' says I, 'let's hope the poor thing is learnin' from the missionaries that there's somethin' better to bow to than that. But, anyhow, *while* he's learnin', let's give him worth-while clothes to bow in. He couldn't do it on skates, I shouldn't think. Scarcely."

Confident that she had made a profound impression by this display of erudition, she added a closing word.

"Of course," she said, "I realize I'm fortunate to live in a house belongin' to people who have nice things to give away and where money isn't any real object."

And again there was a moment of silence and an exchange of looks among her audience. She noticed it and was about to speak when a noise at the door caused her and all the others to turn in that direction. The door was thrown wide open and the lathy figure of Kohath Briggs appeared. Kohath was bearing a mighty package. Behind him, and giving orders as he had been accustomed to give them from the quarter-deck of the old *Sophia,* rolled Captain Barnabas Cummings.

"Steady now, steady!" blustered Captain Barney. "Don't run afoul of them tables. Take your time. . . . Oh, hello, Roxanna! Think I wasn't comin', did you? How are you, Mr. Bacon? I— Well?" once more turning his attention to Kohath, who had paused. "What's the matter?"

Kohath's long neck stretched as he turned to peer over the huge bundle in his arms. "Where you want me should put this, Skipper?" he drawled.

"Put it? Put it down, of course. Standin' there hollerin' right in the middle of the channel! Put it *down.*"

Mr. Briggs obeyed orders. He deposited his burden with a thump upon the heap of goods arranged upon the nearest table. Some of those were, in consequence, pushed off and fell to the floor. Mrs. Noah Oaks, who had spent at least fifteen minutes sorting them in different piles, sprang to the rescue.

"Oh, not right there on top of everything!" she protested. "Oh, dear, dear! Now they're all mixed up again. *Don't* leave it there, Mr. Briggs, *please!*"

Kohath heard, of course, but as usual he required time to understand and act upon the understanding.

"Eh?" he drawled. And added, feelingly, "Say, that had some heft to it, did you know it?"

Captain Barnabas roared impatience.

"Pick it up!" he commanded. "Pick it up! Don't

you hear her tell you pick it up? Oh, good Lord A'mighty! Get out of the way and I'll shift it myself."

He would have tried, in spite of his eighty-two years, but the minister and Kohath between them bore the package to the farthest and least occupied table. Captain Barney superintended the transfer.

"Harnsomely, Mr. Bacon," he pleaded, nervously. "Don't let it go by the run. There's stuff in there that'll break if you heave it around so. Harnsomely, Kohath, you lubber! . . . There, that's it. . . . All the way down from the house," he added, turning to Mrs. Beasley, "he's been givin' me heart disease with that bundle. All but droppin' it, and bangin' it into trees and posts."

Briggs mopped his forehead with a crumpled handkerchief. "So everlastin' big I couldn't see over it to steer," he drawled. "If you'd only have let me hitch up the horse, same as I wanted to, we'd have been here half an hour ago. . . . Whew!" with a gasp of exhaustion. "If I ain't beat out then nobody ever was."

The captain snorted disgust. "Hitch up a horse and team," he sneered, "to tote a little mite of a thing like that. When I was your age I could have lugged two of 'em, one under each arm. Well, there! you can go home now and turn into bed and rest up, if you want to. We don't need you any more."

Kohath promptly sat down on a chair.

"Nothin' I have to go home for 'special," he announced calmly. "Guess likely I'll stay where I be for a spell."

Mrs. Oaks—she was president of the Ladies' Society—took command of the situation.

"Well, it's nice you did get 'em here just this minute,

Cap'n Barnabas," she said. "We're about done sorting the rest and now we can look over what you've brought. I'm sure they'll be welcome, whatever they are."

She was about to cut the cord binding the Cummings bundle, but Captain Barnabas caught her arm.

"That's a good line," he declared. "Don't cut it. A pretty nigh brand-new cod line like that is too good to waste. Let me untie it. I made it fast myself so I know just how to cast it off. Won't be but a second."

This was a rash prophecy, for the succession of sailor knots required time and effort, even for his practiced fingers. He picked and tugged at each one and from the chair upon and around which Mr. Briggs was draped, came a mournful chuckle.

"I told you you was lashin' that up as if you was furlin' a mainsa'l," he observed. "There wasn't no million dollars in it, fur's I could make out."

The Skipper was too busy to retort. At last the final knot was untied and the sheet covering the Cummings donation to the missionary box was thrown back.

"There!" panted Captain Barnabas. "There you be. The dummed missionaries can have all them and welcome. I hope they appreciate their luck."

The members of the Ladies' Society, and Mr. Bacon, crowded up to inspect. Azure was in the background. So far Captain Barney had not noticed that she was present.

No one said a word during that first inspection. They looked and looked; then they looked at each other. Old Mrs. Bean was the first to speak.

"What a sight of old bottles!" she mused, in a sort

of whispered soliloquy. Captain Cummings turned on her like a flash.

"Old bottles," he crowed, triumphantly. "Sartin there's a lot of 'em. There's every one I could find around the house. I guess likely you don't none of you appreciate what store them Kanakas set by bottles, especially the green and blue and red ones like them over yonder. They'd rather have an old empty bottle than they would anything else in the world, unless 'twas a full one. Why, I remember one whalin' cruise amongst them islands—back in 1845, or thereabouts 'twas—when I traded a red quart whisky bottle for half a boat load of coconuts. Yes, sir, I did! And the Kanaka I swapped with offered to give me his daughter for the mate to it. They don't have any glass, you understand, and so a bottle is a kind of miracle, as you might say. If the missionary you're shippin' this stuff to has got any sense —maybe he has, but I never run acrost a missionary that had any—he can start up his whole blessed Sunday school with them bottles. Give 'em out, kind of reward of merit for learnin' lessons, or somethin'. You bet he can!"

This practical suggestion for the propagation of Christian teaching in the South Seas was not greeted with the applause which, perhaps, it deserved. Every one looked at the Reverend Mr. Bacon. He shaded his face with his hand and Mrs. Beasley confided to her daughter afterward that she couldn't tell whether he was laughin' or shocked. His comment when made was, however, grave enough.

"Yes. Yes, of course, Captain Cummings," he said. "I'm sure the bottles—er—some of them, at least—will be very welcome. Now what else have you?"

The captain, it developed, had many things within the compass of that sheet. Most of them were unusual, they had individuality of their own. A set of worn red flannel underwear he exhibited with especial pride.

"Look at that," he ordered, lifting and shaking out the most intimate of these garments. "Why, a Kanaka 'll go crazy over that. He'll rig out in it and strut up and down the main street same as if he was General Grant. Yes, he will. Maybe he won't wear it same as you and I would, Roxanna. Just as liable to tie the legs around his neck and let the rest string out astern. But he'll trade his everlastin' soul for it, just the same. It's the red that'll get him, you understand. If I was a missionary—and I wouldn't be if there was any other job a-goin'—I've seen too many of 'em and they are the ruination of Kanakas—but if I was I'd carry a trunk full of them red flannels. Lord love you! *they* don't know what they're worth. You can cheat the eye teeth out of 'em and they're satisfied. Now here's another thing pretty nigh as good: That old lookin' glass. Oh, I know the quick-silver's wore off the back consider'ble, but that don't count. One of them fool cannibals will roost in front of a lookin' glass for an hour, makin' faces at himself. Ain't it amazin'! If *you* looked like him, Mr. Bacon, you wouldn't want to *see* what you looked like. No sir-ee! You'd be prayin' to be struck blind so's you couldn't ever see and to be allowed to forget what you'd seen afore. But not a Kanaka. Why—"

And so on, with frequent breaks in the exposition during which he expressed his convictions as to the utter uselessness and impractical character of missionaries in general. His hearers cast sidelong glances at each other and shifted uneasily. Finally Mrs. Oaks broke in.

"Yes," she said hurriedly. "Well, I'm sure we all thank you, Cap'n Cummings, ever so much. Now don't you think," turning to Mrs. Beasley, "that we'd better have our little business meeting now? Seems to me we had. And we can finish our sorting and packing by and by—to-morrow, perhaps. There's no real hurry, you know."

Mrs. Beasley accepted the suggestion, and the significant wink accompanying it, with alacrity.

"Yes," she said. "I do. It is gettin' pretty late and some of us will have to be goin' soon. Do let's have the meetin' right off."

So the group about the Cummings exhibit broke up and turned away from the table. And then Captain Barnabas, for the first time, caught sight of Mrs. Crisp. His round, red face broke into a broad grin.

"Why, hello, Azure!" he exclaimed. "You're here, ain't you? Well, well, well! You're here!"

Every one now turned to look at Azure and again she was conscious of that peculiar and, it seemed to her, expectant hush.

"Here!" she repeated, with dignified condescension. "Why, yes, I'm here. I don't look as if I was anywhere else, I shouldn't imagine."

The Skipper was regarding her with the same broad grin.

"You're here," he said again. "I didn't hardly expect you—to-day. Kind of quiet, ain't you? Seems to me I don't remember hearin' you say a word since I made port."

Azure scornfully drew herself erect. "I don't recollect," she observed, sweetly, "that I nor most of the rest of us has had a chance to get in a word of our own for the last ten minutes. . . . Well, Susan," turning to Mrs. Oaks, "if you're goin' to call that business meetin' I should say do it. That is," with severe sarcasm, "if you feel that lookin' at *trash* isn't the only thing we came here to do."

She stalked toward the rows of chairs at the other end of the vestry. Mrs. Oaks and several other women turned to follow her, but Captain Barnabas roared an order to halt.

"Here! Hold on!" he shouted, angrily. "Wait a minute. Look here, Azure Crisp, what are you callin' trash? Who are you hintin' at? Eh?"

Azure scarcely deigned to turn her head. "I'm not hintin'," she replied, in her most ladylike manner. "It ain't *my* business to say what's trash and what isn't. *I* ain't the president of this society."

She moved grandly on. Mrs. Oaks scuttled like a frightened hen toward the official table. The minister lingered to pacify the irate Captain Cummings.

"There, there, Captain—" he began, but the Skipper had no intention of being pacified.

"Huh!" he grunted, loudly. "Ain't president, eh? No, you're right you ain't. You ain't much of anything in this meetin'house. You've been so busy playin' poodle dog at the heels of First Church folks that—"

"Sshh! sshh!" This from Mr. Bacon.

"No I won't sshh. Why should I? She's been fetchin' and carryin' for Mary Brewster so long she's begun to think she was christened Brewster, herself. Humph! That name ain't so much to brag about neither, not just now 'tain't. It's come down some, I'd say. Looks as if Brewsters had to go to work for a livin' these days, like everyday folks. . . . Oh, well, all right, Mr. Bacon. I won't raise a row in the meetin'house. Only," with one final irrepressible outburst, "I ain't goin' to have her puttin' on airs over me."

"Won't you all please sit down and come to order," pleaded Mrs. Oaks, clapping her hands for silence.

But now it was Azure who refused to obey. She turned again to face her detested enemy.

"What was that you just said, Barney Cummings?" she demanded, sharply.

Captain Barnabas was not in the least daunted.

"I said you needn't try out your high and mighty airs on me," he repeated. "That's what I said; and I meant it."

The minister once more essayed the rôle of peacemaker.

"Now, Captain Cummings," he began; but Mrs. Crisp would not let him finish.

"I don't care what he says about me," she proclaimed, scornfully. "I'm above bein' bothered by *him,* I should hope. But when he commences slurrin' those that ain't here to speak for themselves, then I speak for 'em. What did he mean by the Brewster name havin' 'come down'? And about Brewsters havin' to work for a livin'? . . . No, Susan Oaks, I shan't sit down and I shan't come to order till he answers me. What did you mean by that, Barnabas Cummings?"

"Mrs. Crisp—" begged the minister.

"Oh, Azure, now *please*—" persisted Mrs. Oaks.

"Be still! . . . Well, Cap'n Cummings?"

Captain Barnabas looked a trifle foolish. Every person

in the room, including Kohath Briggs, who had been indulging in a short nap in his chair, was now gazing at the couple. The vestry was still.

"Humph!" grunted the captain, grudgingly. "Well, maybe I hadn't ought to have said that. Perhaps it ain't a comedown; that's accordin' to how you look at it. Keepin' books at the bank is a respectable job enough, nothin' to be ashamed of. Only when somebody does it whose family has always acted as if the rest of us was—was bugs that they mustn't mess up their shoes by steppin' on, then—well, then, the bugs can't help bein' surprised, that's all."

The silence was absolute now. The creak of Mrs. Bean's chair, as she lifted a hand to her ear in order to hear better, was the only sound to break it. Azure was staring at the old man in utter bewilderment.

"*What* on earth are you talkin' about?" she gasped. "Yes—and who?"

Captain Barney returned the stare. "Do you mean to say you haven't heard about it?" he demanded, incredulously. "Hasn't anybody told you? Hasn't *she* told you?"

"Told me? Who told me? Told me what?"

"Hasn't Mary Brewster told you that she's got Allie Jones's job at the Wapatomac National Bank and is comin' there to work day after to-morrow mornin'?"

Azure's eyes and mouth opened. She turned pale.

"You—you're crazy," she exclaimed.

"Crazy nothin'! I swan I believe you *haven't* heard it! She ain't told it—ashamed to, probably. Well, it's so. She asked my grandson, Dave, a week ago to get her that place if he could, and he did. The directors voted her in yesterday forenoon and she's to be on hand Wednesday mornin'. . . . You needn't act as if you was struck by lightnin'. It's so. Ask anybody here. They all know it. And if you don't, you're the only one in this town."

Mrs. Crisp gasped. Then she turned to look at the eager faces of the occupants of the chairs. What she read on those faces was proof sufficient. The peculiar behavior when she first entered the vestry, the odd way in which these people had looked at her, their evident expectancy—all these were explained. The amazing disclosure was true, or at least they all believed it to be.

She would not—yet. Her back stiffened.

"Rubbish!" she cried. "Stuff and nonsense! I never heard— Why should Mary Brewster take a job in a bank, or anywhere else? Mary *Brewster!* Bosh!"

Mrs. Beasley rose and came to her side.

"I guess it's so, Azure," she said, soothingly. "Most everybody heard about it yesterday, after directors' meetin', and there's no doubt it's true. We were so surprised to find out—or guess by the way you acted since you came here—that you didn't know, yourself. Now, now, now! Don't look so queer. There's nothin' shameful in it. Of course we *can't* imagine why Mary feels she's got to do such a thing, but—"

She had wound an arm about the Crisp waist, but Azure threw it aside. She turned on her heel and marched to the hook where hung her legacies from Annabelle Brewster, the flowered bonnet and the sealskin cape. She tied the bonnet strings with fingers which trembled, but there was no tremble in the voice with which, at the outer door, she bade defiant farewell.

"Good afternoon," she said, majestically. "I *supposed*

when I came here that this was to be a missionary meetin'. I didn't suppose it was just an excuse for pryin' into people's private affairs. Not that there's the least thing for us to be ashamed of in those affairs, but they are our own business and we *intended* to keep 'em so. As for me, I'll never—*never* set foot across this doorsill again. Considerin' *some* that appear to be head ones and to be runnin' this church," with a glance in the direction of Captain Barnabas, "I'd be ashamed to. Good afternoon."

The door closed behind her. The Skipper broke into a scornful "Ha, ha!" Mr. Briggs, in his seat at the rear of the room, chuckled languidly. The vestry buzzed with exclamations and excited whispers. It was some time before the business meeting was really called to order.

Mary was seated by the table in the sitting room, poring over a book on *Double Entry Bookkeeping,* a relic of her days at the academy, when Mrs. Crisp entered. She was still wearing the sealskin cape and the flowered bonnet, the latter a little over one ear. Miss Brewster looked up.

"Well, Azure," she asked, "did you have a nice time at your missionary meeting?"

Azure ignored the question. Standing directly before her employer she leveled an accusing finger.

"Mary Brewster," she ordered, "you answer me right straight off. Are you goin' to work for that Dave Cummings in his bank? I know perfectly well you ain't—but are you?"

Mary put down the treatise on bookkeeping. The scene she had so dreaded was imminent. The crisis had arrived. Well, she must meet it.

"Yes, Azure," she said, gravely. "I am. I should

have told you before, of course, but I knew how you would feel—at first—and I kept putting it off. Take off your things now. Sit down on the sofa and I'll tell you why I am doing it."

Azure sat down. She did not take off her things, but she sank upon the sofa and covered her face with her hands.

"Oh, my soul! my soul!" she sobbed. "Every day since your poor mother passed away I've been mournin' for her and now I'm ready to say I'm reconciled. The one thing she dreaded more 'n all was insanity and now her own daughter's struck with it. Oh, my soul, my soul!"

CHAPTER V

IT was a dismal evening in the old Brewster house. Mary explained to Azure the reasons which led to the shattering of family tradition, repeated them over and over again. She did not emphasize the most impelling reason, her lack of money, and, of course, she said nothing concerning her rash plunge in the stock market. She dwelt upon her loneliness and her feeling that she must do something to keep her mind occupied. Azure listened, but the end of the session found her in exactly the same position as at the beginning.

"Well," she groaned, rising from the sofa and wiping her eyes with her handkerchief, "no use my sittin' here any longer, I suppose. I had to get supper the day your poor mother died, and I presume likely I must get it now. We all have our duties laid onto us, let the chips fall where they may. And to-morrow mornin' I'm goin' to send for the doctor. If you'll take my advice, which I suppose you won't, you'll go right upstairs and lay down this minute. I'll bring your supper up when it's ready."

Mary was becoming a little weary.

"Nonsense, Azure," she said, "I shall eat supper in the dining room as I always do. I'm not sick and I'm not insane. I know I am doing exactly the right thing and I am going to do it. Now please be sensible. And don't," with a sudden burst of impatience, "stand there weeping over me as if I were in my coffin. I feel much more alive this minute than I have felt for months."

Mrs. Crisp sighed heavily and turned to go. She paused before the portrait of great-grandfather Brewster.

"When I see that grand noble face lookin' at me," she declared, tragically, "and think of—"

Mary interrupted. "Oh, do stop!" she cried. "I am thankful to know that I shall soon be where it can't look at me, and I won't have to look at it from morning till night. . . . Now run along and behave yourself."

Azure did not run. Her exit was that of a martyr on the way to the stake. Supper was a funereal meal and throughout the next day her demeanor toward her employer was that of a humane jailer toward a condemned criminal with but a few hours to live. She was loftily righteous but sorrowfully sympathetic. Only in the evening of what might, judging by appearances, have been Mary's last day on earth, did she utter an observation which showed that her mind was working toward a partial reconcilation with Fate.

"Mary," she said, "there's just one thing I do want to say. Don't you let that old Barney Cummings know you realize what it means for one of your family to go to work for day's wages. He called it a comedown, the impudent old—er—er—Methusalem. Don't you ever give him the satisfaction of lettin' him see you know it *is* a comedown. If he begins heavin' out his hints, you snub him right up. You let him understand you're a Brewster and he's a Cummings. Now you'll do that, won't you?"

"I will, Azure," said Mary, laughing.

"All right. Be sure you do. When he sprung it on me down to that vestry meetin' I can't tell you how thankful I am that I kept my head and didn't let him see how he'd knocked me over. I gave him and the rest of 'em to understand that I'd known it all along and had kept it to myself 'cause 'twas our business—yours and mine—and nobody else's. If I ain't glad I did! Humph! Just let him come around patronizin' and crowin' over me and see what he gets. Oh, if it only wasn't his grandson you was goin' to work for! Seems if I could bear anything better 'n *that.*"

The Wapatomac National Bank occupied a new one-story brick building at the corner near the First Church. It was the only brick building in Wapatomac and the town was proud of it. At a quarter to nine o'clock on Wednesday morning Mary Brewster approached its portals to report for duty. She felt queer and alone and strangely out of place. For just a moment as she stood with her hand upon the heavy door with the gilt letters upon its plate glass panel, she hesitated. It required all her resolution to push it open and enter. Like a child on its way to school for the first time she longed to turn and run home again as fast as she could.

She did not run, of course. She walked in and found Ben Jackson, the bank's errand boy and messenger, dusting the desks and preparing for the day's routine. Ben greeted her with a funny mixture of deference, shyness, and a desire to be agreeable.

"How do you do, Miss Brewster?" he said. "I was expectin' you'd be here. Mr. Hall, he said you'd come to-day. You're kind of early, ain't you? Don't need to get here till nine, you don't. Allie never. Sometimes 'twas ten minutes past before he showed up."

Mary smiled. "I wanted to be on time my very first day, Ben," she replied. "Where shall I put my coat and hat?"

"Eh? Oh, hang 'em yonder in the closet. I'll show you. . . . This'll be your desk; anyhow I suppose 'twill be, it's the one Allie always had. He's goin' to stay for a couple of days, so's to help you get started. Cap'n Cummings asked him to."

Mary inspected the desk which was to be hers. Young Jackson, his shyness disappearing, stood, duster in hand, at her elbow.

"The books are all in the safe," he explained. "Mr. Hall will open it up when he comes. He's always prompt. Don't catch *him* bein' late. No, *sir!*"

Mary shook her head. "I am almost afraid to see them," she confessed, speaking her thought aloud.

"What? The books? Aw, you needn't be. You can keep 'em all right. I heard Cap'n Dave tell Mr. Hall you'd keep 'em fine. Huh! I could do it myself, if I had the chance. Allie Jones, he makes out they're a whale of a job, but they ain't. Allie thinks he's all creation, but I don't think he's so terrible much. I guess likely the Wapatomac National Bank'll worry along without him. We can keep afloat even if he does go to Boston to work. Mr. Hall, he says the same; I heard him."

Mr. Hall, the cashier, himself came in a few minutes later. Mary knew him well, of course. Peter Hall was not a native of Wapatomac. He had lived in the town but five or six years, having been called from Brockton, where he had been one of the junior officials of a trust company. The cashier was a widower, thirty-seven years of age, small, thin and dignified. Azure Crisp had declared that she did like to look at him, he looked just the way a bank cashier ought to look. He was greatly respected in the community, and was a regular attendant at the First Church, as of course he should be, being a distant relative of Mrs. Captain Samuel Freeman.

His greeting of Mary Brewster was dignified—he was always that—but cordial also. They shook hands and he expressed pleasure at having her in the bank's employ.

"We are very glad to have you with us, Miss Brewster," he told her. "Very glad indeed. I see Bennie has shown you the desk which will be yours. Jones is to help you for a day or two—to get you started, you know. He will be here soon. Should be here now," with a glance at his watch.

Allie Jones sauntered in at that moment. He was a self-sufficient youth and his self-sufficiency was not lessened by the knowledge that he was doing the bank a favor by remaining these extra days. The safe was opened, the heavy account books brought forth and distributed by Ben Jackson, and, when Mr. Philander Cahoon, the venerable teller and head bookkeeper, arrived, the Wapatomac bank was officially ready for business.

Mary, under the condescending superintendency of young Mr. Jones, was instructed in what she would be expected to do. She was awed and a little frightened at first by the prospect. Allie noticed her perturbation and smiled behind his hand.

"Pretty sizable job, isn't it," he observed. "Especially for a woman. Well," graciously, "I guess you'll handle it all right, after a while. I'll get you going and Cahoon he'll give you a lift any time you get stuck. Don't get discouraged, that's the main thing. Why," with a smile of amusement, "I remember when I first sat down at these books, they kind of had *me* stumped. Yes, they did.

But, 'twasn't but a week or so. After that—why say!"

He did not add, "And now look at me!" but that, Mary judged, was to be inferred. Unfortunately for him, Mr. Hall, who had, with his customary soft-footed tread, approached the pair from the rear, put in a word.

"Suppose you show her how easy it is, Jones," he observed, dryly. "She knows now how smart you are. Get to work and prove it."

Allie, a trifle discomposed, sat down at the desk. Mary sat beside him, watching, listening and trying hard to learn. The forenoon wore away. People came into the bank, men and women whom she had known all her life. They all peered at her through the gratings. Some of them said "Good morning," the others merely stared. She had a feeling that at least half a dozen of these visitors had come solely to look at her, to make sure she was really there. At first this conviction and the curious stares embarrassed and confused her. Then, in the interest of the new work, she began to forget them altogether. The books were complicated, they were vastly different from her father's simple accounts, but she believed she could master them after a time. If a person like Allie Jones could do it, she could. She would, that was all.

David Cummings came earlier than usual that day from his office at the wharf, to the president's room at the bank, where his hours were from eleven to one. Mary did not notice his arrival. She was busy with a column of figures and was first made aware of his presence by hearing his voice. She started, looked up, and found him standing beside her.

"Good mornin'," he said. "Well, you're hard at it, I see. How are you gettin' along?"

She smiled, rather dubiously. "I don't know," she confessed. "I guess I have been too busy to think of that."

He nodded. "That's a good sign," he observed. "It is interestin' enough to take up your mind so far, I judge; eh?"

She understood the reference to their previous conversation.

"There is no doubt of that," she said.

"Then we've made a start. Allie learnin' you the ropes, is he?"

"He is trying to."

Young Jones put in a word.

"She's starting all right, Cap'n," he said, patronizingly. "She'll catch on, give her time. If I could just be around for a couple of weeks to give her pointers she'd do pretty well. Wish I could, but that's out of the question. They're expectin' me up there to Boston now, I know."

"Certain, certain. Well, you tell 'em we couldn't get along without you. They'll understand that just as soon as they get to know you. I guess likely they'll forgive us after a spell. . . . Yes, Peter, I'm comin'."

He turned away to join the cashier, who stood by his desk, a packet of papers in his hand. Mr. Hall led the way to the inner office, which was also the directors' room, and Cummings followed him. Mary did not see him again that day. She was a little disappointed. He had been cordial and pleasant, and of course he was president of the bank and she only an assistant bookkeeper—not even that as yet. But it was her first day and it did seem as if he might have lingered to talk a little longer. On other occasions, when she had come to ask his advice concerning investments or the like, he had never appeared in the least hurried. Well, it was different now of course. She was an employee of the institution, not its patron. Yes, it was different. Everything would be different.

At twelve she went home for dinner. Jones gave her a parting word of advice.

"You be back here at one sharp, won't you?" he said. "The old man—Cap'n Dave, I mean—he's pretty strict about our being on time. So's Hall, far as that goes. Besides, I go for my own dinner at one, you understand."

Mary, again reminded that she was now a business woman and not a lady of leisure, promised to be prompt. At the Brewster house the door was opened for her by Azure, an outwardly dignified and mutely reproachful Azure, but inwardly a mere mortal consumed with human curiosity. Dinner was ready and they sat down.

"Well?" demanded Mrs. Crisp, after a short interval of eager waiting on her part. "What did you do? What did they say to you? Was that Dave Cummings there? You didn't let him lord it over you, I hope?"

Mary laughed. "No one lorded it over me, Azure," she replied. "Every one was very nice."

"Humph! I should think they better be. They know who you are, I should imagine. Did a lot of folks you know come there? Our kind of folks, I mean?"

"Yes, some of them."

"Who?"

"Well, Captain Freeman for one. I suppose he is our kind of folks, isn't he?"

"Humph! He hopes he is. What did he say to you?"

"He said 'Good morning.'"

"Humph! What did you say to him?"

"I said 'Good morning,' too."

"Was that all?"

"Yes."

Azure was disappointed. "Wan't much of a talk, seems to me," she observed.

"Not much. He was busy, I suppose; and I know I was."

"Umph! Busy! All the business he had was just to come snoopin' for a look at you, so's he can go home and cackle and crow with his wife. That old Cap'n Barney didn't come, did he?"

"No. Or, if he did I didn't see him."

"You'd have seen him if he'd been there. Yes, and heard him, too. . . . My glory!" a few minutes later. "You ain't through dinner so soon?"

"I'm not hungry, Azure. And besides I must get back to work."

Mrs. Crisp's look was expressive.

"You—you are goin' back, then?" she queried.

"Why, of course. You didn't think I was through for the day, did you?"

A long sigh. Azure rose from the table. Mary regarded her wonderingly.

"What did you think?" she asked.

"I thought—I was just hopin'—" Then with a sudden burst of candor: "If you must know I was hopin' maybe you'd had enough of it by this time, and was goin' to stay in this house where you belong. That's what I hoped."

Mary laughed aloud. "I am going to work in that bank

to-day and every week day," she said. "That is, provided I can do the work well enough to satisfy Captain Cummings and Mr. Hall. I thought I had made you understand that, Azure. Now I must hurry. I shouldn't like to overstay my noon hour—the very first one, at any rate."

"Your noon hour! My glory's land! Do you mean to tell me that you have got to eat by the clock? Have your hour's noonin' and no more, like—like a Portygee cullin' oysters down to Dave Cummings's wharf? You—Annabelle Brewster's only daughter? Why, I never—"

She was still choking and sputtering when Mary closed the outer door.

The afternoon at the bank was much like the forenoon, except that she did not again see David Cummings. He had gone home to his own dinner when she returned and from it, presumably, to the office of D. Cummings & Co. She continued to labor at the books, under the airy direction of Allie Jones. It was at times so airy, so loftily condescending, that she was tempted to rebellion. Then her sense of humor came to the rescue and she repressed the desire to retort and smiled instead.

Occasionally Philander Cahoon, in an interval of respite from his duties at the teller's window, came to her side and offered a helpful suggestion. Mr. Cahoon was a thin-faced, pleasant old fellow. He wore a rather seedy blue suit, spoke in a gentle voice and his eyes, behind his gold-rimmed spectacles, were kindly. Mary's acquaintance with him was slight but she had always liked him. He was a cousin of one of the directors; apparently, with the exception of herself and Captain David Cummings, the staff of the Wapatomac National Bank was a family affair. On Sunday mornings he usually sat in one of the rear pews at the First Church. To be what Azure called a "First Churcher" seemed also a necessary qualification for enrollment in the bank's force. Well, she herself possessed that qualification.

Captain David Cummings did not. He was not a regular member of any religious society, although his family had been pillars of the New Church from the beginning. He was not related to a director, even distantly. Yet the powers in this closely knit and exclusive corporation had chosen him as their president. She remembered hearing comments and half-hearted criticisms in influential quarters at the time the choice was made, but even Mrs. Eleazir Bradley, widow of the former president, had not offered serious objections. "Of course he is not our kind," Mary remembered Mrs. Bradley as saying; "not in the least like my dear husband. But, for some reason or other, Eleazir had grown to trust and—well yes, to depend upon him. I think, from some things he said to me before he passed away, that he would have liked to know Captain Cummings was to take his place. After all, I suppose we must admit that business capability and family do not *always* go together."

Evidently this was true. Mary Brewster had given the matter little consideration before, but now, behind the brass grill of the bank, surrounded by "family"—poor relations perhaps, as in the case of Philander Cahoon, but relatives and therefore aristocrats nevertheless—the election of David Cummings to the presidency seemed a miracle, and the fact that he had filled that office satisfactorily since his election another. Why was it? He must be a remarkable man. He must be. But for the life of her she could not divine just what it was that made him remarkable.

At home, and alone in her room that evening, she pondered upon the problem. There was nothing remarkable in his appearance or manner. He lacked the assertive authority and aggressive dignity of—say, Captain Sam Freeman or Captain Frederick Donald. He was very "everyday." He was careless in his English and, as every one knew, his education had ended with his graduation from the local grammar school. Yet these people—Donalds and Bradleys and Freemans—accepted his decisions and yielded to his judgment in financial—yes, and sometimes in political matters. And she, herself, had turned to him for advice in her own trouble. Why? She did not really know. As she had told him, it seemed the natural thing to do. Queer. Very queer. Nothing seemed to answer her "Why?" He was honest, of course, but so were the Freemans and the Donalds. He was capable—but they must be, or they could not have made or added to their fortunes. Every one knew him; every one, high or low, hailed him on the street as Cap'n Dave—or even "Dave," without the title. And, in spite of this never resented familiarity, all seemed to respect him. No, he did not look nor act in any way remarkable, but somehow or other, he must be.

She fell asleep still pondering and speculating. A snobbish attitude of mind, perhaps, but Miss Brewster had been born and reared in the snobbiest circles of "Snob Town."

She was prompt at the bank next morning and began her second day, a day very little different from her first.

Only one caller ventured behind the grill to speak to her. Captain Fred Donald drove over from Ostable, entered the gate of the cashier's enclosure and walked ponderously to her desk.

"Well, Mary," he said, in his usual gruff pompous manner, "you meant it, I see. When Cummings told me I thought perhaps he was building a shark out of a sand eel, as the saying goes. I judged he'd counted too much on your being lonesome and dull up there at home. I could hardly think you were in earnest. Glad you are. Yes, yes, glad enough. Good thing for the bank to have one of your family in it. Glad Dave was able to coax you into coming with us. He said he didn't know as he could, but he'd try."

Mary looked up at him.

"Coax me?" she repeated, in surprise. "It didn't require much coaxing. I am very grateful to you and the other directors—yes, and to him—for giving me the chance."

He patted her shoulder. "Yes, yes, I know," he said, with a chuckle. "Dave told us all about it at Saturday's meeting. He generally gets what he goes after. That's why we let him be president. Smart fellow, Dave; mighty smart, for a Cummings. Well, Mary, I hope you won't get tired of playing at bookkeeping too soon. . . . Oh, say," turning back for a final word, "my wife and I are coming over to call some evening. The old lady is crazy to know just why you did this. I told her all that Cummings said, how you were sick to death of sitting around and wanted something to take up your mind, but she isn't quite satisfied. Woman fashion, she wants to have you tell her. Well, good-by. Have a good time with your new playthings," waving his hand toward the bank's account books.

This speech might have given Mary something more to think about, had not her new duties then excluded all other thoughts. For a moment she found herself wondering why Captain Cummings had conveyed the impression that she was, and apparently with some reluctance, doing the bank a favor by entering its employ. Then the ubiquitous Allie Jones called her attention to more pressing matters.

Allie suggested that he go home for an early dinner that noon and that she wait until his return at one.

"I guess you won't mind this once, will you?" he said. "Got a little business to attend to, you see," he added, confidentially; "and between twelve and one is the best time for it."

Mary, with some inward misgivings concerning her own dinner, which she knew Azure would have hot and ready at twelve, cheerfully agreed to the change. Her cheerfulness was a trifle dampened, however, when, after Jones's departure, Bennie Jackson stooped to whisper at her ear.

"Asked you to let him off for business, didn't he?" he queried. "Um-hum. I thought I heard him. Bosh!" scornfully. "All the business he's got is with Nellie Beasley. She works down to Gallup's store and she has her noon at twelve. He wants to hang 'round a spell with her, that's all *that* is."

Mr. Hall also went home at twelve and the bank, its executive department at any rate, was left in charge of David Cummings, who, as always, had arrived at eleven. The captain had greeted the new assistant bookkeeper just as on the previous day, pleasantly and with a word of inquiry as to how she was getting on. Then, as before, he went into the inner room.

That room, during the noon hour, was the business center of the Wapatomac National Bank. A few callers paused at the teller's window to leave money with Mr. Cahoon or to draw a little on their accounts, but the majority passed on and into the president's office. Often those callers were obliged to wait their turns. Several were personages, male or female, of importance in the town or neighboring towns, and Mary was surprised to see how meekly they accepted notice from Bennie Jackson that they would be obliged to wait and how patiently they waited afterward. Mrs. Phoebe Carleton was one of these. She was Wapatomac's wealthiest widow and her husband, the late Captain John Carleton, had been the nearest approach to a millionaire the community boasted. Mrs. Carleton was cream of the cream of local aristocracy. She was accustomed to have what she wanted when she wanted it. But there she was, sitting on the chair outside David Cummings's office, the same chair which Fletcher Ginn, who was anything but an aristocrat, had just vacated.

She had been sitting there for some minutes when the electric bell, on the wall behind Mary's desk, rang. Mr. Cahoon turned to look over his spectacles.

"That is Cap'n Cummings ringing, Miss Brewster," he said. "Bennie is out on an errand. Would you mind seeing what's wanted?"

Mary entered the inner room to find Cummings seated at the big table about which the directors were wont to gather at their Saturday morning meetings. Ginn occupied a chair opposite. He was a resident of East Wapatomac, owner of a small property near the shore. He went cod-fishing in his catboat part of the year, farmed a little, and cultivated a small cranberry bog. He was a raw-boned, stoop-shouldered man and now, as he sat slouched forward in the bank chair, his gnarled fingers twisting and untwisting, he looked troubled and disconsolate.

He nodded to Mary and muttered an embarrassed "Good day." Captain Dave, who had been writing on a slip of paper, looked up.

"Miss Brewster," he said, "will you just hand that to Philander and bring back the figures he'll give you? Much obliged."

Mary delivered the paper to Mr. Cahoon, who, after turning the pages of a big book on the table behind him, made some penciled jottings upon the back of the slip and returned it to her.

"I guess that is what he wants, or near enough," he said.

She handed the paper to Cummings, who inspected the figures.

"I see," he said, musingly. "Well— Oh, by the way, what time is it?"

He answered his own question by looking at his watch. "Sho!" he muttered. "I didn't realize it was so late. I suppose Mrs. Carleton is outside there, isn't she?"

Mary said she was, adding that the lady had been there for some time. He smiled.

"She'll give me fits for keepin' her waitin'," he observed. "Well, they won't be any worse fits if they are put off a minute longer. You tell her— No, wait! I'll tell her myself."

Mary, who was on her way to the door, paused. He had bade her wait, but she did not know whether or not the order was intended to be taken literally. He turned to Mr. Ginn.

"Well, Fletcher," he said, "I'm sorry, but I'm afraid the bank can't do anything for you. I wish it could, but it can't."

Ginn's long face grew longer still. He sighed and, rising, took his hat from the table.

"I cal'late that's about the way you'd feel, Cap'n Dave," he said. "It's pretty tough on me. If I could get that fish weir for that figger, I know I could make a go of it. But I ain't got the money and if the bank can't let me have it that settles it. It's a darn shame, though. *Can't* you do it, Dave? 'Tain't such a lot, and I'll pay back every cent of it, if I'm spared to live."

Cummings nodded.

"You would try, I don't doubt," he agreed.

"Try! I'd do it. I've always paid my debts so fur, ain't I?"

"I never heard you didn't. But the trouble is you haven't got any security to back up a loan. The bank can't take a lien on the weir, it's too risky. And the shanties on the beach aren't worth anything—to us. You're carryin' a mortgage already on your real property, includin' the cranberry bog."

"I've paid my interest reg'lar and this weir, if it done well, might help me pay some of the principal."

"I know, but that's too big an 'if.' Sorry, Fletcher."

Ginn turned away.

"Well, all right," he muttered. "If you say so, it's fair enough, I suppose. But it's the only piece of luck ever come my way, this chance is. I might have known 'twas too good to be true. Good-by."

Cummings lifted a hand. "Wait!" he ordered. "Hold on a moment. Cahoon's just given me some figures on your balance here. 'Tisn't a big one, but you've generally managed to keep some money with us for the past year. And I judge you've never overdrawn."

"Course I ain't. Think I'm a crook—or a fool, Dave Cummings?"

"If I did I shouldn't say what I'm goin' to say now. I know you're an honest, hard-workin' man and I agree with you that that weir may turn out a bargain at the price. You come down to my office at the wharf to-morrow forenoon, about nine or so, and—I'll see—maybe I'll let you have that money myself."

Ginn turned sharply. His tanned cheeks flushed.

"Let me have it!" he repeated. "Why, you just said—"

"I said the bank couldn't let you have it without security. It can't."

"Well then?"

"But I can, I guess, if I feel like it. If you want to give me your personal note I shouldn't wonder if I'd take it. Maybe we can fix up some sort of partnership in that weir property. You be on hand at the wharf to-morrow at nine. . . . There, there," hastily, "don't stop to talk any more. Phoebe Carleton's fingers are twitching already. She'll comb my hair for me."

Fletcher Ginn departed, his round shoulders straighter and a different look in his eye. Cummings, rising from the table, turned to Miss Brewster.

"Sorry to keep you standin' here," he said. "I thought

perhaps you'd better. Fletcher is one of the kind who might stay and talk for a week if he and I were alone. Just ask Phoebe Carleton to step in as you go out, will you, please? I'll probably want you again soon. When I do I'll ring."

Mrs. Carleton received with a sniff the announcement that the president was ready for her.

"It's high time, I should say," she snapped, rising and shaking her skirts. "If David Cummings thinks I've got nothing better to do than sit around and wait his pleasure he's making a big mistake." She laid a hand on the knob of the sanctum door and then turned to give Miss Brewster a sharp glance with her keen old eyes.

"So you are really here, Mary, are you?" she observed. "I heard you were, but I have lived too long to believe more than half I hear. . . . Well, what are you doing it for? Fun? Or money?"

Mary smiled. "Both, perhaps," she replied.

"So! . . . Think you are going to like it well enough to stay?"

"Yes."

"Humph! You seem pretty sure. You have got yourself talked about, did you know that?"

"I can guess."

"I guess you can. Well, don't let that worry you. It is your business and talk won't hurt you. I'm sixty-eight years old and if being talked about was fatal I should have died long ago. You do what you want to do, what you think is right, and never mind the chatter. Independence shows character. I knew your father, Mary, and his father, too. They had character, both of 'em, and it looks as if you took after that side of the house.

. . . I want you to come and have dinner with me Sunday. Can you?"

"Why—why, yes, I think I can. Thank you, Mrs. Carleton. I should be glad to."

"That's right. And," with a twinkle, "you needn't be afraid that I shall cross-question you about your private affairs, for I shan't. . . . There!" turning the knob. "Now I'll tell David Cummings what I think of him for keeping me perched out here like a hen on a roost."

The door of the private office closed behind her. Mary returned to her desk.

Ten minutes later the electric bell rang. Mary, obeying the summons, found Captain David and Mrs. Carleton seated at the big table, with papers and documents spread before them. The former looked up as she entered.

"I want you to witness Mrs. Carleton's signature, if you will, please," he said. "Now, Mrs. Carleton, if you'll put your name there."

The old lady sniffed. "I declare I've got a mind not to," she announced. "Dave Cummings, you've played a Yankee trick on me and you ought to be ashamed of yourself."

Cummings laughed. "Not a bit of it, Mrs. Carleton," he said. "So far as I can see I've done exactly what you asked me to do. I thought you'd be pleased as Punch."

"Umph!" sarcastically. "You didn't think any such thing. You thought you had a good joke on me and I suppose you have. I've a precious mind not to let them have that stock, after all."

"All right. I'm not advisin' you to let 'em have it. I think it's a pretty fair investment. Seems to me I told you so in the beginnin'."

Mrs. Carleton impatiently shook her head. She appeared

to be in a mood divided between chagrin and amusement.

"Oh, you provoking man!" she snapped. "Mary," turning to Miss Brewster, "do you know what he's done? Yes, I shall tell her, too! If she's goin' to work for you she might as well know what a sharper you are, David Cummings. You see, Mary," she went on, "about a year ago my husband's first cousin, Frank Beals—I guess you don't know him; he lives in Sandwich—asked me to take some stock in the Canning Company there. He was interested in it, himself. So, to help him along—yes, and because this person here," with a wave in the direction of Cummings, who was listening with a broad smile on his face, "told me he considered it a good risk, I took a hundred shares. A month ago Frank had some disagreement with the other heads of the Company and he got out. So, naturally—because they had treated him so abominably—I wanted to get out, too. I tried to sell my stock, but I couldn't. Then I put the matter in his hands," another wave toward Captain David, "and asked him to see if he couldn't make those people give me back my money. And what do you think he's done?"

Mary had no idea, of course, so she said nothing. Cummings, still smiling, answered the question.

"I did just what you asked me to do, Mrs. Carleton," he put in, cheerfully. "I got them to take it back. Now if you'll just sign the certificate on the back there and if Mary here will witness the signature, I'll hand you your check and everything will be settled. And we'll all be happy, I should say."

"Yes," pettishly. "*You'll* be happy, I don't doubt. Mary, do you know what he did? He went up to that Canning Company's place himself, and he looked into their affairs and the upshot of that is that the Wapatomac National Bank is taking a block of that very stock. Taking it themselves because they believe it is a safe investment and a sure profit. And he has the impudence to tell me that he has *sold* mine. Did you ever in your life?"

Mary looked from one to the other. She could scarcely be expected to take sides in the matter. Nor did she understand it very well. Cummings again saved her the embarrassment of replying.

"One of the clauses in the agreement was that they should take back your stock, Mrs. Carleton," he said. "I made that plain. You told me that if I didn't get you out of that concern without losin' a cent you'd never speak to me again. Course I couldn't have that happen. Good friends are scarce."

"Rubbish! Why didn't you tell me the bank was going into that Company?"

"I didn't know it then. Besides, you told me that if Saint Peter himself was runnin' that business you wouldn't have anything to do with it; not after the way they treated Frank Beals, you wouldn't. You said get your money and get rid of your hundred shares, that's what you expected me to do. I was pattin' myself on the back for havin' done it. Now, as I've told you, you needn't sell if you don't want to. You can keep your stock and I'll tell the Cannin' crowd that the deal's off."

"I don't want the stock. You know I don't. I told you I wouldn't have it in the house. I took it to help Frank along. It's only that—that—well, you're altogether too clever, Dave Cummings. Give me that pen!"

She signed the transfer blank on the back of the certificate and threw down the pen.

"There!" she snapped. "Now I hope you are satisfied, smarty."

Mary, as directed by Cummings, signed her name beside that of the perturbed seller of the shares.

"So!" said the captain, with satisfaction. "That's over and done with. The medicine is out of the way; now we can pass around the candy. There's your check for five thousand, Mrs. Carleton."

She took the check he handed her, examined it carefully, and deposited it in her hand bag.

"I suppose you think I am going to thank you," she observed. "Well, I shan't. You don't deserve my thanks. I hope you nor the bank ever get a single dividend from that Canning Company."

She was on her way to the door, when he spoke.

"Oh, Mrs. Carleton," he said, deprecatingly, "I—I hate to trouble you, but—"

"But you're going to. . . . Well?"

"Of course I don't expect you to forgive me."

"I shan't."

"I know. But I was just goin' to say that I've been lookin' into that matter of those bonds of yours and I guess you and I can talk about 'em now with some understandin'. I wouldn't think of askin' you to drop in here to-morrow noon, but if you *should* be passin', why—"

He paused. She regarded him sternly. Then she sighed.

"I'll be here," she said. "You see, Mary?" in mock resignation, "how he winds me around his finger. Why I let him I'm sure I don't know. To look at him this minute you'd think butter wouldn't melt in his mouth, but that's all make-believe; he's as deep as the Atlantic Ocean.

Good-by, Mary. I shall expect you at dinner Sunday. Good-by, David Cummings, you—you wolf in sheep's clothing."

She marched out, closing the door with emphasis. The "wolf" laughed heartily.

"The old lady thinks I put one over on her, I'm afraid," he said. "She's as good a friend as I've got in the world and she comes to me about all her investments and so on, but to hear her talk you'd think I was a schemin' skinflint. She was bound I should make the Cannin' Company give her back the money for those shares, but she can't quite be reconciled to the notion that somebody else may make a profit on 'em. She's a good soul and a fine woman, but a red pepper plaster isn't sharper than she is when there's a dollar goin'. . . . Oh, don't worry," with a glance at Mary's face. "She isn't mad at me. She and I think a sight of each other."

Mary had turned to go, when he spoke her name.

"Yes?" she said. He was turning over the papers before him.

"Why," he began, with some hesitation, "I—er—I just thought I'd ask you how things were goin'? With the books, you know?"

"Oh. They are going as well as I should expect, I suppose."

"Allie and Philander helpin' you the way they ought to, are they?"

"Yes, indeed. They are very patient, both of them."

"Don't be afraid to ask 'em whenever you need help. That's what they are paid for, you know. Hall says you are startin' in first-rate. He's sure you will get along."

"Is he? I am not, but I shall try."

"You ain't—" he paused to fold the Canning Company certificate. "You ain't gettin' tired of your bargain? 'Ain't beginnin' to wish you hadn't come here?"

"No," emphatically. "Of course I'm not."

"Um-hum. Well, if you should, at any time, you must say so. You see," with a smile, "my conscience isn't quite clear yet about lettin' you do it. I can't help thinkin' what your father would say to me if he was alive. . . . Azure Crisp now? She's had somethin' to say once in a while, I presume likely?"

Mary laughed. "Oh, yes!" she admitted.

"She thinks I ought to be in jail, doesn't she?"

"She was considering having me sent to an asylum. Captain Cummings, I wish you would forget Azure and what my father would have said, and everything of that kind. I am happy here and I shall stay here. That is," earnestly, "unless you and Mr. Hall and Mr. Cahoon find I am not capable of doing the work. If you do decide that I am not you must tell me so—at once."

He rose from his chair. "Not much danger of that, from what I've heard so far," he said. He hesitated a moment and then added, a little awkwardly, "you see, I—well, I've tried not to bother you much myself. Thought it might make you sort of nervous to have me hangin' around, lookin' over you shoulder and so on, you understand. But I've questioned Hall and Philander and kept run of you through them and I guess it won't be breakin' any rules if I tell you they are more than satisfied. And —" he refolded the certificate, "of course if, at any time, you *should* like to come to me over any matter that bothers you, I—well, I'm here between eleven and one and down at the wharf or at home the rest of the time. . . . There!

Now if there's anybody else waitin' outside the door yonder just ask 'em to step in, will you, please?"

That evening at bedtime Mary, reflecting upon the day's happenings, found herself beginning to understand a little more clearly the qualifications which made David Cummings a successful bank president.

CHAPTER VI

MARY finished the first week—or half week—in the employ of the Wapatomac National Bank on Saturday at noon. And, for the first time in her life, she experienced the sensation of what Bennie Jackson called "being paid off." It was a distinctly pleasant sensation, even though the sum she received was far from large. Cahoon handed her her envelope with a quizzical smile upon his kindly old face.

"Something new for you, I guess, Miss Brewster," he observed. "My end of it is for me, certainly. I never expected to have the honor of paying one of your family a salary. How does it seem to belong to the working class?"

"It seems very nice, thank you, Mr. Cahoon," she replied. He nodded.

"I'm glad you like it," he said. "I hope you like us, after you come to know us better. Like us well enough to stay for a while, I mean."

It was quite evident that he, too, considered her bookkeeping merely a whim, a new toy to be played with only until its novelty wore off. As a matter of fact, this was now the opinion of Wapatomac in general. Azure Crisp had dropped hints to that effect and Captain Cummings, when questioned, at home and elsewhere, had not denied the insinuation. Kohath Briggs, at the post office, was quoted as saying: "I cal'late it's natural enough. When you've got everything you want in this world then you commence to hanker for things you don't want. About a month of settin' at that bank desk and addin' up figgers and that Brewster girl will be as satisfied to swear off as I was after I stole the old man's pipe to try smokin'. I was eight years old that time and I never touched tobacco again for over two year."

This, coming from a member of the bank president's own household, was accepted by the majority as authoritative.

Allie Jones, who was leaving for Boston on the afternoon train, bade his successor a more or less dubious farewell.

"I hope you get along all right," he said. "I'm sorry I can't hang around a fortnight or so longer to lift you over the hard spots, but I can't. They're waitin' for me up to the city, and wonderin' why I ain't there, I suppose. Don't get discouraged if you make mistakes. Why," with a burst of candor, "I made one or two myself when I first came here. Honest, I did!"

Mr. Peter Hall, dignified and soft-footed, as always, followed her to the door to say a pleasant word.

"I hope you are not tired of us yet, Miss Brewster," he said. "You will be with us again on Monday morning?"

Mary looked at him in surprise. "Of course I shall," she answered.

Mary went home, to be welcomed by Azure as an invalid might be welcomed by a solicitous nurse.

"I suppose likely," observed Azure, "you'll be for tellin' me that you ain't tired a bit. . . . Yes, I thought so. Well, if you'll take my advice, you'll go right upstairs soon as you've finished dinner, and lay down. If anybody comes

—that Dave Cummings or any of his bank slave drivers—I'll tell 'em you're sick."

"But I'm not sick, Azure."

"Humph! Well, *I'm* sick, and I shall be until you come to your senses. I dreamed about your poor dear mother last night. I was ashamed to look at her, even in a dream."

They walked to church together next morning, but Mrs. Crisp, before entering the meetinghouse, announced flatly that she would not sit in the Brewster pew. So Mary was its sole occupant. After service, she made no effort to avoid meeting the Freemans and Bakers and Bradleys and others of her own social set. They asked questions, of course, how she liked being at the bank, and so on, but even in the case of Mrs. Captain Eleazir there was an absence of that anxious pity and patronizing concern which she had found so exasperating at their last meeting in that aisle. She did not know it, but Wapatomac's aristocracy, like its commoners, had reached the conclusion that her amazing departure from class custom was but an eccentricity, a passing whim. "Now that I come to think of it," Mrs. Bradley had told her daughter, "there was always an odd streak in that family. Captain Benjamin was queer, and stubborn too, when he wanted to be."

The most surprising incident of the forenoon was a remark made by Mrs. Bradley's only daughter, Elvira. Miss Bradley was a thin, cowed maiden of twenty-nine, her demeanor and speech usually as precisely orthodox as her appearance. So Mary could scarcely believe her ears when, as she and Elvira were alone for a moment, the latter seized her hand and bent to whisper a confidence.

"Mary," she whispered. "I've been thinking about you

this whole week. I don't see how you dared do it, but I only wish I had your courage. There are times, when I am all alone or with mother, in that big house of ours that I would give anything in this world to get out and do something for myself, something new and different. I believe I wouldn't mind going out washing by the day. It would be heavenly compared to sitting there at home and watching myself grow old."

The Carleton carriage and span were waiting at the foot of the granite steps leading up to the walk of the First Church and Mrs. Carleton herself was on the lookout for her dinner guest. Azure, who could be counted upon not to miss the opportunity, assisted her mistress into the carriage and watched it roll away.

"There!" she said, addressing Elkanah Bearse in a tone sufficiently loud to be heard by such members of the congregation as might be passing, "she's really gone. Phoebe Carleton's been beggin' and pleadin' with her to come to their house to dinner for I don't know how long, but she's been puttin' it off and puttin' it off until I began to be afraid Phoebe's feelin's would be hurt. They will have a lovely time together this afternoon. They're bosom friends, just like David and Absalom in the Bible."

Mary did have a pleasant afternoon at the Carleton house; particularly pleasant because the old lady kept her promise and asked not a single question concerning her guest's reason for entering the employ of the Wapatomac National Bank. When that subject was mentioned, it was Mary herself who mentioned it. Ever since her brief interview with Captain Donald that second day at the bank she had been pondering over something he had said. Now, as they sat together after dinner, in the stately parlor of the Carleton mansion, she broached the matter which had puzzled her.

"Mrs. Carleton," she said, "you own stock in the bank here and you know a good deal about what goes on at the directors' meetings, don't you?"

Mrs. Carleton turned to look at her. "While my husband was alive and on the board," she replied, "I used to hear a good deal. Now I don't hear as much. Why?"

"I'll tell you. When Captain Cummings came to tell me that the board had consented to let me work there, he said that the vote was unanimous. I inferred from what he said that he merely mentioned my name and that was all there was to it. I could scarcely believe it had been so easy and simple, but he said it was. . . . You are smiling. Why?"

The old lady was not smiling exactly, but there was a twinkle in her eye.

"So David Cummings told you that, did he?" she asked.

"Yes, he did."

"Humph! Well, it was just like him. Why are you asking me about it?"

"Because, on Thursday, when Captain Fred Donald stopped by my desk to speak with me he said something that I couldn't understand. He said—or it was perfectly plain he thought—that it required a great deal of persuasion—coaxing, he called it—on Captain Cummings' part to get me to consent to take the position. That wasn't true at all. I was wild to come and Captain David knew it. Now if he told Captain Donald and the rest I would have to be coaxed, why did he tell them so? Do you know?"

Phoebe Carleton's amusement was now open and unconcealed.

"Dave Cummings is a pretty smart politician as well as a good business man," she said. "Am I to understand that you asked him to get you that position if he could, Mary?"

"I asked him to get me any sort of position, provided that it was respectable and paid a salary. You see, I—"

"Never mind your reasons, my dear. I told you I shouldn't ask for them and I don't want you to tell me. You keep those reasons to yourself—always. That is my advice and I have lived in this town all my life. . . . I see. Yes, I guess I see. You didn't know what a fight had been going on among the directors over that place young Jones was giving up."

Mary's eyes opened.

"A fight!" she repeated. "Why, what do you mean?"

"Humph! Well, there is no reason why I shouldn't tell you, although perhaps you had better keep it to yourself. Yes, there was a fight. It was very quiet, hardly any outsiders knew about it, but Mrs. Freeman told me and so did Fred Donald's wife and Emma Bradley and others. I heard both sides. It was a sort of family rumpus and threatened to be a pretty serious one."

She went on to tell of the "rumpus" and its growing seriousness. Then to draw her conclusions as to the part David Cummings had played, first in preventing the disagreement from becoming public and leading to disastrous consequences for the bank; then in diplomatically exerting his influence to bring about the appointment of a compromise candidate, namely Mary Brewster.

"He wanted to help you," she declared. "Of course he did. He told you he would try his best for you and I never heard him say a thing like that unless he meant it; but I rather guess it must have taken every scrap of even his smartness and contrivance and tact to bring Fred Donald to the point of voting with Sam Freeman and not against him. And vice versa. Ha, ha! I wish I might have been behind the door at some of the talks he must have had. And then he told you how simple it was! Oh, dear, that is funny!"

Mary could scarcely believe it. The "simple matter" seemed anything but simple now.

"But why did he wish Captain Donald and the others to think it was doubtful whether or not I would take the position?" she demanded. "That I would have to be 'coaxed'?"

Mrs. Carleton shook her head. "More tact, my dear," she declared. "It wouldn't do to let either side think *he* was trying to gain any end of his own. If they had been sure you would accept, that you were really seeking the place, they might have been suspicious and not have voted so unanimously. Dave led them to think—or, I imagine he he did—that he would have a hard job to get you to do the bank the favor of working for it. Probably—all this is just as a guess—he let each side imagine it was getting the better of the other."

Mary was silent for a minute, thinking it over. She drew a long breath.

"I don't believe," she said, with conviction, "that I should ever have taken the position if I had known all this!"

"Of course you wouldn't. That was why Dave didn't tell you."

More reflection. Then Mary said: "I am beginning to understand what you meant when you said he was as deep as the Atlantic Ocean."

"Oh, he is! But I have never found him anything but true blue all the way through. Between ourselves, right here in this room, Mary Brewster, where no one else can hear us, I don't mind saying that I had rather trust David Cummings with my personal affairs and my money than I would any other person in this town. He makes me cross, he'll do things in his own way—just as he did with that Canning stock of mine—but, if I couldn't have but one friend in Wapatomac to look out for my interests—yes, and 'boss' me for my own good—I'd pick him for that one. And when you consider the family he comes from and that I am John Carleton's widow, you'll admit that is saying a good deal."

Mary left the Carleton house an hour later with a still further revised estimate of the president of the Wapatomac National Bank. The interviews she had witnessed in the directors' room, that with Fletcher Ginn as well as with Mrs. Carleton, had impressed her strongly with his kindliness and common sense. But what she had just learned of the manner in which he had brought about her selection as bookkeeper made even a deeper impression. He had done it all and never told her a word. Behind her liking for and trust in him there had heretofore been a trace—just a trace, perhaps, but still a very real one—of condescension, of unconscious snobbery. He was a Cummings and she was a Brewster. Now this trace had vanished. So far from regarding him with patronage, she was beginning to be almost afraid of him.

On Monday morning, for the first time, she resumed her work at the books without the advice and company of Allie Jones. But she managed to get on without him very well indeed. By the end of that week she had gained confidence. At the end of another she was really beginning to feel at home at the desk. Every one was kind to her, every one was glad to help, and the words of praise which she received from old Mr. Cahoon and the cashier were gratifying and inspiring. She saw comparatively little ot David Cummings and then only in the way of business, but he, too, was pleasant and encouraging. He never again suggested that she come to him with her problems, but she had never found it necessary to do so. Mr. Hall seemed the natural person to consult and he was so very patient, even eager, in helping her past the stumbling-blocks. She liked Peter Hall better than she used. Formerly she had thought him perhaps too stiffly dignified, a trifle too much "just what a cashier ought to be," as Azure put it. Now she was coming to think this but a manner, an unbecoming cloak covering the real man underneath. Yes, she really liked Mr. Hall. And there seemed no doubt whatever that he liked her.

He invariably made it a point to come immediately to her desk on arriving at the bank to wish her a good morning. He was so very indulgent concerning the length of her noon hours. Not that she was in the habit of exceeding her allotted time, but he was so thoughtful in urging her not to hurry back. She saw him often at church on Sunday and he always stopped to speak with her. He was a popular man in the First Church, and was consulted by the minister and the church trustees. Of course, being a relative of Mrs. Freeman, he was prominent in the social affairs of the best families, and, as a widower eligible for "filling in" at whist parties or dinners, his company was much in request.

Mary met him at some of these gatherings. Wapatomac, in general, had recovered from its shock following her stepping from the beaten path of her class, and now settled in the belief that she had done so merely from eccentricity. The most irritating accompaniment to this otherwise satisfactory attitude of mind on the part of Mary's friends and acquaintances was their evident conviction that the eccentricity was but temporary. Captain Sam Freeman, always blunt and outspoken, asked her across the Baker dinner table one evening if she had not had "almost enough of it." "Of course, as a director," added Captain Sam, "I hope you haven't. We're mighty glad to have a Brewster in the bank. But we all know it won't last. Has she hinted to you, Hall, when she is going to give up playing with your books and stay at home like a sensible woman? Eh? Has she? Has she now?"

Mr. Hall's reply was, Mary thought, a trifle too polite and less crushing than it might have been. Yet it was decisive, in its way.

"We are hoping Miss Brewster likes us well enough to forget to be sensible in that way, Captain Freeman," he said. "If any hints of the kind you mention are made we shan't accept them if we can help it; you may be sure of that."

He walked home with Mary that evening. They talked of all sorts of matters, everything except the bank. He said good night at the Brewster step. Azure was awaiting her mistress on the other side of the door.

"Was that Peter Hall?" she demanded, eagerly. "I couldn't see very well through the crack, but I thought it sounded like him."

"Why, yes, Azure, it was Mr. Hall," replied Mary.

"Did he see you home from the Bakers'?"

"He walked home with me, if that is what you mean. It was on his way."

"Humph! He lives up to Snow's—Frankie T.'s—and that's half a mile on the lower road. I'd call it more out of his way than I would on it."

Mary laughed. "He said it was on his way," she explained. "He told me he was coming in this direction. I was very glad of his company. It saved my having to beg a ride with the Bradleys."

Azure smiled. "Um-hum," she said, significantly; and that was all—at the time.

She said more when, a few evenings afterward, the cashier called at the house. The call was quite unexpected and Mary was at first fearful that its purpose was in some way connected with the bank or her work there. But it was not. Apparently Mr. Hall had dropped in merely for a social chat. He had been out for a walk after supper, he explained, and, seeing the lighted Brewster windows, had been tempted to stop on the chance of finding her in.

"I hope I am not interfering with any plans you may have for the evening," he said.

Mary had no plans and said as much. They talked of town affairs, of the new extension the Freemans were adding to their house, of church matters, of the Sunday school. He told her that Mrs. Baker had received a letter from Allie Jones and that that young gentleman had found his new position with the Boston bankers not quite the bed of roses he had counted upon.

"I judge from some things Mrs. Baker said," he went on, "that Allie has to work harder than he expected. Also that he is the least bit homesick. Well, the work won't do him any harm. As for the homesickness, he will get over it in time. I remember very well my first few weeks here in Wapatomac. I had broken up my home in Brockton after my dear wife's death and I came here knowing scarcely any one—except the Freemans, of course. It was a lonely time. This world can be a very lonely place, in spite of all the people in it."

With which not altogether original observation Mary expressed entire agreement. She had been very lonely indeed since her mother's death, she told him, and the position at the bank had come as a heaven-sent opportunity of relief.

"I understand perfectly," he said. "Captain Cummings explained his reasons for believing you might be induced to come with us. Needless to say, I was only too glad to use my influence with the board."

She looked at him. "Captain Cummings gave me to understand that no influence was needed," she said. "He says the board voted for me unanimously."

"Oh, it did! it did, certainly. Was that—er—all the captain told you?"

"Yes. . . . Why?"

"Oh, nothing! He is an odd individual at times, Cummings."

"What do you mean by that, Mr. Hall? Has he told you more than he told me?"

"Oh, no! No, indeed! He told me next to nothing of the whole matter until the vote had been taken."

Mary's next speech was made involuntarily and at once. As she thought of it afterward it was not entirely diplomatic.

"Then I don't see how you could have used your influence for me with the board," she said.

If he was in the least taken aback he did not show it. He laughed pleasantly.

"It may be that I knew before he told me," he said. "Some of the directors take me into their confidence, even if Captain Cummings doesn't always do so. Oh, I am not criticizing him for a moment," he added. "When I spoke of him as odd I meant odd in his habit of keeping his thoughts and plans to himself. He has, I think, the most complete self-confidence of any man I know. His experience in the banking business has not been large, but he makes surprisingly few mistakes. A sterling character on the whole, self-made of course, and a little rough at times, but honest and—yes, a very good president for an institution like ours. Very good indeed."

Mary's interview with Mrs. Carleton was too recent and too fresh in her mind to prevent her detecting and resenting the trifle of patronage in this estimate. And because she, too, had formerly applied almost the same estimate to David Cummings she was the more prompt to resent.

"I admire him and like him very much," she said, crisply.

Peter Hall's agreement was so hearty that her resentment disappeared.

"So do I," he declared, with emphasis. "Rough diamond or not, there is no doubt whatever that he *is* a diamond. I am proud to be associated with him. Why, Miss Brewster—"

He went on to tell her of some incidents connected with Captain David and the bank which were highly to the Cummings credit. His praise was whole-hearted and enthusiastic. When he said good night, which he did shortly after nine, he left a favorable impression behind him.

"I have had a very pleasant call," he told her, as they stood by the door, "I figured that I was in for a 'blue' evening—I have them occasionally—and you have kept me from thinking of myself. I am ever so much obliged."

"You are quite welcome. I know what it is to have the blues. I have them very often."

"Do you? Well, then on my next seizure perhaps I shall come here again. May I?"

She could say nothing but yes, nor was there any reason why she should.

She supposed Azure to have gone to bed, but not a bit of it. Mrs. Crisp was up and wide awake in the kitchen.

"He stayed quite a spell, didn't he," she observed. "For the first time, I mean."

"For the only time, as far as I know," said Mary, not altogether truthfully. "Azure, don't be silly."

Azure's smile expressed much. "Oh," she sniffed, "*I* don't care how long he stays. He's a real nice man. He's the kind of man who ought to be comin' here—*our* kind. I guess likely *his* father never peddled clams. No, nor his grandfather never fetched rum bottles to a missionary meetin' neither."

Mr. Hall repeated his call an evening of the following week. And thereafter those calls were almost regular. He did not come often, but he continued to come and, after a time, Wapatomac took notice and began to comment.

David Cummings was one of the last to hear these comments. And it was his grandfather, old Captain Barnabas, who first called them to his attention. The three—David, Cap'n Barney and Kohath Briggs—were at the supper table when the old man broached the subject.

"I was down to the bank just afore noon," he said. "I stopped in on the way back from the post office to leave that letter for you, the one from them stockbrokers up to Boston. 'Twas addressed just 'Wapatomac, Mass.,' so they put it in our box 'stead of sendin' it along with your other mail to the wharf. I judged it might be important so I cal'lated I'd leave it on the way by. You was out somewheres, so Philander told me."

"Yes. Cap'n Donald asked me to drive over to East Wapatomac with him to look at a piece of land he was thinkin' of buyin'. He and some others are talkin' of layin' out another good-sized cranberry swamp. I found the letter when I got back. Much obliged to you, Skipper."

"That's all right. I didn't wait. Philander, he was pretty busy. And Peter Hall—he, he!—he seemed to be busy, too. Him and Mary Brewster was havin' a nice, sociable time together. He was hangin' over her desk and purrin' into her ear, like a cat coaxin' for fish. He and she have took quite a shine to each other, from what I hear. Don't know's I blame him much. She's a pretty good-lookin' woman. Wonder to me she ain't ever married. Why do you suppose she ain't, Dave?"

Captain David did not seem interested.

"Because she didn't want to, I presume likely," he remarked, shortly. "Any more of these biscuits in the kitchen, Kohath?"

Mr. Briggs retired to the kitchen in quest of the biscuits. Captain Barney chuckled to himself.

"What do you think, Dave?" he asked. "Think there's

anything serious goin' on betwixt them two, her and Hall, I mean?"

"How do I know?" impatiently. "No, no, of course there isn't. Why should there be?"

"Don't know why there shouldn't. She's single and good-lookin' and rich, and Peter he's a widower and his job's handlin' money. Probably he'd just as soon handle hers as anybody's. He, he! Folks are sayin'—"

"Oh, bosh!"

"Bosh nothin'! It's so, ain't it, Kohath? You've heard what they're sayin' about Peter Hall and the Brewster girl, ain't you? Tell Dave what you told me."

Kohath placed the plate of steaming biscuits upon the table and slid his lengthy figure into the chair.

"I don't know's I've heard nothin' that amounts to much of nothin'," he drawled. "There! that's all the biscuits there is. Make 'em go fur as you can."

He proceeded to help them go by shifting two to his own plate. Captain Barnabas hastily pulled the remainder out of his reach.

"Tut, tut, tut!" he snapped. "If you was figgerin' to stow 'em all under your own hatches, why didn't you do it out in the kitchen? Then you wouldn't have had to bother to fetch 'em in. And what do you mean by sayin' what you heard didn't amount to nothin'? If 'twas nothin' then you talked nothin' pretty much the whole afternoon. Which is what you *do* talk most of the time, that's a fact."

Mr. Briggs leaned back in his chair.

"I have to talk what I cal'late them that listen to me is competent to understand," he retorted, with dignity. "All I said was that folks are talkin' about the way Peter Hall is chasin' after Mary Brewster. 'Cordin' to general tell he is callin' up to her house once a week reg'lar, and last Thursday night he took her to the Old Folks Concert over to the Bayport town hall. That is all I said. 'Twas all I had a chance to say; you said all the rest."

Barnabas ignored the fling, for the moment. "Hear that, do you, Dave?" he crowed. "Sounds a little like keepin' company, don't it?"

David Cummings pushed back his chair. "Who's been throwin' overboard all that rubbish?" he demanded. "Rubbish is what it is, of course."

Kohath shook his head.

"No, I guess it's more'n that, Cap'n," he drawled. "I've heard about his callin' from half a dozen different ones who have seen him go there. I understand Melissa Knowles has been watchin' from her front window and she vows he's bangin' the Brewster knocker every Thursday evenin' now, reg'lar as a clock. And as for the Bayport concert, why, I know that's so, because— Eh? Why, Cap'n Dave, you ain't finished eatin' so soon, have you? There's apple pie comin'."

David did not wait for the pie. "I am goin' to my desk," he told them. "Don't disturb me; I have some work to do."

As he closed the sitting-room door behind him he heard his grandfather say:

"Well, if she is cal'latin' to change her name to Hall I don't know's I blame her much. I'd do more 'n that to get rid of havin' to live along with that Crisp woman."

For an hour David Cummings remained at his desk, but the work he accomplished during that period was slight. There was much he had intended to do and there was one matter in particular, a matter not entirely unconnected with Mary Brewster and her affairs, which required deliberate thought and careful consideration. He had been considering it ever since reading the letter which Captain Barnabas brought to the bank that noon. He had reached no decision, but he had meant to do so that evening at home, where he could be free from interruptions. And now he was finding it hard to concentrate. The bit of gossip he had just heard at the supper table kept intruding and, when he should have been thinking of this other and really important matter, kept cutting his thoughts adrift and setting them afloat upon a sea of speculation which was not pleasant—which was even decidedly unpleasant.

A dozen times he halted this tendency to drift with an impatient "Bosh!" and tried to anchor his attention where it belonged. But it was off and away again a moment later. He did not believe the stuff and nonsense connecting the names of Mary Brewster and Peter Hall. It was just "old woman's talk" and there was always plenty of that in Wapatomac, with little excuse or none. And, even if it were true—that is, if Hall had called occasionally at the Brewster home—still that meant nothing, of course. He and she had known each other a long time, they belonged to the same social set, and if he called on her once in a while, if she had accompanied him to the Bayport concert, what of it? It did not necessarily follow that—that— Oh, stuff and nonsense! Besides, what business was it of his, anyway?

None at all, that was undeniably true. Not the least bit his. His relations with Mary Brewster were literally those of business. She had asked his advice and help in a purely business matter and he had obtained for her the position in the bank in the same spirit. The friendship between them was precisely that which existed between him and old Mrs. Carleton or Mrs. Bradley or a dozen other feminine clients. A purely commercial friendship, nothing more. There was not, nor had he or she ever dreamed of there being, any other sort of friendship, friendship of the ordinary, everyday kind such as existed between people of the same environment and association and, above all in Wapatomac, family standing. He remembered two generations of Captain Ben Brewsters, wealthy, well dressed, conscious of position and power. He remembered himself, as a barefooted lad, delivering huckleberries at the Brewster back door and Annabelle Brewster graciously giving him a penny above the price, "to keep for yourself, little boy."

He remembered his own father, the latter's shiftlessness and shabbiness and obsequious willingness to do errands and odd jobs for the Carletons and Brewsters and Bakers and Freemans. He remembered all this and he knew that Mary remembered it just as well. Now he was prosperous and, in his way, as powerful in the community as the most pompous old aristocrat of them all. He was not seeking social position, could laugh at the ridiculous line of demarcation between those who had had money for three generations and those who had recently acquired it—often did laugh at it; but there it was, a fact to be admitted and reckoned with.

He knew himself to be the equal in brains and business acumen of any one of those people who condescended to him. But also he was quite wise enough to realize that they—some of them, at least—possessed qualities which he could never have, culture, ease of manner, refinement, learning.

Mary Brewster possessed all those qualities, as well as good looks and good taste. Peter Hall had some of them. Cummings had always secretly envied the freedom from self-consciousness with which the cashier met strangers, particularly young misses from the city who came to the bank during the summer months. He could chat with them, show them about, always had something to say, was always easily agreeable, yet becomingly dignified. Captain Dave was more awkward under such circumstances. He had not forgotten a remark made by one of those young persons which he happened to overhear. "He is a nice, jolly man, that president of yours, Mr. Hall," the girl had said. "I like him. But he *is* a real countryman, isn't he?"

At the time the remark had amused rather than offended him. He was a countryman from choice, and glad to be. He understood, too, precisely what the speaker meant and would have cheerfully agreed that she was right. But now, somehow, as the recollection came to him he found a trace of bitterness in it. Because he lacked the superficialities of birth and breeding and education, he could never hope to be Mary Brewster's friend in the sense that another—Hall, for example—might be and apparently was. If he should call upon her at the Brewster house, except to discuss a business matter—begin calling regularly, as, according to the gossip which his grandfather and Kohath were reporting, Peter Hall was calling—she would deem him presuming probably, and ridiculous certainly. She might smile at first, but later she would be offended. And he would never have done such a thing. His own sense of the ridiculous was too strong to allow him to make that kind of a fool of himself.

Then why was he thinking like a fool? Sitting there at that desk and making himself uncomfortable because another man was doing what he could not do? Was he jealous of Peter Hall? Was he *that* kind of a fool?

No, of course he was not. Then what was the matter with him? He knew Peter Hall by this time very well indeed, knew his faults as well as his virtues. Hall was not a broad-minded man, not a "big" man, although he made a perfectly capable bank cashier. He was not good enough for Mary Brewster. But who was? And whether he was or not was not the concern of David Cummings.

Which brought his thinking to exactly the point where it started. He summoned every atom of resolution he possessed and succeeded for ten consecutive minutes in centering his attention upon the matter he had sat down at that desk to consider and decide. Having reached a decision he put on his hat and coat and left the house. He, too, was going to call upon Mary Brewster, but as her financial adviser, nothing more.

He made that perfectly clear to Azure Crisp when she opened the door in response to his knock. Azure's eyes were dazzled by the lamplight above her head and for an instant she did not recognize him. In fact, it appeared almost as if she had expected some one else.

"Come right in," she urged. "Mary's to home and— Why, who is it? Oh!" with a decided change of tone. "Is that you, Cap'n Dave?"

Cummings stepped past her into the hall. "Yes, it's me, Azure," he said. "Tell Mary I've come to see her about a business matter. I won't keep her long, tell her."

Azure hesitated. "Well," she said, a trifle defiantly, "I don't know. I ain't sure, but I shouldn't be surprised if she was cal'latin' to go out this evenin'. I'll tell her you're here, but—"

Mary, herself, interrupted. She was hurrying down the stairs.

"Why, good evening, Captain Cummings," she said, hastening towards him with extended hand and a smile. "This is an unexpected pleasure."

Her eyes were bright, there was color in her cheeks, her manner was cheerful, almost gay. She was wearing a becoming gown, one he had never seen her wear at the bank. In all respects she was a marked contrast to the discouraged, careworn woman who had met him in that hall on his two previous visits. And, perhaps because of the gossip he had heard at the supper table or his reflections afterward, this contrast emphasized in his mind the unbridgeable gulf between them. He took the hand she offered him, dropped it, and stood there, conscious that he looked as he felt, awkward and out of place.

Mary misinterpreted his silence. Her manner changed. "Why, what is it, Captain Cummings?" she asked, anxiously. "Is anything wrong?"

He shook his head. "No, no!" he stammered, hastily. "Nothin' wrong at all. I—er—well, a little matter has come to my notice that I thought perhaps I had better talk with you about. It won't take very long, I guess. If you are busy—or it isn't convenient—why—"

Mrs. Crisp broke in. "I told Cap'n Dave I rather guessed you was goin' out this evenin'," she explained.

Cummings would have spoken, but Mary did not give him the opportunity.

"Nonsense!" she protested, with an annoyed glance at the officious housekeeper. "What in the world did you tell him that for, Azure? I am not going out. That is," with the slightest hesitancy, "if I am it won't be for an hour or more. Come in, please. Won't you take off your coat?"

He followed her into the sitting room, but he refused to remove his coat or even to sit down. Standing with his back toward the canvas from which great-grandfather Brewster frowned lofty disdain upon the world in general, he began to state the business which had brought him there. And it was difficult to state.

"I—I—er—don't know as you'll be interested at all in what I've come to say," he began. "As a matter of fact I haven't got any real right to guess you will be. Probably you'll think I'm—I'm. . . . Pshaw!" disgustedly; "I'm makin' an awful mess of this. Might have known I would. Perhaps I better not say it, after all."

She was listening with surprise, curiosity, and a little amusement. Evidently she could not imagine what he was trying to tell her. He set his teeth and began again.

"I—I shouldn't have thought of comin' to you about it," he said, "only—only, you see, I had a letter to-day from my stockbrokin' friends up to Boston. They take care of some of my—well, you might call 'em speculations, I suppose—and they've been takin' care of this one. They enclosed a notice and a statement from a company I was fool enough to buy stock in. I— Eh? What is it? What makes you laugh?"

She was laughing, laughing quietly, and nodding as if she had guessed a riddle.

"Of course!" she exclaimed. "Now I know why you came, Captain Cummings. I am glad you did, for I should have come to you if you had not. I had made up my mind to speak to you to-morrow at the bank. Now sit down. Yes, you must sit down! I shan't say another word until you do."

Reluctantly he seated himself upon the haircloth sofa, great-grandfather Brewster glowering majestically above him. She waited until he had, as he would have said, "come to anchor." Then she went on.

"Your letter," she said, "was about the Boroda Copper stock, of course. And the notice enclosed was to the effect that the company had found it necessary to levy a two-dollar assessment on each share. I know that was it because I received one just like it."

He had not expected confession so soon, had even wondered if she would confess at all. He was practically sure his suspicion was well founded, but, after all, it had been but a suspicion. He ran his hand through his hair.

"Pshaw!" he exclaimed, with a sigh which was an odd mixture of relief and disappointment. "Humph! So you did buy some of that stuff, after all. I was kind of afraid you might have."

She interrupted. "You knew I had bought it," she declared, with conviction. "You have known it all the time. Now haven't you? Answer me truly."

He shook his head. "Why no," he said, earnestly. "I didn't know it. How should I? 'Twas only that I—well, somehow or other I just thought—I was afraid you might have. You see—"

"Of course I see. I didn't lie to you. I never told you I hadn't bought it. But I tried my very best to make you think I hadn't. I was ashamed to have you know I was such an idiot."

"Now, now, now! Hold on, Mary! I'm the same kind of idiot. I bought it myself."

"That is quite different. You could afford to take the risk and I couldn't. Moreover, you told me not to do it. Well, I did, and then I tried to make you believe I hadn't. I should have known better than to try. You are much too wise a man to be fooled by an inexperienced person like me. You saw through my make-believe that very first evening when you came here in answer to my note. Now, truly, didn't you?"

He could not deny it, nor did he try.

"We-ll," he admitted, reluctantly, "I guessed you had bought it, that's a fact. Oh, I didn't blame you any. That stock looked good when you and I bought it. Yes, it did. It's a shame the way it has turned out."

"Don't feel badly on my account. You mustn't. It serves me right and I think it has taught me a lesson. Now, Captain Cummings, you came here this evening to talk to me about that stock. Were you going to ask me if I had bought it? Not that it makes any difference. I had made up my mind to tell you the whole story at the bank to-morrow. But were you?"

Again he rumpled his hair. "I don't know as I should have asked you right out," he said, with an embarrassed smile. "I didn't want to do that, for of course, as I've realized all along, it ain't my business and never could be unless you wanted me to help you with it. I guess likely what I would have done would have been to tell you about that assessment and then—well, then just see if you were interested enough to hear any more."

She nodded. "I am interested," she said. "Very much so. So you may tell me anything you wish and please believe that I am very, very grateful for your interest and help. But," with decision, "you mustn't tell me to pay that assessment because that I am not going to do."

She had surprised him again. He looked at her. She was smiling, but behind the smile was determination unshakable. He whistled between his teeth.

"Sho!" he exclaimed. "You've kind of taken me aback and left me with my canvas shakin'. I was goin' to tell you that I thought you had better pay it. If it ain't convenient for you to—to raise the money for the assessment just at this time I'm sure that can be arranged all right. In fact, I know it can."

She smiled. "Which means, I suppose," she said, "that you—or the bank, perhaps—would lend me the money to pay it with?"

"Why—well, it could be arranged. I don't know as we'd bother the bank about it. No need for any outsiders to know what has been goin' on."

She nodded. "I understand," she said. "You would find the money for me just as you found it for Fletcher Ginn and his fish weir. That is very good of you—and like you—but it can't be done. I have thought this all out, Captain Cummings, and I shall take my medicine. I shall not pay that assessment."

He was greatly troubled. "I hope you don't really mean that, Mary," he protested. "I am pretty sure that Boroda company is goin' to pull through all right. If it does, some day those shares of ours will be worth a lot more than we paid for 'em. I've got some extra cash that is lyin' idle and if you'll just let me—"

"No."

"But, Mary, maybe you don't understand what not payin' the assessment means."

"I think I do. If it isn't paid I forfeit my holdings, or something like that. Very well, then I shall forfeit them. I have made up my mind and, really and truly, I don't greatly care. I have counted that money as good as lost for some time. Now that I know it is lost I am reconciled. It serves me right; I have had my lesson, and I am willing to pay for what I have learned. I am going to forget it."

"But, Mary—"

"No, no, Captain Cummings. Thank you very much, but—*no.*"

She was still brightly smiling, but there was a finality in her refusal which he recognized and made no further attempt to combat. Before he could speak she went on.

"Please don't look so very solemn," she begged. "It isn't such a dreadful thing, after all. I invested—or threw away—about a thousand dollars in that precious copper mine. That is a lot of money to lose, I know, but the loss doesn't mean as much to me as it did. Thanks to your getting me the place at the bank I am earning enough to pay my way and, with my other income, I have a little left over. Last week—just think of it!—I engaged a carpenter to repair the ell roof. I am beginning to feel hopeful of the front fence and—yes, even the henhouse. So you mustn't weep over me. I am contented and prosperous and—thanks to you—happier than I have been for a long, long time. I am going to forget Boroda Copper altogether and, so far as I am concerned, you must do the same thing. Now we won't talk about it any more."

He was silent for a moment. Then he said: "Well, if you feel that way that ends it, I suppose. Ends it so far as your payin' the assessment is concerned. There is one other thing though, that I'd like to say. It is just common sense, just a plain matter of business, and I'd like to have you consider it that way. That stock of yours is worth somethin', you know. May be worth consider'ble to a person who was willin' to take a chance and hang on. I'm takin' that chance with mine and I'd just as soon take it with a little more. Would you be willin' to sell me your Boroda, Mary? If you would I'll take it off your hands."

It was her turn to be astonished. She looked at him as if she thought he must be joking.

"Sell it to you?" she repeated. "Why in the world should you, or any one else, buy that stock now?"

He leaned forward. "Just business, that's all it is," he said, earnestly. "I'm in up to my waist already; might just as well be in up to my neck. I'll take your shares of Boroda off your hands at the price you paid for 'em and be glad of the chance. Now that's just business common sense. What do you say?"

She said nothing at first. Then she laughed merrily. "Oh, Captain Cummings!" she exclaimed. "Why will you persist in treating me as if I were a child? I admit I have acted like one, but I am really very ancient indeed. Why don't you offer to give me a thousand dollars? That is what your 'business matter' amounts to. Thank you ever and ever so much, but no—of course, no."

"But, Mary—"

"No. Now won't you *please* change the subject?"

He did not change it. Instead he changed merely the proposition he had just made for another.

"I was afraid you wouldn't," he admitted. "Well then, how about this? I want that stock of yours. I should really like to have it. I believe in the prospects of that mine and if I can get a few more shares cheap I'm goin' to get 'em. I might as well have yours as anybody else's. I want to buy 'em. What will you sell 'em to me for?"

"But, unless that assessment is paid, they are worth nothing, nothing at all."

"If I buy 'em I shall pay the assessment. The last quotation on 'em that I saw was three dollars and a quarter, or somethin' like that. Will you sell your stock to me at that figure? It will be doin' me a real favor if you will."

She hesitated. "That price you quoted was ever so long ago," she said. "There has been no sale for over a month. I have looked every day, and I am sure of that."

It made no difference. The time for obtaining stock at any price was short and he must act quickly. He urged and argued and, at last, she consented.

"Very well," she agreed. "You may have the stock. I can't talk against you; you are far too clever for me. Only please—*please* don't think you are fooling me again. I know you are doing this just to help me and for no other reason. I know."

He rose from the sofa. "Not a mite of it," he declared, hastily. "Business and that's all. To be honest, I feel a good deal like a swindler for takin' 'em from you at any such price. . . . Well there, Mary! You bring your certificate down to the bank to-morrow, signed in blank with your name on the back and I'll hand you your check. I'm ever so much obliged to you."

She came toward him. She was not smiling now.

"You are obliged to *me!*" she repeated. "Oh, Captain David, how can you?"

"Eh? How can I what?"

"How can you say such things and expect me to believe them? I know you now. I have learned a lot since I came to work in your bank, sir. Indeed I have! I know all about the 'simplicity' of that vote of the directors, and I know a little at least of what you did to make it unanimous for me. I—"

She paused. There was an odd little catch in her voice. He was greatly taken aback.

"Here, here!" he exclaimed. "What's all this rubbish? Who's been tellin' yarns out of school? That vote was unanimous. I—"

He was interrupted by the clatter of the knocker on the front door. He heard it and turned. Azure Crisp was hurrying through the hall. She opened the door.

"Oh, good evenin', Mr. Hall!" she gushed. "I thought likely 'twas you. Yes, Mary's to home. She's expectin' you. Come right in."

The cashier crossed the threshold. Cummings saw him and turned again to look at Miss Brewster. She was not looking at him but at the new arrival. He stepped out into the hall.

"Hello, Peter," he said, pleasantly. "Nice evenin', ain't it. Good-by, Mary. Fetch that—er—paper down when you come to the bank in the mornin'. Good night, Hall. Night, Azure."

He went out, hurriedly.

CHAPTER VII

THE transaction in Boroda Copper was completed next day. Mary brought the certificate to the bank, signed the transfer upon its back, and David Cummings handed her his check in exchange. He thrust the certificate into a compartment of a big pocketbook and the pocketbook into his inside pocket.

"There!" he observed, cheerfully. "*That* child's christened. . . . Eh? What's the matter? Anything wrong with the check? Didn't forget to sign it, did I?"

Mary, who was standing by the table, the check in her hand, looked from it to him.

"Oh no!" she said. "That part is all right."

"That part? Is there some other part that's wrong? Didn't I figure it out as it should be? If I cheated you I vow I didn't mean to. . . . Let's see."

He reached for the check, but she did not give it to him.

"The figure is right, too," she said. "There is nothing wrong with the amount or the signature. I know you haven't cheated me, but I am still far from sure that I am not cheating you, or at least that you are not cheating yourself. I very much doubt if that stock is really worth anything, Captain Cummings."

He smiled. "Don't you believe it," he protested. "I've made a good bargain. Too good to be honest, I'm afraid. One of these days, when Boroda is sellin' around fifty and I'm gettin' rich by the minute, you'll be thinkin' what a cheat I was for grabbin' it away from you for next to nothin'. Sure you won't change your mind? It ain't too late, you know. You've only signed the transfer in blank."

She looked at him keenly and with some suspicion.

"What do you mean by that?" she asked. "I have signed it, haven't I? I have sold that stock to you? Really sold it?"

"Eh? Oh, sure, sure! Only—"

"There isn't any 'why.' I have sold you the stock and I have taken your money—more shame to me. Of course," she added, with a laugh and a shake of the head, "I know perfectly well that, if I were to stay here and listen, you would talk me into believing that I was doing you a great favor and that the obligation was all on your side."

"Well, it is. I—"

"No, no! I am not going to let you talk. Mrs. Carleton has told me how you talk to her and, as she says, wind her around your finger. I know you are doing this thing just as a kindness to me. Well, it is done—I have been weak and selfish enough to let you do it—so we won't say another word on the subject. But you haven't fooled me, Captain Cummings, not a bit."

She went out of the directors' room and to her desk. When he next saw her, a short time afterward, she was seated at that desk, and Peter Hall was bending over her shoulder, apparently assisting her with some problem in bookkeeping. Cummings did not linger to look at the tableau, nor did he break in upon it. He had come out to speak with Hall, but he postponed the consultation until later. Twenty-four hours' reflection had but strengthened his conviction that the private affairs of his cashier and his assistant bookkeeper were not his business. So long as they did not interfere with the welfare of the Wapatomac National Bank—which was his business—they concerned him not at all. He must not permit them to concern him. For the sake of his own peace of mind, and as a matter of the simplest common sense, he would hereafter see and talk with Mary no oftener than the daily routine made necessary.

His interview with her that morning was the last of importance which took place between them for months. He saw her every working day at her desk in the bank, they exchanged casual pleasantries as to the weather or the state of each other's health, and of course she was occasionally summoned to the private room on a business matter. But on these occasions, in pursuance of his firm resolution, he was always the business-like employer and she the clerk. Neither he nor she referred to the Boroda transaction again. The stock was now seldom quoted in the financial columns and when it was the price was very low indeed. At home, around the Cummings supper table, Captain Barney and Kohath chatted of Wapatomac's doings, but they did not mention Mary Brewster nor Peter Hall. They would have done so, of course, for the village was now pretty thoroughly convinced that the cashier's intentions were serious, but Captain David's antagonistic attitude made the subject taboo while he was present.

"It's all bosh," he declared. "And, anyhow, it is their bosh and not ours. I won't have my evenin's turned into tattle sessions. Why don't you fellows join the sewin' circle or Ladies of Honor Lodge or somethin', like the other old women? Be still, both of you. Be good girls, and maybe I'll buy you a couple of new dolls next time I go to Boston."

Captain Barney had on this occasion ventured to remonstrate.

"What's the matter with you, Dave?" he demanded, indignantly. "What's made you so high and mighty all to once? Kohath and me are only sayin' what everybody else says. And some of it comes right straight from abaft the mainmast, too, as you might say. Ain't that so, Kohath? You know what I mean, don't you?"

Mr. Briggs nodded solemnly. "The last time I met Azure Crisp," he drawled, "she as much as said— Eh? What are you lookin' at me that way for, Cap'n Dave?"

Captain David was looking at him, regarding him with an expression of shocked and pained surprise.

"What's the matter?" demanded Kohath, giving his waistcoat a hasty examination. "Spilled somethin', have I? What is it?"

David slowly shook his head. "Well, well!" he exclaimed. "So that is the way of it, and we never guessed, the Skipper and I. So you and Azure Crisp are meetin' each other these days? Well, well!"

Captain Barnabas broke into a roar. The Briggs countenance turned a brick red, partly because of outraged innocence and partly from hot resentment.

"Wh—what—what divilish foolishness is this?" he sputtered, with unwonted animation. "Who's been lyin' about me? Who said I was meetin' anybody?"

"Why, you did. You started to tell us what the Crisp woman said the last time you met her—or she met you, I don't know which it was, of course. And did you notice, Skipper, that he said the *last* time? So it couldn't have been the first time. Dear me, dear me! Kohath, I am—well, I'm surprised."

He shook his head sadly and went into the sitting room. Captain Barnabas was still rocking back and forth and choking over the joke. The cook, however, was not in a laughing mood. He turned upon his hilarious companion.

"You got me into this," he vowed, angrily. "Now I won't have no peace and you know it. He'll be pokin' fun at me from now till next Fourth of July. Why can't you mind your own business?"

Captain Barnabas resented the accusation.

"How did I get you into it?" he demanded. "You was the one that said you'd been meetin' her. . . . Say, look here," with sudden suspicion; "you act mighty funny, now I come to notice it. There ain't any truth in what he said? You *ain't* been meetin' that Crisp thing, have you?"

Kohath's answer cannot be printed here. It was too hot for anything but an asbestos page. The incident had the effect of confirming the taboo upon supper table references to Mary Brewster and Peter Hall. Mr. Briggs was now as averse to dangerous topics of that kind as was his employer.

The winter months dragged by. March, entering like the proverbial lion, made its exit in an equally proverbial lamblike mood. Wapatomac had little of importance to talk about and was now centering its attention upon the usual spring topics, the mackerel catch, the repairing of summer cottages, the results of the votes at town meeting, and the like. Mary Brewster's daily occupancy of the bookkeeper's chair at the bank was now an old story. People had even ceased to speculate as to how long she would remain there. The intimacy between Hall and herself was also beginning to pall as a topic of marked interest. The cashier still called at the Brewster house, but according to Mrs. Knowles and other front line sentries, his calls were no more frequent than they had been. David Cummings knew she was doing her work satisfactorily, and beyond that he made it a point not to inquire. If she cared to consult him at any time she knew, for he had told her, that she was welcome to do so. Of late it seemed to him almost as if she were avoiding him. Between Peter Hall and himself her name was scarcely mentioned.

One April afternoon, however, the cashier mentioned it and in connection with a matter not at all concerned with the bank. He and the captain had been in conference in the directors' room over a somewhat doubtful loan. The conference ended, Hall rose to go. Then he paused. Cummings looked up at him inquiringly.

"Yes?" he asked. "Anything else you had to say, Peter?"

The cashier seemed a trifle embarrassed.

"No-o," he replied. "No, nothing to do with what we've been talking about. It was only that I have just heard—" He hesitated, fumbled with the papers in his hand, and added: "Say, Captain Cummings, do you know much about Benjamin Brewster, Miss Brewster's brother, the one who lives out West? Did you use to know him well when he was here in Wapatomac?"

Captain David shook his head. "Not well, no," he answered. "Why? What started you thinkin' about Ben Brewster, for mercy sakes?"

"Oh, nothing much—only— Well, I just wondered what sort of a man he was, that's all. You didn't know him, you say?"

"I didn't say that exactly. I knew him some, of course. He is—he must be—fifteen years older than I am and when he was a big boy home from college on his vacations I was just a little shaver. Later on, when he used to come here once in a while, I was away fishin'. Shouldn't have chummed with him much if I hadn't been, I guess. His folks and mine were a different breed of cats."

"Yes. Yes, of course. I understand what you mean."

"You ought to; you've lived in Wapatomac seven or eight years. What makes you ask about him?"

Hall did not answer the question, immediately. "You saw him when he came on to his stepmother's funeral, didn't you?" he persisted.

"He didn't come to her funeral. He was sick, they said. And when his father was buried I didn't go to the cemetery and that's the only chance anybody except Mary and her mother had to see Ben scarcely at all. He had to hurry off on the early train next mornin'. I haven't seen Ben Brewster for years and years. Shouldn't know him if I did see him, I expect."

"He is a rich man, isn't he?"

"So I've heard, though I don't know as I ever heard it from anybody who might be supposed to know. He has lived in Denver, or somewheres out West there, for ever so long. Story is he married a woman with a barge load of money."

The cashier nodded. "She is dead," he announced. "He is a widower now."

Cummings was still but mildly interested.

"I want to know!" he observed. "How did you hear that?"

Then Mr. Hall revealed the secret of his information.

"His sister had a letter from him day before yesterday," he said. "It was a long letter and he had a lot to say in it. Seems his wife died last November. They haven't any children, he is all alone in the world, just as Mary—just as Miss Brewster is, and an invalid beside. The doctors tell him he can't live many years longer, or something like that. So—this is what he wrote—he has been thinking that she and he are the only living members of the family and it seems a pity they are separated by so many miles. He thinks they shouldn't be."

Captain David was much more interested now.

"Eh? What?" he asked, abruptly. "Does that mean he wants Mary to come out there and live with him?"

"No-o. At least he didn't say so. He—well, he hinted that he was considering coming on here to make her a visit. Of course, what may be in his mind behind that nobody else knows. He is rich and—Mary has heard that he and his wife had a lovely home in Denver. It is possible that. . . . Well, anyhow, that is all he said in the letter."

His expression was far from happy as he repeated this bit of news. He was not looking at Cummings, but the latter was looking at him, looking and making a shrewd guess as to the cause of the unhappiness. If Ben Brewster was considering offering his sister a home in the western city it was easy to surmise why the thought was far from pleasing to Peter Hall. It was not altogether pleasing to David Cummings, although he did not show his feelings.

"You know all this is so, of course?" he asked.

"Yes, I know it."

"Mary showed you the letter, did she?"

"Why—er—why, yes, she did."

"I see. . . . Humph! Well, I don't know as it is any of our affairs."

"No-o. No, only—well, as friends of Miss Brewster, you and I would, naturally, hate to have her make any mistake—er—do anything she might be sorry for later on."

"I don't know that I'd go so far as to call quittin' a bookkeepin' job in the Wapatomac National Bank to live with my brother such a terrible mistake, even if that brother was a millionaire. Don't hardly seem as if I would. What makes you think it may be?"

The cashier appeared to find this question hard to answer. He turned away.

"Hold on a minute," persisted Captain David. "What makes you think it may turn out a mistake, Peter?"

Hall fumbled with the papers. "Oh, I don't know," he muttered. "No doubt it is all right, only—well, as a friend of hers I should like to know more about what sort of a man this Ben Brewster is. He hasn't seen her for years. He hasn't written her. After neglecting her all this time it does seem queer that he should take such an interest in her all of a sudden."

"I see. . . . Well, did she say she thought it was queer?"

"No-o. I don't know that she did."

"Um-hum. Then I don't see why you and I should worry. Mary's got her share of common sense, same as her father had before her. I don't think she'll let her half brother or anybody else coax her into doin' what she thinks she had better not do. I hope she won't anyhow."

He had not meant to emphasize the "or anybody else," but he had emphasized it just a little. Hall looked at him, seemed about to speak, then turned and, without another word, left the room. Cummings threw himself back in the chair, rumpled his hair, and frowned at the ceiling. What he had just heard concerning Benjamin Brewster was but mildly intriguing. He attached little importance to it. Considering that Mary was the man's only living relative, his half sister, it was perhaps natural enough that, alone after his wife's death, he should think of visiting her. This was not so very surprising. But the fact that Mary had shown the letter—a personal, intimate letter—to Peter Hall was illuminating—yes, and in spite of his philosophic resolve, disturbing. So the intimacy between the two had reached that stage. A few months earlier and, if she had shown that letter to any one, it would have been to him, David Cummings. He was her "sheet anchor"; he had never forgotten her calling him that. Apparently she had another anchor now. He was right in surmising that she had avoided him of late. And, apparently, his grandfather and Kohath were also right when they attached importance to the gossip connecting her name with that of the cashier.

It scarcely seemed possible. He remembered other swains of former years, good-looking, smart young chaps who had called often at the Brewster home and of whom gossip had whispered much. One after the other they had called and called—and then their calls had ceased. "Another one got his clearance papers," said Wapatomac. "She must be fussy if she figures *he* ain't good enough for her." Now, after this long interval, had she at last found one who was good enough? And that one this middle-aged, precise individual with his hair parted in the middle and his shoes always so neatly polished? Who trotted so exactly in the narrow path of orthodox respectability and never, never deviated from it? Whose world was bounded by the four walls of the bank during the week and on Sundays by the cast-iron creed of the old First Church? No, it did not seem possible, but apparently it was. One of his grandfather's favorite aphorisms was that women were queer birds and you never could tell which way they would fly next. Evidently this was true; but for Mary Brewster—for Mary Brewster to—

He left the bank a few minutes later and, as he walked toward the outer door, he caught a glimpse of Mary at her desk and of Mr. Hall solicitously bending over her shoulder.

He asked no questions concerning the letter from the Denver brother, nor did Hall volunteer any further information. As for Mary herself, he saw less and less of her. On the few occasions when she and he were alone she never referred to matters outside the bank routine. This was as it should be, of course, and he never encouraged her to do so, but there were times when he caught himself wondering why. The only answer to the question was one which he did not like to consider.

One Saturday afternoon in early May he returned

from the bank to the wharf and office of D. Cummings & Co. to find his grandfather, Captain Barnabas, the only occupant of that office. The usual number of longshoremen and roustabouts were busy on the wharf, but in the office Captain Barney sat alone, smoking an ancient and odorous pipe. It was the dull season of the year in the shellfish business; oysters had ceased to be in demand, lobsters were not yet on the market, and few clams—"quahaugs," Captain Dave would have called them—were shipped on Saturdays. Nevertheless, this complete desertion of the office was unusual.

"Hello, Skipper!" cried David. "What are you doin' here?"

Captain Barney blew a perfumed cloud in his grandson's direction.

"Me?" he said. "Oh, I'm kind of deputy supercargo here for a spell. Better hurry up home and get your dinner, hadn't you? It's been waitin' for half an hour. Kohath and me have had ours. I was sort of sharp set, so he and I mugged up by ourselves. You cruise right along, Dave. I'll keep the ship afloat till you get back."

David turned to look at the roll-top desk in the corner beside his own, where his manager, Jacob Paine, was accustomed to sit. The desk was closed and locked.

"Why should you have to 'tend ship, Skipper?" he asked. "Where's Jake?"

Then he remembered and answered his own question. "Oh, yes, yes!" he added. "Jake is takin' the afternoon off, isn't he. I forgot."

Captain Barnabas nodded. "Cal'latin' to go to the auction over to Bayport," he said. "Lots of Wapatomac folks goin' to take in that auction, they tell me. They're sellin' off the furniture of the Salters house over there and there's liable to be some good stuff sold cheap. Hannah Salters had some nice things in her day. I remember her when she was a girl, afore she married Dan Salters. Simpson, her name was, and—"

David cut short the flow of recollection. "Where's Jim?" he asked. "He isn't goin' to the auction, too, is he?"

Jim Leathers was the D. Cummings & Co. bookkeeper; had been since the firm went into business. Barnabas shook his head.

"No, no," he explained. "Jim's been here right along, up to a few minutes ago. He was late goin' to dinner. There was a feller here that talked consider'ble and he kept Jim from leavin' sooner." Then, with a chuckle, he added: "Kind of funny, that was, too. You'd ought to have been here, Dave. Jim wished you was, I'll bet."

"Why? Who was this fellow?"

"I don't know who he was. Jim, he didn't neither, seems so. He was a stranger to him, same as he was to me. And yet—and yet," with a puzzled frown, "he didn't look exactly like a stranger, he didn't. Seems as if I'd ought to know him, as if I'd met him somewheres afore."

"Well, who was he? What did he want? Didn't he tell you his name?"

"No. And I didn't have no chance to ask. He was here when I got here and him and Jim was havin' a kind of sharp argument, seemed so."

"What about?"

"About gettin' a check cashed, fur's I could make out. I didn't hear the whole of it. When I come aboard Jim was sayin' that he couldn't cash a check for that much without askin' Jake or you and you was both away just then. The feller, he laughed, kind of toplofty and nasty, seemed to me, and wanted to know if either of you would be back or if all Wapatomac was dead or asleep or havin' a holiday or somethin' like that. Said he'd called at the house where he was goin' and there wasn't nobody there; then he went to the bank and that was shut up; and then he come here to see you and you was out. He said he hated to strain the resources of this concern—that's what he called it, 'strainin' the resources'—but he was liable to need money, even in a town like this one, and so he'd be very much obliged if Jim would cash that check for him. Jim vowed he couldn't do it until you come. The feller said he would be in again and went out. Jim, he asked me to look out for things until you did come and hurried off to his own dinner. I wanted to ask him more about the feller, but I didn't have a chance. I don't hardly blame Jim for not wantin' to cash the check, though, do you, Dave? I judge 'twas a pretty good-sized one."

"Certain I don't blame him. He's had his orders. The last check we cashed for a stranger turned out to be good for nothin' but a souvenir of the money we swapped for it. I told Jake he better frame it and hang it up as a warnin'. This chap was pretty fresh, I should say, who-ever he was. What did he look like, Skipper?"

"Oh, I don't know. Didn't look as if he'd climbed out of the poorhouse window, I'd say that much. Kind of tall; gray hair and a little black mustache; dressed up in a nice suit of clothes and—oh, yes, I remember noticin' it, there was a sort of black band, a piece of black cloth, sewed around one sleeve. Must be mournin' somebody, mustn't he? And I cal'late he was lame or sick or somethin' himself; he was luggin' a cane, anyhow. He wore a pair of them brass-rimmed nose glasses; had 'em moored at the end of a little two-for-a-cent brass chain. I kept thinkin' I'd seen him afore, but I guess likely I hadn't."

"Doesn't sound like any one I know. He said he came here to see me, did he?"

"That's what I heard him tell Jim."

"I can't think— Eh? Why, yes, maybe I can. There was a salesman for a barrel concern comin' to see me this mornin'. The Boston office of that company has been tryin' to get us to give 'em an order for a long while and they wrote their representative would call here at ten this forenoon. Did this chap look like a drummer for a barrel company?"

Captain Barnabas was doubtful. "He was dressed kind of smart, like one of them city drummers," he admitted. "He *might* be sellin' fish barrels, but I swan to man he didn't look as if he'd ever took hold of one. No, nor as if he liked the smell of them you've got out yonder on the wharf, neither. He might peddle cologne or jewelry, but I shouldn't have picked him for fish barrels. No, sir!"

David laughed. "I guess that is who he was, though," he said. "Well, if he wants to get an order here he's started the wrong way. Bein' three hours behind to his appointment, and pokin' fun at Wapatomac, and tryin' to get our bookkeeper to cash a check without knowin' him from Adam, isn't the best kind of introduction, not to D. Cummings & Co., it isn't. Well, Skipper, as long as you started at the job of supercargo I'll let you keep it till I get back. There won't be much doin' and Jim will take over your watch when he comes. See you later."

Kohath was awaiting him when he entered the house at the top of the hill. Dinner, Mr. Briggs announced, was probably "as good as spiled," which calamity, he took pains to add, was not in the least the fault of the person who had cooked it. Cummings ate hurriedly and, as soon as he had finished, took his hat and coat and turned to the door. He had left his grandfather alone in the office and, although the bookkeeper should have returned before this, he was a trifle anxious. Kohath called to him as he was about to leave.

"Ain't goin' to that Bayport auction, be you, Cap'n?" he asked. "Lots of folks are. Peter Hall's goin'. Enoch Hawes, down to the livery stable, told me about every horse 'n team they had was let. Hall, he's hired one. Enoch said Peter was so fussy about the buggy bein' washed and dusted and all that he cal'lated he must be takin' a girl with him. . . . Er—er—Mary Brewster, she didn't say she was goin', did she?"

David did not answer. He strode down the hill, his hands in his pockets and a frown between his brows. There were times when Mr. Briggs' habit of saying the wrong thing in the wrong place made him long to choke the garrulous cook.

When he reached his place of business he caught a glimpse of Jim Leathers, the bookkeeper, giving instructions to a group of laborers at the end of the wharf, so his anxiety concerning leaving the establishment in his grandfather's care had been needless. The door of the office was ajar and, through the opening, he saw Captain

Barnabas and another man standing, their backs to the door, deep in conversation. This other man was a stranger and, remembering the old gentlemen's picture of the barrel salesman, David surmised that it was he. Humph! If this well-dressed individual did sell barrels it seemed evident that the calling was profitable.

Neither the Skipper nor the visitor noticed Captain David's approach. He stood there for a moment, his hand upon the latch. Captain Barney was speaking.

"No," he was saying. "I don't know any more than I've told you. Folks say she went to work in my grandson's bank so's to have somethin' to take up her mind. She's got all the money she needs—anyhow she ought to have—so it wan't on account of the wages. She done it, I guess likely, 'cause she took a notion. All them Brewsters are notional, always was."

The "barrel drummer" tapped his leg with his cane.

"An odd notion, I should say," he observed. "Is it your—er—grandson's idea that her working there was merely to keep her mind occupied?"

"Um-hum. That's what he's told me he thinks 'tis."

"I see. Down at the hotel where I had lunch— What was it? 'The Wayfarer's Curse,' or something like that?"

"Eh? Curse? No, no! The Travelers' Rest, that's the name of it. Give you a real satisfyin' meal there for fifty cents, they tell me."

"They tell you the truth. A very little of it satisfied me. Down there at the 'Curse' or 'Rest,' or whatever it is, I was given to understand that—er—Miss Brewster had gone to some auction or other in Bayport. Had driven over there with a man named Hall. Who is he?"

"Eh? Peter Hall? Why, he's the bank cashier. Smart, able man for the job, too. Makes a good first mate for David, Peter does. So he's took Mary to the auction, has he? Well, well! I want to know! That's one more little mite of proof that there's somethin' doin' in them latitudes. He, he! Sho! Dave'll have to give in afore long, I guess, that me and Kohath know what we're talking about. Yes, sir, he will! I've told him over and over that all hands are sure Hall is keepin' comp'ny with Mary Brewster. I've told him and so's Kohath, but he won't— Eh? Why, hello, Dave! Back again so soon, be you!"

David Cummings had opened the door and entered. He paid no heed to his grandfather's hail. He stepped over to where the pair were standing and his first remark was addressed to the supposed representative of the barrel company.

"Well, sir?" he said, rather brusquely. "You were waitin' to see me, were you?"

The stranger turned deliberately and looked him over. Captain Barney's description was not a bad one. His clothes were good and well cut, although not in the least flashy, his hair was gray, his small mustache black, and there was about him a certain air of patronage, at least of easy composure, which David Cummings, in his frame of mind at the moment, found unreasonably irritating.

"Were you waitin' to see me?" asked Cummings again.

The visitor regarded him through the gold-rimmed eyeglasses.

"Possibly," he observed, with a slight smile. "Who are you, may I ask?"

"My name is David Cummings."

"Oh! . . . Oh, yes! Well, I was—er—hoping that I might see you. Yes."

"What did you want to see me about?"

Captain Barnabas felt called upon to furnish the information.

"He's the feller—I mean he's the one was here afore, Dave," he put in. "The one I told you about. He—"

"Yes, I know. . . . You were to be here at ten, weren't you?"

"Was I? I wasn't aware of it."

"Your people wrote me you would be here then. I waited for you until almost eleven. . . . Well, what can I do for you, now that you are here?"

The caller's smile was broader. He looked the questioner over with that same air of cool and amused interest. Cummings' irritation increased. If the firm had not a barrel in the world, he would not have given an order to this fellow. He was certainly the "freshest" specimen of the genus drummer that had ever called at that office. And his reply now was, although perfectly polite, just as provokingly and languidly indifferent.

"I don't know that you can do anything for me," he said. "I called here before with the hope that you might accommodate me by cashing a small check. Your bookkeeper—I suppose that was who he was—told me he could do nothing of the sort without your consent."

"He was right. Those were his orders. We make a rule here not to cash checks for strangers. We have had a few unpleasant and expensive experiences along that line. You mustn't blame the bookkeeper. How much is your check?"

"Can't say, exactly. I haven't drawn it yet. I was daring to think of a hundred dollars."

"Hum. . . . I see. It is your own check, then?"

"It is—or will be if I draw it. Of course," with the same languid smile, "I can make it fifty if that amount will reduce the strain on your conscience, Mr. Cummings."

This was a trifle too much. David stepped back.

"My conscience can stand the hundred, I guess," he retorted, grimly. "That ain't the question, exactly. You'll excuse my plain speakin', but I don't know who you are. I know the concern you travel for, and they are all right, of course. If you can bring some one in here to identify you I'll cash your check and welcome."

"Dear me! Now that is very good of you, I am sure. So you don't know me? . . . Well, I judged you didn't."

To the surprise of both the Cummingses he turned on his heel and walked toward the door. Captain David strode after him.

"Here! Just a minute," he ordered. "What do you mean by sayin' you judge I don't know you? Why should I know you?"

"Can't say, really. Good afternoon."

"But—here, hold on! Where are you goin'? If you will get yourself identified, I'll—"

A wave of the cane was the only answer. This amazing barrel salesman had left the office and was disappearing around the corner of the building. David Cummings, standing in the doorway, stared after him.

"Well, I'll be darned!" he exclaimed, with emphasis. "If that don't beat all my goin' to sea then I'm a Norwegian. . . . Here, Skipper, who *is* that fellow? I'm beginnin' to believe he never saw a fish barrel."

Captain Barney shook his head. "I don't know who he is," he protested. "I took it for granted same as you done that he was that barrel drummer you was expectin'. He never said 'twas his business though."

"Humph! From what I heard of the talk between you and him he was a whole lot more interested in other people's business. How did you and he get to goin' about Mary and Peter Hall and all that?"

"Eh? . . . Why, I don't know. Seems to me he started it. Mentioned Mary's name he did, and—"

He was interrupted by the entrance of Jim Leathers. Jim had witnessed the departure of the mysterious stranger.

"Did you cash his check, Cap'n Cummings?" he asked.

"No. Why should I? I told him if he would get himself identified I would, and he marched off without another word. Who in blazes is he? Didn't he tell you his name or anything, Jim?"

Leathers nodded. "Um-hum," he replied. "He told me his last name, but no more. He said—and it struck me funny, too—that his name was Brewster. Course I asked him if he was relation to the Brewsters here in Wapatomac and he never answered me. Don't seem as if he could hardly be. Yet I don't know any other Brewsters in the county, do you, Cap'n Dave?"

David Cummings was staring at him, staring as one to whose mind had flashed a new and most disturbing thought. He strode to where his grandfather was sitting and laid a hand upon the old man's shoulder.

"Skipper," he demanded, "do you remember what Ben Brewster, Mary's half brother, used to look like? Think now! Do you?"

Captain Barnabas thought. Then he sprang to his feet and struck his right fist into his left palm.

"By the everlastin'!" he exclaimed. "That's who 'twas. Cap'n Ben Brewster's boy! If it hadn't been that his hair was white and he was walkin' with a cane I'll bet I'd have known him first minute I see him. And I *did* know 'twas somebody I'd seen afore. I told you so, Dave Cummings!" triumphantly. "Don't you recollect I did?"

David did not answer. He was standing by the window, running his fingers through his hair. When he turned it was with a shrug and a rueful shake of the head.

"I put my foot in it this time," he declared, with a sigh. "Yes, sir, I certainly did put my foot in it."

CHAPTER VIII

MARY BREWSTER had accepted the Hall invitation to drive with him to the Bayport auction, but she had done so with some reluctance. In a way she was eager to go. The old Salters home contained some treasures in the shape of fine old furniture and china and such things were even then beginning to be appreciated, particularly by the summer people. It was not likely that she would be able to pick up anything at a price she could afford, but she might, and at least she would have enjoyed looking them over. If she could have gone alone the afternoon would, she felt, have been thoroughly pleasant.

It was because Peter Hall had insisted that she go with him—there was the trouble. She was beginning to feel a trifle uneasy about Mr. Hall, his repeated calls and invitations. At first she had regarded his interest in her and his dropping in at the Brewster house as merely the desire of a lonely man for companionship. He was her superior at the bank, and no one could have been more patient or kind in overlooking mistakes and helping her with her daily work. He had gone out of his way to be of assistance to her and she was grateful for this and his encouragement. She had refused several invitations from him to attend dances and entertainments, but she had accepted others, just as she finally consented to drive with him to the auction at Bayport, because she did not wish to hurt his feelings by refusing.

She had permitted him to call on her for the same reason. She knew Bayport well enough to know that people would soon be noticing and commenting, but since her defiance of convention in the matter of employment at the bank she had learned the joy of independence and to ignore hints and innuendos, just as she ignored Mrs. Crisp's ridiculous speeches. Azure had assumed the attitude of a beneficent but wise and understanding guardian. When she opened the front door to admit Mr. Hall she always greeted him with a knowing smile and an air of confidential patronage. Having ushered him into the sitting room she would pause a moment to smile again upon the pair, a sort of "Bless you, my children" smile which made Mary long to throw something at her. Then she would close the door and tiptoe away with elaborate and squeaky caution. She now made no open references to the consummation which she so devoutly wished and confidently expected. She and Miss Brewster had fought that matter to a finish on one memorable occasion.

Hall's call was a short one on that particular evening and Azure was still up and in the kitchen when he left the house. Mary found her there and commented upon her not having gone to bed. The housekeeper's reply was the speech which started the blaze.

"I've just been sittin' here thinkin'," she said solemnly. "And I'm goin' to ask you to do me a great favor, Mary Brewster. I want you to promise me that when it is all settled and you two are engaged you won't tell a livin' soul afore you do me. I want the privilege of springin' the news on that old Barney Cummings myself. I ain't forgot how he crowed over me at that missionary meetin' about your goin' to work for his grandson! Huh! I want the fun of tellin' him that, no matter if his precious grandson did coax you into actin' so silly, it is somebody else who has put his nose out of joint. I notice Dave Cummings isn't makin' many 'business calls' at this house nowadays. I guess *he* sees how the wind's blowin'."

It was a most untimely remark. Mary herself was beginning to feel a trifle disturbed concerning the persistence and regularity of the cashier's visits. She lost patience altogether and whirled upon the triumphant Mrs. Crisp with heightened color and flashing eyes.

"Azure," she said, sharply, "if I hear any more of this sort of thing from you I shall tell you to pack your trunk and go. I shall! You must understand this once and for all. I have no intention of becoming engaged to Mr. Hall. He and I are friends, and nothing more. And don't you ever—don't you ever *dare* hint to a soul what you have just said to me."

Azure wept. There were hysterical references to her long service in that household, to Mary's sainted mother and to family pride and traditions. The interview ended in reconciliation of course, but Mary did not retract a word of her ultimatum. And, thereafter, Mrs. Crisp managed to refrain from further mention of the, in her mind, inevitable "engagement." Her smiles and knowing nods and shrugs were, however, always in evidence, and she never lost an opportunity to chant the cashier's praises, often on characteristically original and unexpected pretexts.

"My, my!" she once exclaimed, standing at the window and watching Peter Hall disappear into the rainy darkness, "it does do me good to see how that man holds an umbrella when it's rainin' same as 'tis now and same as it was last Sunday afternoon. *He* don't stick it way up in the air as if it 'twas a rake handle and he was haulin' pears off a tree with it. No indeed! He holds it easy and refined, as if he was used to it; and, when he's with you, Mary, he holds it over you, not over himself or the sidewalk. That's one thing," she went on reminiscently, "I could never teach my Obed to do right. He always wore ileskins stormy weather and he hadn't any use for an umbrella at all. So, when 'twas rainin' and we was goin' anywheres and he saw anybody he knew acrost the road or way off in a field maybe, he was just as liable as not to start wavin' signals with the umbrella and leave me and my best hat to get soaked through. Either that or get to talkin' and forget what he was doin' and start twirlin' it 'round and 'round like the paddle on a side-wheel steamboat. Mr. Hall, now, he don't do such things. Rain or shine, he's always so dignified and genteel."

Mary laughed at this, but there were times now when she did not laugh at the idea that the cashier might be seeking more than her friendship. Recently she had begun to fear that he might not be satisfied with that. It seemed to her that there was a slight change in his manner toward her. He was never presuming, never unduly familiar, in fact he was always deferentially and formally polite even to the verge of exaggeration, but it did seem sometimes as if he were assuming a sort of proprietorship over her. And, of late, she had noticed that he was inclined to speak of his own personal affairs, of his salary, of the amount he had put by "in safe, conservative investments," and once—this was during his most recent call—he had hinted that he was even daring to hope that he might again have a home of his own. She had changed the subject hastily, but it had put her on her guard.

It was partially her fault, of course. She realized this now. She had asked his advice in matters intimately personal. The letter she had received from her half brother in Denver she had shown to him. It had come as a great surprise to her, she was impelled to talk with some one about it. David Cummings would have been the natural confident, but for some time Captain David had kept away from her. At first she had tried to think his apparent aloofness was not real nor premeditated, but, as the weeks passed, she became certain that he was avoiding her purposely. She could not imagine why and her feelings were hurt. Then her pride was aroused and she was as coolly indifferent toward him as he was to her—more so. She had dutifully replied to the Denver letter, expressing conventional delight at hearing from her brother and the hope that his visit might become a reality and soon. To this reply she had received no acknowledgment.

And, as concerned Peter Hall, she had reached a definite, if tardy conclusion in her thinking. This drive with him to the Bayport auction was to be their last excursion together. She would accept no more invitations and, if possible, she would discourage his calls at the house. To be independent of criticism and gossip was one thing, to be drawn into an embarrassing complication with this man was another. He had been a good friend to her, but even at the risk of breaking that friendship, and the consequences which the break might entail, this intimacy must cease before it reached a crisis. It had not reached that crisis yet, and it should not if she could prevent it.

The cashier's manner and behavior that afternoon were, for the most part, not such as to strengthen her apprehensions. He purchased several small items at the sale of the Salters effects and she also was tempted by a wonderful pair of antique candlesticks into spending more than she knew she should afford. Mr. Hall seemed rather desirous that she should buy more extensively. "If you haven't the money with you—er—Mary," he said, "I shall be happy to supply it. Your credit with me is A1 you know," he added, as a sort of professional joke.

They had been close acquaintances now for quite six months, but this was the first time he had permitted himself the familiarity of calling her by her Christian name. Every one else in the bank, even Bennie Jackson, hailed her as "Mary," but Peter Hall had always addressed her as "Miss Brewster." She noticed the change, and her refusal of the loan was even firmer than it might otherwise have been.

During the drive back to Wapatomac he kept leading the conversation to the subject she was most anxious to avoid, his present status as cashier, his well-founded hopes of further advancement in his profession, his loneliness, and, once more, his desire for a little home "all my own—or, better still, mine and, perhaps, another's."

Fortunately—or so Mary considered it—his arrival at this dangerously sentimental stage was approximately that of their arrival at the Brewster gate. And, more fortunately still, a figure was standing upon the Brewster front step and peering in the direction of the approaching buggy.

"Why, what is Azure doing out there?" Mary asked.

"Is she looking for me, I wonder? It *is* Azure, isn't it?"

She knew perfectly well that it was, and the question was merely a time filler. Mr. Hall was not in the least interested in Mrs. Crisp's reason for being out of doors instead of in. In fact, judging by his expression, had the housekeeper been at the bottom of the well he would not have hurried to pull her up.

"Mary," he whispered, leaning forward, "I—"

But Mary also was leaning forward.

"It is Azure," she broke in. "And she is dressed in her best clothes, and—yes, I am sure she has been watching for me. What is it, do you suppose? What can have happened? Azure! Azure, here I am. What is the matter?"

Mrs. Crisp came hastening down the walk. She was, as Mary said, arrayed in all her Sunday-go-to-meeting grandeur, including the black transformation and the gold breastpin. Also, in spite of her evident desire to appear genteelly dignified in the presence of the cashier of the Wapatomac National Bank, she was aquiver with excitement.

"My glory's land!" she exclaimed, with a sigh of relief. "I'm so glad you've got here. I've been standin' watch at that front door, like the lookout on a swordfish boat, off and on for the best part of an hour. Mary Brewster, I—I—don't you ever tell me again that miracles don't happen. Don't you dare to. And here I've been waitin' and waitin' tellin' him: 'She'll be here pretty soon; she'll be here pretty soon,' and seems if you never would. Well, He moves in a mysterious way His wonders to perform. He plants His footprints on the—er—the—well, there, I don't know! . . . Come right in. You mustn't keep him waitin' another single minute. Come *in!*"

She paused, panting. Hall looked as if he were considering shouting for help and a straight jacket. And even Mary, accustomed as she was to her housekeeper's vagaries, looked a little alarmed.

"What in the world, Azure?" she demanded. "Have you gone completely crazy? What is all this about? Stop waving your hands and tell me."

Mrs. Crisp's pride was touched. She drew herself erect. "So far as that goes," she said, loftily. "I ain't crazy and you know I ain't in the habit of bein', either. I've had a surprise, that's all. And you are goin' to have a bigger one in a minute. That is," with asperity, "if you will be so kind as to get out of that buggy and come into the house where he's been waitin' for you 'most three hours."

"He? Who? Who has been waiting for me?"

"That," with a toss of the head, "I ain't allowed to tell you. I've had my orders not to. He wants to surprise you. Now won't you please come?"

Mary alighted from the buggy. The cashier would have assisted her, but she was too quick for him.

"You'll excuse me, won't you," she said, turning toward him. "Evidently some one—I can't imagine who—is waiting for me. I enjoyed the auction very much. Thank you, Mr. Hall. Good-by."

Peter Hall was plainly disconcerted and disappointed.

"But, Mary," he stammered, "I—I had hoped—I meant— When shall I see you again?"

"Oh, perhaps at church to-morrow. At any rate, at

the bank on Monday. Good-by. Thank you again for the drive and the auction."

She hurried up the walk. Hall, frowning, slapped the horse with the reins and drove away. Mary paused an instant to look after him. It was her turn to sigh with relief.

"Azure," she said, impulsively, "I think I was never gladder to see any one than I was to see you on the step just now."

"Why? . . . You didn't know—"

"Of course not," hastily. "Now tell me! Who *is* this person who is waiting to see me and who has put you into such a state? It isn't—it isn't Captain Cummings, is it?"

Azure was at the door, but she turned now, indignant astonishment in her stare.

"Cap'n Cummings?" she repeated. "Dave Cummings! Do you suppose he, or any of his tribe, would—would—oh, my land of glory! . . . You come along and see for yourself. Then I guess I won't be the only one in a state."

The door leading from the hall to the sitting room was closed. She threw it open.

"There!" she announced, triumphantly. "Here she is, finally."

Mary entered the sitting room. A tall, gray-haired gentleman, who had been sitting in the rocker by the table, rose and extended both hands.

"Well, Mary, my dear," he said, with a smile, "here you really are. And are you as glad to see me as I am to see you?"

Mary looked at him, at first in bewilderment and then with dawning recognition.

"Why—why, Ben!" she cried. "Why, *Ben!*"

CHAPTER IX

AND now Wapatomac was once more furnished with a new topic of conversation and again it was a person bearing the aristocratic name of Brewster who had supplied it. But this time that person was not Mary—she was but secondary in the public interest; the real hub about which rumor and speculation revolved was her half brother Benjamin, the unexpected arrival from the far and romantic West. The noon train of Saturday brought him to town and by the evening of Monday that town knew all there was to learn about him and a great deal of which it is quite probable he himself was unaware. He was a widower, his wife had been dead but a few months. He was rich. He was "real sick," that is to say he was "not a bit well," there was something the matter with his heart, or his lungs, or some important section of his interior. He had come on to visit his half sister and the old house where he had spent his boyhood and the visit was a tremendous surprise to Mary. As for Azure Crisp, she was reported to have said at Gallup's store, whither she had come that Saturday evening to purchase additional supplies for the next day's dinner, that she was never "struck dumber" than she was when she answered his knock and found him standing on the step. And a surprise which struck Mrs. Crisp dumb must have been, all agreed, a surprise indeed.

Cross-questioned concerning the length of his visit Azure was obliged to confess that she did not know.

"As far as I'm concerned," she declared, "I hope he'll stay a year. It'll seem good to have a man around the house again to cook for. And especially such a man as he is. He's a real Brewster, and when you've said that you've said all that's needful. So gentlemanly, and so pleasant and genteel spoken, and yet, with it all, all his money and everything, so pleasant and everyday. You'd think, to hear him talk to me, this afternoon afore Mary got home, that he wasn't any more 'special account than—well, than you are, Noah Gallup. No, sir, you wouldn't! He knew me and called me by name the minute he laid eyes on me and he said that now, since his own dreadful loss had come to him, he could appreciate how I felt when Obed was took. And, you talk about the judgment of dumb animals! Why, Galahad—that's our cat—he climbed up into his lap—I mean the cat climbed into Mr. Benjamin's lap—within the first fifteen minutes after he came in where he was. I mean after the cat came in, of course. And he'd have stayed there to this minute, I guess, only Mr. Benjamin got up because he sheds his hair so this time of year. . . . What say! Oh, don't talk so ridiculous! You didn't suppose I meant Mr. Brewster was sheddin' *his* hair, did you? Come, come! Do hurry up with that tea and the rest of the things. I came here shoppin', not to stand and chatter half the night."

From this it may be inferred that the visitor from Denver had already made a favorable impression upon his sister's housekeeper.

And that impression soon became general throughout Wapatomac. In the old First Church on Sunday morning all heads turned when Mary and her brother walked up the aisle together. It seemed natural enough to the older people for a Benjamin Brewster to be sitting in that front pew. And, although this particular Benjamin could not be hailed by the title "Captain" and although there was about him no flavor of the sea, although his step had in it no trace of the deep-sea roll with which every other adult male Brewster had approached that pew, there was a certain something about him which stamped him as a member of the family.

Mrs. Captain Sam Freeman whispered to her husband: "I haven't seen him for years and years, and he has changed so I don't think I'd ever have known him, but just the same he looks like a Brewster, doesn't he, Samuel?"

Her husband nodded. "Looks a good deal more like Cap'n Ben's first wife than he does like his father," he whispered in return. "But he's got a sort of hint of Ben in him, that's a fact. Thought you said he was sick or somethin'. He looks hearty enough to me."

After the service there was a crowding about to shake hands and to welcome the long absent one back to his native village. And here, as in Azure's case, Benjamin Brewster proved himself the possessor of that quality so valuable to politicians and public men, and so much envied by those not possessing it, the faculty of remembering and connecting names and faces. Again and again he called former acquaintances by name the moment they approached him.

"Why, how do you do, Mrs. Baker? Well, well! It is certainly good to meet you again. Know you? Why, of course I did! You haven't changed an atom. You don't look a day older. And Captain Eben, too! How are you, Eben? Yes, I'm at home again, for a time anyhow. All Wapatomacites come home sooner or later, don't they? No, I can't say just how long I shall stay. That depends. I am not quite as strong as I look, as a matter of fact. But this air, and meeting with old friends like this, ought to build me up if anything can. Is there a doctor in this town nowadays? There is? What on earth does he find to do? You people don't need him; that is obvious enough."

Yes, there was no doubt that Wapatomac, most of it—and particularly its "best families"—were favorably impressed with Ben Brewster. Mrs. Eleazir Bradley, on her way home and in conference with her daughter, said: "He is a gentleman, there is no doubt of that. Of course he should be, being a Brewster, but considering how long he has lived away out West there, I couldn't be sure until I saw him. Elvira, you have been complaining about there being so few nice men in town nowadays. Here is one. You ought to cultivate him. . . . And he is a widower, too."

Miss Bradley colored. "Mother, don't be foolish," she protested. "He is old enough to be my father. But you can't help liking him, can you? He hadn't seen me—to talk with, I mean—since I was a young girl, but I didn't have to tell him who I was at all. He says he isn't well—his heart isn't strong, or something. I hope it isn't true. Mary Brewster is lucky to have a brother like him. She is lucky in a lot of ways, *I* think."

The fortunate one, herself, at home with this brother whom she scarcely knew, was beginning to get acquainted with him. Even yet it was hard to realize that he was her own father's son. Annabelle Brewster during her widowhood and while she and Mary were alone together in the old house seldom mentioned his name. When she did it was slightingly. Mary knew that the second Mrs. Brewster and Ben, Junior, had never been friendly. He was away at school and college when she, Mary, was a young girl and he had left for the West soon after his graduation. He came on to his father's funeral, but not to that of his stepmother. His wife had telegraphed that he was ill and could not come. Judge Baxter had settled the estate and sent to him at Denver the sum which he inherited under his father's will.

So to Mary he was practically a stranger and a stranger of whom she had heard little that was good. He had ignored her and her mother, had not even written at the time of the latter's death. So it was little wonder that she felt no affection for him and had thought of him scarcely at all. His recent letter, stating that he was thinking of coming on to visit her, had aroused no enthusiasm in her mind. She had written him that she would be glad to see him, but she knew that she would not be really glad at all. She did not care whether he came or not; in fact would have preferred that he remain away.

And now he was here, his trunks—five of them—were here also, so it was evident that he intended to remain for some time. He frankly said as much. "I have been away for a thousand years, it seems to me," he told her, with that pleasant smile of his; "and, if you can put me up, Mary, and put up with me, I shall stay for a while."

She, of course, told him that she would be delighted to have him stay as long as he wished.

But the delight was not too keen. She could not help feeling a slight suspicion of the motive behind this visit. He had spoken of his loneliness since his wife's death, of how he had been sitting there in the "desolated home" in Denver, with no one of his own near him, and how there had come over him the desire to see the place where he was born, the home of his boyhood. "And I thought of you," he said. "You and I scarcely know each other and yet we are brother and sister. There is no truer proverb than the old one which tells us that blood is thicker than water. It is when a man is alone and in sorrow—or in ill-health, or all three—that the truth of it is forced upon him. I felt that I must see you again before I died. I tried to make that plain in my letter."

She nodded. "Yes," she said. "That is what you wrote me."

He seemed to guess the thought in her mind. "But you wonder at my not coming or writing before," he suggested. "You are wondering why I have neglected you for so many years. It is natural you should. I am ashamed of myself. But there are excuses, even if not too good. I have been a busy man, I have been away from Wapatomac since I was twenty-one. And—for we may as well speak the whole truth—there was another reason. Your mother, Mary, father's second wife, was—please understand I am not dreaming of blaming her; no doubt it was my fault quite as much as it was hers—but she and I did not get on well together. But perhaps we had better not talk of that; God knows I am sorry for my part of the misunderstanding. Now let's talk about you. I was—well, I confess I was very much surprised to learn on my arrival that you were—er—employed as bookkeeper at the bank here. I wondered why. It can't be because you needed money. Surely father's estate supplied you with a sufficiency of that."

She did not answer the implied question then.

"How did you learn that I was working at the bank?" she asked.

He told her. Upon his arrival in Wapatomac on Saturday he had boarded the "depot wagon" and had alighted from it at the Brewster gate. There was no one at home. Mary was away and Azure was out on an errand. He had, therefore, called at the next house, Mrs. Knowles's, and that lady had told him of his sister's employment and where she was likely to be found. So he walked to the bank and found that closed for the day.

"The Knowles woman," he added, "is a garrulous soul. She informed me that David Cummings—I remember him slightly as a boy, of course—was president of that bank, so I went down to his place of business at the wharf."

Mary interrupted. "Oh, did you see Captain David?" she asked.

He smiled. "Yes, I saw him," he said.

"Did you tell him you were my brother?"

"No-o. No, he and I had a few words concerning a—er—little business matter, and I left without telling him who I was. He didn't recognize me. Naturally he wouldn't."

"A business matter? What sort of a business matter?"

"Oh, not an important one. I needed a little money, or thought I did, and I asked him to do me the favor of cashing a check."

"He did it, of course? He is always cashing checks for people."

Another smile. "He didn't cash this one. He was—well," with a sudden sharpness, "I thought him countrified, a boor, swollen with his own importance. He annoyed me and, as it didn't seem worth while losing my temper because of a fellow like that, I walked out. The check could wait. I could depend on you to temporarily finance me, Mary; at least I hoped I could. You would have taken that chance with your long lost brother, wouldn't you?"

She did not say whether she would or not. He turned to look at her and was immediately aware that he had made a mistake.

"Captain Cummings is not a boor," she said, firmly. "He may be a countryman—he is, of course—but as far as that goes I am a countrywoman. He is a very able man and has been a good friend to me. I am sure I don't know why he didn't cash your check, but I know that he must have had a reason, or thought he had. . . . You didn't tell him who you were, you say?"

"No. . . . No. I didn't. I should have, of course, but—oh well, I was tired and out of sorts generally. Most of it was my fault, no doubt. When you know me better, sister," he added, with disarming frankness, "you will learn that there are times when I am—well, hard to bear, I'm afraid. Testy, and fussy, and generally impatient. It is this confounded disease of mine, so the doctors tell me. They are continually preaching at me not to get overtired, or permit myself to fret about little things, all that sort of stuff. In fact they have served me a pretty plain notice that my days in the land are numbered—and not a large number, at that."

He sighed, then shrugged and smiled once more. Mary was conscience-stricken. In his letter he had written something like this.

"Oh, I am so sorry," she cried. "And I am awfully

sorry you and Captain David had a disagreement the first time you met. He will be sorry, too. If you had only said you were my brother."

"Yes," soothingly, "Yes, yes, certainly. My fault, or my infirmity, most of it, I'm sure. I was a little sorry myself, after I thought it over. I shall explain to Cummings when I see him. If he is a friend of yours he must be my friend, too. Now do tell me about yourself. Why did you decide to become a business woman? It is getting to be quite the fashion nowadays, but—well, I am a Brewster, you know, and I haven't forgotten what it used to mean to be a Brewster in Wapatomac."

She did tell him, not mentioning her stock speculations, but of her loneliness, her need of more money for household requirements, and her desire to do something which would keep her busy. He was very understanding and sympathetic. Her shortage of money seemed to surprise him, but, rather to her own surprise, he did not appear to regard it seriously. In fact, if such an absurd idea were possible, she might have imagined him as more pleased than disturbed by the disclosure. He patted her shoulder as they rose in answer to Azure's summons to the supper table.

"Never mind, Mary, my girl," he said, cheerfully. "Don't let the lack of money trouble you. And, so far as your straining those bright eyes of yours over bank ledgers and things—well, we'll see about that by and by."

She looked to see if he were in earnest. Then she laughed. "That is a very pretty speech, Ben," she said, "but my 'bright eyes' have already stood the wear and tear of thirty-five long years. If the strain of looking for the extra dollars I needed to keep this old house in repair didn't dim them I should imagine the ledgers wouldn't. Besides, I like my work at the bank. I really enjoy it."

He nodded. "You mustn't think I am interfering," he protested. "I have no right to interfere and I shouldn't dream of doing so. But if, later on, matters shape as I hope they may, I shall probably have something to say to you. . . . No, no! Later on, not now. Now we must eat the nice things Mrs. Crisp has cooked for us. My dinner was proof enough that they will be nice," he added, addressing the gratified housekeeper. His and Azure's renewed acquaintanceship had been brief, but she was already his worshiping slave. And although Mary was still a trifle doubtful, her vague suspicions not entirely dissipated, her impression of Mr. Benjamin Brewster was thus far not unfavorable. He was a fascinating talker and he had a way.

He did not walk down to the bank with her next morning. At first he had expressed the intention of doing so, but thought better of it. He would remain at home most of the forenoon, he said. "Unpacking, you know," he explained. "A nuisance, but a necessary one. And, there are those blessed doctors to be considered. Rest—rest—that is their text for me. Well, after I have rested I may take a stroll and drop in on you. When does your friend Cummings usually arrive there?"

Azure Crisp was favored with much of their guest's society that morning. He had evidently changed his mind about unpacking the five trunks, for, later on, when she went to his room to put it to rights, she found four of them unopened. He spent the greater part of the forenoon seated in a chair in the kitchen chatting with her. She characteristically did most of the talking and he encouraged her to do so. When she paused—when, as old Captain Barney would have said, "her clockwork ran down"—he set it going again with a question or two. By eleven o'clock she had told him all she knew of Mary's reasons for entering the bank's employ, a great deal about David Cummings, the latter's standing in the community, and of Miss Brewster's trust in him as financial adviser.

"Why on earth she should pick him to talk over her money affairs with I vow I never could make out," Azure declared. "I give you my word, Mr. Benjamin, there was one spell there, when he kept callin' and callin' at this house, that I began to be real worried. Foolish of me, of course 'twas, for there could never be nothin' between them—more than just business, I mean. She was a Brewster and he was nothin' but a Cummings and you know what that means as well as I do."

"Certainly."

"Yes, I knew you would. But pretty soon Peter Hall began payin' attention to her and that did relieve my mind consider'ble. Mr. Hall, now, he's different. He's *our* kind of man—yours and mine, Mr. Benjamin."

"I am sure he must be. So he is interested in Mary, is he?"

Interested? Azure should say he was! She sang the cashier's praises for the next half hour. When, at eleven o'clock, Benjamin Brewster left the house for his stroll, he had learned much.

He sauntered down town, swinging his cane, and pausing occasionally to rest and to inspect landmarks which had once been so familiar to him. Standing before the new building of the Wapatomac National Bank he looked that over. The average Wapatomac citizen gave, figuratively speaking, three proud cheers when he exhibited that bank building to a visitor. Azure Crisp had delivered a panegyric concerning it during their morning's conversation. The gentleman from Denver should, therefore, have been greatly impressed by its grandeur. He did not appear to be. For some reason or other it seemed to amuse him. He entered its portals with no unusual reverence and, inside, looked about him with a nonchalant interest.

Mary was at her desk behind the counter. She did not look up from her books. Philander Cahoon peered from behind the grill of the teller's window, but, being rather nearsighted, did not recognize him. Brewster noticed Philander carelessly, and only for an instant. Peter Hall was seated at the roll-top desk inside the rail beyond the brass sign "Cashier." Hall had not attended church the day before, a most unusual omission for him, so the pair had not met. At him Mr. Brewster gazed appraisingly for some moments. Then he sauntered to the rail and spoke his sister's name.

She rose and came to meet him. He was introduced to Mr. Cahoon, to Bennie Jackson, and, of course, to the cashier. They shook hands. Brewster's shake was hearty and his greeting pleasantly informal. Hall's was less so. Mary had told him, although he had heard it before, of her half brother's arrival in town and he was not overjoyed at the news. A wealthy kinsman in the Brewster home did not fit in with Mr. Hall's carefully matured plans at all. He foresaw all sorts of possible complications. He tried hard to seem genial and hearty, but he did not succeed very well. There was a constraint in his manner which contrasted unfavorably with Ben

Brewster's ease and gracious cordiality. They chatted for a few minutes. Then Brewster said:

"Is your president about, Mr. Hall? If he is I should like to meet him. We met Saturday, but," with a glance at Mary and a laugh, "we didn't know each other then."

Captain David was in the directors' room, it appeared. Mary offered to conduct her brother there.

"That is, if you can spare me for a moment, Mr. Hall," she said.

Hall's consent was granted and, a minute later, she rapped upon the door of the inner office. She was asked to come in. The two Brewsters entered the room together. Cummings, who was seated at the big table, the usual pile of papers before him, rose. He looked at Mary first, then at her companion, and the expression upon his face changed.

"Why—why, hello!" he exclaimed. Then, with a rueful smile and a shake of the head, he added: "I guess probably my conscience might stand the strain of cashin' that check for you this mornin', Mr. Brewster. Don't seem to be quite as stiff in the backbone as 'twas on Saturday, for some reason or other."

For just a moment Mary wondered how her brother was going to take the joke. His own backbone appeared to stiffen as it was spoken. Then he, too, smiled.

"Well, Cummings," he observed, "you will have to admit that I have the best sort of identification here with me. You know Mary—at least she tells me she knows you very well indeed—and she will swear to me a hundred dollars' worth, I think."

Captain David came around the table and held out his hand.

"Don't say another word, Ben," he protested. "I was a fool for not knowin' you the minute I laid eyes on you. I was expectin' somebody else and I'm sure I wasn't expectin' you. I acted like a jackass, but what's bred in the bone is liable to break out on the hide, so they say. Forgive me for showin' my spots, will you? They ain't catchin', at least I hope they ain't."

The Brewster forgiveness was graciously granted and the proffered hand accepted. Cummings urged his visitors to be seated. Benjamin took the most comfortable arm-chair, but Mary hesitated.

"I don't know that I ought to stay, Captain Cummings," she said. "Mr. Hall may need me."

David's reply was almost brusque. "I guess he can do without you for a few minutes," he said. "He sees a good deal of you and I don't so much—not lately. There, there," his brusqueness vanishing, "you sit down. I'll tell Peter I ordered you to stay and you can shift the responsibility to me. . . . Well, Ben, so you've come back to Wapatomac and home folks for a while. Glad to see you. They tell me you aren't feelin' as shipshape as you might be. I'm sorry to hear that, I am so."

Mr. Brewster dismissed his ill-health with a wave of the hand. He was not well—no, but what could not be cured must be endured, endured to the end, whenever that might be. He spoke of his delight at revisiting his native town and in enjoying once more the society of his sister. Cummings nodded.

"Yes," he observed. "You and she haven't had each other's company for a long spell, have you? . . . Well, Denver is a good way off, that's a fact."

"Yes," a trifle curtly, "it is."

"Um-hum. And a pretty fine city, they tell me. Some different from Wapatomac."

"Somewhat—yes. . . . Oh—er—Cummings, while I am here I want to thank you for your interest in my sister's affairs. You have advised her well, she tells me. Very kind of you indeed."

"That's all right, that's all right. I wouldn't say that my advice was worth much, but such as it was you can be sure she was welcome to it."

Mary put in a word. "Captain Cummings has been more than just an adviser," she said; "he has been a very real friend. I told you that, Ben."

"Yes, yes, certainly you did. I understand."

"I guess likely," observed the captain, "you were a little mite surprised to find her keepin' books for us here in the bank, eh?"

"I admit I was very much surprised. There again your advice and friendship were responsible, I hear."

David looked at him quickly. So, too, did Mary. The former's hand moved upward toward his hair.

"I was responsible for gettin' the bookkeeper's position for her," he said, slowly. "I wasn't responsible for her goin' to work. She was set on that, herself."

"I begged him to get the place for me," declared Mary. "I told him that, if he couldn't, I should go to Boston and try for work there. It was my own business and no one else's. I thought it all out and I had made up my mind. . . . I am quite capable of doing that at times, Ben," she added.

Her brother may have noticed the crispness of her tone. If he did he chose to treat it as a joke. "Most of your sex are, according to my experience," he rejoined.

"Eh, Cummings? . . . What charming quarters your establishment has here, hasn't it. Very attractive indeed. A new building, so I understand. You should be proud of it."

Captain David was proud of it and did not hesitate to say so. He offered to show the visitor about. The tour of inspection did not take long, of course. Brewster was gratifyingly interested in the mahogany fittings, in the new vaults with their time lock, in everything.

"Wonderful!" he said. "Wonderful! And remarkable for a town of this size."

"Best bank building in the county," said the captain, with satisfaction. "Well, I guess you've seen the whole of it now, Ben. Is there anything else I can do for you? How about that check?"

The check was drawn, for two hundred dollars instead of one, and, in accordance with his president's orders, Mr. Cahoon promptly cashed it. Brewster did not trouble to count the money. He thrust the bills in his pocket as if two hundred dollars was a sum too trifling to be particular about.

"Much obliged," he said, carelessly. "Oh, by the way, Cummings; if I stay here for any length of time I shall probably find it convenient to open an account with you. That will be all right, I suppose?"

"Sure thing! But, so far as that goes, it won't be necessary. We'll be glad to cash your checks any time. Now that I know you ain't peddlin' fish barrels I shan't be nigh so fussy. I didn't tell you I figured you to be a barrel drummer, did I? Well, 'twon't take but a minute and it was a good joke on me. Ha, ha! yes, 'twas so."

He told the story, pausing to laugh between sentences.

It was funny, as he told it, and Mary laughed, too. Her brother's amusement was less pronounced. He smiled, of course, but toward the end of the recital he seemed, or so Cummings thought, a little impatient. He looked at his watch and the action prompted David to look at his own.

"My, my!" he exclaimed. "It's noontime, isn't it. Time for you to be goin' home for dinner, Mary. Run right along. I'm sorry I kept you."

"But it isn't quite time, Captain Cummings. I almost never go until half past twelve. I have kept Mr. Hall waiting with his work as it is. I must go back and finish with him before I think of dinner."

Benjamin Brewster shrugged. "If Cummings tells you to go I should say that was sufficient," he said. "I shall be glad of your company." Turning to the captain he added, "I am beginning to realize what I have missed in not having that company for twenty years."

"But, really, Ben—"

Captain David interrupted. "You run right along with your brother, Mary," he urged. "I'll square you with Peter, if it's necessary. You go this minute."

Mary, still with some reluctance, hurried away to don her hat and jacket. Cummings looked after her.

"A fine, smart woman, that sister of yours, Ben," he said. Mr. Benjamin picked up his own hat and the cane.

"Glad you think so, I'm sure," he observed. "Well, no doubt I shall see you occasionally, Cummings—here at the bank. Good morning."

A few minutes after he and Mary had gone the cashier entered the inner office. He had some papers in his hand, but they were but an excuse.

"Well, he came, didn't he," he said. "What did you think of him?"

David reached for the papers. "Think of who?" he asked, casually.

"Why, that half brother of hers from Denver. What did you think of him?"

"Eh? Oh, I don't know. What did you?"

Peter Hall, for once, forgot to be either diplomatic or dignified.

"I think he is a stuck-up snob," he snapped. "That's what I think."

Cummings was looking over the papers.

"You don't say," he observed, absently. "Well, well; I want to know!"

Which concluded that part of the conversation.

CHAPTER X

MR. HALL'S estimate of the gentleman from Denver was not in accord with that of the majority of Wapatomac's population. During that week and those immediately following the village either made or renewed acquaintance with him and the almost universal opinion was that he was a "fine man." The aristocratic section, the Bradleys and the Freemans and their sort, were favorably inclined toward him from the beginning. He was a Brewster and, therefore, by heredity and early training, should be all right. It is true that Brewsters were sometimes eccentric—witness Mary's absurd bookkeeping venture—and it was also true that he had spent many years far from the chastening influence of his native town. But unless, or until, time proved him to be unworthy, they were glad to welcome him back among them for the sake of the family name.

And as they came to know him they liked and admired him for his own sake. He was always so polite and agreeable. The punctilious manner in which he returned calls made upon him, returned them neither too soon nor too late, was gratifying. He was a charming table companion. Mrs. Bradley and Elvira invited him and his sister to dinner and, after the guests had departed, Elvira expressed her feeling concerning him, a feeling with which her mother agreed heartily.

"I declare, mother!" sighed Miss Bradley. "I feel as if I had been listening to the most wonderful lecture I ever heard in my life. Yes, and a lot of lectures on all sorts of subjects. He knows *so* much about literature and pictures and—oh, everything! And the way he talks about them! I could listen forever. The only thing is he makes me feel so ignorant. Oh, mother, why can't *we* go to Europe? Other people do. You used to go, of course—on father's ship when you were first married—but I have never been anywhere but to Niagara Falls."

Mrs. Freeman was just as enthusiastic after an evening at the Brewster home. So were the Bakers and the Coltons. From almost the very first the people who "counted" in Wapatomac, particularly widows, wives and daughters, stamped "Approved" upon the forehead of Benjamin Brewster. Mrs. Phoebe Carleton was practically the sole feminine member of the upper circles whose approval was qualified.

"Oh, I guess he is all right enough," she admitted. "He can talk, I'll say that for him. Yes, he is all right, probably. I wish he weren't so dreadfully certain of it himself, that's all."

Some of the men were less agreeable in their comments. A portion of this may have been due to envy; praise of one of his own sex served with breakfast, dinner and supper has a tendency to antagonize the average male. Then, too, many of those ancient mariners had met all sorts of men in all sorts of places, where judgment of character was a part of their business.

"Yes, yes, yes!" snapped Captain Fred Donald at his own breakfast table. "Heavens and earth, yes! He's as slick as a barrel of sperm oil and he could talk a tin peddler into making him a present of his cart, I guess, if he set out to. Now give me another cup of coffee—

and a rest on Ben Brewster, until dinner time, anyhow."

Mrs. Donald obliged with the coffee although she postponed the "rest."

"Why don't you like him, you unreasonable thing?" she demanded. "You can't find one real objection to him anywhere and yet you're so obstinate that you won't own up to being wrong. What is there you don't like about him? Come now!"

Her husband found it hard to answer. He did his best, however.

"I never said I didn't like him," he declared. "I haven't seen him times enough to know whether I like him or not. All is, I—well, after I'm dead I may see the Lord A'mighty, kind of looked for'ard to it, anyhow. It sort of takes the edge off to see a copy of Him walking around down here."

Mrs. Donald was shocked at his irreverence and said so.

With the larger group of Wapatomacites, those not of the select few, the Brewster manner was but slightly different. It was not quite as familiar, perhaps, but it was always affable. And his faculty of remembering old acquaintances was gratifying. He made it a point, when meeting these people who had known him in boyhood, to chat with them of their personal affairs, to inquire concerning their families, and to call to mind happenings of the old days in which he and they had been concerned. With the great majority of these people also he was rapidly becoming a favorite. He met Captain Barnabas Cummings at the post office one noon and, although the old man was prejudiced at the beginning, remembering the scene with his grandson in the latter's office, the interview ended with Captain Barney's at least partial surrender to the Brewster charms.

"He's quite a feller," he told Kohath, "when you come to know him. He recollected things about me that I swan to man I'd forgot myself. And he wouldn't believe it when I told him how old I was. 'It's the air down 'round here,' I told him. 'You'll last long as I have if you stick to this town, Mr. Brewster.' He as much as said he was cal'latin' to stick long as he did last. He's sick, did you know it, Kohath? Don't look so 'special ailin', but he is. Well, I thought as much when I fust see him walkin' with that cane. Told Dave so, I did."

Brewster had a sufficiency of money, there was no doubt of that. He was a liberal spender; bought a whole box of cigars at Gallup's store the first Monday after his arrival and the best they had in stock, at that. And passed them about among the citizens present, which did not injure his popularity. A week later he opened a checking account in the Wapatomac National Bank and his first deposit amounted to more than a thousand dollars. There were many suits of clothes in the five trunks and Azure multiplied that number when she told of the unpacking.

From Mrs. Crisp, Wapatomac learned something of his life there in the West. He had not been engaged in active business for some time. He had married late in life; he had idolized his wife, and her death was a frightful blow to him. They had no children. Their beautiful home in Denver he had sold and the furniture with it. His plans for the future were rather indefinite, so Azure gathered; he did not choose to talk of them—to her.

Nor did he with Mary. "Let's forget everything but

the present *for* the present, sister," he said. "I am having a happy time, thanks to your hospitality and kindness. Later on I may—well, as I told you before, we'll see."

One evening of the first week of his visit Mary came home from the bank to find him reading in the sitting room. He threw down the book when she entered and the expression upon his face was anything but pleasant. His reply to her greeting lacked its usual suave geniality.

"Why, what is wrong, Ben?" she queried. "Something, that is plain enough."

He scowled. "Why is it," he asked, snappishly, "that all doctors are such confounded old women? They are all alike. They all paw you over and look wise and then preach the same old platitudes. If you are careful you may live twenty years. But you mustn't eat this, or drink that, or take violent exercise, or get overexcited, or— Bah! If being careful means doing none of the things that make life worth living at all, then I am certainly careful, all right. I've a precious good mind to quit it and enjoy myself again. Careful! If I wasn't trying to be careful is it likely that I would sentence myself to—"

He stopped in the middle of a word. Mary was amazed. She had never heard him speak like this before. "Why, Ben, what is it?" she urged. He looked at her, shrugged, and then, with a smile, rose and patted her shoulder.

"I beg your pardon, my dear," he said, contritely. "I warned you that I could be a good deal of a nuisance at times. I dropped in on Hamilton this afternoon, your doctor here in town. My own doctor at home made me promise to consult one of his professional brethren occasionally. It's a part of the game; they all stand together, confound them. Hamilton insisted on doing what they all do, making an examination. That is part of the game, too. And, after I had been punched and pounded and stethoscoped and the rest of it for half an hour, the best the fellow could do was to deliver the same lecture I had heard twenty times before. . . . Bah!" angrily. "The fool!"

"Doctor Hamilton isn't a fool," said Mary, gravely. "He is a very good doctor indeed."

"Eh? . . . Oh, yes, I have no doubt he is. Well, sister, we'll just forget him and all his tribe. And you must forget my bad temper. How are the Wapatomac masters of high finance to-day? Brother Cummings and the rest?"

Mary did not forget Doctor Hamilton as she was ordered to do. The next time she met him she asked him about her brother. The doctor looked grave.

"Mr. Brewster is not a well man," he confessed. "He must take care of himself. I have told him so and other doctors have said the same, I judge. If he is careful, why then—bar accidents, of course—he should be safe enough. Wapatomac ought to be just the place for him, if he is content to stay in it. If I were you, Mary—that is, if he were my brother—I should try hard to make him stay."

To his wife he said more than this.

"He is like a hundred men who have come to me since I began practice," he said. "They dance and keep on dancing, but they resent having to pay the piper. This Ben Brewster has rolled high, or I miss my guess. A good quiet sanitarium, with the door locked and the right kind of nurse to manage him, would be my prescription, but I'll be hanged if I can imagine his taking it. I'll bet my Sunday hat that those Denver doctors ordered him to the country for rest, and that is the real reason why he is here. But don't you dare tell any one I said so."

The two conversations, that with Ben himself and the later one with the doctor, made an impression upon Mary Brewster. They made her feel more kindly toward her brother. Little flashes of irritability on his part, a certain testy peevishness which she noticed occasionally, and a tendency to consider his own comfort first and Azure's convenience second, she now understood to be due to his ill-health. Her mother had been fretful and perhaps a little selfish during her last years. Invalids were like that.

And, on the whole, she surely had no reason to complain of Benjamin's selfishness where she was concerned. He was kindness itself in so many ways. And generous, too. During the second week of his visit little delicacies began appearing upon their table, expensive dainties which she had not, for a long time, felt that she should afford. Ben had bought them and had ordered them sent home. And had paid for them himself. "Let me do at least that much," he begged. "I feel like an interloper here, goodness knows, sponging on the sister I have neglected—yes, neglected is the word—all these years. Well, I think—yes, I am almost sure I see a way to atone for a little of that neglect. You and I will have a heart to heart talk before long. A business talk. You aren't the only business Brewster, young woman."

So Mary's favorable impression deepened. It was pleasant to have his society when she came home from work. It was distinctly nice to chat there at home with some one beside Mrs. Crisp, some one who knew and enjoyed books and music and who had seen much of the world. And it was not disagreeable, the consciousness that he was of her own blood, the son of her father. He and she spoke often of their father and of the time when she was a little girl and Ben at college or home on vacations. She began to like him, even to feel affection for him. Blood *was* thicker than water. He had said so when he came and it was true. And practically every friend whom she met told her what a wonderful person her half brother was.

Mr. Peter Hall did not. Aside from banking hours Hall had had no opportunity to tell her anything since their drive to the Bayport auction. He had suggested calling, had asked several times if he might drop in that evening or the next, but she had always found an excuse for postponement. Benjamin's name was usually mentioned in these excuses and possibly this was why the cashier himself so seldom mentioned that name. And one evening, the Friday night of Ben's second week in his sister's house, Hall came unannounced and found Mary in and alone. Her brother was out, paying a dinner call on the Bradleys. She should have accompanied him, but she was tired and had begged to be excused.

Ben's call was not a lengthy one and he returned home before ten. As he came up the walk to the front door that door was opened and a man came out. The lamplight shone upon his face as he emerged and Mr. Brewster recognized him.

"Good evening, Hall," he said, carelessly. "Nice night; eh?"

Peter Hall grunted acknowledgment, but barely that. He brushed by almost rudely and strode on down the path. Flinging the gate open and, without taking the trouble to close it, he disappeared in the darkness. Ben turned to look after him. The cashier was one of the few people in Wapatomac who had never wholly yielded to the charm of the captivating gentleman from Denver. Between them, or so it seemed to Brewster, there was always a certain restraint, entirely on Hall's part of course. For some reason or other—and Ben imagined he could guess that reason—Peter did not like him. Brewster was amused, rather than disturbed, by the dislike, but now he was surprised. Heretofore the cashier had always been at least polite.

He stood there on the step, tapping his boot with his cane, and speculating concerning the cause of the visitor's rudeness and hurried exit. Then he opened the front door with his latchkey—he had a key of his own now—and entered the hall. The sitting room door was closed and, after a moment, he rapped upon one of the panels.

"Are you there, Mary?" he asked. "It is Ben. May I come in?"

She answered, but not immediately, nor was her tone eager.

"Yes," she said.

He entered. She was sitting in the chair by the table and it needed but one glance at her face to confirm his suspicion. He did not comment upon her look, but threw himself back upon the horsehair sofa and crossed his knees.

"It is a wonderful night," he said. "And I had a pleasant call. Too bad you didn't go with me."

She stirred in the chair.

"I wish to goodness I had," she said, impulsively.

"So do I. Our precise little friend from the bank has been here, hasn't he? I met him as I came up the walk."

She did not speak. He removed his eyeglasses, rubbed them with his handkerchief, readjusted them upon his nose and continued.

"Another business call, I suppose?" he suggested. "I confess it seems a trifle inconsiderate to me, this pursuing you with bank affairs day *and* night."

Still she was silent. He tried again.

"Peter the—er—Little seemed rather out of sorts, I thought," he said. "Something gone wrong at the temple of finance?"

She spoke then, but without looking at him.

"It was nothing to do with the bank," she said, shortly. "No, don't ask me what it was. Please don't. I had rather not talk about it."

He nodded. "Then we won't talk about it," he agreed, cheerfully. "Shall we discuss Mrs. Bradley? Or the fascinating Elvira? Come now! *There* is a subject; there is a pair of subjects."

But the Bradleys were not destined to be discussed that evening. Mary Brewster turned her back upon him. He waited a moment, then rose and crossed quietly to her side.

"Sister," he said, gently, laying a hand upon her shoulder, "you mustn't cry over that fellow. He isn't worth a tear. Believe me, he isn't."

She whirled and looked up at him. Her eyes were wet, but they were flashing with alarmed inquiry.

"Why, what do you mean?" she demanded.

He stroked her hair. "Just what I said," he affirmed. "The pestiferous Peter isn't worth a thought, to say nothing of a tear. You sent him about his business, of course. Your mistake, if you will forgive my saying so, was in ever permitting him to see you except at his place of business."

She sprang to her feet. "What *do* you mean?" she cried. "Who told you? How did you know?"

Firmly, but still gently, he forced her back into the chair again.

"There, there, my dear," he said. "Please don't excite yourself. And don't look as if you thought I had been listening at the keyhole. I have been in Wapatomac but a short fortnight, but I needed to be here only a day to learn that this Hall person was more than suspected of—what do they call it?—of courting you. . . Sshh! Sshh! I never imagined that you suspected any such thing. Considering who the fellow is, and who you are, you would not dream of it. And as for your encouraging his confounded presumption, that, I knew, was too ridiculous to waste a serious thought upon. If I had been here longer and had felt that I had the right to speak, I should probably have warned you to be careful. I have had some experience in the world and I know the lengths to which conceit may carry a pompous little nincompoop like this chap. . . . But there! it is over now. Of course he did ask you to marry him? Asked you here, this evening?"

Concealment or denial were useless. He knew, this brother of hers. And apparently all Wapatomac knew, had been eagerly waiting for the announcement confirming its whispered prophecies. Mary's cheeks flamed as she thought of it. And it was her own fault, her own blind, self-sufficient fault. She had squelched Azure when obviously Azure was but repeating what the whole town was saying. She had been too proud to listen, to heed, and when, at last, she herself began to fear and almost believe, it was too late. Oh, it was humiliating! And the consequences were certain to be most disagreeable.

Ben Brewster was still stroking her hair, in his fatherly —or brotherly—fashion.

"He proposed to you, of course?" he repeated. "And you sent him packing."

"I suppose there is no use pretending. He asked me to marry him and I said no."

"Naturally. Well, that explains his manner when we met just now. He looked as if he had been kicked. The blackguard!"

She shook her head. "You shouldn't call him that," she protested. "He isn't a blackguard. He is a good man, and he has been very, very kind to me at the bank. The rest of it has been my fault. I am to blame. When he first began calling here, I—well, of course I did not realize. And I couldn't tell him not to come. How could I? I didn't imagine— It is only recently that I have begun to feel anxious and to wonder if— Oh, Ben, it is dreadful! What shall I do?"

He laughed lightly. "Do?" he repeated. "Do nothing, of course. It is done, and so is he—well done. You won't be troubled by him again."

"But I am troubled. I am sorry for him, in a way. And I shall have to meet him and work with him. Oh, it is bound to change everything! I—I almost think I should leave the bank. But, how can I, after Captain Cummings went to so much trouble in getting me the place?"

He took her arm and led her over to the sofa.

"Sit here by me, Mary," he said, gently. "I have been hinting that, some of these days, I should have something important to say to you. I am going to say it now. And you mustn't interrupt until I have finished. I have a proposition to make which will, I hope and believe, settle your problem and mine for the rest of our lives. Now be patient and listen."

She tried to listen. What the "proposition" might be she had, of course, no idea whatever. Apparently it must be, as he said, important, for his tone and manner were grave. He began by speaking of his wife's death and his loneliness in the great house in Denver. She had heard it all before and found it hard to keep her attention from wandering to Mr. Hall and the distressing interview just ended. When, with an effort, she did force herself to concentrate upon him he was speaking of his ill-health and what his doctors had told him. This, too, was not new, although he had never before referred to it as seriously and in detail. Apparently they considered his condition serious indeed.

"They gloated over me like a flock of buzzards over a dying horse," he said, with increasing irritation. "If I had believed all they said I should have ordered my tombstone months ago. Well, I didn't. I may fool them yet, confound them! . . . But," more quietly, "I'm afraid there is no doubt that I am in bad shape, very bad shape. . . . Well, realizing this, and being so all alone out there, with the one who had been all the world to me gone forever, I—I got to thinking. And I thought of you, sister."

The result of his thinking was a definite scheme, a plan of which his visit to the old home in Wapatomac was but the preliminary. Convinced that, whatever happened, he could never live in Denver again, he had disposed of all his western property.

"I told you," he went on, "that I was here merely as a visitor, planning to stay but a little while. I had to say so. I realized that, considering how neglectful and unbrotherly you must think me after those years of separation, I could not be sure that you did not hate me, or that we should get on together, you and I. But behind it all was this plan of mine. We *have* got on together, haven't we? You don't hate me, do you, Mary?"

"Of course I don't, Ben."

"I know it. My fortnight has convinced me of that. And it gives me courage. Mary, suppose I should tell you that I hoped to stay here with you the rest of my life, what would you say?"

She could say nothing. She merely gazed at him uncomprehendingly. He went on to explain. He did not mean that he contemplated staying as her guest—scarcely that. What he did mean was that, provided she thought well of the plan, he would make the Brewster home—the home of his ancestors as well as hers—his permanent abiding place. He would pay all the household expenses, Azure's wages, and those of another servant provided one was needed. He would keep the place in repair, and of course it did need repairs. Her own income would be her own, to spend as she pleased for personal necessities or luxuries. "I will pay all household bills," he said, in conclusion. "You need never think of them again, provided you can bear the company of this brother of yours for—" with a shrug and a sigh, "as long a time as the fates allot him. There! that is my proposition. What do you think of it?"

She could scarcely think at all as yet. The proposal was so sudden and so amazingly unexpected. The thought uppermost in her mind she did, however, express.

"But—but, Ben," she faltered, "I don't see— Why are you doing this? You—you don't seem to me to be— Ben, are you sure you would be contented to live in a place like Wapatomac—always? Somehow I can't imagine your being contented to do that."

He assured her that it was the one thing which would content him. "It may not be very long," he added. "According to those doctors it isn't likely to be. I have had a hard, nerve-racking, striving life. This old town and this old house, and you, my dear, spell contentment for me; the rest of the world doesn't count any longer. There is rest here and I want rest—yes, and peace and the companionship of my only near relative."

"But—but can you afford to—to do all these things? To pay—"

He interrupted her. "I haven't quite finished," he said. "Yes, I can afford it. I am not a millionaire exactly, but—well, between ourselves, Mary, I have an assured income of over ten thousand a year. That, I should say, might keep us going. Eh?"

She gasped. This was in 1905, when the purchasing power of the dollar was more than double its present capacity. He saw her expression and smiled.

"It will do, you think," he said. "Well, so do I. And now what do you say?"

She was silent, trying to realize what it meant, or might mean. After a moment she asked another question.

"And if I agree— Oh, it is wonderful, of course, and you are wonderfully generous and kind and—and—"

"Oh, not at all, not at all," with a wave of the hand. "I am asking a good deal and offering to pay for it. . . . Well, is it settled?"

She hesitated. "Not quite," she said. "I— Ben, you have told me what you hope to do. What do you expect me to do in return?"

He seemed a trifle taken aback. It was, she surmised, a question he had not looked for.

"You?" he asked. "Why—why, nothing. Nothing at all—except have general supervision of the housekeeping and," with a laugh, "of me."

"Aren't there *any* conditions? Any at all on my part?"

And now he hesitated, but only for an instant.

"None worth mentioning," he replied. "Of course I shall expect you—well, to give up that whimsy of yours, your bookkeeping. You will be glad to do that, I imagine. Particularly after this little affair with the sentimental Hall person."

Her silence now was longer. He leaned forward to look at her.

"Surely," he added, with a hint of impatience, "you won't mind giving *that* up?"

"Won't I?"

"I can scarcely imagine that you will. You are a Brewster, a Brewster woman, and I confess it hurts my pride a bit to have my sister accepting wages from a

Cummings and his crew in a country bank. . . . Oh, oh!" hastily, "I quite understand why you went there in the first place. You were tired of sitting here alone and, as you explained to me, the trifle you earned was a convenient addition to your spending money. Now you won't need that trifle. All your income will be yours. The house will not need a cent of it."

She sighed. She hated to seem in the least ungrateful, but she could not bring herself to the point of instantly relinquishing her new-found independence and the happiness it had brought her. And she had so enjoyed her daily work in the bank.

"I—I don't know what to say, Ben," she faltered. "I guess—I feel as if I mustn't say anything definite just yet. I must think it over. Do you mind if I do?"

He was plainly disappointed and, for a moment, she thought he was going to be angry. Instead, however, he smiled and patted her shoulder.

"Not in the least, sister," he said, heartily enough. "Quite right. Just what you should do. Now there is one more point I am asking you to consider. That is your future. I may live three months, or," with a snap of his jaws, "I may, as I said, fool those doctor idiots and live twenty years. But if I *should* be unlucky I have provided for you. Yesterday afternoon I drove over to Ostable and saw a lawyer there. He was more or less of a country jake but he managed to understand what I wanted. This was the result."

He took a long envelope from his pocket and from it drew a folded document. He handed it to her.

"Not a cheerful bit of paper, exactly," he observed,

"but a rather important one. My—ahem—my last will and testament. Read it, my dear."

She read it. It was brief and to the point. Upon the death of the testator, Benjamin Brewster, all the latter's property, real, personal, etc., etc., was bequeathed to his dearly beloved half sister, Mary Brewster of Wapatomac, Massachusetts.

"There is your insurance clause, Mary," he said. "If—I say *if*—or when—I step out of this vale of tears all that I leave is yours. Just consider this when you are considering the rest of this proposal of mine. While I live I pay all expenses. When I die—well, sister, there you are. . . . Oh, no, no! you mustn't thank me. It is a simple matter of duty on my part. I am a poor 'risk,' speaking like a life insurance agent, but so far as *your* risk is concerned—well—"

And again he waved his hand.

All that night Mary lay awake thinking of the surprising offer. Even Peter Hall's proposal of marriage was, for the time, driven from her mind. She understood the significance of her brother's proposition. Its acceptance meant for her comfort, freedom from worry, her own money to use as she pleased while he lived, and—although she would not permit herself to seriously consider such a contingency—the assurance of wealth should he die. It was a wonderfully generous offer, so wonderful and unselfish that she could scarcely believe it to be as simple as it sounded. She found herself speculating, guessing, as to what might lie behind it. The old prejudice against Benjamin Brewster, the prejudice engendered by her mother's dislike and fostered by the years during which he had evinced no interest in either of them or the old home for which he now professed such fondness—these were not even yet entirely dissipated. But their return brought with them sharp twinges of conscience. She ought to be ashamed of such suspicions, vague though they were. She had no reason to think him anything but the kindest, most generous of brothers. It was only that, somehow, she could not understand his being contented to spend his days in sleepy, quiet Wapatomac. He did not seem to fit in Wapatomac—for any length of time, that is. But he was not well—no, he was not well at all, that must be the explanation; that and the fact that his own conscience was troubling him and he wished to make amends.

If she said yes to him she must resign from the bank. He expected her to do that. And she did not want to resign. What would David Cummings think of her if she did? He would at least think her remarkably changeable and more than ungrateful. And she knew that by this time she was a competent bookkeeper and that the bank needed her services. If she should leave, the question of her successor would arise and, no doubt, Captain Cummings would have all the old jealousies and bickerings again on his hands.

Morning found her no nearer a decision. She told Benjamin so at the breakfast table.

"I— Oh, I don't want you to think me too ungrateful, Ben," she said. "But—may I have a little longer to consider? Just a—well, perhaps a week, or even two?"

His reception of this request was not as gracious as she had hoped, but she could scarcely blame him.

"Very well; as you like," he said, shortly. Then, with a lift of the lip, he added: "I shall be curious to learn how the broken-hearted Peter greets you. It ought to be an interesting situation, I should say."

CHAPTER XI

MARY dreaded meeting Peter Hall that morning. Her brother's reminder that the meeting was likely to be embarrassing for them both was quite superfluous. She realized only too well how embarrassing it must be. Hall had not received his dismissal graciously. Once convinced that her refusal of his proposal was definite and final he had stalked from the sitting room and from the house without a word of farewell. She had tried to be considerate. She had spoken of her gratitude toward him, the gratitude she should always feel. She should never forget his kindness and patience. She valued his friendship and seriously hoped that they might always remain friends. As to marrying him, however, that she could not do. It was impossible.

In his expression and manner as he made his abrupt departure was more than bitter disappointment. There was anger, too. His pride was hurt. The little cashier possessed a self-esteem entirely out of proportion to his stature. He considered himself an important personage in Wapatomac and a large percentage of the town's population agreed with that estimate. That percentage would have appraised an offer of marriage from Peter Hall as a high honor and its recipient as a very lucky woman. Mary Brewster had been unappreciative of that honor. Would Hall be broad-minded enough to forgive, even if he could not forget? Or would he hold a grudge? Mary did not know, but she was fearful. Had her half brother not disclosed his plan for their future the situation would have been distressing indeed. As it was, if her position as bookkeeper became intolerable, she could always accept Ben's generous offer. Perhaps she might come to feel that she should accept it in any event. That remained to be seen.

She was at her desk and busy when the cashier entered the bank. She greeted him with a "Good morning" which she tried to make as pleasantly everyday as if there had been no unpleasant evening preceding it. He acknowledged it with a stiffly formal "Good morning, Miss Brewster," and, seating himself at his own desk, opened the letters which Bennie Jackson had placed there. When, later on, he required her services on a matter of business connected with one of those letters, he did not, as had been his custom, rise and come to her; instead he called her to him and stated his requirement curtly. All through that day his manner was coldly business-like. There were no more pleasant smiles, no more leaning over her shoulder, no confidential chats about this or that connected with her work or his. If Philander Cahoon noticed the difference—and she felt sure that he must notice it—he said nothing. Bennie Jackson, however, was less reticent.

"What's the matter with the boss," he whispered. "He's sour as a green apple. Ain't hardly said aye, yes or no to any one of us all day, has he? Has he told you what ails him, Mary? He'd tell you if he'd tell anybody. You're his pet in this bank. Guess you know that, don't you?"

Mary went home that afternoon with her apprehensions partially dispelled. If Mr. Hall chose to keep their relations entirely upon a business footing she was content. It might be best if he did so. She would have preferred that they remain friends, but perhaps that was too much to expect.

Before the week ended she was forced to realize that even this strictly business relationship might become unendurable. The cashier's manner toward her was frigidly dignified, he never spoke to her except in the way of duty and not then if he could convey his wishes through the medium of Cahoon or Jackson. All this she did not greatly mind. In fact she found his behavior amusing, at times. The studied way in which he avoided looking at her, or refused to meet her eye if she looked at him, his pompous walk—outraged dignity in the line of his stiff little back—as he passed her desk, were really funny. They had the effect of salving her conscience. She had been truly sorry for him, but now she was not. His behavior was absurd and, more than anything else could have done, gave her his real measure as a man.

If he had been content with ignoring her she would have smiled and ceased to think of him at all. But it was soon apparent that his resentment would not stop there. It became, in an impalpable, indefinite way, a persecution. He began to find fault with her work, to be hypercritical, to find mistakes where, it seemed to her, no real mistakes had been made. If he had spoken to her directly concerning these real or fancied lapses it would not have been as bad. This, however, he never did; he reported them to Philander Cahoon, who, plainly acting under instructions, conveyed the reproof to her. Philander was always tactful, always kindly and considerate of her feelings, and it was evident that he disliked the duty laid upon him; but Peter Hall was cashier and Cahoon was his subordinate, and the poor old fellow was acutely conscious of his age and the fear that some younger man might be chosen to sit in his place at the teller's window.

Mary bore—or tried to bear—these criticisms patiently, but they made her nervous and, being so, and though trying to be more than usually careful, she did at last make an actual and somewhat important blunder. It was on a Tuesday of the second week following the rejected proposal of marriage and when Philander, of course acting under instructions, called it to her attention, she was very much disturbed.

"Oh, I'm sorry, Mr. Cahoon," she said. "I am so sorry! I don't see how I ever did it. How could I have been so stupid?"

The teller fidgeted uneasily. He glanced towards the cashier's desk. Mr. Hall's back was as rigid as always, but Mary, also glancing in that direction, was perfectly sure that he was listening to every word.

"Well—we—well, you see, Mary," faltered Philander, "Mr. Hall seems to think that—that—er—perhaps you were in a little too much of a hurry yesterday to get away for your dinner. He thinks—well, he thinks maybe you had better not leave any day until twelve and—er—get back prompt at one, you know. He—"

Mary interrupted. "Did he tell you to tell me this?" she demanded.

"Why—why—"

"Never mind. I can see that he did. Thank you, Mr. Cahoon. He won't be troubled by my hurrying away again, you may be sure of that."

The moment Philander moved toward his window, she

rose and walked into the enclosure beyond the rail. If Peter Hall heard her approach he gave no sign of doing so. He did not look up until she spoke and then looked immediately down again at the papers on his desk.

"Mr. Hall," she said, and although she did not raise her voice, she took no pains to lower it, "I understand you think I am not particular enough about my dinner hour. You think I am in the habit of going too soon and staying too long. Is that so?"

She heard Bennie Jackson, behind her, halt in his walk and she saw Captain Eben Baker, who was waiting outside the grill, turn his head and look in her direction. Hall, however, did not look.

"Is it true?" she asked again. "Is that what you think?"

Peter Hall cleared his throat. "This isn't the time to talk about such things," he said, with stiff reproof. "I am busy, Miss Brewster."

"So am I. But I want to know if it is true. Do you think that, Mr. Hall?"

Still he did not look at her. He did, however, look at Captain Baker and the expression of surprised interest upon the latter's face seemed to annoy him exceedingly.

"See me after banking hours, Miss Brewster," he snapped. "All right, Cap'n Baker. Come right in."

Baker moved toward the gate of the cashier's enclosure. Mary, however, remained where she was.

"Mr. Hall," she said, crisply, "it may be that I haven't been particular enough about the time of my leaving the bank and my coming back. I am sorry for that, but I am sure you must remember that it was you, yourself, who urged me to go whenever I pleased and stay as long as I liked. You told me so not only once, but several times. I supposed, of course, you meant it, and so perhaps I did not watch the clock as carefully as I should. I shall, hereafter."

She went back to her desk. Captain Eben entered the cashier's pen. Philander Cahoon suddenly became very busy at his desk by the window. Bennie Jackson hurried off on his interrupted errand; but, catching Mary's eye, he grinned broadly as he made his exit.

That evening, for the first time since he broached to his sister his carefully thought out plan for his future and hers, Benjamin Brewster referred to it.

"Well, Mary," he queried, "how about it? You have had more time than you asked for to consider that proposition of mine. Have you decided to say yes and make us both happy?"

As a matter of fact Mary was nearer to saying yes then than she had been since the surprising plan was explained to her. She had thought of it in every spare moment during the days and evenings and lain awake thinking of it after she had gone to bed. It was very alluring, it seemed to offer a solution of almost every difficulty, she was sure that any friend whose advice she might ask would say she should accept. And yet—well, somehow or other, she had not been able to bring her mind to the consenting point. Always, when she was near that point, came the thought of David Cummings and his disinterested, painstaking planning and effort to get her the position in the bank. Certainly she must tell him first of all if she were going to give up that position and—well, she hated to do so. It seemed so ungrateful. Also—and up to those last few days it had been an undeniable fact—she could not bear the thought of giving up her work for its own sake.

But Peter Hall's outrageous behavior was killing that reluctance. The interview between them that afternoon had been humiliating and her cheeks flamed whenever she thought of it. How dared he speak to her in that way? With Captain Baker and the others looking on and listening! How dared he? After all, although she was his hired subordinate, she was still a Brewster, and this ridiculous little Hall person had himself told her what an honor he considered it to have a Brewster in the bank's employ.

She and Ben were in the sitting room when the latter asked his question. She had scarcely spoken since they came in from supper. She did not answer and he repeated the query. Then she turned to look at him.

"I don't know, Ben," she said, with a troubled shake of the head. "I don't know. I—I think—well, yes, I am almost sure that I shall say yes in the end, but—but I—I don't believe I can say it now. I know it is unreasonable to ask you to wait any longer. It is just that— Oh, dear! I don't know how to explain it."

He had not been in the best of humor that day. At dinner and again at supper he had eaten little and even the adoring Azure had confided to her mistress that he was "kind of grumpy and out of sorts, seems so." Azure, of course, had an excuse for him.

"It's his heart or kidney, or whatever he's got, that ails him," she said. "He was out late last night, you remember. I knew how 'twould be when he told Cap'n Sam Freeman he'd come over and have dinner with him. Mrs.

Sam's away, up to Boston, and I cal'late them two set up all hours. Mr. Benjamin ate too much, or got too nervous or somethin' and now he's payin' for it. Land of glory! *I* don't mind a bit. Men are liable to get that way when they're sick. You ought to have seen my Obed after one of them Red Men collations or Fourth of July celebrations or somethin'. *He* wan't fit to live in the house with. In a way," she added, thoughtfully, "I s'pose you might say Obed was sort of a sick invalid 'long in his last days. I didn't think so at the time, but I realize it now. I shouldn't be surprised if he'd been took mortal any minute—if he'd lasted out, instead of gettin' drownded."

Whatever the cause of Mr. Brewster's mental or physical indisposition his humor was not improved by his sister's procrastination. His brows drew together and his tone was almost sharp as he spoke.

"Far be it from me to hurry you," he observed, with some sarcasm; "but really, Mary, I can't see what you are waiting for."

Again she shook her head. "I know," she admitted. "You have made me a wonderful offer and I ought to accept and be thankful. And, as I said, I suppose I shall accept in the end. It is only that—"

"That what? Surely you are not hesitating out of regard for the unspeakable Peter. You are not reconsidering *his* proposal, are you?"

She straightened in her chair. "I despise him," she said, her eyes flashing.

"Indeed? Really? You surprise me a little. I have refrained from mentioning his name because you haven't mentioned it, but, as I remember, you were far more tolerant of his confounded presumption than I was. Has he been a little—er—difficult since his hopes were blighted?"

Her lips tightened. "He has been hateful!" she exclaimed.

"Ah! Has he so? Well, I am not paralyzed with astonishment. I judged he would be as disagreeable as he dared. But, unless I am very much mistaken, there will be limits to his daring. You—our family—have some influence in Wapatomac and he knows it. What has he done, or said, in particular?"

She had not intended to tell him or any one, but now she did. She told of the incident of the afternoon. He rose to his feet.

"The little blackguard!" he snorted, his face crimson. "The impudent upstart! I will walk in on him to-morrow morning and—"

She interrupted. "Oh, no, no!" she protested. "You mustn't do that, Ben. Don't you see you mustn't? It will only make trouble. You mustn't do it."

He was pacing up and down the room. She had never before seen him like this.

"Trouble!" he repeated, wheeling toward her. "There will be trouble for *him;* you are right there. Insulting you—my sister—in that way! Why—"

"Wait! Wait, Ben, please. I don't mean trouble for him."

"Then what do you mean? . . . Come!"

"I mean trouble for—for every one. There will be a scene and—oh, so much talk and—and gossip! I can't bear that. You know I can't."

"Humph! . . . Well, perhaps. But, Mary, I insist upon one thing. That is that you leave that picayune bank to-morrow morning. For the sake of our family you must. I insist upon it. . . . Here, I'll attend to it myself. I will go down there in the morning and tell them you are through."

"No. . . . No, Ben."

"Why not? In heaven's name what is the matter with you? Do you *enjoy* being treated like a—like a fisherman's girl who is afraid of her job?"

He had gone too far. Her tone was crisp and her reply emphatic and unmistakable.

"I mean," she said, "that I prefer to attend to my own business. When—or if—I give up my position I shall tell them so myself."

"*If* you give it up! Good Lord! you don't intend to stay there to be insulted *again,* do you?"

"I don't know yet what I intend."

"When will you know?"

"By to-morrow night, perhaps. I must talk with—" she hesitated and then added: "I will try to give you your answer then, Ben. It will probably be yes. And I *am* grateful to you; truly I am."

He was watching her intently. "I don't exactly understand," he said. "Why will you be more certain to-morrow night than you are now? You said you must talk with some one. With whom?"

"Captain Cummings. I begged him to get me this bookkeeper's position and he went to a great deal of trouble and on my account. Naturally I must tell him, before I tell any one else, that I am leaving the bank—if I do leave."

The flush upon his face deepened until it became almost

purple. "Cummings!" he cried. "For heaven's sake, what—"

He paused. To her surprise and alarm, his expression changed. She heard him catch his breath, saw him seize a chair back as if to steady himself, and then sit heavily down. She sprang to her feet and hurried to his side.

"Why—why, Ben!" she cried. "What is it? What is the matter? Are you sick? Tell me?"

He was breathing heavily and his voice, when he answered, had a peculiar quaver, like that of a frightened child. All its petulant irritation had gone.

"I—I don't feel well, Mary," he gasped, looking up at her. "I—I— It is this trouble of mine."

She was very much frightened and ran to the door to call for Azure. Mrs. Crisp came hurrying and she and Mary assisted him to the haircloth sofa, after which the housekeeper rushed away to return with a hot water bottle and another bottle, the latter containing cherry rum.

"You lay right still where you be, Mr. Benjamin," she commanded. "Put this hot bag to your feet now and take a swallow of this. It'll do you good. Nothin' ever done my Obed so much good, when he had a spell, as cherry rum. He used to crave it, poor soul. . . . There! Now you feel better, don't you?"

Apparently he did. The purple flush was fading from his face and he breathed more easily. After a little he insisted upon sitting up.

"I'm all right now," he said, some of the petulance returning. "There, there! Take that confounded thing away," referring to the hot water bottle. "It's scalding me. . . . Here! Give me another drink of that stuff."

He helped himself to a second liberal dose of the cherry rum. Then he rose to his feet.

"I'll go to bed, I think," he said. "Yes, yes; I am all right, I tell you. Indigestion, I suppose. The stuff I had to eat last night at Freeman's was enough to kill any one. . . . Well," defiantly, "it hasn't killed me and it isn't going to."

Mary insisted upon going with him to his room upstairs. There she left him, after exacting a promise that he would go to bed immediately. When she came down to the sitting room Azure was waiting her.

"Tut, tut, tut!" observed Mrs. Crisp, with a shake of the head. "I told you so, didn't I? You take a man with his wife gone away up to the city, and another man comin' to eat dinner with him, and—well, 'most anything's liable to happen. Every time I left my Obed he was a reg'lar wreck when I got back. And poor Mr. Benjamin has always got his infliction to remember. He can pretend it ain't there, but it is, just the same. You may break, you may scatter the vase all you want to, but the scent of the roses will hang to it still. That's what *I* always say."

Next morning Mr. Brewster, although quite recovered, had breakfast in his room. Mary went up to see him and found him cheerful, his ill temper apparently gone. He did not refer to the subject they were discussing the previous evening and, because he did not, neither did she.

Nor did he at dinner. Mindful of her statement to Mr. Hall and Philander, she left the bank just as the clock struck twelve and she was back at her desk at a quarter to one. The cashier had gone home for his own dinner and Captain David Cummings was in the directors' room and, for a wonder, alone. It seemed to her that the opportunity she had awaited had come. She rose and walked to the door of the inner office.

Cahoon looked up from his books.

"Eh?" he queried. "Did the cap'n ring for you, Mary? I didn't hear the bell."

"No. He didn't ring."

She did not wait for him to ask another question, but knocked. Cummings' voice bade her come in. She entered and closed the door behind her.

He was seated at the big table, the usual litter of papers and letters before him. He looked up.

"Who wants me now?" he asked, with a shrug of resignation. "I kind of hoped they would let me alone for a few minutes. Phoebe Carleton, is it? The stock market's been a little stirred up lately and I've been expectin' her to drift in."

Mary shook her head. "No," she replied. "It isn't Mrs. Carleton. I can see you are busy, Captain Cummings and I am sorry I disturbed you. Another time will do just as well."

She turned to go, but he detained her.

"No, no," he protested, rising. "I ain't so busy as all that. What is it? Somethin' you wanted, yourself?"

"Yes. But it can wait."

"There, there! Sit down, sit down. I'm glad to see you, honest I am. Now what's on your mind?"

She still hesitated. "You said you were busy and hoping to be left alone."

"I wanted some folks to leave me alone, but you aren't one of 'em. Sit down in that chair. That's right. Now what is it?" Then, noticing her expression, he added, more gravely: "Nothin' gone wrong in the bank here, has there? I hope not."

She tried to smile. A great deal had gone wrong, but she did not intend to speak of that.

"Captain Cummings," she said, "I am thinking that, perhaps, I had better give up my position here in the bank."

It was not the way she had meant to put it, and of course he misunderstood. He looked at her in astonishment.

"What!" he exclaimed, sharply. "What's that you say? You're goin' to give up your position? . . . Why, what's all this?"

She hastened to modify her abrupt statement. "I didn't mean that exactly as it sounded," she explained. "I don't know that I shall give it up. I meant to say—I think I did say—that I am thinking perhaps I had better do so, that perhaps I ought to."

He ran his fingers through his hair. His gaze was fixed upon her face and it was evident that he was struggling to find the reason behind her entirely unexpected announcement.

"Humph!" he observed, after a moment. "Humph! So somethin' *has* gone wrong. . . . Dear, dear! . . . Look here, Mary, has somebody been talkin' to you? You haven't heard—well, you haven't heard any talk about things here in the bank, have you?"

She could not imagine what he meant.

"Talk?" she repeated. "I haven't heard any talk. No one has talked to me. Why, what do you mean, Captain Cummings?"

He was still regarding her keenly. Then he nodded. "No," he said. "No, I guess you haven't. So it isn't that.

. . . Humph! Well, then, it is somethin' else. Mary, has anybody here been—I don't know how to say it exactly—has anybody been sayin' things to you they shouldn't? Hurtin' your feelin's or anything?"

This was perilously close to that part of the truth which she had no intention of revealing. She colored slightly and he noticed it. Aware that her embarrassment must be obvious, she tried to cover it by a hurried, and untruthful, denial.

"Oh, no! No, indeed!" she said, quickly. "It isn't that. I have had an offer made to me that I am almost sure I should accept."

She heard him catch his breath. His glance strayed toward the door leading out into the banking room.

"An offer!" he repeated, uneasily. "Oh! . . . Well?"

"I think if it had not been for you," she went on; "I mean if you hadn't been so kind to me, had worked so hard to get me this place when I needed it so badly, I—"

"Never mind that," almost sharply. "That doesn't amount to anything. . . . Go on! You have had an offer?"

"Yes. An offer from my brother. . . . What? What were you going to say?"

Apparently she was mistaken in thinking he was about to say anything. He leaned back in his chair.

"Well, well!" he observed. "From your brother, eh? That's some better, anyhow."

"Better? Better than what?"

"Eh? . . . Oh—er—better than if it was from somebody else—another bank, say. So Ben has made you some sort of offer that you think you ought to accept? What is it?"

"That is what I came here to tell you."

She went on to tell of Brother Benjamin's plans for their joint future. She told it all, even of the will she had seen which, in case of Ben's death, left all his wealth to her. David Cummings listened intently, breaking in occasionally to ask a pointed question. When she finished his hair had been rubbed and twisted until his head bristled like a thistle top.

"There," she said, in conclusion, "that is the offer I have had. It seems very wonderful to me. Don't *you* think I should accept it? Honestly, don't you, Captain Cummings?"

He was deep in thought, his fingers toying with a pen-holder. Now he nodded.

"Yes," he said, slowly. "It sounds like a mighty fine chance." Looking up, he added: "I'm almost surprised you haven't said yes before this. Why didn't you, Mary?"

She scarcely knew how to answer. Her reason for post-poning the acceptance seemed vague enough, or at least hard to put into words.

"I—well, really, I hardly know," she admitted. Then, with a burst of candor, "Why, yes, I do, too! First of all I hated to give up my work. I loved it, I really did."

"Eh? Loved it, you say? Does that mean you don't love it now as much as you used to?"

Again he was hitting close to the truth.

"Oh, no, no!" she stammered. "And there was another thing. I couldn't say yes to Ben until I had spoken to you. If I were to leave I must tell you before I did any one else. And, besides, I wanted your advice. I want you to be my sheet anchor again. Please give me your straightforward, honest opinion. Don't hold anything back. This is very, very important to me."

He was silent. She bent forward to watch his face.

"I think," she said, after a moment, "that there is some doubt in your mind. Please tell me what it is."

He gave his tousled hair another scrub. "I don't see why there should be," he confessed. "No, I don't, Mary, that's a fact."

"But there is? What is it?"

Another pause. Then: "I guess there really isn't any. I just—well, I've been knockin' around and against all sorts of folks since I was knee-high to a fish barrel and I shouldn't be surprised if it made me too suspicious. When anybody comes to me with a proposition that's so blessed perfect that there *can't* be anything wrong with it I commence to look for holes."

"Then you think there may be a hole in this one?"

"Don't seem as if there could be. Your brother offers to live along with you and he'll pay the bills. He doesn't propose to touch a cent of your own income and he don't intend takin' title to your house and land; that too, will stay yours. He's got, or he says he has—and judgin' from the checks he deposits here with us, I guess it's true enough —a big income of his own. And he's made a will leavin' everything he owns to you if he dies. That's good enough. . . . Yes, indeed, that's good enough."

"Then what is the trouble with it?"

"Why, nothin', I should say. If it wasn't quite so everlastin' good I'd be happier about it, but that's my mean disposition. . . . Mary, just how much do you know about this half brother of yours? About what he's done and how he's lived since he left here twenty odd years ago?"

She was obliged to admit that she knew very little. Ben had told her a good deal, but she had no proof beyond his word.

"Although," she added, rather defiantly, "I see no reason to doubt that he has told me the truth. Do you?"

"Eh? Oh, no, no! not a mite!"

"Well, then?"

And again he did not speak. She began to resent these silences. "Captain Cummings," she said. "You don't like my brother, do you?"

She had caught him unawares and he was confused. "Why—why," he stammered, "you mustn't say that, Mary. Why shouldn't I like him?"

"I don't know, but you don't. Perhaps you are prejudiced because of what happened that day when he arrived, when he asked you to cash that check."

He laughed aloud. "No, no!" he declared. "I don't hold that against him. No, indeed!"

"You shouldn't. I think if any one should be resentful about that he is the one. But he isn't. He thinks you are a—" she hesitated and then finished the sentence with, "a very able man. I have heard him say so."

"Have you? Well, now, that's first-rate. I'm afraid he's too liberal in his estimate, but I'm much obliged."

"Why don't you like him? Tell me."

He put down the penholder. "I don't know a thing against him, and that's straight truth, Mary," he said, earnestly. "But, to be as right down honest as you ask me to be, I don't know much more *for* him. And, except for what he's told you himself, I should judge that you don't, either. . . . Now hold on, please, just a minute. Let me finish. You and he haven't been livin' in the same house very long yet and, as it is now, you're the skipper and he's a passenger. If you fall in with this plan of his—and, mind you, I'm far from sayin' you shouldn't—things are bound to be a little different. He'll be in command then, at least he's goin' to pay all the bills, and it is you who'll be passenger."

She was inclined to resent this. "He doesn't say that at all," she declared. "It will be my house and I am to manage it, just as I always have."

"Yes, but with his money. He wouldn't be human if he didn't give an order once in a while. Perhaps you and he will get along first-rate. Maybe it will be all smooth sailin', very likely 'twill, but I do feel sure the whole situation is goin' to be different from what 'tis now. It's the difference between havin' a good friend visitin' you and contractin' to take that same friend as a regular payin' boarder. That I *do* know about, for I've seen it happen a good many times. It changes things altogether. It puts the boot on the other foot."

This, or something like it, was precisely what had been in the back of her own mind from the beginning. It was one of the causes of her hesitancy in accepting her brother's proposal.

"I see," she said, slowly. "You think I won't be as independent as I am now. I suppose you are right."

"I guess I am. But you mustn't take that as meanin' you should say no to Ben. If you could wait a little longer, if you could just wait a while and get to know each other better, then—well, then, seems to me you could be surer of not makin' any mistake."

She was troubled. "He can't understand why I have waited as long as I have already," she said. "That doesn't make any real difference, however. I am as anxious not to make a mistake as you can be not to have me. Your advice, then, is for me to put off the decision?"

He seemed to hesitate. Then he said: "I don't want to let my personal convenience have any real bearin' on this affair, Mary, but—well, it would be a little help to me if you *could* keep on here in the bank for a few weeks longer. There are things goin' on that— Humph! But they don't count, and shan't, against your doin' the right thing for yourself. Nothin'," very earnestly, "could count in that way with me. I'd like to have you believe that."

"I do. You are a wonderful friend, Captain Cummings. And, you must believe this, if you need me here in the bank I shall stay. Neither Ben nor any one can change my mind in that respect."

The statement, made as earnestly as his had been, seemed to please him greatly. He flushed and when he next spoke it was without looking at her.

"I might as well confess my sins—or part of 'em," he said, with a half smile. "When you come to me for advice about a thing like this I'm afraid that advice may not be quite as impartial as it ought to be. It's pretty hard for me to keep myself out of it. I—well, I guess I'm jealous. It makes me proud to have you call me your friend and maybe I don't like to think that your brother, or anybody else, can be a better friend. That mean disposition of mine again, eh? . . . Oh—er—what's Peter Hall's notion of this scheme of Ben's? What does he think you ought to do?"

She rose from her chair. "I haven't asked his opinion," she said, crisply. "I have no intention of doing so."

He looked up then. "Eh?" he queried. "Oh! . . . Well, I didn't know but—"

She broke in. "Mr. Hall has nothing whatever to do with my personal affairs," she said, with emphasis. "Nothing whatever, now or in the future. . . . Captain Cummings, please answer one more question. Will it really help you, as president of the bank, if I stay on as assistant bookkeeper for a while longer?"

He hesitated. "I can only answer that in one way," he said, slowly. "If it won't hurt you with your brother to wait a little while—say a couple more weeks—or three, maybe—before you take up with his plan—why, yes, it would."

"Then I shall stay."

"Understand, Mary, I do honestly think you probably ought to take up with it in the end. I know I've talked a lot, tried to raise objections and all that, but I haven't raised one yet that will hold water. If you and he keep on gettin' along with each other as well as you do now, and nothin' we don't know about turns up, no friend such as I want to be could tell you not to do it. . . . And," with another rueful smile, "that wasn't as easy for me to say as it sounded. I—I'm goin' to miss you around here."

She was at the door, but she paused. "And I shall miss you," she said, impulsively. "I am very glad I am going to be here for a few weeks longer, at least."

Her hand turned the knob. "And I shall miss Mr. Cahoon and Bennie," she added, as if in afterthought. "They have been very kind, too."

Left alone in the director's room, David Cummings sat, with the pile of letters and papers before him, regarding them with unseeing eyes. He sighed, heavily. She was going to leave the bank, which meant, of course, that she was going out of his life. With Benjamin Brewster as her future "skipper" he, Cummings, would see her not even as frequently as he had before she came to the bookkeeper's desk. She had said she would miss him, but he was wise enough to realize that she would miss him only a little while. Just about as long as she would miss Bennie Jackson and Philander Cahoon.

But—and somehow he found absurd comfort in the thought—she had not said that she should miss Peter Hall.

CHAPTER XII

AT nine o'clock that evening a caller came to the Cummings house on Nickerson's Hill. David was, as usual, at his desk in the sitting room when Kohath announced the arrival. Captain Barnabas was out, attending a deacons' meeting in the New Church vestry. Mr. Briggs was very much impressed when he announced the visitor.

"It's Mr. Ben Brewster," he whispered. "Says he wants to see you, he does. Must be pretty important, don't you think, 'cause he's walked way down here, 'stead of comin' to the bank or askin' you to come to see him, or anything. What do you cal'late he's got on his mind, Cap'n Dave?"

Cummings shrugged. "I'll know better after he tells me," he said. "Send him in her, Kohath."

"But ain't you comin' out to fetch him in yourself? Seems as if—well, considerin' who he is, and his walkin' way down here and all, you'd—"

Dave, without waiting for him to finish, rose and threw open the dining-room door. Mr. Brewster stood by the table. He was well dressed as always, and carried the cane which, borne by another, would have seemed a foppish affectation. In his case it was, of course, regarded as the necessary aid to an invalid.

"He wouldn't set down," breathed Briggs in his employer's ear. "I asked him to but he wouldn't."

"Good evening, Ben," hailed Cummings, cheerfully. "Glad to see you. Come in here where it's more comfortable."

Brewster acknowledged the greeting with a curt "Good evening," and entered the sitting room. David closed the door behind them and waved toward a chair.

"Sit down, Ben," he said.

But Brewster refused that invitation as he had Kohath's.

"No, thank you," he said, stiffly. "I shall stay only a few minutes. . . . Cummings, I believe my sister told you this afternoon of a certain proposition I had made to her. She says she did."

Captain David nodded. "Why—yes, Ben, she did," he admitted.

"Yes. And you agreed—or she says so—that my offer is a good one, a liberal one, and that she ought to accept it, for her own sake quite as much as mine."

"Well—yes; something like that. I told her that it sounded to me like a mighty fine offer. . . . Sit down, Ben, do. I'm glad of this chance to talk with you."

"Thanks, no. I can't stay and I didn't come here to talk with you about that. It is a private matter and—well," with a hint of irritation, "I confess I can't see why she thought it necessary to mention it at all outside of the family."

"Maybe she shouldn't. I presume likely she felt—yes, I know she did—that, as I was responsible for gettin' her into the bank, she ought to give me her reasons for thinkin' of leavin' it. She told me of her own accord. I shouldn't have asked her, you understand."

"Yes? Well, I am a little surprised that she did, nevertheless. It is her affair, and mine, and neither of us would wish it to be discussed by outsiders, at least until after she has left the bank. We shall both be obliged if you will keep it to yourself until then."

The tone of Cummings' next speech was a little sharper.

"Did she give you to understand that she thought I was likely to talk about it with outsiders?" he asked.

"I don't know that she did. I am asking you not to, that is all."

"All right. I shan't."

"Thank you. Now—and this is why I came here—she tells me that you wish her to remain in your establishment for some time longer. She seems to feel that you need her there; in fact, she says you told her so."

"I told her that, if it didn't make any great difference to her, it would help me and the bank consider'ble if she could hang on for two or three weeks."

It had been evident to the captain from the beginning of the interview that his caller was not in good temper. This mild reply seemed, for some reason, to increase his vexation.

"So she says," he snapped. Then, more calmly, he added. "Cummings, I feel that she shouldn't stay. I am in poor health, my nerves are shaky, and this unsettled condition as to my future is not good for me. Miss Brewster will, in the end, give up your bookkeeping—she should never have taken it on, of course; she wouldn't if I had been here to advise her—and I wish her to give it up at once and live at home with me, as she should do. What I am asking of you—what I came here to ask—is that you will oblige me by telling her to do that very thing."

Captain David rubbed his hair. "It looks to me as if you hadn't got hold of this quite right, Ben," he said, earnestly. "I told Mary right off that she must do just what she thought best for herself. I told her she mustn't let me or the bank stand in the way of that for a single minute. If she feels she ought to leave to-morrow mornin' she must leave. There'll be no teasin' her to stay, so far as I'm concerned."

The Brewster cane tapped the Brewster shoe.

"Will you tell her to-morrow morning that you feel she should leave at once?" he asked.

"I've told her already to do what she thinks right."

"That scarcely answers my question, does it? She is staying on because you told her you needed her, and she considers herself under some obligation to you. I confess it seems to me that she has more than canceled any obligation, real or fancied, by working as long as she has already—particularly at the—er—magnificent salary your bank has seen fit to pay her. . . . However, we won't discuss that at this late date. I—"

"Wait there! I don't know as I like that very well. No, I don't. Her salary isn't very big, that's true, but it is as much as we've ever paid anybody in her place and she understands that. She has never complained about it."

"She wouldn't be likely to. She doesn't know much about such things. . . . But there, there!" more impatiently still. "Never mind that. It isn't material. Your telling her that you have changed your mind and think she should leave at once *is* material—to her welfare. I ask you to tell her that, and I am asking it as a favor, Captain Cummings."

"I see. . . . As a favor for her—or for you?"

"For her, of course. And—why, yes, certainly—in a measure, for me, too. I am her brother. But I am thinking of her future and it is for her sake that I ask it."

"Yes," dryly. "Well, I am glad you told me that. I am thinkin' about Mary's welfare just as much as you are—yes, just as much. She told me this afternoon that she loved her work in the bank. And she has told me before that she is happier there than she has been at any time since her mother died. And another thing—and almost the last thing she said—was that she was glad to know that she was goin' to stay at her desk for a few weeks longer. I am glad she is. I haven't changed *my* mind. If she has changed hers then all she's got to do is say so and she can leave the next minute. But—well, she must say so to me. I hired her and it's my right."

The blood was mounting to the Brewster forehead.

"Does that mean you doubt my word?" he cried, indignantly.

"Why should I? I take your word for granted, same as I expect you to take mine. But I took her word this afternoon. I thought she meant what she said. All she has to do is tell me she didn't. Then the matter's settled, for all hands."

Benjamin Brewster stalked to the door.

"Cummings," he proclaimed, turning. "I might have expected this from you. As a matter of fact, I did expect it. I can do no more now. My sister is inexperienced and she may be innocent enough not to see what is behind your damned selfishness. I do."

Captain David had risen to his feet.

"Here, here!" he demanded. "What's that you say?"

"Selfishness was the word I used. It is good English, isn't it?"

"I guess likely 'tis, but you're puttin' it in the wrong place."

"I think not."

"I know yes, if you're pinnin' it on me, so far as Mary is concerned. What I told her was—"

"Oh, bah! . . . I don't know exactly what you told her. I wasn't there to hear it, worse luck. I wish I had been."

"So do I. But, now that you've started this sort of talk, you'd better hear a little more. There wasn't one grain of selfishness in what I said to your sister. Whether there is any in this offer of yours to her I don't know, either. I guess likely I know as much as she does and that's what you told her when you made it."

"What the devil do you mean by that?"

"What I said and no more—yet."

Brewster raised his cane to point it at his adversary.

"You have hypnotized my sister," he declared, his voice shaking with anger. "You have made a fool of her, somehow or other. But you haven't hypnotized me. *She* may believe in your disinterested advice and your kindness and all that rot, but I am no such idiot. I know what you're up to, just as I knew from the beginning what that runt Hall was working for. Well," with a sarcastic laugh, "she put him in his place, I'll say that for her."

He would have continued but Captain David lifted a warning finger.

"Stop!" he ordered, sharply. "I don't know what you mean about Peter Hall and I don't much care. But—"

Another scornful laugh interrupted him.

"The devil you don't!" sneered Brewster. "Then if you are the remarkable bank president some of these hayseeds claim you are, you had better keep your eyes open. If you haven't noticed how that cashier of yours has been persecuting my sister for the last week then you must be blind.

And you talk about her being happy in that bank of yours! You, standing in her light and working against her interests to gain your own ends. I know what you've got up your sleeve. I know. And it didn't need the hints I've had to put me wise either."

He slammed through the dining room and out of the house. Kohath hastened from the kitchen to open the door for him, but he had gone.

David Cummings, his face almost as red as that of his late caller's, was looking after him.

"Godfreys!" exclaimed the astonished Mr. Briggs. "He seemed to be in consider'ble of a hurry, didn't he, Cap'n Dave?"

The captain grunted. "No more of a hurry than he'd better have been," he growled.

Then he went back to his desk in the sitting room.

CHAPTER XIII

DAVID CUMMINGS did a great deal of thinking before, and after, he retired that night. And when, the following noon, he entered the bank he glanced toward Mary Brewster's desk with strong misgivings. He even wondered whether or not he should see her sitting at that desk. Benjamin had had an opportunity to tell his side of their interview and it was highly probable that the tale had thrown a most unfavorable light upon him, Cummings.

But Mary was there and nodded pleasantly as he entered. When, a little later, he found occasion to summon her to the directors' room on a business matter, her manner was free from embarrassment or constraint, and, although he purposely mentioned her brother's name in the course of their brief conversation, and watched her intently when he did so, that manner remained unchanged. It was hard to believe that Ben Brewster had not told his sister of his call at the house on Nickerson's Hill, that she was unaware of the scene which had taken place there the evening before, but he was forced to believe it. Nothing else could explain her attitude. She was as friendly and pleasant as always, and the reference to Benjamin merely caused her to mention the fact that he was not at all well that morning.

"He hasn't been very well for a week or more," she said. "This morning Azure and I insisted that he stay in his room and I sent for Doctor Hamilton. He says there is nothing seriously wrong—nothing new, that is—but he thinks Ben has been going about too much of late and needs rest. I think he is right, but Ben is a man, and men don't know how to be sick, I suppose. It makes them cross."

She laughed as she said it. Cummings looked up.

"Oh, he is cross, eh?" he observed. "Nothin' happened to make him that way, special, is there?"

"No, indeed! And he isn't very cross. Just a little impatient sometimes, that is all. And he doesn't mean anything by it. Usually no one could be nicer than he is to me."

"Hum. . . . Well, I'm glad of that."

"You don't speak as if you were too glad. I don't see why you are so prejudiced against him. You are, you know."

"I don't want to be. . . . Oh—er—what did he say when you told him you had decided to stay here at the bank a while longer?"

Mary's brow clouded slightly. "He didn't like it very well, of course," she admitted. "I told him I had talked it over with you, that you needed me for a time, and so I must again put off my decision for a few weeks. He was disappointed, and said so, but I am sure he understood why I feel I ought to do it."

So Benjamin had not told her, either of his intention of calling upon him, Cummings, or what had taken place when he did so. David wondered why, but he decided to remain silent also, for the present at least.

Later on, when the cashier had gone home for dinner, he called old Mr. Cahoon into the directors' room.

"Philander," he said, "I want you to give me a list of

our correspondents in some cities out West. I've written their names on this paper. Look 'em up when you get time and hand 'em in to me. Don't bother Mr. Hall or Miss Brewster about it, do it yourself. . . . Oh, and say," he added, carelessly, "there's one other thing I want to speak to you about. How is Mary gettin' along with her work nowadays? I've been too busy to notice much myself. Nobody findin' any fault, is there?"

Philander seemed a trifle confused, even a little troubled. "Why—why, I guess she is getting along pretty well, Cap'n Cummings," he stammered. "I guess so. Far as I'm concerned she is, sure."

"Humph! What do you mean by as far as you are concerned? Is somebody else concerned the other way?"

"Well, you see—I guess it doesn't amount to much—Mr. Hall, he—well, lately, he seems to think she isn't quite as careful about—about little things as she was. I haven't noticed any difference, but, two or three times this last week he's made me—he's asked me to tell her about some mistake he thought she'd made. And—well, the other day she *did* make one. He thought—Mr. Hall did—that she'd been takin' too much time off for her dinner. He had me tell her that, too. She was dreadfully upset. I was real sorry for her."

Cummings was rumpling his hair.

"Anything more?" he asked. "Go ahead and tell me, if there is."

"No-o. I guess that's all, so far. Only— Say, Cap'n Cummings," in a troubled whisper, "there hasn't any—anything gone wrong between them, she and Mr. Hall, has there? It seems to me that he's been—well, kind of down on her lately. . . . I don't know as I ought to say this to you, but—"

Cummings interrupted. "Philander," he said, "the next time Mr. Hall thinks she has made a mistake, or has any fault to find, and orders you to tell her about it, instead of goin' to her you come in here and tell me. If I ain't here you put it off till I come and tell me then. Understand?"

"Why, yes, sir, I guess so. Only, if Mr. Hall—"

"I'll stand between you and Hall. Now make out that list for me."

The very next day when, at his regular hour, eleven o'clock, he entered the bank, as he passed the teller's window Cahoon spoke his name.

"I've made out that list you wanted, Cap'n," he said. Then, with a look which, or so the captain fancied, meant more than his words, he added: "I'll bring it in to you in just a minute."

Cummings paused, as was his custom, at the gate of the cashier's enclosure. "Morning, Peter," he said. Mr. Hall's face was primly stern and his back very straight indeed. His reply to the salutation was punctiliously polite, as always. "Good morning, Mary," said the captain. Mary looked up from her work. "Good morning, Captain Cummings," she said. There was color in her cheeks and, or so Cummings thought, a slight tremble in her voice.

When, a few minutes later, Cahoon entered the directors' room, bringing with him the list of western correspondents, Captain David was ready for him.

"That's all right, Philander," he said, taking the papers from the teller's hand. "Much obliged. . . . Well?

What's the trouble now? There has been some, I judge. Tell me about it."

Mr. Cahoon was nervous. "I've done something you told me not to do, Cap'n Dave," he said. "I'm awfully sorry, but I couldn't very well help it. Mr. Hall ordered me to do it right away, and you weren't here, so—"

"All right," hastily. "What was it?"

Mary had been fifteen minutes late that morning, Philander explained, whereas Mr. Hall had been unusually early. The cashier had required her services in some matter connected with the morning mail and, when she did not put in an appearance, he had been, so Mr. Cahoon said, "a good deal put out."

"He called me over," went on the teller, "and said that there was altogether too much slackness on the part of the people who worked in this bank. He made it a point, he said, to be at his desk at nine o'clock and he expected the rest of us to be at ours. I was to tell Miss Brewster that she must be more prompt. I tried to put off doing it, but no, that wouldn't do. I must tell her then. So, of course, I had to. She was all broke up about it. Seems her brother—Benjamin, I mean—had a sort of ill-turn and she stopped to see the doctor on the way down. He was busy and she had to wait and—well, that was the reason. When I spoke to her she did same as she did before, went right to Mr. Hall and told him. He didn't say much, scarcely answered a word as a matter of fact, but he wasn't very forgiving seemed to me. It's all kind of queer because a while ago I've heard him tell her, three or four times over, to take just as much time away from the bank as she needed. He's always been fussy about Bennie's being on hand early—yes, and with me if I ever happened to be the least bit late. But with her—well, that was different. Of course, she being a Brewster, I could understand why he would be different. But now. . . . Well, that's all, Cap'n Dave. You told me to tell you and so I have."

Cummings nodded. "Thanks, Philander," he said. Shortly afterward Peter Hall came in for his daily conference with the president. When the conference was over the latter asked him to wait a moment.

"Peter," he said, slowly, toying with the penholder, "I judge that you and Mary Brewster aren't hittin' it off as well as you were a while ago. That's so, isn't it?"

The little cashier's face turned a fiery red. He seemed to find it difficult to reply.

"What—what do you mean?" he blurted. "Hitting it off? I don't understand."

David's smile was innocence itself. He understood, or believed he did, but the complete understanding had nothing to do with what he intended to say just then.

"I mean here at the bank," he explained. "My eyesight is fairly good, but a fellow would have to be pretty nigh-sighted not to notice that you and she weren't as satisfied, either of you, as you used to be. Isn't she keepin' up with her work, or what is the matter?"

The Hall face was still flushed.

"If—if Miss Brewster has told you—" he began, but Cummings raised his hand.

"She hasn't told me anything," he put in. "Not one blessed thing. Suppose you tell me, Peter."

Mr. Hall was relieved by this emphatic statement, that was obvious, but it was just as plain that he still was not happy.

"I—er—I am sorry this little matter has come to your attention, Captain Cummings," he said, stiffly. "I have tried not to bother you with it. Of course I realize that Miss Brewster's position in the bank here is a little different from that of the—er—ordinary person."

"Different? How?"

"Well, she is who she is. Her family—"

"There, there! She hasn't got any family—or she hasn't had any up to Ben's gettin' here. She came here to work just as anybody else might have come. You used to tell me that she was doin' that work as well, or better, than it was ever done before. Now she isn't, is that it?"

Mr. Hall would scarcely go so far as to say just that. The work was being done well enough—well enough. A few mistakes of late, and these he had felt should be called to her attention. Then there was the matter of punctuality. Punctuality, as the captain knew, was one of his own, Hall's, pet hobbies. Mary had not been—yes, that he felt he *must* say—as careful in keeping bank hours as she should have been. And he had considered it his duty to tell her so. There was much more, all rather involved and not very definite.

"Of course," he said, in conclusion. "I realize that perhaps I have been rather—perhaps I shouldn't have taken it on myself to say a word to her about these things. I should have done it to anybody else, of course, but" with a momentary tang of bitterness in his tone, "I realize that she is a favorite of yours, Captain Cummings."

The captain's tone also changed slightly.

"What do you mean by 'favorite'?" he demanded.

"Why—why, she is, isn't she? You were responsible

for bringing her here. She always spoke of you as a particular friend."

"I am her friend, at least I mean to be. I always supposed you were as much her particular friend as anybody, yourself. . . . Well, well!" good-naturedly, "I guess likely she has a good many friends besides you and me, Peter. Now about her mistakes and bein' late and that sort of thing. Just now it seems to me we had better not pay much attention to all that. We've got this bank to think about, you and I, Hall. You know," lowering his voice, "what's goin' on in the board pretty nigh as well as I do, I guess. I thought when I got Mary in here I had settled things and brought the ship into smooth water. Now it's gettin' squally again. I want her to stay where she is for a little while longer, anyhow. If she should up and leave us just now, with the pullin' and haulin' that's goin' on, I'm afraid of that open split and the town row I've been dreadin' so long. So I want you to do your best to keep her happy and contented and not find any fault with her. Will you do that?"

Peter Hall rose. His reply was not graciously given. "You are the president of this bank and what you tell me to do I shall do, of course," he said, curtly.

"Fine! Fine! I knew you'd see it as I do. Much obliged, Peter."

The cashier's exit was not quite as dignified as usual and the sharp click of the latch as he pulled the door shut behind him was loaded with repressed feeling. Cummings smiled to himself. Benjamin Brewster's pointed hint the night before, coupled with Cahoon's disclosures concerning the changed relations between Hall and the assistant bookkeeper, to say nothing of the former's marked confusion when his superior first mentioned that change, were sufficiently illuminating. Captain David felt certain of what had happened. He did not know how or when it had happened, but Benjamin's statement that his sister had "put Hall in his place" meant just one thing to his mind. He found an almost wicked satisfaction in the thought. She was not going to marry Peter, at any rate.

But his smile was merely transient. There were too many other urgently unpleasant matters pressing upon his attention. What he had just said to the cashier concerning trouble in the board of directors was true. It was a trouble which had been growing for almost a month, and again, as at the time just prior to Mary Brewster's entering the bank's employ, it was the ordinarily unimportant position of assistant bookkeeper which was its cause. When Cummings brought about Mary's appointment he thought he had, as he expressed it to Hall, piloted the ship into smooth water. That particular storm was weathered, he believed. He was mistaken; the storm had risen again and was now as threatening as ever.

Captain Fred Donald's wife's cousin, one of the two former candidates for the assistant bookkeeper's place had, fortunately, found employment with a Brockton furniture house, so he was eliminated. Mrs. Bradley's nephew, young Henry, was, however, still desirous of working in the bank. And—this was the new and irritating complication—Allie Jones was eager to return to the desk he had quitted in Mary's favor. Allie was not happy with the Boston bankers, or they were not happy with him—or both. He was a relative of Mrs. Small, whose husband was a director, one of the Donald faction, and the settled conviction of that faction was that anything greatly desired by the group headed by Captain Sam Freeman and backed by the powerful influence of the widow of the ex-president, Captain Eleazir Bradley, was wrong.

Jones was pleading to return to the Wapatomac National Bank. Mrs. Small was certain he should do so, and whatever she wished her husband found it sound judgment to wish likewise. His opinion was shared, as always, by Cahoon and Captain Fred Donald. They had not the least fault to find with Mary Brewster's bookkeeping, but they shared the conviction of most of Wapatomac that she did not really need the position, that she had taken it merely for fun. If she knew that Jones wished his old place again, Small was sure she would be glad to resign in his favor; he said so in board meeting. But Mrs. Bradley had heard of Allie's desire and had summoned Captain Freeman to council. If there *should* be a change, if any one were to take Mary's place, her nephew must be that one. So when Small proposed Jones, Captain Sam, backed by Colton and Baker, countered by insisting upon Henry. And once more David Cummings held the balance of power and again he was fighting to avoid open rupture, and the news of the disagreement from becoming public property.

This was, of course, his reason for telling Mary that her remaining in the bank for at least a week or two longer would be of help to him. Neither the Small nor the Freeman faction would go so far as to order her dismissal. What the leaders of each side hinted in private conference with him was that he, Cummings, as president, should tactfully explain the situation to Mary, who would, naturally, understand and be glad to resign in favor of the right person, the latter being Jones or Henry, according to which side was arguing its cause at the time. And this Cummings would not do.

"I worked like a deck hand to get her to come to this bank," he said. "And you fellows all agreed her helpin' with our books would be a wonderful thing for the bank. How can I go to her now and tell her to get out, when you know that we haven't got a particle of fault to find, but just want to chuck her to let somebody else in? I can't—and I won't. Of course you can go to her yourselves, but if you do—well, then I guess likely you'll have to get a new president along with your new bookkeeper, that's all."

He told Captain Freeman that and Freeman was, as Cummings expected him to be, very much disturbed. He snorted in disgust.

"That *would* be like choppin' down the mainmast to save reefin' tops'ls, wouldn't it!" he exclaimed. "We'd have a fight on about a new president then. Come, come, Dave! be reasonable. Nobody wants you to fire Mary—at least none of my crew do; the old Harry himself couldn't tell what Fred Donald and Small and their gang may want. What I'm tryin' to say is that you just drop a hint in Mary's ear and she'll settle it herself. See if she don't."

"Yes," dryly. "Well, Cap'n Donald was around yesterday beggin' me to drop the same kind of hint so it could be settled his way. If Mary Brewster should lay down her pen and walk out of our door this minute the only thing settled would be that the fight had just commenced to begin. Be reasonable yourself, Sam. That's all I ask."

Freeman was scowling.

"Well, well!" he grumbled, impatiently, "you needn't get mad about it. Look here, Dave, you're bull-headed enough about what you won't do. Is there anything you will do? Come now."

Cummings' answer was prompt.

"I say do nothin' for the present," he declared. "Let things slide and I shouldn't wonder if they calmed down. Allie, now, he might be offered a good place somewhere else. He *might,*" with a wink. *"Then,* if Mary should leave, why, there wouldn't be likely to be any objections to Jim Henry, would there? You might tell Emma Bradley I said that, if you feel like it."

Captain Sam grinned. "I'll tell her," he agreed. "I don't know what course you've set in your own mind, Dave," he added, "but you're steerin' somewhere, I can see that. . . . Darn the women!" getting up from his chair. "They're behind this fuss, just as they were behind the other one. My wife is as good a woman as ever lived, but when it comes to taking sides and sticking up for her relations she's as stubborn as Hulda Small or Emma Bradley or any of 'em. And we men have to take our orders or else we're in hot water at home. Good thing if we were all old baches like you, Dave. . . . Say, speaking of the like of that, they tell me Peter Hall isn't wearin' out the Brewster doorstep the way he was a spell ago. The women are all clacking over that now."

The interview with pompous Captain Donald had been almost a replica of that with Freeman, except that, to the former, Cummings had hinted of the possibility of young Henry's having some other position offered him which might cause him to withdraw his name as candidate. And

Captain Fred had chuckled over this and agreed to wait another fortnight before passing the Jones claim.

A fortnight, however, was but two weeks and, although David Cummings might now count upon that as a period of truce, hostilities were but deferred, not ended. Mary had put off the acceptance of her brother's offer; Freeman and Donald had agreed to wait; so much was satisfactory. And much might happen even in two weeks. David had already written letters to business acquaintances in Boston and Providence asking if any of these acquaintances knew of an opening for a likely young fellow. It was his idea that, should he learn of such an opening, he might transfer the information to Henry or Allie Jones. If one of the two could be tempted into accepting employment elsewhere his complex problem would become a simple one. Then, should Mary leave the bank, he was certain a majority of the board would vote for the remaining candidate. Of course, should Mary definitely decide to reject Ben Brewster's alluring proposition and wish to remain as assistant bookkeeper, he, Cummings, would fight for her to the final gun. His threat to give up his own position if the directors took open action against her had been in the nature of a "bluff," but there was truth behind it. If they did a thing like that, in the face of his opposition, they could elect a new president, and be hanged to them.

He did not, however, consider that extremity a likely one and so did not worry about it. After Peter Hall had stalked from the directors' room, he wrote more letters to other business friends and the necessity of finding a good job for a young chap of his acquaintance, and finding it at once, was stressed in each of them.

He wrote another letter also. Denver was one of the

western cities upon the list he had handed Philander Cahoon the day before. And Philander had, as requested, returned the list with the name of the bank's correspondent in each city written opposite that city's name. David Cummings' letter was addressed to the Denver correspondent. In it he asked for confidential information concerning one Benjamin Brewster who had, until recently, resided in that city. Information concerning Mr. Brewster's record, character, credit, anything and everything. Promptness in reply would be considered a favor. He dropped all the letters in the post office as he walked to the wharf after leaving the bank.

The week which followed should have been for Mary a much more agreeable one, both at the bank and at home, in the old Brewster house. It had begun badly enough. Benjamin was ill and Mr. Hall has been intensely disagreeable that one morning. But Ben's indisposition lasted only a few days and the cashier had not again taken her to task, either personally or by proxy. He was still frigidly formal and loftily superior, but she could laugh at that. Her estimate of him now was that he was a narrow-minded little pomposity and she lost patience with herself when she remembered she had once considered him a valued friend. As long as he did not criticize nor publicly insult her she was happy in having as little to do with him as possible.

But it seemed that she was destined no longer to be entirely happy inside the walls of Wapatomac's financial institution. Apparently, as one disturbing element was removed, another took its place. Peter Hall, for some unexplained reason, had ceased to annoy her, but now it was David Cummings whose behavior was strange.

Cummings did not, of course, find fault nor publicly humiliate her, as the cashier had done. But he avoided her altogether. Yes, he did. Once before she had fancied him doing that very thing, but this time it was more than fancy, she was sure of it.

He had been so kind, so friendly and considerate, during their interview in which she broke the news of her half brother's wonderful proposition. If he had been irritated and vexed with her for thinking of giving up the position he had worked so hard to obtain for her she would have understood and found an excuse for that feeling. But he had not. He had even told her that he was inclined to feel she should accept and that she would do so, he was almost certain, in the end. She had expected him, as the days passed, to call her to the inner office and ask her if she had yet made up her mind concerning her problem. He did not; in fact he seldom sent for her at all; usually, when he did ring, it was to summon Bennie Jackson or Mr. Cahoon. She began to wonder if he had been hurt and offended, after all. Why should he behave so oddly? She was remaining at her desk because he had asked her to do so, as a personal favor. One might expect him to be more than ever friendly on that account. And her mind, even yet, was not made up. She would have liked to tell him so, to consult with him further, but he never gave her the opportunity. He was offended—that must be the reason. And he had no right to be; if anything he should be grateful to her for yielding so graciously to his wishes.

His behavior was the one unpleasant item connected with her work. And her half brother was, by his good nature and patience, offsetting this at home. He was unusually kind and better tempered than he had ever been, to her. He had, at the time she announced her further postponement of the decision, been resentful and almost angry. Now he appeared to have forgotten the matter; at least he never referred to it. Once, when she herself did so, he shook his head.

"You must decide for yourself, sister," he told her. "I thought it all out pretty thoroughly while I was lying up there in bed, wondering if those doctors were right and that I really had come to the end of my rope, and I decided that I must not let the least atom of personal consideration on my part weigh in the balance. You must decide. And when you do you must tell me, that is all."

She was touched. She laid her hand upon his.

"Thank you, Ben," she said. "I shan't keep you waiting much longer, I promise you that."

She was ashamed of herself for having kept him waiting as long as she had. Nor was she quite certain why she did so. Usually she had little trouble in making up her mind on any point, no matter how important. She had a will of her own, like her father before her, and prided herself on using it. Now she was as absurdly vacillating as Elvira Bradley, of whom Azure had remarked that she couldn't make up her mind what kind of cake to choose at the church supper till the kind she finally decided on was all gone. What *was* the matter with her?

The second week of the promised two or three began and drew nigh to its Saturday. She had not spoken more than a dozen words with David Cummings during that week. On Friday noon, however, Cahoon was out and when the president's bell rang she felt obliged to answer it.

"I don't suppose you wanted me, Captain Cummings," she said, as she faced him across the directors' table. "Mr. Cahoon isn't here. I'm sorry."

He smiled. "You'll do first-rate, Mary," he said. "This is what I'd like done, if you can spare the time."

She listened to his instructions, which were brief, and turned to go. Then, acting upon impulse, she turned back.

"Captain Cummings," she demanded, "what have I done that you don't like?"

He stared in amazement. "Don't like?" he repeated. "Why—why, nothin'. I don't know what you mean."

"I think you do. Are you angry with me because I am going to leave the bank?"

He raised his hand to his hair. "Oh!" he said, after a moment. "Then you are goin' to leave?"

"I think I am—yes, I haven't told Ben so, but I think I shall before long."

"I see. Well, I supposed likely you would. I don't blame you at all."

"Why do you say that?" resentfully. "Of course you blame me! You have scarcely spoken to me since I told you about it. I tried to explain how important it all was and then—yes, *then* you seemed to understand."

"I did understand. I do now."

"Oh, don't pretend! You know how very important this was to me and how undecided I was, and how I counted upon you as the one friend who would give me honest, unselfish advice. I thought you had given me just that, and then it seemed as if you had. And now—yes, ever since—you have been as indifferent—you haven't asked a question about it, you— Oh, well! never mind! I have hurt your feelings, I suppose, and I am very sorry. But—well, mine are hurt, too. . . . Which is ridiculous. . . . I will give these papers to Mr. Cahoon when he comes in."

He had risen from his chair. "Wait!" he ordered. "Wait, Mary! I can't have you sayin' that to me. It isn't right."

"Oh, I know I shouldn't say it. You are my employer and I am only a clerk. I forget that sometimes."

She was at the door but he strode from behind the table and caught her arm.

"And that is worse than the other," he said, very earnestly. "That you *mustn't* say. I realize—I guess nobody could realize it more than I do—that I'm no more fit to be your employer, as you call it, than a fo'mast hand is to be cap'n of a yacht. That is, in one way I ain't. I'm rough and I haven't got much education and—well, you're a Brewster and I'm a Cummings, which is all that needs to be said in this town. But you mustn't say that I've ever taken advantage of my job and yours to—to treat you as if—as if—"

She broke in. "I don't say it," she said, repentantly. "And I'm sorry I said what I did a moment ago. I knew you didn't mean it that way. You have been wonderfully patient with me and wonderfully kind. I shall never forget it, no matter where I am."

She reached for the knob, but still he detained her.

"And I—I'm terribly sorry if I've hurt your feelin'," he went on, his voice shaking as his own feeling got the better of his usual restraint. "I wouldn't do that for the world. I have—yes, I have kind of kept out of your way since you and I had that talk because I was afraid of—afraid of myself—afraid I'd say more than I ought to. You've had a fine offer made to you and I—I'm selfish inside, I guess—and when I'd had time to think it over I realized that I'd said too much already. I coaxed you into stayin' here these extra weeks just because I—well, mainly because I couldn't bear to let you go. It seemed as if I couldn't, that's all."

She was gazing at him in astonishment. Never before had she seen him like this. He was usually so calm, so deliberate in speech and manner.

"But you told me my staying another fortnight would help you, would help the bank," she faltered. "That is what you said."

"Yes, I know I did. And it was true, too. It does help the bank, it has helped it already. But, just the same, when I sat down and looked myself in the face, I knew that wasn't the real reason, the whole reason, anyway. The plain fact was that I wasn't man enough to give you up to anybody—your brother or anybody else. . . . There! that's the truth. I know what you must think of me."

He could not know, because she did not know, herself. She was not at all sure of his meaning. She was silent, and he, after an instant's pause, went on.

"Just selfishness, that's what 'twas," he said. "So, when I made myself see how selfish it was, I decided I wouldn't risk talkin' with or seein' you any more than was just needful. If I did I might weaken again and keep on standin' in your light and doin' or sayin' something which would work against your best interests. I was accused of doin' that and it made me mad, at the time. 'Twas true though; I see it now."

She did not understand, of course.

"Accused!" she repeated. And then again, with rising indignation, "Accused of standing in my light and working against me! You? Who said such a wicked thing? Oh! Was it—was it Mr. Hall?"

He shook his head. "No," he replied, with an attempt at a smile. "No, 'twan't Peter. Peter don't accuse folks of much, not out and out, not your kind of folks, anyhow. . . . Never mind who it was. 'Twas true enough."

She looked at him steadily. He avoided her look.

"I can't imagine who it could have been," she said, slowly. And then: "Captain Cummings, I don't understand all you have just said, but—but I am sure now that you aren't offended with me; that you haven't avoided me because you were angry."

He shrugged. "You can be sure of that much," he agreed. "Yes."

"And—and am I to understand that you now feel sure I should accept Ben's offer?"

He drew a long breath. "Yes," he said. "Yes, I can't see any good reason why you shouldn't. In fact," more firmly, "I guess likely you'd better, Mary. It might be best for—for all of us."

"But the bank? You said—"

"Never mind the bank. That don't count at all."

"But you—yourself? You told me you needed me here?"

"I thought I did. But that doesn't count, either. . . . There! Now perhaps you'd better give those papers to Philander."

All the rest of that day Mary's thoughts were far removed from the books of the Wapatomac National Bank. They were concerned with other matters and were a curious mixture of relief, doubt, and other, and much stranger, misgivings. That evening Benjamin led her from the supper table to the sitting room and, as always when he had something important to say, closed the door.

"Sit down, Mary," he began. "I have heard some things to-day—I had heard some of them before but I heard more this afternoon—which I think you should know. They concern your—our good friend Dave Cummings, and, in a way, they concern you, too."

She turned toward him. "What?" she asked, sharply. "What do you mean? What have you heard?"

The shadow of the lampshade fell upon her face and she was thankful for it. His speech was so exactly in line with her thoughts. And yet, he could not mean—

"I am going to tell you," he said. "Cummings, I'm afraid, is in trouble with his directors there at the bank. Oh, yes, it is true! And, in a way, my dear, you are involved."

Before she could ask another question he went on to explain. He told her of the disagreement in the board, of Jones's wish to return to his former position, of his strong backing, of young Jim Henry's renewed fight for the place and who was behind him. The name of his informants he did not disclose, although he intimated there were more than one.

"Cummings, of course, is standing firmly for you," he added. "The others seem to think you don't need the trifling salary you are earning—which of course you don't—and that you would really care very little if you gave it up. But Cummings—I suppose because he got you the place—is fighting hard to keep you in it. A fine thing for him to do, but perhaps a little impolitic. At any rate, the resentment against him is growing. I have even heard—I don't imagine there is much truth in it—that his own position as president may be contested next year if he remains stubborn. Now that is bad, very bad, isn't it?"

She gasped. "Oh! Oh, why didn't he tell me?" she cried. "He didn't say a word of all this."

"He wouldn't, naturally. He wouldn't, because he's a stubborn sort of fellow—personally I admire him for it—and the others don't mention it to you because they are your friends and are afraid you may misunderstand their motives. . . . Oh," with a laugh, "it is all two-for-a-penny stuff and couldn't happen anywhere else, but Wapatomac has been like that ever since I can remember. So far the row has been kept quiet, but it is bound to get out soon. And then—well, almost anything may happen then. You see what I mean, sister?"

She saw plainly enough. "Oh, why didn't he tell me?" she said again. "Then you think, Ben, that it would help him, help Captain Cummings if I resigned now, at once?"

"Don't you think it might?"

"I—I don't know. You see, he told me it would help him if I stayed a while longer."

"Yes? But don't you imagine he thought you wanted very much to stay?"

"Perhaps. But if I do leave I can't see that his trouble will be ended. Allie wants the place and so does Mr. Henry. That question won't be settled, will it?"

"Not immediately, I suppose. But one thing will be

settled and I think it will help us all. Mary," with a snap of his jaws, "I'm ashamed to tell you what I have heard is being whispered about town, but I must. There is a whisper that this man Cummings is—well, very keenly interested in you, personally. That he—humph!—may be hoping to have better luck than the late unlamented Hall."

She sprang to her feet. Her face was crimson. She looked at him and then, turning, walked to the door. He was there before she could open it.

"For heaven's sakes, sister," he pleaded, "don't think *I* believe such rot. I'm not an absolute fool. He, old Barney Cummings's son, and you—well, I should laugh if I didn't feel more like committing murder. I thought at first I wouldn't mention it, but— Don't go! Don't be angry with me, please."

She brushed him aside. "I am not angry with you," she said. "Good night."

He saw her at breakfast, but she was silent and spoke scarcely a word. That evening, however, she spoke and to the point.

"I resigned my position to-day, Ben," she said. "I am through at the bank. I shan't go back there again."

He came to her side. "And that means," he asked, "that you are going to accept the offer I made you?"

"Yes, Ben."

"Good! Good! Why, the old Brewster house is coming into its own again. Kiss me, sister. I am happy. . . . Aren't you?"

"I ought to be. Yes, I am happy."

CHAPTER XIV

MARY BREWSTER'S entering the employ of the Wapatomac National Bank caused at the time of her doing so a very real sensation in the town. Her leaving that employ caused little or none. The expected had happened, that was all. Two-thirds of Wapatomac had prophesied that she would "get sick of working for a living" after the experience ceased to be a novelty, and although there was some chuckling over the fulfillment of the prophecy, few were greatly surprised. There was considerable speculation as to who would be her successor as assistant bookkeeper, but that question was soon answered. Ten days of uncertainty and then Allie Jones reappeared in his native village and announced that he was to resume his former duties.

"They sent for me," Allie explained confidentially to bosom friends, "and I judged they needed me pretty bad, so I thought maybe I'd better come back. I ain't complainin'. No, sir-ee! Boston's all right enough, but it ain't like Wapatomac. If anybody brags to you about the city bein' the only place for a risin' young fellow you can tell 'em I say there's nothin' to it. There's just as good chances right here in a growin' town like this one, if you've got the stuff in you to take advantage of 'em."

The Jones statement was not taken very seriously, for it was the general opinion that Allie was thankful enough to get back. The bank officials and its directors had little to say—publicly, that is—on the subject. Peter Hall's answers to questions were curt but satisfying. "Miss Brewster decided to leave us and Jones was anxious for his old job. So we took him on again, for a while, anyhow," said the cashier.

This statement was true, so far as Hall's knowledge went, but there was more which he did not know. Cummings' letters to his Boston, Brockton and Providence friends had—one of them, at least—produced results. The very day when Mary announced her resignation came a letter from a Providence brokerage firm saying they had an opening for a young man of the sort Cummings described. The next afternoon, Sunday, David drove to Bayport, saw young Henry and, after exacting a promise of strict secrecy, told him of the opportunity which, so the captain explained, he had "happened" to hear of. Jim Henry took the Monday morning train to Providence and, when he returned home on Wednesday, he had accepted the position there.

There was indignation in the Bradley household when he broke the news to his Aunt Emma. She had a good deal to say about "ingratitude" and "not knowing your own mind for a week at a time," also she was particularly desirous of learning why he did such a thing without telling her a word beforehand. His explanations concerning the need of haste were not too graciously received. She declared he had made her look perfectly ridiculous before "that Fred Donald and his crowd" and that never again might her nephew expect help from her, no matter if he were crawling to her on his knees begging for it. As his new salary was to be considerably larger than that which he might have received from the Wapatomac bank Henry saw no reason why he should ever approach his aunt in that uncomfortable posture. Mindful of his promise to Captain Cummings he did not tell her how he learned of the Providence opportunity.

So the board meeting the following Saturday ended peacefully. When the president explained the immediate need of some one to help Cahoon with the books and suggested that, maybe they might as well hire Allie Jones and be done with it, the Bradley faction—through its leader, Captain Freeman—acquiesced and Allie's appointment was confirmed. Captain Sam even went so far as to pat Cummings on the back when the meeting had adjourned.

"I'm almighty glad *that* wrinkle is ironed out, Dave," he said. "Far as I'm concerned I'd just as soon have Allie here as anybody else. So long as Jim thought he wanted the job and Emma and my wife and the rest of 'em was bound he should have it, I had to fight for him, of course. I hate to see Fred Donald and Small strutting around all puffed up and vainglorious, but I can stand it, I guess. It didn't work out, though, just as you and I thought it might when we had our talk, Dave, did it? Queer that it should be Jim Henry instead of Allie who got another job. This is a funny world and you can't count too much on what's liable to happen in it."

Cummings gravely agreed that you could not.

"No," said Freeman. "But sometimes," with a grin and a wink, "you can help to make it happen. Mind you, Dave, I ain't asking whether you helped this to happen or not. So long as our board meetings stop being Kilkenny cat fights, I'm contented."

So David Cummings' problem—that problem—was

settled and settled with far less disturbance than he had dared hope. Jones was not likely to be a perfect bookkeeper, he never had been, but he would do for the present. And Mary had settled her own problem and he had no honest reason for doubting that she had settled it for the best, so far as she was concerned. When the reply to his letter to the Denver banker came it contained nothing of marked discredit to Benjamin Brewster. Brewster, so the letter said, had lived in Denver for a number of years. When he first came there he had been in the book business—merely a book agent, some people said, though that might not be true. Then he married the wealthy widow of a retired silver mining magnate. He gave up his book business shortly after his marriage. He and his wife had a fine home, but were seldom in it. They traveled a great deal. When she died—she was older than her husband—the house and the other real property were sold. Soon after that Brewster had left Denver.

"From what we can learn," the letter continued, "and of course that is not much on such short notice, the Brewsters did not mingle with the best society in the city, the exclusive crowd, that is. Mrs. Brewster was a good, honest woman, so they say, but not too cultured and her manners and English were more useful than ornamental. Her first husband was decidedly self-made, a rough-and-ready old-timer, and she married him before he got his money. But, in spite of this, she seemed to have been more popular among their acquaintances than Brewster himself, although his manners are particularly good and he is a very interesting talker. The only definite thing we have heard against him, and that is gossip and not really definite, is that he was a high liver and something of a gay boy in his day. For a year or two he has been under the doctors' care and in a pretty serious condition, at least that is the story. They had no children and Mrs. Brewster seems to have had no near relatives. Her husband must be a rich man, if he inherited all his wife's property. That is all we have learned so far. If we learn more we will, of course, communicate with you."

David read the letter carefully and then reread it. Ben Brewster had been a "gay boy" in his day. Well, Cummings had guessed that already. And he had married an elderly widow for her money. That offense was not in the penal code. Nothing in all this to back a shadowy doubt, certainly nothing warranting honest counsel against accepting such a proposition as had been made to Mary. Cummings was thankful that he had stifled his distrust and prejudice and had been honest with her. Nevertheless, the letter was disappointing. Perhaps it should not have been, but it was. The captain was no Sunday-school book hero, no paragon of perfection. He was a man, with a full share of human failings. He had taken a dislike to Brewster the first time they met, in the office of D. Cummings & Co. Subsequent meetings had increased the dislike. And now he was disappointed and chagrined to learn that Benjamin was no more, nor less, than he professed to be.

And he was not satisfied even yet. He knew men, he prided himself on knowing and judging them. And he knew fish—that was his business. And there was something fishy about Ben Brewster. Yes, sir, there was!

He tore up the letter and threw it in the wastebasket. Then he walked up and down the directors' room, thinking.

And the result of his thinking was not flattering to his self-respect or his common sense. His principal reason for disliking Brewster was that he was jealous of him. He had begun to dislike Hall for the same reason. And he had—or he was afraid he had—said enough to Mary, in that one interview when she had accused him of resenting her even considering leaving the bank, to let her glimpse the other feeling behind the jealousy.

He tugged savagely at his hair as he thought of it.

She had been cool and very brief in announcing her resignation. She had given him no chance to argue, even if he wished to do so. She said merely that she had definitely decided to accept her brother's offer and thought it best to leave the bank at once. She thanked him for his kindness, expressed a hope that he would soon find some one to take her place and had gone away. Well, at least, he had said no more foolish things. He had forced himself to be as business-like as she was. And business-like he would be from that moment on. The Brewsters should trouble his thoughts no longer. He would put them both from his mind.

So when Benjamin next visited the bank and Cummings happened to meet him, Captain David's greeting was pleasant, if rather offhand. And Ben's was more than that. He mentioned the weather, chatted of town happenings and seemed to have forgotten altogether his short and snappy call at the Cummings' home. That he had not forgotten, however, was proven by his final words before leaving with the roll of bills Cahoon handed him in exchange for a check.

"I say, Cummings," he said lightly. "I'm afraid I let my temper get away from me that evening over at your house. I was half sick and unfit for human society, I guess. Just forget it, will you? Wouldn't have hurt your feelings for the world, of course."

David nodded. "Oh sure!" he said. "Don't worry about that. It takes somethin' important to hurt my feelin's. I'm busy these days."

Mr. Brewster had taken pains to inform his friends among Wapatomac's elect of his decision to become a permanent resident of his native town. "Sister and I have decided that the place for Brewsters is in the house where Brewsters have lived for a hundred and fifty years," he said. "It is her house, of course, but she is good enough to ask me to share it with her. Considering what a crotchety creature my various ailments make of me at times she is something of a martyr, don't you think?"

Of course no one thought anything of the kind. Shrewd guesses concerning the arrangement between the Brewsters were made, and some of these guesses Benjamin did not contradict, although he would say nothing definite. Mary was even less communicative. But it came to be generally understood throughout Wapatomac that, although the old Brewster house was, of course, Mary's property, it was her half brother's money which would hereafter pay its bills. A wonderful arrangement for them both, said the Bradleys and Freemans and Bakers and the rest of the élite, but particularly wonderful for Mary.

"It is perfectly splendid for you, my dear," said Mrs. Bradley. "I can't begin to tell you how delighted all your real friends are to see you out of that bank, where you never did belong and back here again in your own lovely home. I am sure your dear mother must be happy up where she's gone to know things have turned out as they have. And we all think you brother is one of the finest men that ever lived. You ought to be proud of him and of course you are. And grateful, too."

Mrs. Phoebe Carleton, who always had an opinion of her own, was not in entire accord with that of the majority in this case. She called one afternoon when Benjamin was out and she asked some pointed questions.

"It's not my affair, Mary," she said, "and you can tell me to mind my own business whenever you like. But are you sure you haven't made a mistake? Just why did you do it!"

Mary explained. She told her old friend what she had told no one else except Captain David. To her surprise Mrs. Carleton had apparently heard it, or most of it, before.

"Yes," she said, "that's just about the story as it came to me. Ben is to run the house and pay all expenses, and when he dies, if he dies before you do, you are to be his heir. Yes, I have heard that."

Mary was astonished and annoyed. "Why, how could you have heard it?" she demanded. "I have never told a soul, except Captain Cummings. He didn't—no, I am sure he didn't tell you."

Mrs. Carleton smiled. "Indeed he didn't!" she agreed. "Dave Cummings knows how to keep his mouth shut. If he didn't know that he wouldn't be where he is to-day. No, he hasn't told any one, you may be sure of that."

"But he was the only one who knew . . . except Ben, of course. I can hardly believe *he* would tell."

"Probably he didn't really tell much. You can drop a hint here and there and raise a surprising crop of fact and fancy in Wapatomac. And you think you've acted for the best, do you, Mary?"

"Why, don't you?"

"I hope you have. Only—well, I gloried in your spunk when you went to work in Dave Cummings's bank. It was a brave thing to do, and, to my mind, it proved you had a good deal of your father's grit and common sense. I liked your father, Mary. . . . Well, he's gone, so we won't talk about him. . . . Now, you see, even if this new arrangement turns out to be as lovely as it looks for you, you've lost one thing by it, that's your independence."

Mary resented this, perhaps because it was precisely the thought which had so long delayed her acceptance of Ben's proposal.

"I don't see that I have," she said, defiantly. "I was working for others there. Here I am in my own home. I can do what I please."

"Provided it pleases Benjamin. . . . Now, now, don't be cross. I shan't let you be, that's all."

"But I am, rather. I can see that you don't like my brother. Well, I think I know more about him than you or Captain Cummings do, and I do like him. And, as for losing my independence, I tell you now, Mrs. Carleton, that I haven't lost it. And I don't propose to lose it. . . . Why do you smile?"

"Eh? Was I smiling? I beg your pardon, my dear. So Dave doesn't like Ben Brewster. Did he say why?"

"No, he didn't. But I am sure he doesn't. And I'm just as sure you don't. And if you wish to be my friend you must."

"Well, I am your friend. I haven't got a worth-while thing against Ben, nor against this plan of his and yours either. Only I've lived a long while and I'm sure and certain that an arrangement like this one changes matters altogether. He isn't your visitor any more; he is—well, your partner, if you want to put it that way. . . . But there, I must run along. Kiss me, Mary Brewster, and don't you dare hold a grudge against me for doing as I'm likely to do, that is say plain things in a plain way. If I didn't like you I never should take the trouble to say them. Probably all this will work out well enough, perhaps better than well enough. If you ever feel you must talk to somebody—well, you know where I live. And if I'm out of town—or dead—why, there's always David Cummings; talk to him."

CHAPTER XV

THE summer days and weeks slipped by. Mary became accustomed to the change in her daily routine. It was not so very different from that she had known prior to her assuming the duties of assistant bookkeeper in the bank. There was one marked difference, however; she was no longer worried over financial matters. Benjamin was faithful to the letter of this agreement. Her own income was hers, to spend as she pleased, and he never asked concerning it. With the old Brewster home, the house and grounds, he was more interested. They were Mary's of course, but he seemed to have taken charge of them. At first, before improvements and changes were made, he consulted her, asked her advice. She almost never disagreed, and perhaps because of this, he began to make them without consulting her. The house was painted, the fences repaired, the flower beds trimmed and shrubbery uprooted or planted where, in Ben's opinion, it should be. And, after a little, he began to make changes inside as well as out.

Oddly enough, it was Azure, more than Mary, who objected to these latter. She was more intimately concerned in them, of course, for Benjamin gave his orders directly to her and insisted that they be carried out. Azure's rejoicing over the fact that the wealthy and cultured relative from Denver was to live right there in the house with them "forever and ever" had been quite as great as her jubilation at Mary's giving up her work at the bank. Her manner when meeting Mrs. Noah Oaks or Roxanna Beasley or any of her New Church acquaintances was no longer defiantly apologetic. She was condescending even to the Reverend Mr. Bacon when she met him.

"Yes," she said, in answer to the minister's question, "we're all nicely, thank you. And dreadful busy. What between havin' the Bakers and Donalds and all comin' to supper and Emma Bradley or Elvira runnin' in to ask our opinion about this and that, and carpenters and hired men all over the place—well, we can't scarcely find time to set down and read a book, and you know what a loss of privation that is to *me,* Mr. Bacon. Still, I don't mind much, because this is the way it was when Cap'n Ben and his wife was alive. I said to Mr. Benjamin only yesterday, I says: 'This,' says I, 'is home again.' And says he, 'Yes indeed, Azure,' he says, 'be it ever so humble, eh!' I knew what he meant—you know how I do love poetry, Mr. Bacon—so I finished it out for him. '"Oh, give me my lowly patched cottage again,"' I says. Not that I'd call our house 'lowly'—ha, ha!"

Mr. Bacon ventured to suggest the hope that Mrs. Crisp might by this time have reconsidered her vow never to set foot within the doors of the New Church.

"That affair the day of our missionary box meeting was most regrettable," he said. "Captain Barnabas Cummings is a very good man and a great worker for the church, but he is—well, stubborn in his likes and dislikes and his experience with missionaries must have been unfortunate. He thinks, however," he added hastily, "that Mr. Benjamin Brewster is a remarkable man and he suggested my asking him if he would not speak in our vestry some evening on any subject he may chose. I understand he is to deliver an address in the First Church next month."

Azure stiffened. "Yes," she said, "he is. But there ain't any Cummingses in *that* church."

"Of course," went on the minister, diplomatically, "I came to you first with the suggestion. I thought perhaps you might use your influence with Mr. Brewster and his sister."

The stiffness relaxed a trifle. "Well," sniffed Azure, "I don't know. I did say I'd never demean myself by comin' to that church again, but I'm a Christian, I hope, and we're commanded not to lay up treasures—er—or whatever 'tis, against them who despitefully use us. I'll think it over and maybe I'll speak to Mr. Benjamin. . . . Oh, yes!" genteelly. "I'm sure we'll be glad to have you call, Mr. Bacon. Only perhaps you'd better let us know a day or two ahead. We're pretty well dated up these days."

This was at the beginning of the new régime in the old Brewster house. Now, although Mrs. Crisp was still as elegantly condescending and serenely lofty when in converse with outsiders, inwardly she was increasingly unhappy. Since Mrs. Brewster's death, and more especially during Mary's employment at the bank, Azure's rule as housekeeper had been practically supreme. Mary seldom interfered with that rule, or, if she did, it was tactfully done. Occasionally of course, she said no and said it with decision, but she seldom found it necessary to do so. Azure usually had her own way—or thought she did—and with tradespeople, grocers' boys, and scrubwomen or other "hired help" hers was the way of an autocrat.

But now her sovereignty was sometimes disputed. Benjamin Brewster was particular in his eating and he was forming the habit of supervising the choice of dishes served. As a general thing he merely suggested, but once in a while—especially when he was suffering from one of his "ill turns"—he issued orders and not always with the best temper in the world. He could be, and occasionally was, sarcastic and sneering. He required much waiting upon and very often had breakfast brought to him in his room. Captain Ben Brewster, in his day, had always risen by six, winter and summer, and Annabelle, his wife, except toward the end of her last illness had invariably breakfasted with Mary and Azure in the dining room. Doubtless Mr. Benjamin, in his Denver mansion, had not been accustomed to early rising, but nevertheless Mrs. Crisp found it irritating to be, as she thought of it, "trottin' upstairs with a passel of stuff on a tray, like a baby's nurse." And, when she did so, she would have enjoyed sitting and chatting while he breakfasted, but he did not encourage her remaining. Once he asked her pointedly if she hadn't anything to do downstairs. Azure did not like it. She might work for wages, but she did not consider herself a servant.

And, too, he seemed to be dissatisfied with the arrangement of the furniture, sometimes with the furniture itself. He ordered a new bed and mattress from Boston for his bedroom, also a new and luxurious armchair. The old maple bedstead and the feather bed and the Salem rocker with the painted flowers on the back he consigned to the attic. He did this without consulting his sister, but she did not seem to mind, at least she raised no objection. To Azure, however, every stick of furniture in that house was a part of the house, and displacing it was sacrilege. If the reproving wraiths of generations of dead and gone Brewsters had met her as she bore that Salem rocker up the attic stairs she would not have been greatly surprised.

Then he began to tamper with the fitting up of the first floor. Azure was attending a meeting of the Ladies of Honor Lodge one afternoon and returned to find the ancient haircloth sofa in the sitting room replaced by a modern and expensive davenport. Benjamin chuckled at her outcry of horrified astonishment.

"A little surprise for sister," he said. "Something of an improvement, eh! That other thing," referring to the haircloth sofa, "gave me the mollygrubs to look at and the backache to sit on. What have I done with it? Well, I sold it for five dollars and I figure that four dollars and ninety cents of that was sheer profit. Oh, we'll make the family ark moderately comfortable in time."

It seemed to Mrs. Crisp that Mary was not overjoyed when she first saw the new davenport. She did, however, agree that it was ever so much more comfortable than the old sofa. Azure wept that night. What would be the next item of discard! She, herself, perhaps. She could not believe that Mary would ever consent to her dismissal, but she might; she had not resented the unceremonious throwing out of the sofa which great-grandfather Brewster had bought as a part of the original fittings of his grand house. And Mr. Benjamin had once casually mentioned that, in his Denver home, there had been four servants. "And they were trained servants, who knew their places and kept themselves *in* those places," he had added. This was that morning when he had ironically inquired if she had nothing to do downstairs.

She said nothing to her mistress of her wounded feelings and her misgivings. But there came a day when these could be repressed no longer. Mary came back from a tea at Mrs. Bradley's to find Azure awaiting her in the hall when she opened the door. One glance at the Crisp face was enough.

"For goodness sake, Azure," she cried in alarm. "What is the matter? Are you sick?"

Azure shook her head. "No," she said.

"Then what in the world—? . . . Oh!" as the thought came to her: "Is it Ben?"

Benjamin was a trifle indisposed on that day, which was his reason for not accompanying his sister to the Bradley tea. As that function had been arranged principally in his honor, Mrs. Bradley and her daughter, particularly the latter, were greatly disappointed at his absence.

"Is he worse?" asked Mary.

Mrs. Crisp's back stiffened.

"No," she snapped, fiercely. "He ain't. He's better, I guess. Far as that's concerned he ain't never been any sicker than a man with a tender stomach who eats hot biscuits and cranberry pie for supper has a right to expect to be. He's been up and around ever since you left. . . . Oh, my glory's land, I should say he has!"

The last sentence was in the nature of a wail. Mrs. Crisp wrung her hands and looked as if she were about to cry. Mary spoke sharply.

"Azure," she commanded, "stop acting so. And looking

so, too. Stop it this minute. Now tell me what has happened."

Azure seized her arm. "You come right along with me, Mary Brewster," she ordered. "You come and see for yourself."

She led, almost dragged, her mistress into the sitting room. "There!" she proclaimed. "*Now* what do you say?"

Mary said nothing immediately. She was prepared to find almost anything in that sitting room, even a dead body. But instead there was nothing unusual there. Mrs. Crisp's patience was on a hair trigger.

"Well," she demanded. "Well! Don't you see it? Don't you—my land of glory! Haven't you missed it *yet?*"

And then Mary did miss it. The wall above the new davenport was blankly empty. There was a large rectangle where the wall paper was fresh and unfaded. The portrait of great-grandfather Brewster had covered that space, but it covered it no longer. Nor was it anywhere in the room.

"Why!" exclaimed Mary. "Where—"

Azure interrupted. She waved an arm in the general direction of the second floor. "*He* took it down," she cried, hysterically. "He did! He told me to do it and I wouldn't and so he did it himself. He—he said he was sick of seein' the damn thing glowerin' at him. That's what he called it, a damn thing. He—he's lugged it up attic and chucked it in a corner same as if 'twas a—a old rat trap. And that picture has hung there since—oh, ever since this house was built. And—and that ain't all! Oh, dear! how can I tell you what he said to me! To *me*—

when I've worked for his father and yours and—and—"

Mary put an arm about the shaking shoulders. "Sshh! Hush, Azure," she said soothingly. "There, there! You mustn't, you know. Now tell me all about it."

They sat together upon the new davenport and Azure, between sobs, told the story. When Mr. Brewster had ordered her to take down the picture and carry it to the garret and she had refused he had been very angry. He had said dreadful things, had reminded her that it was he who was paying her wages nowadays. He had added other caustic comments. He was tired, he said, of being tormented by a person who was neither a relative, an intimate friend, nor a capable housekeeper, but seemed to consider herself a combination of all three. If she didn't care to do what he told her to do, do it and keep her mouth shut, she might go. He even told her where she might go.

Mary heard it all, to the very end, her lips tightening and her color rising as she listened. Then she rose from the sofa.

"Azure," she said. "I want you to go to the garret, bring that portrait down and hang it where it has always hung. Do it now."

Azure was frightened. "But—but he said—" she faltered.

"Never mind what he said. He shan't say it again. Don't worry any more. Go and get that picture. . . . Where is he?"

"He's—he's up in his room, I guess. . . . Oh, dear! Now *you're* goin' to get into trouble. I almost wish I'd just packed my things and gone without sayin' a word."

"You are not going anywhere, except to the garret

and back again. Now run along. Mr. Benjamin is not well and he has said things he didn't mean. No doubt he is sorry already that he said them. . . . If he isn't," she added with emphasis, "he will be."

Ben, arrayed in bathrobe and slippers, was lounging in his new easy-chair when she, after knocking, entered his bedroom. He put down the book he was reading and looked up with a smile which, or so she fancied, was a trifle forced.

"Hello, sister!" he hailed, cheerfully. "Back again, eh? How was the tea? And how, especially, is the fascinating Elvira?"

She did not answer the question. Instead she took the chair opposite him and spoke her mind.

"Ben," she said. "I have just told Azure to bring great-grandfather's portrait down from the garret and hang it in the sitting room again. And I have told her, too, not to worry about anything you may have said to her. This is my house and everything in it is mine. That, unless I am very much mistaken, was understood when you and I made this new arrangement of ours. Ben, I think we had better have a plain talk, don't you?"

He did not say whether he did or not. He reached toward the box at his elbow and selected a cigar. Doctor Hamilton had strongly recommended his smoking less or, better still, not at all, but he had paid no attention to the recommendation. He lighted the cigar and laid the match on a tray beside the box. There was an empty glass also on that same tray.

"So Azure has been making trouble, has she," he observed. "That is the worst of these old family retainers, they get to think they are part owners of the place."

"Azure has been our housekeeper here for forty years. If she considers herself a part of it I don't wonder she does. I think she is, myself; at any rate she should be. She has earned the right."

Benjamin smiled. "As for that horrible portrait," he said, "it has been getting on my nerves. I can remember that thing glaring at me when I was a kid. Perhaps that was one reason why I cleared out. Come now, Mary; you don't like that—er—work of art any better than I do. I know you don't."

Mary had never admired or loved the portrait. There were times when its corpselike, waxen stare had affected her nerves. But she did not meet her brother's smile with one of her own.

"Why did you take it away without consulting me?" she asked.

He blew a smoke ring. "I did it for your good, my dear," he replied. "I knew you would never do it yourself, because you have grown up with it. Honestly, sister, it is a very good thing for you that I happened in here no later than I did. You had lived in this house, and this town, with haircloth furniture and sign-painters' portraits and Azure Crisp until you were in danger of getting to be as out of date and *passé* as they are. You are too clever a woman—yes, and too good-looking a woman, if you don't object to your aged brother's saying so—to do anything of the kind. You are entitled to live a real life in a real world. I am going to see that you do it."

She was silent. After a glance at her face, he went on. "That portrait doesn't really count of course. I was sick of the sight of it, that's all; but," with a laugh, "if you actually enjoy sitting in a chamber of horrors I'll see that it is hung up again. We won't quarrel over that, Mary, I promise you."

She nodded. "No, we won't," she agreed. "You have forgotten what I said in the beginning. The portrait is already back in the sitting room. . . . Ben, I hope we shan't quarrel over anything, but—I don't like this attitude of yours. I think I am entitled to know of changes in the furniture, and about the house, before they are made."

"Don't you like those that have been made already? Surely you aren't shedding tears over the tomb of the late haircloth sofa?"

"That doesn't make any difference. But I very much dislike your hurting Azure's feelings. You have hurt them. She was crying when I came in. I imagine she is crying now."

He seemed amused. "Really?" he asked. "Pshaw! I wish I could see her do it. I didn't suppose anything as dried up as she is had a tear left in its system. Mary, you let that woman run this place to suit herself and she runs it as she might have run it for great-grandfather Brewster. Her housekeeping and that portrait belong in the same age."

"She is as good a housekeeper as any in Wapatomac."

"Perhaps so, but," impatiently, "what does that signify? This town scarcely knows that the Revolution has ended yet."

She leaned forward. "If that is your opinion of Wapatomac," she asked quickly, "why did you come back to it—to live?"

"I came back," with increasing irritation, "because you were here. And I am living here, with you, for the same reason. I have told you that several times, I believe."

"I have lived here all my life and for twenty years you didn't know, or at least you didn't seem to care, whether or not I was living at all. I have told you *that,* at least once . . . we won't go over it again now. I have accepted your offer and we are to live together, but I do expect you to keep your half of the agreement."

He shrugged. "Half, did you say?" he repeated. "Only half? A little too generous, aren't you, sister?"

"What do you mean?"

"Oh, nothing—nothing. My—er—half, it seems, is to pay all expenses, including the salary of your beloved Azure, all the bills for work necessary to be done if this rattletrap of a house is to stand up and shed water, and to keep my mouth shut. Your half is to spend your own money on yourself as you please, and to give me the devil if I venture to make, and pay for, an improvement once in a while. I like your half better, myself."

She rose to her feet.

"If that is you feeling," she said icily, "our agreement is ended."

"Here! Wait a minute! Does that mean that you are ordering me out?"

"I am not ordering you—no. I couldn't do that now, and you know it. If it is necessary I can go, myself."

"Where? Back to the bank to your—er—dear friend Cummings? That will make it a little difficult for him, won't it? I understand there is a new assistant bookkeeper already in your place."

She did not deign to answer, but turned away. He watched her for a moment. Then he sprang from his chair and caught her before she reached the door.

"Here, Mary, Mary!" he cried. "Don't go like that. I am sorry. I didn't mean it. . . . Come now, forgive me, there's a good girl."

He put his arm about her waist. She tried to free herself, but he held her tight."

"Don't be angry," he pleaded. "Come now, don't! I am a beast. I know it. When my nerves, and the rest of me, are in this state I am not fit to live on the same earth with you, to say nothing of sharing the same house. I beg your pardon, dear."

Still she did not speak. He released his hold and stepped back. "Oh, well!" he sighed. "I can't blame you. You have borne with me longer already than I should have expected, probably. . . . I have no right to ask more of you. I thought—I hoped—but there!"

She said nothing, even yet. But she remained where she was and he took courage from that.

"You can see how it is with me," he continued sadly. "I am a wreck to-day. I am a sick man. Not that that is a real excuse for my hurting your feelings—or Azure's either, but—well, it is a fact. You ask me why I came back to live—came back to you. I have tried hard to make that clear. I thought—I hoped you believed me."

And still she was silent. He went on, his voice shaking with an emotion which seemed real enough. "I—I," he stammered. "Oh, I don't want to sound foolishly sentimental, but you might call me a sort of prodigal son, I suppose. The other prodigal had to be on the point of starvation before he turned home to the family he deserted. I wasn't starving, but I was very ill, dying or next door to it, the doctor said. My making you this proposition, our living together, was sort of atonement, in a way. I did not mean to be selfish in making it, I meant to be even generous. . . . I—oh, well! We'll forget that. What is the use? Perhaps I expected too much. More than I should expect from any one. I will go away if you wish me to."

It was the one touch which could have been effective, just then. Mary turned to look at him. He was abjectly humble and, certainly, he did look far from well. Her conscience smote her.

"You have been generous, Ben," she said, though still coldly and with reluctance. "Goodness knows I am grateful to you. You mustn't think I am not."

He waved his hand.

"I know, I know," he said. "It is all my fault. Well, I'll go."

"No, I—I don't want you to go. Perhaps I have been too—too unreasonable or oversensitive, or something. You *are* paying for everything and I do appreciate all you are doing to keep the place and this house as they should be. I didn't really care about the sofa—no, nor the portrait, very much. Perhaps if you had spoken to me before you took it down I should not have objected—perhaps I shouldn't, although I am old-fashioned, I suppose, and I do love these old rooms to be as they always have been. But when I found poor Azure so heartbroken and miserable, I—Ben, you must *not* interfere with her. Probably she isn't the best housekeeper in the world; but she is a part of our family. If she goes, *I* go. I mean that."

There was no doubt that she meant it. Benjamin Brewster sighed.

"I will apologize to Azure," he said. "Just as I apologize to you, Mary. I was in a mood—or state of health—to insult any one who contradicted me and she happened to be that one. I am very sorry. Don't worry. She shall rule the wave, as she always has. When it came to the point I could never have let her leave this house. Why," with the smile which was so winning when he wished to make it so, "she is as much a part of my memories of the old life here as that absurd portrait. They shall both remain where they belong, of course. And now you will forgive and forget, won't you?"

There was more, but of the same trend. The quarrel was over, peace reigned. Mary left the room, still conscience-smitten, but still doubtful and much troubled in mind. Her brother's last remark was an entreaty to her not to worry.

"I shall try to be more decent hereafter," he assured her. "Please tell Azure that I am on my knees to her, so to speak. . . . Oh, yes! and just ask her to be good enough to bring my supper up here this evening, will you, sister? I don't feel quite up to getting down, if you don't mind a poor joke."

So Mary departed to console and reassure Mrs. Crisp. The invalid waited until he heard her step upon the stair. Then, walking to the open window, he savagely flung the stump of his cigar into the clematis vine below. His next move was to take the glass from the tray; cross to the cupboard by the head of the bed, unlock it with a key from his pocket, take a bottle from a shelf and pour until the glass was a third full. He drank, relocked the closet and returned to his chair. There were several bottles in that closet which contained medicines prescribed by Doctor Hamilton. This particular bottle, however, was not one of these.

So the portrait of great-grandfather Brewster continued to hang where it had always hung in the sitting room. And Azure was, for the time at least, mollified and soothed by the generous, if slightly offhand, apologies of Mr. Benjamin. And that gentleman himself was for a whole week good-natured, polite and very, very agreeable.

But, as other weeks followed, and his moods varied, and he became increasingly exacting, particular as to his food and his time for rising and retiring, caustic in his comments upon Wapatomac and its people, pleasant when it suited him and sarcastic and irritable when that suited better, requiring constant waiting upon and compliance with his whims—Mary's doubts grew to certainties. She remembered only too well, now when it was too late to make remembering worth while, the fears expressed by both Captain Cummings and Mrs. Carleton.

"Things are bound to be a little different," Captain David had declared. "He'll be in command then; at least he's goin' to pay all the bills, and it is you who'll be passenger."

And it was true. Nominally, legally, the old Brewster house was hers, but actually it was her brother who commanded. And she had, in the face of these warnings from her two best friends, entered into the agreement.

She had done it with her eyes open, she had given her promise—she must abide by it.

She would; and she would not complain. Neither they nor others should know of the mistake she had made. She was proud and she was a Brewster. She had, as the captain himself might say, made her bed and she must lie in it.

CHAPTER XVI

MR. BENJAMIN BREWSTER'S address, or lecture, in the vestry of the old First Church was a huge success. It was postponed several times, owing to the lecturer's uncertain health, but at last it was given. The vestry held a distinguished audience, the very best people of Wapatomac and select delegations from Ostable and Bayport. The subject was "Art," a somewhat vague but gratifyingly uplifting topic. Some of Mr. Brewster's hearers, particularly of the masculine persuasion, were far from certain what it was all about, but they kept their uncertainties to themselves. And their wives and daughters hung enraptured upon the words which fell from the speaker's lips.

Brewster had traveled, although neither as much nor as far as some of the retired captains who listened to him. But their travels had not included foreign picture galleries and they knew nothing of the "French School" or the "Dutch School," of Rembrandt, nor Van Dyke, nor Raphael, nor Michelangelo. Benjamin's gifted tongue dealt lightly with "distance," and "handling," with "feeling" and "depth" and "touch." Elvira Bradley's virginal bosom thrilled with strange emotions as she looked and listened and Captain Eben Baker mopped his perspiring forehead with his handkerchief and whispered in his wife's ear: "Good Lord! how that fellow can wrastle the dictionary. I didn't know there was so many long words in the manifest."

The lecture was interesting and clever, even if, perhaps, a carping critic might have found it a trifle superficial. It was profound enough for those who heard it and the applause at its finish expressed genuine enthusiasm. Also it was the inspiration which resulted in the formation of the "Raphael Club," an organization which for four whole years met weekly in Wapatomac to discuss art and artists.

There was but one yellow leaf in the wreath of laurel which that evening placed upon the Brewster brow. The lecture was over and the Reverend Mr. Sampson had mounted the platform to express the thanks of the audience to the speaker, when Miss Gertrude Wise, the new teacher of the "downstairs," that is, the primary school, rose and claimed his attention. Miss Wise was young and the Wapatomac school was her first charge. She had come to the village directly from the "Edgewater Normal" and she lacked discretion. They did not teach that at the Edgewater Normal.

"Mr. Sampson," she said, while every one turned to stare at her, "may I ask Mr. Brewster just one question?"

Benjamin, himself, answered. "Certainly, Miss—er—Miss Wise, isn't it? Yes. Ask it, by all means," he said, graciously.

"Mr. Brewster, did I understand you to say that the 'Winged Victory' was in the gallery at Florence? I thought you said it was, that you had seen it, there."

Brewster nodded. "I did—and I have," he replied, with smiling toleration. Elvira Bradley's eyes flashed as she turned again to gaze at the presumptuous teacher. What was *she* interfering for? Impertinent thing! As if Mr. Brewster had time to bother with *her*. And expressions upon faces all about showed that their owners were thinking precisely the same thing. If Miss Wise saw these expressions she was, apparently, not a mind-reader, for she marched serenely on to destruction.

"Are you certain about that?" she asked. "I think—yes, I am sure that I saw the 'Victory' in the Louvre in Paris. I was there last summer, you see. Of course I mean the real 'Victory,'" she added. "There are lots of imitations."

There was a rustle throughout the vestry. Then every head turned back again to face the platform. It would be delightfully thrilling to see their Jove launch his thunderbolt.

But it was not launched. The Brewster smile faded and the Brewster face, slowly, but quite perceptibly, turned red. Benjamin caught his breath, swallowed, coughed and then managed to smile again. There was no patronage or condescension in this smile, however. It was not even a healthy one.

"I—er—well," he stammered, "I—Miss Wise, I am—er—yes, I confess you are right. The 'Victory' *is* in the Louvre. I—er—well, my locating it in Florence was a—er—*lapsus linguæ,* if you know what I mean."

If Miss Wise did know she was in the minority, but her learning did not add to her popularity. That school term was her last in Wapatomac.

Aside from this trifling, if unpleasant, incident the Brewster triumph was complete. Even Mrs. Crisp, who, in her black silk and with breastpin and transformation much in evidence, sat on one of the rear settees, gloried in the adulation poured upon one of her household. Azure's attitude toward the gentleman from Denver was no longer worship. Daily contact with an idol, especially if one is obliged to keep house for him, is likely to prove disillusioning. The gilt upon this particular idol was wearing off in spots, but those spots were still invisible to the public eye and she would have been the last to call attention to them. In Wapatomac, Benjamin Brewster was a very popular man, and his lecture added to his popularity and his reputation. He shed a new radiance upon the house of Brewster, and Azure, who considered herself a Brewster in all but name, basked in the reflected glow.

She had already conveyed to Brewster the Reverend Mr. Bacon's suggestion that he speak before a New Meetinghouse audience. He had been in one of his ill humors that day and he had dismissed the idea with an impatient "no." Now, while Wapatomac was congratulating him on his success and itself upon the intellectual treat he had given it, she ventured to repeat the suggestion, and he was much more receptive. It seemed that Mr. Bacon himself had come to him pleading that he deliver another lecture, in the New Church this time.

"My congregation," said the minister, "is, I grant you, neither as wealthy nor perhaps as cultured as Mr. Sampson's. But, for that very reason, I hope they may have the privilege of listening to you, Mr. Brewster. We can't afford to pay for such lectures as yours, but if you will help us to improve our minds and widen our horizons you will be doing a very gracious act."

This was very pleasing to hear, just as the praise he was receiving from the First Church people was pleasing, and Benjamin's objections melted. He promised to think the matter over and when Azure approached him the second time he consented. He would lecture in the New Church vestry some evening within a month, the exact date and the subject to be announced.

So Azure had the gratification of bearing the news to Mr. Bacon and she made the most of it.

"I had consider'ble of a time coaxin' him," she said, with dignity. "He wouldn't do it for everybody, I can tell you that. And I do think I'd ought to say this, Mr. Bacon. I hope and trust that you'll make it plain to Barney Cummings and Roxanna and the rest of 'em that I was responsible. Not that I want any credit, you understand, but I've had things said to me by some of that crew that hurt my feelin's. I shall come to that lecture, of course, but it's got to be understood that I ain't comin' in sackcloths and ashes. Indeed I ain't! I may be heapin' coals of fire, but that's neither here nor yonder. Duty is duty, and a primrose by the river's brim a primrose is to me and that's all there is to it."

The clergyman seemed a little bewildered by this declaration, but he departed to spread the glad news and to arrange for the sale of tickets at twenty-five cents each. The date was finally set and the subject announced. Mr. Brewster was to speak on "Beauty—What Is It?"

The day before that on the evening of which the important event was to take place he did not come down to breakfast nor to dinner. Azure carried the meals to his room and she reported that he was "all upset, growlin' and frownin' and generally unlikely." "He's sneezin' and barkin' around," she reported, "and I'm guessin' that he caught cold last night down to them billiard and pool parlors. Yes, that's where he was; Gallup's boy told me when he fetched the things from the store. That's a draughty old hole, that pool room is, and always was even in my Obed's day, and 'twas new then. He hadn't ought to be there, playin' billiards in his shirt sleeves. . . . 'Tain't a befittin' place for a Brewster to be at, anyhow," she finished, with asperity.

Mary was incredulous. "He didn't go to the pool room, Azure," she said. "He went to the Odd Fellows' meeting. He has joined the Odd Fellows, you know."

Mrs. Crisp sniffed. "Odd Fellows' meetin' was over by half past nine," she declared. "And he never got in until 'most twelve; I know, 'cause I was awake and heard him. Gallup's boy told me he saw him at the pool room, himself, and he's seen him there afore, too. He was playin' with Sidney Small and Sidney ain't much account, even if he wears tailor clothes and is cousin to a director in the Wapatomac bank. And, anyhow, that pool room has a bad name. The story is," she went on, lowering her voice, "that they sell drinkin' liquor there on the sly. Mr. Benjamin ought to be more careful, a man that everybody looks up to, same as they do him."

Mary tried to find an excuse. "There is nothing very wicked about a game of billiards," she said. "Ben is fond of the game, I've heard him say so. He had a table of his own in his Denver house."

Azure did not seem entirely satisfied. Mary thought she could guess the reason.

"Was he cross to you, Azure?" she asked, smiling. "You must forgive him if he was. A cold is likely to make one fussy and short-tempered. I hope he hasn't got one."

"Well, he has. I'll bet on that. . . . And," suddenly, "if 'twas anybody but him I'd say he had somethin' worse.

I'd say he'd been—oh, well! Never mind! Of course he hasn't."

"Wait! What do you mean?"

"Nothin' much. Only—well, don't you ever smell anything when you go to that room of his? I do. . . . And I lived with my husband long enough to know 'tain't cologne neither. Perhaps he's takin' it for his cold. Folks do. . . . No, I shan't say another word. But I'm—I'm worried, just the same. I've seen a minister's wife's own uncle go to smash from—from what I smelt."

She hurried away, nor would she wait when Mary called after her. A few minutes later Mary herself knocked at her half brother's door. He called to her to come in. She found him in the easy-chair by the open window, smoking. Pages of the Boston paper of that morning were scattered about and one section, that containing the financial reports, was in his hand. He was much interested in the rise and fall of the "market," in fact, laughingly mentioned it as a sort of hobby of his. Frequently, when in conversation with Baker or Donald or Freeman, substantial citizens who enjoyed the thrill of occasional small speculation, he had referred to certain transactions of his own in the "Street," transactions which, due to his intuition and foresight, had resulted in profit. These more or less confidential revelations were repeated, of course, and it had come to be the accepted belief in Wapatomac that Ben Brewster was a man who had whipped Wall Street at its own game and whose opinions on such matters were well worth consideration.

Mary's first remark, when she came into the room, was concerning the open window.

"Why, Ben!" she protested. "You shouldn't be sitting

there, with that breeze blowing on you. Azure says you have a cold."

She would have closed the window herself, but he lifted an impatient hand.

"Let it alone," he ordered. "You people down here seem to think fresh air is poison. So Azure told you I had a cold, did she? If that woman could learn to mind her own business I'd raise her wages. I haven't got a cold and I don't intend to have one."

He ended this declaration with a snort which became a sneeze. His face was flushed and his tone irritable. His sister sniffed, almost without knowing that she did so. Azure's hint concerning "smelling something" in that room was alarming and—yes, there was in it a strengthening of certain vague suspicions of her own. Several times during these recent weeks she had fancied detecting a peculiar odor in that room when she visited it, and once, when her brother came home late from a walk down town in the evening, it had seemed to her that his speech and manner were a trifle confused and queer. She had dismissed these fancies as ridiculous and unworthy, but the disquieting suspicion had remained, nevertheless.

The breeze from the window was rustling the newspapers on the floor and the bedroom was sweet with the perfume of clematis from the blossoms outside. There was nothing suspicious in that smell, certainly. Benjamin drew his bathrobe closer about his shoulders.

"I suppose you trotted up here to see if that Crisp woman was right, didn't you?" he queried. "Well, she isn't. Where have I been to catch cold, for heaven's sake?"

Mary shook her head. "I don't know, unless it might

be the billiard room," she suggested. "You were playing there with your coat off last night and perhaps—"

He interrupted. "Who told you that?" he demanded, sharply. "What's all this? Can't I even play a game of billiards in this dead and alive place without some one running to you about it? I— How did you know I was there?"

"Gallup's boy told Azure and she told me just now. She thinks you may have taken cold there. She says the room is very draughty."

"Humph! How does she know? What else did she tell you?"

"Nothing, except that you were there, playing with Sidney Small. I'm sure I don't care, except about your health. Good-by."

"Here, wait a minute! . . . You are mad again, I see. I did think I was the only touchy one in this house, but I guess it runs in the family. Come back here and sit down. I want to talk to you."

She obeyed, though with some reluctance. He took several sheets of paper from the table.

"I've been making a few notes for that lecture of mine to-morrow night," he said. "I have been trying to get together something to penetrate the skulls of the crowd I shall have to face. Most of them are fishermen or clam diggers, I judge, so I am going to be as nautical as the deuce. You'll be surprised, Mary, to learn what an old tar I am. Wait until you hear me."

His smile of self-satisfaction was broad. She, too, smiled, but she seemed doubtful.

"You must be very careful, Ben," she continued.

"Those people know more about such things than you do. If you *should* make a slip—"

"Bah! Don't worry. There'll be no primary school-teachers showing off down there. . . . Oh," with an angry gesture, "I wish to the Lord I could get away from this bunch of narrow-minded little—er—beach crawlers and go somewhere where I could breathe in comfort. I'd like to pack up and clear out for a month. I'd have one good time, I promise you."

"Well, why don't you?" she asked, quickly. "Don't let me detain you."

"Eh? . . . No, you'd be glad to get rid of me, I don't doubt. Provided I left my money where you could reach it. . . . There, there!" leaning forward to seize her hand, "don't go up in the air. I didn't mean it. I can't go because your confounded doctor won't let me. The last time I saw him he told me I was as good as dead if I didn't stay here and vegetate. Well, he's a liar, for I'm the livest dead man *he* ever saw. . . . Oh, don't be cross, Mary. I'm sorry. The fact is I'm particularly sore to-day. If I were where I could have been in touch with the right people in the stock market I could have cleaned up fifty thousand in a fortnight. Say," picking up the newspaper from his lap, "have you noticed what has happened in the market lately? Have you?"

"No."

"Well, you should. I don't know what you've got your money invested in. You haven't seen fit to tell me and I haven't asked. I don't even know how much you've got of your own. Oh, don't be frightened," carelessly, "I'm not trying to get any of it. What's yours is yours. . . . But you haven't any Coppers, have you?"

"Coppers?"

"Yes, yes. Copper stocks. You haven't any, of course?"

She smiled. "I had some once," she said, "I haven't any now."

"What did you have?"

"Oh, nothing you ever heard of, I imagine. I had a few hundred shares of a stock called Boroda, but— Why, Ben! what in the world is the matter?"

He had risen to his feet. "Boroda!" he cried, excitedly. "You had Boroda? Where is it?"

"I sold it. They called an assessment which I couldn't afford to pay."

"Good Lord! Tell me about it."

She told of her one speculation and its disastrous ending. He could scarcely wait for her to finish.

"You sold for three dollars and a quarter a share!" he cried, fiercely. "Why, you idiot! Do you know what it is worth now? It closed yesterday at fifteen and a half and they say it will touch a hundred inside of a year. They have struck one of the richest veins in history. And you let it go for three and a quarter! Why? For heaven's sake, why?"

"I told you. I couldn't afford to pay the assessment. . . . So it was a good stock, after all, just as he said. . . . Oh, dear! Well, I didn't know, so there is no use weeping over spilt milk. It serves me right. I shouldn't have speculated at all and I never shall again, you may be sure of that, Ben."

The assurance did not seem to gratify him greatly. He was walking up and down the room, scowling and muttering to himself.

"You sold it for three dollars," he repeated. "You

gave it away, that's what you did. Yes, and whoever bought it knew perfectly well what he was doing. Did you sell on your own responsibility or did some slick swindler coax you into letting him have it?"

"No one coaxed me. I was advised not to sell, as far as that goes."

"Who advised you? The broker who bought it for you?"

"Yes. He and—some one else. The person I did sell it to told me he thought I should keep it, but I had no money to spare for that assessment. Now, Ben, don't glare at me like that. It can't be helped now. Besides, don't you imagine I am as sorry as you are?"

"Humph! Well, who was this crook who took it away from you? Some one here in town?"

She hesitated. "He was a good friend," she said, firmly. "I can't tell you his name because I don't think I should. He was anything but a crook, and you mustn't call him so."

"I'd call him worse than that if I had him here. Who was he? I want to know."

"I can't tell you. . . . And I must go now. I think you should be careful of that cold of yours. I hope you will be."

He consigned the cold to a place where cold is supposed to be unknown. "See here, Mary," he said, "have you got any more stock like Boroda? If you have, for mercy's sakes let me take care of it for you. Where do you keep your securities, whatever you've got?"

"In my safe-deposit box at the bank."

"Humph! You and I must go over them together. You have a list of them somewhere in the house, of course? Yes; well, let me see that list now. Go and get it."

She did not go. She had no real objection to his seeing the list, but she did object to his peremptory order to fetch it. And his manner throughout the whole interview had been irritating in the extreme. Then, too, the tidings of the rise in Boroda Copper, and the thought of the profit which might have been hers were unpleasant. She had a share of the Brewster family temper and she had been holding it in by sheer force of will.

"Get me that list, will you?" he repeated.

"No, I won't."

"Why not? Are you afraid *I* might try to cheat you out of something? You needn't be. I'm not like your Boroda 'friend.' I am your brother; don't forget that."

"I'm not likely to forget."

"What? . . . Oh, well, don't be stuffy. I want to help you keep what belongs to you, that's all. Go and get that list for me, there's a good girl."

"No."

"What! Why won't you?"

"Because—well, because I don't choose to."

She left the room and this disagreeable session ended there and then. Benjamin did not come down to supper and until seven o'clock the following evening he remained in his room. Azure reported that neither his cold nor his temper was greatly improved. At half past seven, however, he appeared, dressed and ready, and the trio, for Mary insisted that Azure accompany them, were driven to the New Church in a rig hired from the livery stable.

The New Church vestry was packed to the doors when they arrived. Captain Barnabas and the other leaders of the society were determined to show the First Church crowd that the latter were not the only ones who appreciated culture and uplift when these graces came their way and that no subject, even "Beauty—What Is It?", was too highly seasoned for their appetites. So the advance sale of tickets was tremendous and, as always in such cases, each buyer was on hand to get his or her money's worth.

Seats in the very front row had been reserved for the Brewster party and it was a magnificent sight to see Azure march grandly up the aisle between the tightly jammed settees. She had waited for this. Memories of her humiliation at the missionary box meeting in that very vestry were never absent from her mind. Some day, some time, she would show these people what was what, and who was who. And here was her opportunity. She was glad they were a few minutes late, proud to be walking immediately in the rear of the lion of the evening, and her greatest thrill came when Kohath Briggs, at the end of the Cummings settee, dared to whisper: "Hello, Azure! Some crowd, ain't it!" Azure looked at Kohath, and through him, and answered not a word. This was triumph. She wished she might walk up that aisle again and repeat the experience.

The Reverend Mr. Bacon escorted the speaker to the platform and, after what the county weekly described as "a few well-chosen words of esteem," introduced Mr. Brewster to his audience. The greeting of that audience was gratifying. During the hand-clapping Mrs. Crisp turned and saw Captain Barney and Kohath applauding with the rest. More glory! They knew—they must know —whose persuasion had brought Benjamin Brewster there.

They might not be willing to own up to it, but a share of that applause belonged to her. The bosom of the black silk rose and fell with a sigh of pure happiness.

The lecture began. Beauty, said Benjamin Brewster, was a vague thing, an indefinite thing, easy to locate in some instances, but permeating so much of life that the careless eye was likely not to notice it in passing. There was beauty in a great picture—yes. In a lofty mountain, in a roaring cataract, in a placid little pond at sunset, in the ocean waves beating upon the shore. All this was beauty and recognized as such. But it was not all of beauty, far from it. Beauty was in our everyday life, in our humblest tasks. Why, there was beauty even in a well-ordered room, a cleanly swept floor. The capable housewives of Wapatomac beautified the world daily.

This was a good beginning, for in that particular audience were many beautifiers of the broom-wielding variety. Mrs. Noah Oaks leaned forward to nod triumphantly at Mrs. Beasley, who returned the nod. Caleb Hammond's wife nudged her husband. Susan Hapgood, sitting next to Mrs. Simeon Bean, whispered loudly, for the old lady was, although she would not admit it, somewhat hard of hearing: "That is a lovely thought, ain't it, Mrs. Bean?" Mrs. Bean's reply was snappish. "Why don't he talk up?" she demanded. "I can't hear more 'n one word in a dozen. I didn't spend my quarter to come to no deaf and dumb show."

The lecturer, having paid his tribute to the feminine toilers in beauty's vineyard, proceeded to lay a wreath at the feet of the men. There was beauty, he said, in the labors of those who followed the sea. Who, as it was written, went down to the sea in ships. They, too, made the world a beautiful place in which to live. What was more beautiful than a fishing boat going out in the morning, the light of the dawn upon her canvas? Captain Jabez Eldridge tapped Captain David Cummings on the shoulder. "I got the answer to that, Dave," he whispered. "She is ten times as beautiful comin' home at night full of cod at fifteen cents a pound." There were indignant orders to "Sshh" all about the irreverent Eldridge person.

Mr. Brewster went on and on. And, true to his promise to his sister, he interlarded his sentences with sailor phrases and nautical metaphor. Most of these were received with favor. This particular audience did know the sea and they appreciated and understood. Once or twice when the speaker mentioned some particular sail or some point of seamanship there was a slight rustle and an old salt leaned forward to look at his neighbor with a doubtful expression, but, on the whole, Benjamin steered a safe course and avoided the more dangerous reefs and shoals. He moved on toward his peroration.

He spoke of a fine new vessel, a magnificent clipper of the old days, leaving port on a long voyage. He described her breasting the billows, her clean new canvas bellying in the wind. He carried her thousands of miles, through calm and storm, to tropic ports in southern seas. And, at last, he headed her home again. But she had been afloat too long. Above the water line she was as stanch and seaworthy as ever, but beneath that line—ah, it was different. The little creatures of the sea had been at work, unseen, undreamed of. Her hull, friends, was riddled; the millions of tiny sea worms had bored into it. They had eaten their way into her timbers. She began to leak; then came a hurricane. She was seaworthy no longer.

And so on—to her finish. "A sad tale," concluded Mr. Brewster, "but true. It is the little things of life, the little things which we are so prone to forget, to consider as beneath our notice, which count in this voyage of ours from the cradle to the grave. If there are thoughts which I would leave with you to-night they are these: First, that beauty is not alone to be found in greatness and in grandeur; second, that no beauty is so secure that it may not be destroyed, if we permit it to be. Beauty is all about us—yes, but so are the gross, the evil things. As we look above, to the towering masts, the snowy sails, the fleecy clouds, the blue sky, we must not forget that below, as those worms were gnawing the hull of that great ship, so petty trifles and ugly little commonplaces may be destroying our sense of the beautiful. And, in the end, what should have been a glorious voyage, may end in wreck. Think in terms of beauty, set your course by beauty's star, but don't forget to search for and cast out the unspiritual and the earthly. . . . I thank you."

Is it a wonder that a hush followed this "I thank you"? That that hush was followed by applause which grew and grew to an ovation? That Mr. Bacon shook the orator's hand and could scarcely find words in which to express his gratitude and admiration? That Elvira Bradley's eyes were like stars in a mist? And Mr. Brewster bowed and bowed again as the applause continued.

But there were small sections of the audience which did not applaud, where—or so it seemed—arguments were going on. And one of these sections centered about the bulky form of old Captain Barnabas Cummings. Captain Barney was, apparently, much excited. The grumble of his voice was audible in the lulls of the hand-clapping, and people were turning to look in his direction. And when the minister stepped to the front of the platform to express his own thanks and those of his congregation, he had scarcely opened his lips when Captain Barnabas opened his.

"Ladies and gentlemen," began Mr. Bacon. "I— Why— Yes, Captain Cummings? Did you wish to say something?"

Captain Barney did wish that very thing. "Just a minute, Mr. Bacon," he hailed. "I liked that speech fust-rate. Yes, I did. 'Twas fine and elegant as ever I heard. But there was just one thing I wanted to say. Somethin' kind of troubles me and I can't quite make it out. I guess likely some of the rest of us old sailors can't nuther, from what one or two have been whisperin' 'round here. I'd like to ask Mr. Brewster a question. Can I?"

Captain David Cummings, three or four rows back, stood up.

"There, there, Skipper," he said, with a smile, "don't bother with questions now. It's late and Mr. Brewster's tired. You can ask him some other time."

He sat down again, but his grandfather did not. "You be still, Dave," he ordered, irritably. "Can I ask that question, Mr. Bacon?"

The minister turned doubtfully to the other occupant of the platform. Benjamin Brewster stepped to the front.

"Very happy, I'm sure, Captain Cummings," he said. "What is it you want to ask?"

Captain Barney looked about him for support. "Some of us fellers down around here," he said, "don't quite understand about that clipper ship you was tellin' us about, Mr. Brewster. She was pretty nigh brand new, you said, and yet the worms got into her hull and et her up. Was that it?"

"Yes," with a smile. "That was—er—essentially it."

"Um-hum. Well, what we can't understand is how them worms could have got into her hull if she was coppered right. She was a new vessel and her copper 'd ought to have been new 's the rest of her. Worms can't chew through new copper, can they? I never see none that could. How about it, Mr. Brewster?"

There was a moment's silence. Then some one, one of a group of boys and young fellows at the rear of the hall, laughed. There were orders to "Hush!" and "Be still!" from other indignant listeners. "Oh, sit down, Barney!" shouted Noah Oaks, prompted by his wife. More laughter.

Mr. Brewster was still smiling. "I—er—don't know that I get your meaning exactly, Captain Cummings," he said.

"Why not? Didn't I make it plain enough? I say if this was a new ship with new copper no worms ever *I* see could get at her plankin'. . . . Let go of me, Kohath. . . . No, I won't set down, Noah. You've been to sea. You know I'm right just as well 's I do. . . . I wisht you'd explain that, Mr. Brewster."

Benjamin waved a hand. "I'm afraid I haven't time to go into that with you now, Captain," he said. "Some other time, perhaps. The hour is late."

"'Tain't ten o'clock yet. And I ain't the only one

would like to know about that. I've had some consider'ble experience with ship worms and them critters. Why, one time when I was on a tradin' voyage down in the South Pacific we—"

"That'll do, Skipper." This from Captain Dave. "That's the boy, Barney!" "Go it, old pickle tub!" from the back seats.

"I'm a-goin' to go it," defiantly. "I guess I know what I'm sayin'. Nobody can tell me how a ship's bottom ought to be coppered. And when anybody starts spinnin' yarns about worms eatin' up through a brand-new vessel's hull *I* say it couldn't happen."

"Three cheers for the worms!"

"Hooray!"

These were more back seat interruptions. The audience was in an uproar by this time. Laughter, angry commands for silence and general disorder. One of the deacons was pushing his way toward the turbulent group by the door. The minister took command.

"The meeting is dismissed!" he shouted.

Every one rose to go, but every one was talking. There were a dozen lively arguments in various parts of the hall. Benjamin Brewster, angry and keenly conscious that his triumphant evening had been turned into a joke, was pushing his way through the assemblage when his arm was seized.

"Hold on! Just a minute, Mr. Brewster," panted Captain Barnabas. "I'm sorry I started the rumpus, but I—I couldn't keep still when you told about that clipper. I'm a crank on copper, as you might say. . . . Just another second. Let me tell you what I mean."

Brewster tried to pull free, but the crowd was too great. Captain Barney was still at his elbow.

"Copper's one of the things I *am* a crank about," he reiterated. "I've kind of specialized in it, in a way of speakin'. Good copper's good stuff, that's always been my motto. And it runs in the family, I guess. My grandson, Dave, he's always been great for buyin' copper stock. Funny, ain't it? But it's so. Why, he's bought I don't know how much copper stock in his time and he's always made money by it. Other folks that had it they might want to sell, but when they did he'd always buy what they had. Course that hasn't got nothin' to do with copperin' a vessel, you might say, but what I mean is— Eh? What?"

A heavy hand descended on his own shoulder.

"That's enough, Skipper," said David Cummings, firmly. "You come home now and finish the sermon there. Sorry, Mr. Brewster. Heave ahead, Skipper! Come!"

Benjamin, in the carriage on the way home, was morosely silent. Mary, too, had little to say. Only Azure was voluble. Her finest feelings had been outraged.

"The idea!" she snorted. "That old Barney Cummings! You might know 'twould be him! After you had made such a *beautiful* speech and then he had to go and spile it all. Shovin' his 'copper' into it. Mr. Benjamin, I—"

Benjamin snapped at her like a steel trap. "Shut up!" he ordered. Then, turning to his sister, he added, with a savage sneer: "That driveling old fool is the grandfather of your—umph!—particular friend. You must be proud of them both."

Mary ignored the sneer, but she spoke the thought that was in her mind.

"I told you, Ben," she said, quietly, "that I didn't think you were wise in speaking of ships and seafaring matters to people who know so much more about them than you did. I feared you might get into trouble."

CHAPTER XVII

THE next day was Sunday and she went to church alone. Her brother's cold was no better, so Azure reported, and he did not leave his room. When Mary returned home she went out into the kitchen to speak with Mrs. Crisp, but the latter was not there. Mary came back to the front hall and, as she did so, Azure descended the stairs.

"Azure!" cried Mary. "Why, Azure! What is it? What has happened—now?"

Azure shook her head. "I—I can't tell you what's happened," she burst forth. "I—I'd be ashamed to. . . . But—but I tell you this, Mary Brewster," with desperation, "either he—that man up there—goes out of this house, or I do. I—I can't stand it any longer. No, not for your sainted mother's sake, nor yours, nor—nor nobody's. I—I am goin' to leave."

Mary tried to detain her. "Azure," she pleaded. "Please, Azure, now—"

"No! No! . . . I mean it. Don't you ask me what's the matter, neither. You—you better ask what's the matter with *him*. . . . And you needn't ask even that. You go up there and you'll see for yourself, I guess likely. . . . And *smell* for yourself, too."

She rushed into the kitchen. Mary looked after her a moment, then she went up the stairs. The door to her brother's room was ajar and she entered without knocking. He was sprawled, as usual, in the easy-chair. His face was red and, beside him, on the table was a glass, not empty this time. These things she noticed, but what particularly caught and held her attention was something he was holding in his hand. A small, leather-covered memorandum book, with initials—her own initials—on the cover. This she saw and it was of it she spoke.

"Ben," she asked, sharply, "what are you doing with that book?"

He looked up at her with a mocking smile.

"Oh, reading it, sister," he replied, airily. "Just reading it. Very interesting reading it is, too. Pity I couldn't have read it before. Might have saved the family a few dollars if I had. . . . Oh, well! may save some of them yet. You can't tell."

She would have seized the book, but he held it out of her reach.

"That is my own private memorandum book," she said, hotly. "You have no right to look at it without my permission."

It was the book in which she kept the list of the securities in which her own money was invested; the names of those stocks and bonds, their numbers, when, and of whom they were bought, or to whom or by whom some of them were sold. It had been in the drawer, a locked drawer, of the desk in her own bedroom.

"Ben," she declared, with seething indignation, "you got that book from my desk. And you must have broken the lock to get it. What do you mean by doing such a thing as that?"

He laughed. It was a foolish laugh and it, and his manner and the glass beside him, made her certain that the suspicions which she had dismissed as vague and unworthy were only too true.

"It's all right, sister," he said. "Quite all right. High time I found out a few things, you know. They've been making a monkey out of you, but that's over. Yes, indeed! They'll have a man to deal with now. They won't *wheedle* me into selling a hundred-dollar stock for three and a quarter. Not much they won't."

"Give me that book this instant."

"Wait a minute, Mary; wait a minute. Can't give it to you just yet. Want to look it over a little more before I do that. I'm the head of this family now, and nobody—no Cummings, or any other crook—can swindle my sister and get away with it more than once. No," savagely, "nor even that once without a fight. . . . Here! don't go! I want to talk with you. . . . Stop! There, that's a good girl. Now we'll have a—well, call it a family conference, eh?"

She had stopped, but only for an instant.

"I don't wish any conference with you now," she said, with cold contempt. "You are in no condition to talk with any one."

"What! . . . Here, what do you mean?"

"You know what I mean. You've been drinking. When you are sober you and I will have a conference, and one that neither of us will forget; I promise you that."

She hurried out into the upper hall and to her own room where, after closing and locking the door, she sat down before the rifled desk and tried to think, to decide what to do, to see a way out of the situation in which her own foolish trust and, as she then considered it, her stubbornness in the face of friendly counsel, had placed her. It was an impossible situation, but any alternative she could imagine was almost as impossible. An hour passed and she was still sitting there, dry-eyed, humiliated and hopeless. No one else was to blame, no one but herself. She had walked into the trap with her eyes open. How could she now, with honor, escape from it?

Captain David Cummings was, on this particular afternoon, a Sabbath breaker. Some important matters connected with his shellfish business were engaging his mind and, after dinner, he had walked down to the wharf of D. Cummings & Co. and there, at his desk in the office, he was wrestling with them. He had been there nearly three hours when, to his astonishment, the knob of the outer door was turned, the door was shaken, and, a moment later, a loud knock echoed through the rooms.

Cummings could imagine no one, except Kohath or his grandfather, who would come to that office on Sunday afternoon. They were the only ones who knew he was there. He rose and, walking through the outer room, unlocked and threw open the door. The person who had knocked was neither Captain Barnabas nor Briggs, but Benjamin Brewster.

Captain David was surprised but he tried to be cordial.

"Why, hello, Mr. Brewster!" he exclaimed. "Tracked me to my hole, did you? Well, that was smart. Glad to see you. Come in."

The invitation was superfluous for Brewster was already in the room. He had pushed by Cummings without the least ceremony. David, more astonished than ever by this rudeness on the part of one usually so very punctilious, turned to look at him. What he saw did not lessen his amazement.

Brewster's manner was not the only thing about him which was strange. His collar was rumpled, his hat was set at a—for him—careless angle, his waistcoat was buttoned awry. He carried the cane, it is true, but, instead of swinging it jauntily, he appeared to be actually leaning upon it, using it as a support instead of an ornament. And his face was more than red, it was a dark purple, with the veins at the temples standing out like rivers on a map. He was breathing rapidly—panting.

Cummings' astonishment turned to alarm.

"Good Lord, man!" he cried, stepping forward. "You're sick. Here! Here! Sit down."

He would have led him to a chair, but Brewster pushed him away.

"Take your hands off me!" he gasped, savagely. "Let me alone, you—you crook."

Captain David stepped back. The man was apparently more than ill—he was insane.

"Why—why, there, there, Mr. Brewster—" he began, but his caller would not let him finish.

"You thought you had hid where I couldn't find you, didn't you?" he sneered, still panting heavily. "Well, that's all right. I found you, damn you, I found you! Now then, you listen to me, Cummings."

With an insane man one must temporize. The captain tried his best.

"Sure, sure," he said, soothingly. "Now you sit down and we'll—"

"No. I—I wouldn't sit down in the same room with

you. I'm a gentleman and you're a dirty crook. Y' understand that? You're a crook and I know it."

Cummings' diagnosis of the situation was changing. He had been at sea, he had seen and handled many men who suffered insanity of the sort he was beginning to reckon this. He made no further effort to coax his visitor to a chair.

"Humph!" he grunted. "Humph! Well, I'll be hanged! . . . You!"

Then he remembered that the man before him was Mary Brewster's brother and the shock of the thought was overpowering. His disgust and anger vanished. He tried again.

"Ben," he pleaded, "Ben, you—you *are* sick. You come into the back room with me and—well, we'll see if we can't fix you up somehow. Come along, there's a good fellow."

Benjamin evaded him. He staggered as he did so and his hat fell off, but he did not pick it up. The sweat was standing in drops on his forehead, but he did not seem aware of it. He wheezed as he breathed.

"I tell you to keep away from me," he shouted. "You're a low-down swindler and I came here to tell you so. I've been sick and I may be sick now. But, sick or not, I walked all the way down here to let you know what I think of you. You stole my sister's stock from her. Palavered her into letting you have it for next to nothing when you know it was worth a hundred. Now I want that stock back, do you see?"

"Sshh, sshh! What's all this? Take it easy, Ben. You'll burst a boiler or somethin'."

The humor in this advice was unintentional. Cummings

was now too much alarmed to be funny. The man was half tipsy—yes; but he was more than that. He was very ill indeed. He was on the verge of—of something, the captain did not know what, except that it was serious. And the man was Mary's brother. That was the one unforgettable thought.

"Give me back that Boroda stock," shouted Benjamin. "You stole it from my sister. I want it. I—I'm here to get it."

Captain David understood then, or partially. The rise in Boroda had been extensively commented upon in the Boston dailies. He understood, and in a way, he was relieved. The fellow was not insane, at any rate.

"Oh!" he exclaimed. "Oh, yes, now I see. Well, I'm glad you came to see me about that Boroda, Ben. I'd like first-rate to tell you all about it. Come along in and we'll—"

"We'll do nothing. Understand, Cummings? Are you going to hand over that stock or—or aren't you?"

"Why, I can't tell yet. . . . Does," trying hard to make the question seem casual, "does Mary know you've come here to get it?"

"None of your business. . . . *No,*" with a snarl which would have been more fierce were it not for the gasping wheeze with which it was delivered. "No, of course she doesn't. She's a soft-headed fool of a woman and she doesn't know anything about such things. But *I* know—and—and— Are you going to give me that stock now?"

Further temporizing seemed useless with this man, in this condition. David shook his head.

"Not this minute—no, Ben," he said, firmly. "I'll be glad, as I say, to talk it over with you when you're fit to talk about anything. You're not fit now, and you know it. . . . Here! Where are you goin'?"

Brewster had turned toward the door. Now he swung back. The eyes, in the purple of his face, were congested. He gasped inarticulately.

"I—I—I—" he panted, "I'm going to—to—" He swayed on his feet. "I'm going to put you in jail by and by," he declared, with an effort. "Now I—I. . . . Ah! Oh! I—I've got to go home and—and rest."

But Cummings was at his side. "You're not goin' home now—to your sister—in this state," he vowed, with emphasis. "You stay here with me for a spell and—rest, if you want to call it that."

Brewster wriggled free. He lifted the cane above his head. Then a change came over his face, a curious change. The fierceness and drunken rage were wiped from it as if with a cloth. The cane fell from his hand to the floor. He reeled.

"I—I am dizzy," he murmured, feebly. "I—I—Cummings! . . . Cummings!"

Captain Dave sprang forward, but only just in time to catch him as he collapsed.

There were few telephones in Wapatomac at that period, but of those few D. Cummings & Co. had one and Doctor Hamilton another. The doctor's phone rang and Hamilton heard the captain's voice begging him to come to the wharf at once. Mr. Ben Brewster was there and very ill.

The doctor hurried, ran almost every step of the way. But when he reached the office of D. Cummings & Co. his services were not needed. Benjamin Brewster was ill no longer. He was dead.

CHAPTER XVIII

MARY, in her own room on the second floor of the old Brewster house was seated in a rocking chair, her aching head pillowed upon the cushion at its back, and her eyes closed. Hours of thinking and fruitless striving to plan for the future had brought only the headache and utter exhaustion. Suddenly she started and sat up. It seemed to her that she had heard an unusual sound, a stifled scream, from somewhere in the house. She listened intently. The sound was not repeated and she was beginning to think she had imagined it, when footsteps approached her door.

"Mary, Mary, are you in there?"

It was Azure's voice and there was a peculiar note in it. Mary rose and opened the door.

"Yes, Azure," she said. And then: "Why, Azure!"

Mrs. Crisp's face was white and her hands, as she extended them toward her mistress, were trembling.

"Oh! Oh, you poor soul!" she gasped. "Oh, how will you stand it? Mary Brewster, when you and I got up this mornin' we little thought—no, and he didn't neither, and why should he! Oh, Mary, I—I don't know—"

"Azure! What *is* it? Tell me."

"Oh, I can't tell you. He made me promise I wouldn't. But when he told *me*—! Dave Cummings—"

"*What?* Has something happened to—to Captain Cummings?"

Azure stepped back. "To who?" she repeated. "What in the world—? Why, Dave Cummings is the one they sent to tell us. He's down there now waitin' for you. Oh, you poor child! I—"

But Mary had pushed by her and was on her way downstairs.

Captain David was standing by the center table when she hurried into the sitting room. His face, she noticed, lacked a little of its usual color and his greeting was very grave. He took the hand she gave him and led her to the davenport.

"Sit down, Mary," he said, gently. "Yes, do. I—I've got somethin' to tell you. Doctor Hamilton is really the one who should have come, but he is—he has a lot to do and—well, he asked me to do this. Mary, you must be brave. I know you will be. You're a Brewster and the Brewsters are always plucky when it's needful. I can depend on you to be, I know."

He paused. She, too, was pale now, but she bowed her head in assent.

"I shall try," she said. "I will be brave, I think. Go on. Tell me."

He held her hand tightly. "Somethin' has happened," he said. "Your brother, Ben, was taken sick, very sick, down in my office a little while ago. He—"

She interrupted. "Wait—please," she said. "Wait, just a moment. . . . Is he—is Ben—*dead?*"

He nodded.

There was an interval of silence. He was watching her anxiously but, to his relief, she did not cry out nor even exclaim. Her pallor deepened, that was all, and, for an instant, she closed her eyes. Then she said, quietly: "Tell me about it, please."

"But—but don't you want to wait? Can't I get you a—a glass of water—or anything? Shall I call Azure?"

"No. . . . No. Tell me. I want to hear."

He did tell her, of Benjamin's unexpected call at the office of D. Cummings & Co., of his odd behavior, of his own conviction that the man was ill, of his attempts to calm him, of Brewster's sudden seizure, of his almost instant death.

"I telephoned for Hamilton right away, of course," he went on, "and he came as soon as he could, but Ben had gone when he got there. A sort of shock—apoplexy, the doctor thinks. Hamilton is there with him now. They'll bring him home here in just a little while. Somebody had to come and tell you and—and, well, it looked as if I must be that one. I've made a poor job of it. I knew I would."

"No, you have been very considerate. I am glad it was you who came. Thank you, Captain Cummings."

He did not speak immediately, he did not dare try. A moment later, however, he attempted to express a little of his feeling. His voice shook.

"I can't say what—what I'd like to say to you, Mary," he stammered; "what ought to be said at a time like this. I do wish, though, that you would believe I'm dreadfully sorry for you and— Oh, pshaw! that doesn't mean anything, they'll all say that. . . . What I'm tryin' to say is—what I *hope* you'll believe is that I want to do more than say, I want to really help, if I can. Isn't there somethin' I can *do?* Anything in the world? Just tell me what it is and it will be done. You know that, don't you?"

She smiled wanly. "I know," she answered. "I know what a friend you are, Captain Cummings."

"No, no! Don't talk so. I haven't done anything yet, and I want to, the Lord knows. Can't I do anything now, this minute, Mary? Can't I?"

She did not answer. Then she turned and looked him in the face.

"There is one thing you can do," she said, "and I am sure you will. You haven't told any one—any one at all—of my brother's—of Ben's condition when he came to see you this afternoon? You haven't told any one that?"

He started and stared at her in alarmed consternation. "Why—why—" he stammered. "I—I don't know as I know what you mean, Mary."

She broke in. "Oh, yes, you do," she said. "Of course you do."

He was speechless. She did not wait for him to reply.

"He has been drinking a good deal of late," she said. "I hope—yes, I think that I—and Azure, of course—are the only ones who knew of it. Doctor Hamilton may have guessed, but he will say nothing. You see," pathetically, "I am still a little proud of the family name. You haven't told any one, have you, Captain Cummings?"

Cummings was greatly agitated. He seized her hand again. "No, no, no," he vowed, "of course I haven't. And I shan't. . . . I mean I shouldn't even if it was so. Probably it isn't so, Mary. He was awful sick when he came there and—and—"

Her steady look was too much for him. He did not

finish the sentence. She withdrew her hand and rose from the sofa.

"Thank you again," she said. "By and by, some day, I shall wish to talk with you again about—all this. I think I know why he went to your office and I can imagine some of the things he may have said to you. Oh, never mind," quickly. "I can't speak of them now. Perhaps I shouldn't have mentioned them at all. You see," with a lift of a hand to her forehead, "I can scarcely realize that he is—is dead. . . . Now perhaps you had better go. There is so much to be done and," with a shuddering glance toward the window, "at once—now. . . . I am grateful to you for—for everything, Captain Cummings."

Wapatomac's older residents will still talk, if asked, of Benjamin Brewster's funeral. The whole town talked of little else for a fortnight after the ceremony. His death, so sudden and so entirely unexpected, created a tremendous sensation. The news spread from Gallup's store to all four corners of the township, and beyond to Bayport and Denboro and Ostable. The county weekly did not depend upon its local correspondent but the editor himself came to the old Brewster house for particulars and a biographical sketch. The Wapatomac lodge of Odd Fellows called a special meeting, passed resolutions and voted a floral tribute. So did the Knights of Honor and the Red Men. The trustees of the First Church also met to resolve and deplore and order flowers. The deacons of the New Meetinghouse, memories of the lecture on "Beauty—What Is It?" fresh in their minds, followed suit. Captain Barnabas Cummings himself put the motion to purchase "a wreath or harp or somethin' that will do us proud and that will take the wind out of the sails of them First Churchers with their 'Gates Ajar' piece, or whatever 'tis they 've ordered."

Captain Barney had forgiven the deceased for his error in the matter of the protection of a ship's hull. "He was dead wrong there," declared the old man, "but I don't hold it against him now that he's dead himself. I said to Dave that very evenin', I says: ''Twas a first-rate lecture, take it by and large, and Ben he'd have made port with it if he'd overhauled his copper.' That's all I said then and I ain't sayin' even that now that he's been ordered aloft."

The parlor and sitting room and dining room of the old Brewster house were crowded with mourners. People were sitting in the hall and even on the stairs. The coffin was half buried in flowers. The "Gates Ajar" sent by the First Church trustees stood at one end of the bier and was commented upon as "perfectly lovely," but the huge anchor selected by the New Church committee, headed by Captain Barnabas Cummings, propped against the opposite end, made it almost insignificant. All that forenoon Azure had been rushing to her mistress with the news of the arrival of another "set piece" or "another great big box from Boston full of the loveliest callas and things." Azure was wild with excitement. Her resentment against Benjamin Brewster while he lived was a bygone as she gloried in the tributes paid him and the Brewster family, after his death.

And Mary, in her room above, the only one of that family left in this world, was beginning to realize something of the popularity which her half brother had won in the community to which he had so recently returned. Envy and petty criticism seemed to have been forgotten. She listened with something like amazement as the Reverend Sampson delivered the eulogy. Benjamin Brewster had been a successful man, a high-minded, sincerely honest man, a gracious gentleman, a patron of the arts, a kind brother, a public-spirited citizen, a deep religionist. His short residence in his native town was a pattern to remember, his sudden taking off by an inscrutable Providence a calamity beyond human understanding. "Sad indeed for us, his friends and associates, but for the dear sister upon whom the blow falls heaviest a loss irreparable."

She wondered what David Cummings, who of course was also listening, and who also knew a little of the truth, was thinking as he heard all this. And Doctor Hamilton —he, too, knew. There were times when she was on the point of smiling. Even Ben, himself, might have smiled, and yet he would have graciously accepted it as his due. This was precisely what he had striven for all along. He might sneer at Wapatomac and its people in private, but in public he had never missed an opportunity to gain their favor.

Then she remembered that he was dead, that, after all, he was her father's son, and therefore, according to all that humanity deemed fitting and proper, she should forget his faults, remember his virtues and be grief-stricken. But the words "high-minded" and "sincere" recalled recent happenings and, in the light of these happenings and the disclosures they had brought, they sounded hypocritical, ridiculous. Azure Crisp, sharing the room with her, broke down and wept under the spell of the speaker's eloquence. Mary looked at her in wonder. How could she?

The great crowd, afoot, or in buggies and democrats and carryalls, followed Benjamin Brewster to the cemetery, left him there and dispersed. And at a hundred houses that evening the dead man's praises were chanted.

Azure chanted them, during the late and hurried supper in the Brewster dining room. It was a perfunctory sort of meal, for they were very weary. Azure poured the tea and looked sadly at the vacant place where Ben had been wont to sit on the occasions—infrequent of late—when he had chosen to eat with them.

"Just think of it!" she observed, with a mournful shake of the head. "Only think, Mary! He'll never sit at this table any more. It don't seem possible, does it?"

"No."

"Well, we'll have his memory, that's a great comfort. *We* know what a man he was. Nobody knew him the way you and I knew him. I'm proud of that."

Mary looked at her. Apparently there was no sarcasm behind this statement, it was made in all sincerity. She did not reply. Azure went on.

"And when I think of that funeral," she declared, "I vow I'm satisfied—yes, I'm satisfied. I only wish he could have lived to see it, himself. When I saw that great crowd pourin' into the graveyard all I could think of was the 'Burial of Moses' in the Fourth Reader.

> *"And when the warrior dieth*
> *His comrades in the war,*
> *With arms rehearsed and muffled drums,*
> *Follow the funeral car.*

"There wasn't any car, of course, but I was so thankful the new hearse got here in time for him to be the first one to use it. That's a—a kind of precious thought for us, ain't it."

"Is it?" absently.

"I should say 'twas! And when I heard all those lovely things Mr. Sampson said about him I kept noddin' my head. '*This,*' thinks I, 'is beautiful to listen to, and so comfortin'.'"

Mary leaned back in her chair.

"Azure!" she exclaimed.

"Eh? . . . Yes, that's what I thought. And to see all the folks who came! Folks from Bayport and Ostable and even the Badgers from way over to Harniss. And the best kind of people. Bradleys and Donalds and Bakers, and Lawyer Baxter—oh, everybody! Mr. Peter Hall was standin' right close to the grave. I hadn't seen him nigh to for ever so long. He did look so sad."

Mary rose, impatiently. "Oh, Azure, don't!" she protested. "Peter Hall hated my brother. They scarcely spoke when they met. And when you say you are proud because you and I knew Ben better than any one else, it is— Oh, you know what it is as well as I do."

Mrs. Crisp gasped. "Why, Mary Brewster!" she cried, aghast. "How can you! With him scarcely laid in his grave! It—it isn't decent."

"It's more decent than the other thing. At least it isn't dishonest. . . . There! I am going to bed and so must you. We are both tired out. Good night."

Azure shook her head. "I know you're worn out, poor thing," she said. "Well—we must forget all the bad—if there was any—about Mr. Benjamin and just remember the good. That's the duty laid onto us. And he's left you all he had in the world. You're a rich woman now, Mary. We ought to remember *that,* if nothin' else."

It was what Wapatomac was beginning to remember. And talk about. Just how the knowledge that Mary Brewster was the sole heir to her half brother's fortune became public no one seemed to know exactly. Mary had never mentioned it except to David Cummings and he, certainly, had kept the secret. Jonathan Baxter, the Ostable lawyer who drew the will, had revealed its contents to no one. Possibly Ben, himself, had dropped hints here and there, or, just as probably, people had guessed and talked and the guess had become a conviction. At any rate, it was now a universally accepted fact. Mary had inherited goodness knew how much money and was a very rich woman.

Callers were very frequent. Wapatomac's "best people" came to express sympathy, to assure her of their devotion and friendship, and, in almost every case, before leaving they expressed gratification at the thought that the Brewster money was to remain in Wapatomac, the town where it belonged. Mrs. Emma Bradley was almost tearful in her expressions of satisfaction.

"It's such a comfort," she declared, pressing Mary's hand. "I knew your dear mother so well. And your father, too—yes, and his father and mother before them. And they were so proud of the Brewster name and of this place and—and all like that. And—I can say it now, though I couldn't say it as I wanted to before—your friends, all your *best* friends, the right kind of people, were *so* troubled and worried when you went to work in that bank. Of course, my dear, we understood you were doing it just for something to do, as you might say, but still we were worried for fear—well, for fear— Oh, you know what I mean, Mary. And now that worry is all done away with. Poor Benjamin has been taken from us, and the loss of a man like him is something we never, never can be reconciled to; but you are spared and so there'll be a Brewster left. And left in the condition a Brewster ought to be in. Of course I don't know whether the upwards of a million that is being talked around is true or not, but—"

She paused here. Mary's answer was no answer at all and, therefore, unsatisfactory.

"Must you go, Mrs. Bradley?" she said, rising from her chair. "Thank you very much for calling."

Mrs. Bradley rose also, but not with alacrity. "I shall run in almost every day now," she gushed. "And just as soon as you feel able to get out at all, you must come and have supper with Elvira and me. Yes, indeed, you must. Only," lowering her voice, "you must be careful how you mention—er—*him* in front of Elvira. Poor child, this has been a terrible shock to her. She—he and she—well, there's no use talking of such things now."

Baxter, the lawyer, came to the Brewster house the day after the funeral, discussed with Mary business details, her brother's will, the settlement of his estate, payment of outstanding bills, and the like. She was only too glad to leave all such matters in his hands. He went away, promising that she should hear from him as soon as he had anything to tell her. A large estate like this, with property, a good deal of it doubtless located in the West, could not be adjusted, nor even estimated in a day or two, but he would do his best. In a fortnight, certainly, he should have something, even if not very definite, to report.

But, apparently, he did not have even that. At all events she did not hear from him. By the end of the third week she was becoming a trifle uneasy. The household expenses she was now paying with her own money—she had been able to save a little from her income of late; but other and unexpected bills made their appearance on the first of the month. Bills for repairs in the old Brewster house had not, all of them, been paid. Carpenters, the local plumber, and the Ostable paperhanger sent in memoranda of sums owed them. Purchase of the new davenport had not been, evidently, a cash transaction. A Boston furniture house sent a statement and a request for payment. Mary was troubled. She wrote to Baxter, explaining the situation. His reply was brief. She must wait a little longer, another week perhaps. There were matters connected with the estate concerning which he had, so far, been unable to obtain satisfaction. Meanwhile, simply as a precaution, he advised her to be careful in expenditures.

What could that mean? Her vague uneasiness was changing to alarm and a dread of—she could not imagine what. The lawyer knew she needed money to pay those bills, she had made that plain in her letter. Benjamin had been a wealthy man, his income, she knew, had been large and his checks came regularly. And all he had possessed was now hers. Why then, should Mr. Baxter urge her to be careful? Was the estate involved in some way? Had other heirs, hitherto unheard of, put in claims? She had read of such things in the papers.

On an evening of the following week the lawyer drove

up to the Brewster gate. Azure admitted him and Mary was awaiting him in the sitting room. His greeting was cordial, but when, after Mrs. Crisp's departure, he rose and closed the door leading to the hall and turned again to face her, she knew that what he had to tell was not pleasant news.

"Well, Miss Brewster," he began, with a poor attempt at a smile. "I am here at last. Of course you have wondered why I did not come sooner."

She nodded. "Yes," she said.

"Yes. Well, you see, I—" he hesitated, faltered, frowned, and began again. "This settlement of your half brother's affairs is—well, it has proved not as simple as I expected it to be. The will itself was so very plain and direct that I thought. . . . Humph! Suppose we sit down and talk this over. Shall we?"

She rose and so did he. Her gaze was fixed upon his face and he seemed to find it hard to meet.

"You see," he went on, after a moment of silence, "I—Ah well! this is going to be hard for both of us. Miss Brewster, you must be prepared for a surprise and—a disappointment. I hate to have to say this, but I must because it is true."

"Please don't keep me waiting any longer than is necessary, Mr. Baxter. There is something wrong with the will, I suppose. Your letter made me suspect there might be. What is it?"

"There is nothing wrong with the will. The will is all right. I drew it myself. The trouble is— Pshaw! Miss Brewster, did your brother show you that will?"

"Yes."

"Did he explain—did he say anything definite as to the

size of his property? Tell you what he owned or how much he owned or anything like that?"

"No. He told me that his income was more than ten thousand a year, that was all. And it must have been. Checks came to him regularly. He deposited them in the bank here."

"Yes. Yes, all that is true. His yearly income was a trifle over ten thousand. But—"

"But what? Do please tell me."

"It ended at his death. It came to him under his wife's will. She left a certain sum in trust to him. He was to have the income from that sum while he lived. Aside from that—well, to make the mean story as short as possible, I haven't so far been able to find that Benjamin Brewster had any property of his own at all. He had a liberal income from that trust fund while living. Now he is dead and—"

He waved his hand.

Mary spoke not a word. He waited a moment, but still she said nothing. He sighed.

"There!" he exclaimed. "Now you know the worst, the very worst. And perhaps it may not really be as bad as it seems. I am still investigating—and hoping. I am as surprised as you are. I can't understand—"

She motioned him to silence. "Please," she begged. "Let me think—I can't see— Oh, are you *sure?*"

"I am beginning to fear that I am. And yet of course, as I say, there may be some mistake. I certainly hope there is."

The hope was so faint as to be negligible, his expression showed that. She drew a long breath.

"He had nothing of his own?" she murmured. "Nothing at all?"

"Well, so far—"

"Wait! I can see you are sure he did not. And yet he came back here to Wapatomac—to me—and— Why did he do that, Mr. Baxter? Why?"

The lawyer shook his head. "That is the greatest puzzle of all," he admitted. "I confess I can't understand his doing that. . . . That is, I couldn't, but Captain Cummings seems to think—"

She interrupted. "Captain Cummings!" she repeated. "Captain David Cummings? Does he know? Did you tell him, Mr. Baxter?"

"No, no, of course I didn't. I haven't told any one but you, and shan't. The fact is—well, Captain Dave seems to have known this, or feared something like it for some time. He drove over to see me day before yesterday. It appears that sometime ago—before you left the bank, I judge—he wrote to a friend, a business acquaintance, in Denver, and asked for information concerning Mr. Brewster. Why he took it upon himself to do this I can't imagine and he didn't tell me. Possibly your brother may have asked some favor at the bank and he—"

Again she broke in. "I think I know why he did it," she said. "I had told him of Benjamin's offer to me and asked his advice. . . . Never mind that. Go on."

"Yes. Well, Cummings' first letter from the Denver banker contained nothing important in Mr. Benjamin's disfavor. It told a little of his life out there, of his marriage to a rich widow and so on. He was supposed to have inherited all her property and to be very wealthy. But about ten days ago, after your brother's death, a second letter came. The Denver man had made, or had had made, a much more thorough investigation. It seems that— Humph! I don't know that you will care to hear this, Miss Brewster. We are expected to speak nothing but good of the dead."

"Oh, don't!" wearily. "I want to hear everything, of course."

"You should, I suppose. It is the sensible thing to do. Well then, it seems that—"

He went on and at length. Benjamin, according to the information in the second letter, had lived a wild life. There were stories of various dissipations, tales of gambling, of fast horses and ladies quite as fast and even more expensive. At one time his long-suffering wife had contemplated divorce. Then his health broke, there was a reconciliation, and the pair lived together until her death.

"But," continued Baxter, "even though she took him back and waited upon him by inches—she worshiped him, so Cummings's friend says—she did have sense enough to change her will. She left him amply provided for during his lifetime, but she obviously did not trust him beyond the ten thousand a year and she did not give him the handling of her property, nor the disposal of it. Now that he is dead it all goes to hospitals and that sort of thing. There! that is the truth, according to Captain David's correspondent. What little I have so far been able to learn bears it out. I am trying to learn more, and shall soon, of course. It may be that—"

Again she lifted a hand. "All this doesn't exactly answer my question," she persisted. "Why did he come back here to Wapatomac? To live here with me? The rest I can understand, I suppose. And it isn't as hard to believe as you may think. For some time— But why did he come here—to me? That I *can't* understand, Mr. Baxter."

The lawyer nodded.

"I couldn't understand it either," he confessed; "but Cummings seems to think he does. Mr. Brewster was in a wretched state of health. He was a very sick man indeed. The doctors had warned him over and over again that he could live but a short time and not even that unless he—well, changed his way of living entirely. And—all this was in Captain David's letter—it seems that he was not popular out there. His wife's friends would have nothing to do with him. His own crowd he could not associate with—and live. He needed constant nursing, attention, comfort, and all that. He believed he could have all these in Wapatomac in this house, with you, and at a comparatively low figure. Denver had, as you might say, thrown him out. Here was a safe berth, a comfortable home, and—well, you and your housekeeper to take care of him and pamper him like a sick baby. And he could come back here and be a big man in his native town. So he did. And, by George, he was a *great* man! If you don't believe it ask any one in Wapatomac. They are holding praise services over his grave yet. . . . Bah!"

His true feelings had got the better of him and he snorted in disgust. Then he remembered that he was saying these things to Ben Brewster's sister and he hastened to temporize.

"Probably I ought to be more careful," he explained. "I don't know all this. Perhaps it isn't more than half true. You *were* his only near relation and he may have—"

He stopped for, to his astonishment, he saw that she was smiling.

"I see," she said, with bitter contempt. "Then it is your opinion—yours and Captain Cummings'—that he was simply a thoroughly selfish, heartless hypocrite. He needed a sentimental innocent to give him a home and take care of him without a great deal of expense and he thought of me. Well, it was clever of him, wasn't it? You will admit that he was a good judge of character."

Baxter was a trifle shocked. "Oh, I wouldn't say that," he protested.

"It is no more than you have said already and apparently it is the truth. . . . Now have you any more to tell?"

He had not. He went on to say, as he had said several times before, that he did not intend to give up hope. All this, or the worst of it, might be a mistake. His investigations had scarcely more than begun. She paid little heed.

"Of course," he added, in conclusion, "even at the very worst, there should be something left. The money in the Wapatomac bank was his and he must have had *some* personal property. All that will be looked into, I promise you, and at once. . . . Miss Brewster, I do hope that, if what we fear proves to be true, it won't—er—make too serious a difference to you. I mean—that is—"

She stepped to the door and opened it. "Don't worry about me, Mr. Baxter," she said. "I shall get along. . . . Of course you won't tell others—yet?"

"Certainly not. Nor will Cummings. You may rely on that. And the moment I have news to report I shall do so. Keep up your courage."

He said good night and walked down the path to the

gate. He wondered at her bravery. He had dreaded this interview. Here was a woman whom every one reckoned an heiress, whose inheritance was generally estimated in six figures, who had had every reason for so estimating it, herself. And she had listened to the crushing news he had to tell with less outward agitation than he knew he had shown in telling it. Those Brewsters were a wonderful family. Yes, they were.

Mary stood there at the door until she heard the gate click behind. Then she turned and slowly climbed the stairs to her room.

The next morning she came down to breakfast at the usual time and, when Azure commented upon her lack of appetite, she said merely that she had not slept well and did not feel like eating. All that day, while in Mrs. Crisp's company, she was outwardly calm and cheerful. It was only when she was alone, facing the situation as it was, that her courage faltered and she was on the verge of breaking down. What should she do? What could she do—now?

And even yet it was not the crisis in her financial affairs, the questions of where she should live, and how, the bills and all the rest of it, which were racking her mind most and which caused her to clench her hands and walk up and down the floor of her bedroom. It was the blow to her self-respect, her pride—the knowledge that she had been such a silly, trusting, complacent idiot, weak when she should have been strong, and stubborn when she should have listened to the advice of others. David Cummings had more than hinted against her yielding to Benjamin's smooth persuasion. Mrs. Carleton had warned her. And—this was the worst of all—she herself had never been completely convinced, never wholly satisfied. Always, before she accepted it and afterwards, the lurking suspicion that behind her half brother's generous proposal was something covert, something hidden, had remained with her.

As she was feeling then she would not have accepted the legacy even if it had been real. The humiliating knowledge that she *had* counted upon it was unbearable. He had waved the ridiculous will before her eyes as a bait. And she had risen to it. There was no use in pretending she had not—she had. She had never given serious thought to his dying; that had been, in her mind, a very remote contingency—but nevertheless the knowledge that he had drawn that will before even making his offer to her had been the most potent factor in her acceptance of that offer. It had seemed such a generous act on his part. There had been no string tied to the legacy. Whether she gave up her position in the bank or not, whether he came to live permanently with her or not, he had made her his sole heir. It was the least he could do for the sister he had neglected so long, he said. How solemn, how close to tears he was when he said it! And all the time he was laughing in his sleeve.

She had never loved him, never wholly liked him, although for a short time, at first, she fancied she did. And of late she had begun to glimpse the cheap material beneath the polished veneer and to realize how cheap it was. She could not, now, feel sorry that he had died. It was well that he had, before all of Wapatomac came to know him as she was learning to know him. They would soon know, however. Sooner or later they would have to know—about her wonderful legacy, at least. And then they, too, would laugh in their sleeves.

Her shoulders squared and her eyes flashed at this realization. Well, they should never learn from her. And if they came to pity and offer mock consolation they would be given no satisfaction. Perhaps they might never know, after all. Mr. Baxter would keep silent; so would David Cummings. And she could—no doubt she would have to—leave Wapatomac before they found out, if they did. And, hereafter, she *would* be independent. A poor sort of independence perhaps, but real. She had traded that independence once for ease and position and money. Never again. Never again—with any one.

So, although Azure was curious concerning the Baxter call of the previous evening, Mary told her not a word. Just some matters concerning the settlement of Ben's estate, she said lightly. Azure, who would have given all she possessed, including the black transformation and the gold breastpin, to learn exactly how rich her mistress was to be, had to be satisfied with that.

"Only I do hope, Mary," she said, feelingly, "that you'll tell me as soon as you can. When folks keep askin' how it feels to be a millionaire I'd like to be able to tell 'em. This sayin' that it ain't the fittin' time to feel anythin' but mournin' and sorrow ain't as satisfyin' as I suppose it ought to be."

After supper that night another caller lifted the knocker of the Brewster front door. "Dave Cummings, come to pay his respects and offer sorrowin' congratulations, I presume likely," sniffed Mrs. Crisp. "It's high time he did, but I guess you wish he hadn't. I'll tell him you ain't feelin' well, if you say so."

Mary did not say so and so the captain was shown into the sitting room. Mary found him there, sitting as usual beneath the portrait of great-grandfather Brewster. He was, she noticed, dressed with unusual care, in what appeared to be a new blue suit. Also he was very solemn and, for him, fidgety and nervous. She closed the door after her and greeted him with a smile.

"Well, Captain Cummings," she said, "how do you do? It is a pleasant evening, isn't it?"

He agreed that it was, but absently and without enthusiasm. It was evident that he was not in the least interested in the matter and was surprised that she should be.

"I have been expecting you to call," she said.

"Oh! . . . Have you?"

"Yes. Mr. Baxter was here last evening. He gave me to understand that you and he had been—in conference."

He started and flushed uneasily.

"So I was not surprised to see you," she went on, still smiling.

He lifted his hand to his hair. "Mary," he blurted, in confusion, "I—I hope you don't think I've been interferin' where it wasn't any of my business. I wouldn't want you to think that."

"Oh, not at all. My business is every one's business just now, of course. . . . And is likely to be more so before long, I imagine."

That he caught her meaning was obvious, also that the bitterness of the tone behind her smile troubled him.

"I—I thought I ought to come," he stammered. "I wanted to come. You see—you see—"

"Captain Cummings, if you are trying to tell me how

sorry for me you are, I'd rather you didn't. I will take that for granted."

He was scrubbing his hair until it stood on end.

"But—but I *am* sorry," he blurted.

"I know. So am I, though perhaps not for the reason you imagine. Don't trouble yourself, Captain Cummings. I admit that a woman who has been the fool that I have been deserves your pity. That is true enough. But don't," sharply, "tell me you are sorry that I am not going to be rich, because that I don't wish to hear."

"It is almost too bad to talk about," he groaned. "When that Denver fellow wrote me—Baxter told you that he wrote, of course?"

"Yes."

"And how I came to write him in the first place?"

"Yes."

"That has worried me considerable. I'm so afraid you think I was buttin' in. I did it all on my own hook, and without tellin' you, but—well, I did it before you had decided to take up with Ben's offer."

"I know. So Mr. Baxter said. . . . Oh, if you only had told me! If I had known I should have waited—perhaps. I think I should, at least until you had an answer to your letter."

"But I did have one, and there was nothin' in it to warrant my interferin'. Everything in that first letter bore out what Ben himself had already told you. And the second one, the one that did tell the important things, never came until just the other day, after he was dead. I ought to have asked for more information right off, I guess. I am afraid I was too easy satisfied. My conscience troubles me about that. I'm some to blame, I know."

"Nonsense! I am the only one to blame. You know it, so why pretend anything else. Oh," scornfully, "I am so sick of pretense and hypocrisy! I am to blame. I wouldn't listen to you, or to Mrs. Carleton, the friends who warned me to be careful. The only one I listened to and believed was— *Don't* talk about it! Don't!"

He tried, nevertheless. "You weren't really to blame," he urged. "It sounded so—so plausible. And perhaps even now we're misjudgin' him."

"Hush! It is true—and it is exactly what I deserve. But, let me say this, Captain Cummings; it isn't the fact that I am not going to be rich that makes me so—so furious at him and at myself. It is because he lied to me, tricked me, counted on my doing the very thing I did do—that is what I can't bear to think of. Oh, don't you *see!* I was such a weak, silly fool. He never rang true to me, I never wholly trusted him. Yet I allowed him to— Oh, why did he do it? He needn't have. If he had come to me and spoken the truth I should have given him the home—and, I suppose, the comforts and attention he was after. If he hadn't cried over me, and talked about his love and how sorry he was for his neglect and. . . . And all the time he was laughing at me. . . . *Oh!*"

She turned with a gesture of disgust, and walked to the window. Cummings, anxiously watching her, would have spoken but she went on.

"I was beginning to find him out, of course," she said. "I was on the point of doing something—I don't know what. The very day he died he and I had— But there! What is the use of saying all this now, when it is too late? That will was the cream of his joke, of course, but it is only an anticlimax. If he had been worth millions, feeling as I do now, I wouldn't take a cent of it. . . . Yes, I was surprised when Mr. Baxter told me, but—oh, never mind! I shouldn't have been. I had learned enough about him to expect anything."

She turned again to the window. The darkness outside was dense, but she raised the shade and stood peering out into it. David Cummings gave his hair another rub.

"Mary," he asked, earnestly, "what are you goin' to do—now? Provided this all turns out the way we are afraid it may?"

She did not turn. "Do?" she repeated. "I don't know. Go to work again somewhere, I suppose—if I can. Oh, I don't expect you to give me my place in the bank. You couldn't do that anyway, and I shouldn't let you if you could. You have done enough, goodness knows. . . . Don't worry about me. Probably I shall sell this house, if any one will buy it, and go to Boston or Brockton or somewhere. I may find something to do there. Other women have."

"But I—we wouldn't want you to do that."

"It isn't exactly a question of what you or I want, is it?"

She heard him rise from the davenport.

"Mary," he faltered. She turned then to find him standing beside her. Even in her state of mind at that moment the expression upon his face startled her.

"Mary," he stammered, "I—I've been thinkin' a lot since—since I got that Denver letter and—and I've got a—a sort of suggestion to make. Will you—will you let me make it?"

She gazed at him. It must be a very unusual suggestion to cause him to change color and fidget and stammer as he was doing now.

"Why, certainly," she said. "What is it?"

"I'm goin' to tell you. It may sound crazy. I guess 'tis crazy and I'm out of my head to even think of makin' it. But—but, you see, in a way, it's—it's a sort of business proposition for—for both of us."

"Oh! For both of us? . . . Is it about the bank?"

"No. . . . It's just about us two, you and me. You see, you're all alone in the world. Well, so am I, except for the Skipper, and he's an old man. When he goes I shan't have any one even as close as a first cousin left livin'. I've got—well, I ain't what you'd call rich, but I've got somethin', quite a little you might say, laid up in the locker. It is more than I'll ever need alone. . . . I was—I was—Mary, do you suppose it's possible you could ever think of—of marryin' me?"

She stepped back. "Why—why, Captain Cummings!" she gasped.

"Yes—yes, I know. I told you 'twas craziness. But—but—well, there it is. I could take care of you—make you comfortable, I hope—and the Lord knows I'd try to be a good husband."

She did not speak. He waited a moment. Apparently he dreaded to hear her answer, for he went on.

"You see," he continued, desperately. "I've been thinkin' and thinkin' about this. I know everybody will say you're throwin' yourself away if you do it. You're a Brewster and I'm a Cummings; they'll say that, too. But they don't know—about the will and all. They'll think I'm after your money. Well, let 'em think so. If you had had the money you expected to have I never should have asked you, you can be sure of that. But now—well, you've got to do somethin'—you said so yourself. If you could do this 'twould settle things, wouldn't it? You wouldn't have to worry. You could keep this place, if you wanted to. That would be taken care of and—and so would you. Try and think of it that way, if you can."

She was trying to think, as well as she could think of anything just then.

"It's a business proposition, same as I said," he urged. "That's the way I want you to look at it. Just as—as a business offer I'm makin' to you; that's all."

She looked as if she were about to cry—or laugh, he could not be sure which. "It certainly does sound like one," she said, impulsively.

"Yes. Well, it *is* one—for you. That's the way you must consider it. Think about it for yourself; don't think about me at all."

"I should have to think of you—a little—if I married you, I should imagine. . . . Captain Cummings, I wish—Oh, please tell me why you are doing this? Why?"

"Eh? . . . Why, because I—because I've been thinkin' of you about every second since things turned out as they have. I've been goin' over and over what you would do, and who would look out for you, and—and—"

"And you were sorry for me?"

"Yes. Yes, I was. But—"

"Wait! And you thought that, situated as I am, and being quite incapable of looking out for myself, some one must look out for me. And so you offered to be that one."

"Eh? . . . No, no, Mary," anxiously. "That wasn't it. We'd—we'd sort of look out for each other; that's what I meant."

"I see. Captain Cummings, it is very generous of you. I don't know what more you could have offered, unless it was to promise to leave me all your money when you died."

"Mary!"

"I beg your pardon. You see, I recently accepted one business proposition that contained that clause. . . . Forgive me. Yours is not that kind, I know. Captain Cummings, I can't accept. Thank you very much. You are a good man, a generous, kind man, but I can't say yes. I have sold myself once. I shan't do it again."

"But, Mary, I'm not askin' you to sell yourself. You shouldn't say that."

"You're quite right, of course. I shouldn't—to you. But—no."

He looked at her for a moment. Then he turned away. Almost instantly, however, he turned back again and, to her surprise, he smiled and held out his hand.

"You'll shake hands with me?" he asked. "You won't hold this against me? We'll be friends just the same, Mary?"

She took the hand he offered. "Why, certainly, we will," she said, with feeling. "I am—really I am sorry, Captain Cummings. And I do appreciate your—your generosity."

"Sshh! It wasn't generous. It was just foolishness—or worse. I never really thought you would—could, I mean. And I suppose Wapatomac would never have got over it if you had. . . . Now, Mary, there's just one thing more that I must say to you. Forget that I was crazy enough to say the other and listen to this, please. It's about that Boroda stock of yours."

"Of mine? Of yours, you mean. I haven't any Boroda stock. I wish I had."

"Why, yes, you have. I've got that stock in my safe-deposit box now. It's in your name, same as it always was; I've never had it transferred. You see, I—well, I never felt right about that deal. Fact is, I never considered it a real trade at all. I just took it off your hands, or made believe take it, because I was pretty sure you was bound to sell it to somebody just as soon as you could and, the way the market was then, you'd have got little or nothin' for it. So I made believe buy it, you know."

"Made believe! You did buy it. You paid me for it."

"I advanced you a little money on it, that's all. You can just call that a—a loan, if you want to. 'Twas a loan, and on good collateral security, that's all 'twas. I only wish all my loans were secured as good as that one," he added, with an attempt at a smile.

She was looking at him in utter amazement.

"Captain Cummings!" she exclaimed. "What *is* this you are trying to make me do? Take back those shares I sold you? Is that it?"

"You didn't really sell 'em. At least I never really bought 'em."

"Certainly you did. And," as the thought came to her, "if you have them now you must have paid the assessment on them. You did, of course."

He was hoping she might have forgotten the assessment. "Why, I did pay that—yes," he admitted, reluctantly. "It didn't amount to much, anyhow, and I paid it along with my own. You can count that in as part of the loan, if you'd rather. That stock's worth considerable now and, although I don't know as I'd advise you to sell it, still if you do need the money right off, there'll be quite a lot comin' to you. Now what do you say, Mary? Shall I sell it for you, or had you rather hang on a little longer? If you can I'd say hang on."

She turned again toward the window. She did not wish him to see her face just then. He waited anxiously for her answer.

"Well?" he asked, after a moment. "What do you say? Is it sell—or stick?"

She spoke over her shoulder. "It is neither, of course," she said. "The stock is yours."

"No, no, it isn't. I tell you—"

"Please don't."

"But, Mary, this is important. This is—is—"

"Another one of your business propositions, I suppose. I shall have to say no, just as I did to the other."

"But, Mary, this is different, altogether different."

"Is it? . . . I confess I don't see much difference. You are sorry for me and—being you—you will make any sacrifice to help me. No, Captain Cummings, what I have done is done. Every important mistake I have made of late has been against your advice."

"Then for mercy sakes don't make another one! Mary—"

"No. No, no, *no!* . . . Oh," in desperation, "please don't argue any longer. Perhaps you had better go now. I—I'm afraid I am not equal to any more to-night. . . . You understand, don't you?"

He picked up his cap from the table.

"Why, sure! sure I do," he said. "Sho! I'm afraid I've made another terrible mess of everything. Seems somehow as if I always do when I try to talk with you. I— Oh, good Lord! Well, don't hold it against me if you can help—that other foolishness of mine, I mean. I was a little out of my head, I guess, and—well, you just forget it, please, and I—I'll try to. . . . As for the Boroda, we'll take that up a little later."

"No, we won't. . . . Captain Cummings, don't worry about me. I shan't starve. I am not an old woman yet and I can earn my bread and butter—somehow. I am not, and I don't intend to be, dependent upon charity—even such charity as yours."

"Charity! Don't talk so. There's no charity about it."

"Oh, *please* don't argue. . . . Good night."

"Good night, Mary. . . . You're sure we're goin' to be friends, just the same as if I—I hadn't made a fool of myself?"

"Yes. Oh, yes, yes! . . . Good night."

He went out. She closed the door upon him. Then, leaning against its panels, she sobbed hysterically.

The next morning, as he cleared away the breakfast dishes after David's departure for the office, Kohath Briggs spoke to Captain Barnabas.

"Cap'n Barney," he asked, "did you notice anything queer about Cap'n Dave this mornin'?"

"Eh? Queer? No, what crazy notion have you got in your head now? Why should there be anything queer about Dave, for the land sakes?"

"*I* don't know. But there was somethin' queer last night. He came home a little after ten and I was settin' here in this room readin' the *Item.* I says 'Hello,' but he didn't say nothin', just went right by me and upstairs. He looked—well, I snum he looked as if he's had a stroke of palsy or been hit over the head with a hand-spike or somethin'. What do you cal'late was the matter with him? Where had he been to; do you know?"

CHAPTER XIX

AND now, once more, as at the time when her speculations in copper ended in disaster, Mary Brewster was facing a crisis. Then, when David Cummings had called in answer to her summons and she had announced her intention of finding work of some kind, she had described her position as desperate. If it was desperate then what was it now? Then she was pinched for money—yes; but she owed practically nothing. Now she owed much, for more and more bills contracted by the late Benjamin Brewster were arriving almost daily. Apparently he had had a constitutional aversion to paying cash for anything. The tailor in Ostable sent in a bill for an expensive suit and an overcoat. Gallup's store presented an account for cigars and table luxuries. Even Solomon Jaynes, who had planted the new privet hedge, and the row of Lombardy poplars which were to shut off the unsightly view toward the henhouse, had not been paid either for stock or labor. "Mr. Ben he told me he always liked to settle his bills first of every month," explained Solomon. "He didn't do it last month, but he was goin' to this."

Very likely he had intended doing so. Mary knew that he had been expecting a check. Now that he was dead that check would, of course, not be sent. Yet the bills were there awaiting it. All creditors, the local ones especially, were apologetic. They were in no great hurry for their money. It was perfectly safe, of course. "I don't never fret much about what a millionaire owes me," commented Jaynes, with a chuckle. "I only wish you owed me more, Miss Brewster."

The Brewster account at the bank had been drawn to the last few hundred dollars. And, except for this, and Benjamin's own personal possessions, including those still unpaid for, Baxter had so far been unable to locate any assets whatever. He was still trying, he wrote Mary, but he was obliged to confess that the outlook was unpromising. The bills must be paid, they must be. No Wapatomac Brewster had ever caused an honest creditor to lose a dollar. And many of these creditors Mary had known all her life. No, they should be paid, even though the paying took the last penny she could rake or scrape. And then—what?

The worst of it, the very worst, was the fact that every one—Cummings and the lawyer excepted—rated her as immensely wealthy. She had told no one the truth, not even Azure Crisp. She would not tell—until, somehow or other, those bills were paid. And the thought of telling even then was too humiliating to dwell upon. The Brewster pride—the disgrace to the Brewster name! The things that would be said! The sneers that would follow her wherever she went! The suave, cultured and rich and dignified Ben Brewster had been a sort of god in the community. A few former idols whom he had displaced, might, prompted by envy, have sniffed skepticism behind his back, but even they had bowed low before his face. Under such circumstances, when the tin god tumbles, the chagrin and wounded self-esteem of disillusioned worshipers are bound to seek a scapegoat. Mary knew she would be that goat. The fact that she suffered most from the upset would not count at all.

She hated the thought of running away. It seemed cowardly and perhaps it was. If she could only, somehow, by hook or crook, by the strictest economy, even parsimony, remain in Wapatomac, in the old house, she would have considered nothing else. She would face the sneers and the insinuations and taunts scornfully and with a brave front. But there was no such way. When the debts were paid, as paid they should be, she would be poorer than she had ever been. She could not keep up the place. She must find work—almost any sort of work that paid—at once. Because of her own silly trustfulness and weak will she had given up her place in the bank and there was no other position for her in Wapatomac. She must, as she had told Captain Cummings, seek employment elsewhere; the city was the most likely chance.

She wrote to Bolles and Snell, the Boston bankers. Mr. Snell's reply was kindly and courteous, but perfunctory after all. There was no prospect of a vacancy on their staff at present. Of course there might be in the future, and if so—etc. Evidently he did not take her application very seriously. She wrote to other of her father's friends in Boston, in Brockton and in New Bedford. All answered and all were kind, but they had nothing to offer.

Meanwhile her days and nights in Wapatomac were becoming harder and harder to endure. Her friends, real and pretended, among the aristocracy of "Snob Town" were continually calling, running in for afternoon chats or to spend the evening. They were so sympathetic, they knew how dreadfully lonely she must be. They, themselves, could not be reconciled to the taking away of that grand man, and if they—who, after all, were only friends

—felt the loss so keenly, what must she be suffering, she who had been privileged to live with him, her own brother? Well, she had the memory of those last months in his company and a sacred memory it would always be, of course. They talked of almost nothing else—except to throw out an occasional hint concerning the size of Mary's inheritance, hints which brought them no information whatever. Mary was either tremendously dense or provokingly close-mouthed, one or the other.

"What I *can't* understand," declared Mrs. Captain Eleazir Bradley, on her return home after her third call in a week, "is why she hasn't gone into mournin' yet. There she sat, this very afternoon, wearing that same blue dress Mrs. Holway made for her a month before Benjamin died. Not a sign of black about her anywhere. It isn't decent and I was tempted to tell her so. You don't suppose she is one of those 'advanced' women who pretend not to believe in wearing mourning, do you, Elvira? She might be; goodness knows she can be stubborn enough to go her own gait if she sets out to, no matter what respectable people think. Look how she acted about going to work in that bank."

Elvira sighed. Her own spirit had been hung with crape ever since Benjamin Brewster's death.

And there were other well-meant persecutions even harder to bear. Being accounted rich Mary was asked to contribute to every possible charity, local or county. The Reverend Mr. Sampson called to suggest her increasing her annual subscription to the church. "And it occurred to me," he said, "that possibly you might wish to donate a family memorial window, or something like that. To bear the names of your father and his—er—wives and that of your dear brother, of course. It would be a gracious act. He would have approved of it, I am sure."

If the reverend gentleman could have read the thoughts in the mind of his listener just then he would have been surprised, to say the least. But, by sheer force of will, Mary kept those thoughts to herself. "All that must wait, Mr. Sampson," she told him. "I do agree with you that Ben would have approved of a memorial window bearing his name. I am quite sure of that."

She had not seen David Cummings since the evening when he made his astounding "business proposition." And she was determined not to see him, if she could help it. She did not like to think of that evening at all, yet she did think of it, over and over again. He had asked her to marry him. What would her blunt-spoken, autocratic father say—or perhaps do—if he were alive and aware of it? What would her genteel, elegant mother have said? What would Azure Crisp say if she knew? Something funny, and a great deal of it. Funny! It was all funny—in a way.

And yet, in another, it was not funny at all. She was far from laughter and much nearer to tears when she remembered that evening. He had meant to be kind—that was it; kindness and pity for her had made him say such things. The fact that he had kept the Boroda stock in her name all these months, that he considered it hers and had planned from the first to return it to her, was—well, it was amazing, but, after all, it was like him. And—yes, she might even have accepted it—in her present state of despairing hopelessness she might have done even that, if he had not put his other "proposition" first. After that she could not—she could not, of course.

Charity, that was what he offered, he had admitted that, or what amounted to the same thing. He would give her a home and take care of her as long as she lived. Precisely what Benjamin had offered. Charity—from a Cummings to a Brewster! Why— And then she remembered Ben's boastful glory in the family name. He was a Brewster, too. Very little to be proud of in *that*.

There were other feelings. Feelings which she could scarcely define and which she tried to repress. At all events she must not meet and talk with David Cummings again. She would avoid him while she was obliged to remain in Wapatomac. That would not be long. It simply could not be.

He came to the house one evening and she, fortunately, had seen him from the window. She bade Azure say that she was tired and had gone to her room. Azure was only too happy to say that very thing. Since her mistress's rise to millionairedom she was more than ever disdainful of common people like the Cummingses.

It was the next day when Mary told Azure the plain, overwhelming truth. Mrs. Crisp herself was responsible for the disclosure. Her always dignified walk was now almost a strut and her attitude toward seven-eighths of Wapatomac even more high and mighty than during Benjamin Brewster's reign. This particular morning Mary came down to breakfast, hollow-eyed, pale and with her nerves at their extremest tension. When Azure referred to the Cummings call as a "piece of impudence" the storm clouds rose.

"You'd almost think he'd be ashamed to come nigh the place," observed the housekeeper. "After the disgraceful way his grandfather behaved at that lecture—

and before everybody. If you ask me I'd say that had more to do with poor Mr. Benjamin's carryin' off than anything else. My glory's land! Standin' right up there in meetin' and hollerin' out that he knew more than the man who'd made that perfectly lovely speech about Beauty and all. I'll never forget that lecture long's I live. Whenever I catch myself gettin' tired of sweepin' or moppin' up floors, or washin' dishes or whatever 'tis, I say to myself: 'Azure Crisp,' I say, 'what's the matter with you? You're beautifyin' the world, that's what you're doin'. Ain't that enough to satisfy *any*body? Suppose you was paralyzed or crippled or somethin' and couldn't do beautiful things like this—what then?' Ah, hum! Well, it's a sustainin' thought to have a hold of, I can tell you; 'specially when you know you've got money enough to hire a dozen other folks to do the work for you, if you felt like it. And we owe it all to that poor, dear man up there in the cemetery lot, Mary. He's gone to the reward he deserves, you can be sure of that."

Mary looked up. "Do you think so, Azure?" she asked, with a peculiar intonation.

Azure was horrified. "Why how you talk, Mary Brewster!" she exclaimed. "Of course he has. . . . But, speakin' of Dave Cummings," she went on, with a characteristic quick change of subject, "I was glad when you wouldn't see him last night. You can't afford to start folks talkin' again, not in the position you hold now, you can't. You've got lots and lots of money and Cap'n Dave is as keen after a dollar as the average, he's shrewd as they make. Twice he's come to this house since Mr. Benjamin died, not countin' the time when he brought the news that he was dead. He used to come to talk business, of course; but now—well, I want you to think of that, Mary."

Mary laid down the spoon with which she had been listlessly stirring her coffee.

"Azure," she demanded, "are you insinuating that Captain Cummings is trying to get money from *me?*"

Azure turned her head. "I ain't insinuatin' anything," she said. "But your sainted mother's last words to me was—"

"I know what they were. I ought to by this time."

"Yes—well, all right. And as long as Mr. Benjamin was here to watch and take care of you I didn't have to worry. But now, when he's gone, and you are a rich woman, I—"

Mary struck the table with her palm.

"Azure," she ordered, "sit down in that chair. It is high time you heard what I have to tell you. Sit down. And keep still until I have finished."

The telling did not take long. Mary did not mince matters. At the end she rose.

"Now you know as much as I do," she said. "And I shall expect you to tell no one until I give you permission. Mr. Baxter knows, of course, and so does Captain Cummings. He came here to help me, if he could. He knows, just as you do now, that when my bills—or Ben's bills—are paid I shall have practically nothing left; oh, a little, but very little. And if I don't find work—somewhere—or even if I do, I shall have to sell this house and go away from Wapatomac. . . . There! you can think it over. And sitting there and wringing your hands and crying won't help at all. I know, for I have tried it."

She went out soon afterward and did not return until

supper time. Then Azure, a shaken, very much transformed Azure, came to her in the sitting room.

"Mary," she said, humbly, "I've been thinkin' it over, same as you told me to."

"Have you? Well, I hope your thinking has been more satisfying than mine has been so far."

Azure shook her head. Her cheeks were tear-stained and her eyes were red. "You poor, poor child," she wailed. "I don't know what to say to you."

"Of course you don't. There is nothing to be said."

"And when I think of that—that pompous, orderin'-folks-round, white-washed tombstone! . . . O-oh! *Oh!*"

"Why, Azure! I am surprised. Didn't you remind me that it was our duty to forget the bad and remember nothing but the good?"

"Good! My land of glory! If you'll tell me where the good is I'll like to have you. Comin' back here and—and cryin' all over the place one minute 'cause he loved it so, and cartin' his own great-grandfather up attic the next. *That* ought to have been enough to open my eyes to him. Well, it was—and I said so, didn't I? . . . No wonder he took to drink; I should think he would. And tellin' you he'd left you all his money! Yes, and tellin' me so, too! . . . Oh, my land of glory!" with a groan. "*How* will I ever hold up my head in front of Barney Cummings and the rest of 'em when they find *this* out?"

"There, there, Azure! There's no use making yourself sick over it. It doesn't help matters any."

"'Beauty—What Is It?' Oh, my land of glory!"

"Azure, be quiet. Is supper ready?"

"Oh, yes! It's ready. When I think of how I 'beautified' my poor tired feet carryin' his suppers upstairs to him— But there! . . . Mary Brewster, what will you do now?"

"I told you I didn't know."

"You ain't goin' to sell this house?"

"I may have to sell it—if I can."

"You shan't do any such thing. . . . Mary, I've been thinkin' this whole afternoon. You must go to Dave Cummings right straight off. Maybe he can get you back into that bank again."

Mary had reached the point where she believed herself incapable of being surprised at anything, but she was surprised now.

"Go to David Cummings!" she repeated. *"You* tell me to do that?"

"Yes, I do. Oh, I know he's that old Barney's grandson, but we're past bein' able to afford rememberin' that. All you and I must think of is savin' this house and keepin' a Brewster in it. Dave got you into that bank afore, I guess likely he could do it again if he set out to. And from what I've heard lately there might be a good chance. They say Allie Jones ain't makin' out with his bookkeepin' even as well as he did before he went up to Boston. They say—"

Mary had heard enough. She faced the housekeeper with a determined mouth, and eyes which snapped indignation.

"Azure," she announced, with compelling emphasis, "I don't want to hear any more from you on that subject. I shall *not* go back to the bank."

"Oh, why not; if you can get back, I mean? If you'll only go to Cap'n Dave and tell him—"

"Stop! I shall not go to him. . . . That is final. Now stop talking about it."

"But—but Mary! To save you from sellin' this house! For the sake of your poor sainted mother's memory. She loved this house so. And your father and your grandfather and—"

"No. Not for the sake of any one—including myself. And if you keep on tormenting me I shall go up to my room and stay there and you may eat supper alone."

So Azure urged no more that night. She continued to think, however, and the result of her thinking brought her to a determination, rash, desperate and upon the consequences of which she did not dare dwell, but which, nevertheless, she meant to carry out. And two evenings later, she again marched into the sitting room and stood facing her mistress across the center table.

"Miss Mary Brewster," she announced, "can I talk to you?"

Mary, who was reading, or trying to do so, looked up.

"I should be surprised if you couldn't, Azure," she answered, dryly. "Why, of course you may," with a smile. "Why do you ask?"

Azure did not smile. Mary waved her toward a chair, but she did not sit. She remained standing, her face wooden in its solemnity.

"I asked," she replied, "because I wanted to. Bein' as this is the last talk you and I may have, Miss Mary Brewster, I didn't want any misunderstandin's to start it with."

"The last talk. Azure! . . . And why on earth are you calling me 'Miss Brewster'?"

Azure became more stiffly erect than ever.

"I call you Miss Brewster, Miss Brewster," she announced, "on account of its bein' more fittin', as I see it. I may be out of a job when I get through sayin' what I've got to say to you and—well, there 'tis. . . . Miss Mary Brewster, I went to see Cap'n Dave Cummings this afternoon."

Mary's book slipped from her lap to the floor.

"What!" she cried. "*You* went to see David Cummings! . . . You don't mean you went to talk with him about—about *me?*"

Azure's expression changed not in the least. She nodded.

"Yes, I do," she declared. "Oh, I know what you'll say and I hadn't forgot what you said afore, but I went. I dreamt about your mother that night after you told me. I see her just as plain as I see you now. She didn't say anything, but she looked, and if ever a look said: 'Azure Crisp, I'm dependin' on you to save this house and land,' 'twas hers. I got out of bed the very next mornin' with my mind made up. 'Annabelle Brewster,' says I, out loud, I—"

"Oh, stop! Stop! . . . You went to—to Captain Cummings, when I told you— What do you mean by doing such a thing?"

Azure lifted a hand. Hers was a planned and carefully rehearsed speech and she had no intention of abbreviating it.

"'Annabelle,' says I, out loud to myself, all alone in that bedroom, 'I'll save 'em or die a-tryin'.' That's what I said and I meant it. It's a duty laid onto me, thinks I, and, as Congressman Billings said in that lovely Fourth of July speech—I'll never forget it long as I live—let us dare to do our duty providin' we know what 'tis. So—"

"Oh, Azure, *will* you stop! *Why* did you go to him, of all people? How could you when you knew how I felt?"

Azure went straight on. "I thought all that day and all yesterday, and all that came to me was the name, 'David Cummings—Dave Cummings.' Thinks I, he got her a place before; he can get her one now, if he will. And he's got to. You wouldn't go to him; you said you wouldn't even see him. So I said again, out loud to myself: 'Annabelle,' says I, 'I'll go.' And I went."

She paused. This time Mary said nothing. What could she say—now? Mrs. Crisp continued.

" 'Twas too late to catch him at the bank, so I went to his office at the wharf and I found him there. I told him just how things was with us."

"But you *needn't* have, Azure. He knew it."

"And he promised me he'd do what he could to get you back in the bank. He said he'd think it all out and have somethin' to tell you when you came to see him to-morrow afternoon."

"What! When I came to see him? You didn't tell *I* would come to *him?* Oh, you didn't tell him that, Azure?"

"I did. He would have come here to see you to-night—that's what I wanted him to do—but he didn't feel as though he'd ought to leave his grandfather. Seems the old man is sick, ate too much of Kohath Briggs's cookin' or somethin'. That," with a sudden relapse from the grand manner, "is enough to make anybody sick, I'd say. . . . Anyhow, Dave'll be at the fish wharf to-morrow afternoon at two o'clock and I promised him you'd be there. I hope and trust you will. Anyhow, my duty's done. . . . That's all, Miss Brewster. I shall be in the kitchen, waitin' your commandments whether I'm to go or stay."

She stalked majestically from the room. If she expected her mistress to call after her, or detain her, she was disappointed. Mary did not speak. Nor did she say more than was necessary when they met next morning. Azure's only solace lay in the fact that, so far at least, she had not been discharged. And when, at half past one, Miss Brewster came downstairs, dressed for the street, she could not restrain her anxiety.

"You are goin', ain't you?" she begged. "You are goin' to Cap'n Dave's, same as I told him you would, Mary?"

Mary's answer was not altogether reassuring.

"Yes, I am," she said. "He will be expecting me, so I must, I suppose. But I shall make him understand that, under no circumstances, will I go back to the bank. And that I shall leave Wapatomac just as soon as I possibly can. I don't know that I shall ever forgive you for interfering, Azure."

CHAPTER XX

DAVID CUMMINGS was not at the office of D. Cummings & Co. when she arrived there. Jim Leathers, the bookkeeper, was expecting her, however.

"Cap'n Dave is awfully sorry," explained Jim, "but his grandfather isn't any better to-day, in fact I judge the cap'n thinks he's a pretty sick man. He sent down word by Kohath—Cap'n Dave did—that, maybe, if it wasn't too much trouble, you'd just as soon come up to the house and see him there. He's very anxious you should. Said if you couldn't do that I was to let him know and he'd try and come here anyhow. He wants to see you particular, so Kohath said."

Mary stood, for a moment, after leaving the office, deliberating whether or not she should visit the Cummings house. Then she decided that her not doing so would be but a postponement of the interview which was inevitable. It might as well be gone through with then as later. So she climbed Nickerson's Hill and knocked at the side door beneath the lattice.

Kohath opened the door and bade her enter. Mr. Briggs looked more than ever like a seedy undertaker. He was wearing the shiny black suit and his long face was depressingly solemn.

"I've been kind of expectin' you," he said, bending toward her to whisper. "Cap'n Dave said you was liable to come. Have a chair, won't you?"

"What in the nation do you cal'late he wants now?" he demanded, forgetting to whisper. "Wants you to come up there. Wants to see you, he says he does."

"Wants to see *me!*"

"Um-hum. He knew somebody was here—heard the outside door shut or somethin', I presume likely—and afore he got through with me I had to tell him 'twas you. Then he ordered me to fetch you up. Says he wants to talk to you."

"But why? Why should be want to talk to me? . . . And do you think he ought to talk with any one?"

Kohath waved his long arms once more.

"No, no, course I don't," he wailed. "But he's made up his mind to, and nothin' short of a charge of buckshot could get him off the notion. If he don't see you he'll raise so much Old Harry that it'll be ten times worse for him than if he did."

"Kohath!" came the shout from the room above. "Kohath! Fetch her up. You hear me?"

"There! You see?" groaned Briggs. Mary hesitated. "I don't think I should," she said, doubtfully. "But . . . oh, well, I will."

The cold light of the autumn afternoon was streaming into the bedroom through the window, the shade of which was hoisted to the very top. Captain Barnabas, wearing a gray flannel nightgown, was propped up in bed, a parti-colored patchwork "comforter" covering the lower two-thirds of his bulky body. Mary had expected him to look like a sufferer at the last extremity, but he did not look like that at all. The color in his face might be the flush of fever, but his eyes, behind his spectacles, were bright and keen with understanding. And his greeting was sur-

prisingly casual and cheerful. Obviously his illness had not affected his brain.

"Hello, Mary," he said. "Glad to see you. Glad to see anybody, fur's that goes. I've been anchored up here in this darned bedroom, with nothin' to think about but my sins, till I'm ashamed to look myself in the face. That's why I made Kohath take away the lookin' glass. . . . Sit down, sit down. . . . Kohath, you clear out."

Mr. Briggs uttered a protest, several protests. "No, I shan't clear out neither," he vowed. "You ain't fit to be left alone and you know it."

"Well, I ain't goin' to be alone, am I? . . . Get out!"

"Look at yourself! Look what you've done! Hauled them pillows around and stuck 'em under your shoulders; just the thing the doctor said you mustn't be let do."

"Blast the doctor! Suppose I'm goin' to lay flat on my back when I've got a lady visitor? Got to show my manners, if I've got any to show—eh, Mary?" with a wink.

"And look at that tray! You ain't touched the milk! No, nor your medicine neither!"

"I will touch 'em in a second, if you don't clear out of here. I'll heave 'em at you, that's what I'll do. Milk!" scornfully. "Fetchin' me milk to drink. Be givin' me a baby bottle next, I suppose. . . . Well, are you goin', or ain't you?"

"Don't you think you had better go, Mr. Briggs?" suggested Mary. "I shan't stay long, I promise you."

"You'll stay long as I want you to—now you're here. . . . Humph!" with a grunt of relief. "He has gone, finally, ain't he? . . . Whew!" panting. "He's a well-meanin' feller, Kohath is, but he ain't what you'd call a

bracer for a sick man. Rigged up in those durned Sunday black clothes and tiptoein' around— Tut, tut! I said to him a while ago, I said: 'Are you makin' up this bed or what are you doin'?' ''Course I am,' says he. 'What did you think?' 'Thought you might be practicin' takin' your last look,' I told him. You act as if you was.' You'd ought to have seen his face! Ho, ho!"

Mary's face bore an expression almost as shocked as Kohath's must have been. The old man may have noticed it, for his next speech was less frivolous.

"There, there," he said. "Don't you mind my cackle. I've always had my joke, and there's no reason why I shouldn't have it now. Haven't got much time left to joke in. Mary, I'm glad you're here. How did you happen to come, anyway? Tell you I was on my last legs, or off of 'em, did they?"

Mary, still shocked, explained the reason for her call at the Cummings house. She and Captain David had a business appointment, she told him.

"I am so sorry you are not well, Captain Cummings," she added. "I didn't know of it—until—"

He interrupted. "Never mind, never mind," he said. "They've whistled for me this time. Oh, yes, they have! No use makin' believe. Well, that's all right. I've stuck around for eighty-odd year and that's a good sight more than the usual allowance. About time I tried some other cruisin' ground. *I* ain't findin' any fault, fur's I'm concerned. . . . It is goin' to be hard for Dave though. Dave's goin' to be kind of lonesome—yes, he is."

She tried to protest, to say something about his not being so very ill, but he would not listen.

"Don't waste your breath," he ordered. "And I can't

afford to waste any of mine. It's Dave I want to talk about—with somebody. And it come acrost me, when Kohath said 'twas you below there, that maybe you was as fittin' a somebody as anybody else. You and Dave were always pretty good friends, down there at the bank and all. Eh? Wasn't you?"

"Why—why, yes," she agreed. "Captain David has been a very good friend indeed."

"Sartin. Well, he's been more 'n that to me. If I was his father instead of his cranky old granddad, he couldn't have done more to keep me comf'table and contented. He thinks a sight of me, Dave does. And I think a sight of him. Yes, I do."

He paused. Mary made a move to rise, but he leaned from the bed and laid a hand on her knee.

"Stay where you are," he ordered.

"But, Captain Cummings, I—I don't think I should. I don't believe the doctor would—"

"Sshh! Be still! It ain't the doctor I want to talk with—it's you."

"But I'm afraid you shouldn't talk with any one—just now. It must tire you, I know."

"Rubbish! Just now is liable to be my only chance *to* talk. And talkin' with Kohath, or listenin' to him talk, tires me a whole lot more. . . . Come, Mary, do stay, to please me, won't you?"

She surrendered, conditionally. "I'll stay—a little while," she agreed.

"That's a good girl. I'll cut it short as I can. The worst of it is," with an impatient movement of his head on the pillow, "what I want to say ain't apt to sound like anything particular to you, I'm afraid. But it is particular to me—and it worries me. I don't know what's goin' to happen to Dave after I'm gone."

He stopped, apparently expecting her to speak. "Happen to him?" she repeated. "I don't understand."

"No, probably you don't. You think, same as they all do, that Dave's a big man in Wapatomac and that he's happy and satisfied. Well, he ain't. Not lately, anyhow."

"Oh, but Captain Cummings, I—"

"Sshh, sshh! Better let me do most of the talkin'. I want to get this off my mind. No, Dave ain't happy, hasn't been for a good while. I've noticed it, though I've pretended to Kohath that I haven't. You'd say he'd ought to be—well, maybe, so would I. He's made himself what he is out of nothin'. Perhaps that doesn't sound much to you. You're a Brewster and your folks have always helped boss the deck here in Wapatomac. Well, our crowd haven't. They've been, most of 'em, decent and honest and all that, and once in a while—same as with Dave—your gang has patted one of 'em on the head and give in that he's a good dog, considerin'—considerin' he was a Cummings, I mean."

"Oh, please now—that is—"

"It's the truth. You know it, same's as I do. That don't amount to nothin', either; it's Snob Town, that's all. . . . Give me a swallow of that dratted milk, will you?"

She handed the glass to him and he drank a little. Then he lay quiet for a brief interval, apparently mustering strength to resume. She watched him, her feelings divided between fear that she was doing wrong in allowing him to talk at all and curiosity. A moment later he went on.

"Now Dave," he said, "he don't mind all that a mite. He just laughs and lets 'em pat and patronize. When they made him president of the bank—not because they wanted to, but because they knew darned well he was by fifty fathom the best man for the job and they must give it to him for the good of the bank—it never puffed him up at all. He wasn't proud; seems as if he didn't have a speck of that kind of pride in him. And he's got a right to have *all* kinds—by godfreys, he has! He's done it all himself. And what have *they* done—the heft of 'em! Nothin'. Their fathers, or their grandfathers, did it for 'em, that's all. All they've done is take what was handed down to 'em. Why, there ain't a Baker nor a Bradley nor a Donald nor a Brewster—none of 'em—fit to make a splice in my boy's shoestrings. He may not be proud of himself, but, by the everlastin', I'm proud *of* him. Yes, I am."

She glanced uneasily at the clock on the table by the bed. "Really," she said, "I must go."

He caught at her skirt as she rose. "No, no," he panted; "you stay—you stay. I need you, I tell you. I—I'm wanderin' off my course, I know, but I'll get back in a minute. . . . That's it. Sit down again. . . . This—this blasted biler of mine is kind of leaky and it takes me a jiffy to get up steam again. . . . Set still and wait. . . . Humph!" with a combination of chuckle and gasp, "I've been sayin' things right out in meetin', haven't I. Cal'late I forgot 'twas a Brewster I was talkin' to. Ain't mad, are you?"

"Oh, no, no! Of course not. But I'm sure I should go."

"You stay. . . . Now about Dave. I want to stick

to him. Dave's goin' to miss me like fury. No brothers, no sisters—no anybody in this house but Kohath, and he's about as much company for a man like Dave as a poll parrot. He talks enough but nothin' comes out. If Dave had a lot of friends, but he hasn't."

She was surprised. "Oh, I'm sure you are wrong there, Captain Cummings," she protested. "It seems to me that he has more friends than almost any one I know."

"No. No, he ain't, not of the kind that count. He's got plenty amongst the other kind—my kind and what was his kind once—but they ain't his kind any more, not in the way I mean. If he'd only married a first-class woman, same as I've preached to him for years—but no, he wouldn't listen to me. Just laughed, that's all. Never seemed to care for women, he never; anyhow he didn't care for them he could have had as well as not. . . . Eh? Off my course again, ain't I. Well, what I'm tryin' to say is that all Dave has seemed to really care about was me and his business and the bank and helpin' other folks get along easier. He's done that all his life. Oh, yes, he has! I could tell you about fifty men and women that would be a hundred miles nigher the poorhouse if Dave hadn't helped 'em up when they was down. Well, now he's down, and who's goin' to help him? That's what's worryin' me."

She was really surprised now, surprised and troubled.

"Down?" she repeated. "Captain David down? Has he lost money, do you mean?"

"No, no," impatiently. "He's fixed all right, fur's money goes. That ain't it. He's going to be so all alone, that's the trouble. And—well, lately, he's acted as if he felt alone. For a month he's been, for him, blue and discouraged like. Sort of don't care and what's the use—that way. I believe somethin's happened to him; he's had some big disappointment or somethin', somethin' that has upset him. You ain't heard anything around town, have you, Mary? Anythin' that would account for it? 'Specially durin' the last ten days or so?"

"No-o. . . . No, I—I haven't."

"I wish I knew what 'twas. He don't act no more like himself than Phoebe Carleton acts like your Crisp woman. I said to him t'other night: 'Dave,' says I, 'what's the matter with you? What makes you so down by the head lately? Nothin' worth while ails you, I hope?' He kind of laughed at me. 'Is anything worth while in this world, Skipper?' says he. 'Don't talk so foolish!' I hollered at him. 'You—president of the biggest bank in Ostable County—talkin' like that. Think of yourself and what you are in this town.' He laughed again. 'Is that your idea of what's worth while, Skipper?' was all he'd say. Now that ain't like Dave. No, it ain't. . . . Eh? Is that that Kohath hailin'? Yes 'tis. . . . You shut up!" raising his voice to a shout. "She'll come down when I tell her to go and not afore. And don't you come up here neither. . . . Stay where you are, Mary. I'll be through in another shake."

His clutch upon her skirt was tighter than ever and she could not, except by force, break away. He lay panting.

"Pour me another shot of that milk," he ordered. "Thanks. . . . Well, I'm about done—and high time, I guess you're thinkin'. Probably you can't understand why I'm tellin' you all this anyhow. Maybe I don't neither, but—well, it's this way: Somebody's got to help

Dave along after I'm gone and I didn't know but you might—try to, anyhow."

Her gaze had been fixed upon the rag carpet at her feet, but now she looked up and at him.

"I?" she said. "Why—why, Captain Cummings, what—what can I do?"

"Nothin' perhaps. Somethin' maybe. You say you figger Dave is a good friend of yours. Maybe you don't know just how good a friend he has been. When you wanted that job in the bank he got it for you. And it took some maneuverin'. And, even while you was there, there was schemin' to get you out and get Jim Henry or that Allie Jones in. There was talk at directors' meetin's, talk I guess likely you didn't know about. Dave told me a little of it. 'Why do you get yourself into hot water fightin' her battles?' I asked him. 'She don't really need the job and you may start 'em into puttin' you out of the presidency if you go against 'em too much.' His chin squared, I tell *you*. 'If she is put out 'twon't be till I've gone first,' he says, and you bet he meant it. Yes, ma'am, he thinks a sight of you. I believe now—honest I do—if you should ask him to get you that job back—which you won't, naturally, bein' rich—and he knew he'd be fired for doin' it, 'twouldn't stop him one minute. That's the kind of friend you've got in my grandson, Mary Brewster. There ain't a selfish bone in him. I know it—and you ought to."

She was silent. He fought for breath a moment longer and then went on.

"What I'd like to have you try to do," he said, "after I'm put on the scrap heap, is see if you can't make things easier for him. You're a big bug in Wapatomac, bigger than ever now that you've come in for your million or whatever 'tis. Your say will count for a lot in town. You stick by Dave and get some of your crowd to take up with him and—and kind of make of him. . . . Oh, not because they are high-toned, but because, outside of their money—and he's got as much of that as they have—they're his kind of folks now and maybe their takin' an interest—outside of business, I mean—would cheer him up a little mite, keep his mind off himself and how lonesome he is. Don't let 'em do any head-pattin' and 'good dog' stuff, I don't mean that. He wouldn't stand for it a minute. You just let 'em see you're his friend, that's all, and they'll chase after him because you do. . . . Could you do that, think?"

"I—I could try. I would if—oh, you don't understand!"

"That you're a Brewster and he's a Cummings, you mean?"

"No! Oh, no! Please don't think that. Indeed I don't mean any such thing."

"Hope you don't, 'cause that's just Snob Town pride and it's darned foolishness. I'm a pretty wise old bird, even if I am an old Cummings, and I tell you that's bein' stuck up over a secondhand nothin' and it ain't worth a hurrah in Tophet. Dave has risked losin' his other friends and the bank president's place he is—or would be if he was anybody else—so proud of, fightin' for you. And he'd do it again if he thought 'twould help you. Now it's no more 'n right for you to do what you can to help keep him happy, is it?"

"No. . . . No, I suppose it isn't. But—"

"Sshh! Don't argue with me. Maybe you can do

somethin'; I hope so. You just forget your name and his, and— Oh, well, there! you think it over, Mary. 'Tain't everybody I'd say all this to, but you've got sense, even if you are one of the grand panjandrums in Snob Town. I'm goin' to rely on you—long's I'm able to rely on anything. . . . Whew!" with a gasp of exhaustion, "I'm beat out. . . . Maybe you had better run along now. . . . And—and tell Kohath to tumble up here when you run afoul of him, will you?"

She hastened to the door. He spoke again.

"Good-by, Mary," he said, feebly.

The tone was significant and it caught her unawares.

"Oh, no, no!" she protested, trying desperately to smile. "It isn't good-by. I shall see you again soon."

He smiled, too. "Good-by," he said, again. "Much obliged to you. . . . Now don't you forget."

She hurried down to the sitting room. Mr. Briggs, who had been nervously pacing the floor, raced up the stairs when she delivered her message. As she opened the outer door she heard, from the sick room above, the voice of the indomitable Captain Barney issuing orders to his subordinate.

CHAPTER XXI

THE next day she learned, from Gallup's boy, that he was better; the New York doctor had helped him a great deal. And the day after that the reports were even more reassuring. Then they were not as good. And on the following Saturday Azure met her mistress at the breakfast table with a face even more solemn than hers had been of late.

"Wapatomac's been hit again," she announced, with a sigh. "Well, I've been expectin' it, but it's always a shock when it comes. Cap'n Barney Cummings was called about three o'clock this mornin', they say. Went out peaceful as a lamb."

Mary, too, had been expecting it, but she looked up with a gasp.

"Oh, no, Azure!" she exclaimed.

Azure nodded. "Yes, it's so," she said. "He's gone. Well, there was a time when I'd have been pretty nigh reconciled, if it ain't irreverent to say so. Nobody could get me riled up the way that old—"

"Azure! Stop!"

Azure lifted a hand. "*If* you'll permit me to please be allowed to finish what I was going to say," she suggested with dignity. "What I was *goin'* to say was that lately I'd sort of changed my mind about him. He was the one person, so far as I know—and except you and me, of course—who had the common sense to imagine that Ben Brewster might not know everything there was to know on this earth, and the spunk to stand right up in a meetin'house vestry and tell him so, too. . . . Yes, my opinion of Barney Cummings changed consider'ble after that. And *I* shall go to his funeral. I hope you will, Mary."

They both went. It was not the grand assemblage which had gathered to follow Benjamin Brewster to his select resting place inside the iron fence, but the Cummings lot in the New Church burying ground was crowded, and some of Wapatomac's "best people" were among those present. Mary saw Captain David standing by the grave. He looked white and drawn, and older than she had ever seen him look. She remembered Captain Barnabas's word to her: "It's goin' to be hard for Dave. . . . Dave's goin' to be lonesome." He looked lonely, indeed he did.

Azure left her after the ceremony was over, she had an errand at the store, and Mary walked home alone. Her thoughts, during that walk, were strange—very strange indeed for a Brewster. No stranger, however, than other thoughts which had filled her mind since her session with Captain Barney in the house on Nickerson's Hill. Where they were leading her she was not sure, nor did she attempt to follow them to any definite conclusion. She had been doing a great deal of self-analysis since that talk with the old man, or his talk to and with her. The results of the analysis were not flattering. If there had been any false pride left in her they would have wiped it out completely.

She had not, of course, made any further attempt to see David Cummings. The day of her call at his home he had written her a brief note. He was very sorry, he wrote, not to have been able to keep the appointment which Mrs. Crisp had made. His grandfather's serious illness had prevented—she understood that—and it would probably continue to prevent his seeing her or any one except Kohath and the doctors, as long as the crisis lasted. But, just as soon as he could, he would call at the Brewster house. And she must not be discouraged. He would be thinking hard, in his spare minutes he should think of but little else, and it was "a lot more than probable" that he could find a way of getting her back in the bank. It might take a little time, and perhaps some managing, but it could be done. In fact, he believed she might safely count on it. "And I do hope, Mary," he added, "that you have thought over that matter of your Boroda stock that I am holding here for you, and that you have changed your mind and will be sensible and take it back; I can sell it for you now at a good price and the money might come in handy to pay bills, if nothing else. It is yours, you know. I never considered it anybody's else's. We will talk about it again when I see you."

The note caused her to do some thinking, a great deal more. Oh, if she did not know what she knew! If she were as rich as people thought her—if she were not a pauper, a subject for charity—his charity! If it were not charity. But it was just that.

So when, on an evening in the latter part of the week following Captain Barnabas's funeral, he called at the house, her mind was still struggling in a fog of desperation. She dreaded seeing him and yet she must see him. It was Azure who had taken it upon herself to go to him begging another favor, a greater favor than ever, to pile the debt of obligation and charity still higher. If only Azure had minded her own business!

So when Mrs. Crisp climbed the stairs that evening to announce excitedly that Captain Dave had come and "I shouldn't be a mite surprised if he was going to say that the job was at the bank waiting for you, Mary, this minute," she was not received with cordiality.

"Very well," said Mary, coldly. "I'll be down in a few moments. I suppose I shall have to."

"Have to! My glory's land! Don't you *want* to?"

"No. . . . Oh, go away!" impatiently. "Go away, before I hurt your feelings. They deserve to be hurt but—oh, what *is* the use? You are impossible."

Cummings was occupying his usual seat on the davenport, beneath the portrait, when she came in. He rose to greet her. Even then, in the midst of her own confusion and embarrassment, she noticed how worn and tired he looked. And the dark suit and black tie he was wearing accentuated that look. Yet his tone was cheerful.

"Well, Mary," he began, "I guess you've been wonderin' whether or not I was ever goin' to get here, didn't you?"

She put out a hand. "Of course I haven't," she protested. "I didn't expect you to come. You shouldn't have come now. . . . Captain Cummings, I—I am so—so sorry for you. You got my note?"

She had written him a few words of sympathy. He nodded. "Yes," he said. "Thank you for writin'. I appreciated it a lot."

"It was the least I could do, and I couldn't write as I felt. Others have written, I suppose, many of them."

He nodded again. "Why, yes, they have," he replied. "You'd be surprised to know how many. Real nice letters, too. Sounded as if they meant what they said."

"I'm sure they did. Of course they did."

"Yes. Well, the poor old Skipper had lived here in town a long while. He knew about everybody. Most of 'em he'd squabbled with, one time or another, but those who wrote didn't seem to hold any grudge. Seemed as if they realized the old fellow said a lot of things he didn't really mean. It was fine of 'em to take the trouble to write. I've told a good many of 'em so."

It was plain that the letters pleased him. He seemed to be thinking of them, for he did not speak again for a moment. Then he looked up.

"Humph!" he observed, musingly, "I can't seem to believe even yet that he's really gone. I go home nights and open my mouth to give him a hail, and then it comes over me that he isn't there—and won't be. Queer feelin' 'tis, too."

"You miss him dreadfully, don't you?"

"Eh? Oh, yes, yes! Odd how I do miss him. Of course I realized he was an old man and likely to step off 'most any day, but—well, he was always so lively, you know. His mind, up to the very last night, was as sharp as ever."

Mary nodded now. "I know it was," she agreed.

"Eh? You know it? . . . Oh, yes, yes! He told me you made him a nice long call that day when you came to the house. He said he'd had a fine talk with you. It was good of you to stay there with him."

"He insisted on my staying. Then I was feeling that I shouldn't. Now I am very glad I did."

"Yes, so am I. Have a lot to say, did he? It wouldn't have been him if he hadn't."

"Yes, he talked a good deal. Mostly about you."

"No! . . . Well, that couldn't have been very interestin'."

"It was. . . . Captain Cummings, what will you do now?"

"Me? Oh, I don't know yet. Stay there with Kohath for the present, I suppose. Afterwards—well, I haven't thought much about it."

"Will you still live there in your house?"

"Doesn't seem much else for me to do. I don't like to think about it. Now is the time when I almost wish I could get back on salt water again. Aboard a vessel a man can find enough to keep his mind busy. He can keep tryin' to sail away from his troubles even if he doesn't make much headway."

"But you must have a great deal to occupy your mind. Your business—and the bank, and so many other things."

"Yes, I know. I am thankful for those, of course. They don't seem to take hold of me, just now, as I'd like to have 'em, but probably they will be a comfort by and by."

"Surely they will. . . . I only wish I had some—comforts, of the same sort."

He straightened on the davenport. "There!" he exclaimed in disgust. "What is the matter with me? I came here on purpose to talk about you and all I've done is mope over myself. Well, Mary, I've done a lot of thinkin' about you since—since I saw you last. Not as much as I would have done, of course, if—if things had been different, but a good deal. And I was glad when Mrs. Crisp came to tell me you would take back your job in the bank, if I—as soon as we can get it for you. She said—"

Mary interrupted. "I think you had better not tell me what she said," she declared, sharply. "I am sure she said practically everything she shouldn't. Captain Cummings, I want you to understand that I never gave her permission to go to you at all. She went on her own responsibility and I never, never should have permitted it if I had known."

He was surprised—and troubled.

"Oh!" he said. "Oh, is that so! Then you didn't—"

"Certainly I didn't. How *could* you think I would!"

"Hum! . . . Dear me! Why, Mary, that doesn't mean you—you won't take that place when I get it for you? It doesn't mean that, I hope?"

"It does. It does. . . . And how can you get it? In only one way, by risking your own position as president, by antagonizing your directors, by making more trouble for yourself. Just the same trouble—or worse—that you had before when you got it for me in the beginning and that you had on your hands all the time I was there. Oh, I know all about it. Your grandfather told me."

He ran his hand through his hair.

"Did the Skipper tell you that?" he cried, aghast. "Oh, pshaw! Tut, tut! What made him do it?"

"Because he should. I imagine he thought it high time I knew and realized a little of your sacrifice for me."

"Sacrifice! Why, that's nonsense. I wanted to do it. I had a fine time doin' it, I like that kind of a game. It's politics, sort of, and I've often thought I should have enjoyed playin' politics, real man-sized politics, if I could have spared the time for 'em. I had a first-class session while I was gettin' you into that bank and keepin' you there. And I'll have just as good a one puttin' you back again. You leave it to me, Mary."

"No."

"Don't say that. . . . Why, it'll take up my mind—help to, anyhow. Please now, be sensible."

"I mean to be. No, Captain Cummings, I shall not go back to the bank. We won't talk about that any more."

He rubbed his head, then his knees, opened his mouth to speak, and closed it again.

"Well," he said, at last, with a sigh, "we won't, if you say so, of course—not now, this minute. And yet 'twas the very thing I came to talk about—that and one other."

"And the other?"

"That wasn't so important, but pretty important, just the same. That was about your Boroda stock."

"Not mine. Yours."

"It never was mine. I never thought of it as mine for a single minute. Come now, don't let's have any debatin' about that. I'll sell it for you—"

"No. Not for me."

"Yes, yes, I will. Of course if you'd rather keep it—and it is bound to go higher—you could hang on. If you need a little ready money before you come back to the bank—or," hastily, "whatever you decide to do—I could let you have it just as well as not. That's a thing to think about, too. Maybe it's the best thing. . . . Don't shake your head—you mustn't."

She had shaken it, and now she was regarding him with a peculiar expression, apparently, of wonder.

"Captain David," she asked, impulsively, "don't you *ever* think of yourself? Of yourself—and no one else?"

"Eh? Surely I do. Think about myself seven-eighths of the time, I guess. But—"

"Wait! You never seem to think of yourself when you talk with me. All you think about then is what you can do to help me—what you can lend me—or give me. . . . That is all."

"Give you! This isn't givin'. I wouldn't dream of offerin' to give you anything. Is it likely I would?"

"But you do, whether you dream it or not. . . . Why," with a laugh that sounded quite as much like a sob, "that other evening, a week or more ago, when you came here, you were so bent upon giving me everything—money and help of any and all kinds—that you even offered to—to marry me. It was the only respectable way you could think of to provide my board and clothes with the rest, I suppose. Hasn't your generosity *any* limits?"

He was shocked and horrified. His face turned a brick red and he sprang to his feet.

"What!" he cried. "Why—why, Mary Brewster, do you—do you mean to say you thought I—I was beggin' you to marry me just because I—I— Oh, how can you talk that way!"

"That is what it sounded like. Surely it didn't sound like begging on your part. I was the beggar. I *am* a beggar—or pretty nearly that. And you pitied me and— Oh, well! you moved your limit of self-sacrifice on to the very end. I'm sure I don't see how you could have carried it further."

"Why, Mary Brewster!"

She was really sobbing now, her head resting upon her arms on the chair back.

"Is—is *that* the kind of fellow you think I am?" he demanded. "Is it?"

"You—you did it. . . . Yes, you did!"

"Did it? Asked you if you could think of—of marryin' me, you mean? Yes. Yes, I did."

"And you thought I— Oh, how could you humiliate me so! How *could* you!"

He took a step toward her and then stopped. He drew a long breath.

"I didn't mean to humiliate you, Mary," he said, his voice shaking. "God knows I didn't mean to do that."

"But you did. . . . Why? Oh, why?"

"Why? . . . Why, because— Ah hum, I guess I can see now how you might take it that way, but I didn't mean it so. I—well, ever since I got that letter from Denver, and went to Baxter and found out he'd just got the same information, all I could think of was you—and what was goin' to become of you. I knew Ben had been livin' high and spendin' lots of money. I guessed likely he owed a lot and, knowin' you, I was sure you'd be for payin' every cent, no matter what became of you afterwards. I was afraid you'd say just what you did say, that you must sell this house and go away from Wapatomac. I couldn't bear to face that somehow—and yet I was facin' it every minute, night and day. So—so I went crazy, I guess—or what amounts to that."

He paused. Her only answer was another stifled sob from behind the arms upon the chair back.

"I went crazy," he repeated. "I vowed: 'She shan't go. I can't have her go.' And I thought—I was foolish enough then to think most anything— 'Maybe if I put it to her just as a plain business deal, which for her it would be, she'd see it that way and—and let me take care of her the rest of her life.' I ought to have known better, of course, but—well, the idea of your leavin' here and my never seein' you any more was too much for me. . . . Oh, it wasn't anything new, my thinkin' about—about the other thing wasn't. Ever since you were a girl and I was a young fellow I've thought pretty much the same thing. Not as anything that could ever be, you know. Your people don't pick their husbands and wives from my crowd—not in this town, they don't. And I'm just a rough-spoken, uneducated fish dealer, and you're what you are—which is about everything I'm not. I never considered it as a sane notion, but I—I played with it, same as a child plays with the idea of Santa Claus after he's old enough to know there ain't any. . . . You were my idea of heaven, I guess; have been since I was a kid."

Again he paused. She was still weeping, but more quietly. Then, with a sigh, he went on with his confession.

"So I fooled myself into believin' I might say what I did to you and you'd understand. I forgot how humiliatin' it must sound to you—Dave Cummings, the clam peddler's boy, hintin' to Ben Brewster's daughter that maybe she might marry him. I forgot that. . . . Yes, maybe I forgot everything except myself—and what you meant to me. That was it, I guess. . . . Well, I'm sorry I hurt your feelin's. I might have known I would. But I should like to have you understand I didn't mean to."

He sighed again and picked up his cap from the table.

"I'll be goin' now," he said. "Havin' made a worse mess of things than ever, I'll move along. . . . If, after I'm gone, you can just forget the rest of it and remember that the Boroda stock is yours to sell or do what you want to with, I'll feel easier. And if you *should* change your mind about coming back to the bank—well, that will be arranged. You won't have to see much of me there, I'll arrange that, too. . . . Well, good night."

"Captain Cummings."

He turned. She had risen and was standing by the table. She was not looking at him, however, but at the tablecloth. The lampshade cast a shadow upon her face.

"Yes?" he asked. "What is it?"

"I—I have changed my mind."

"Eh? You have? About workin' in the bank? Good!"

"No, not that."

"Oh! I see. You mean about the Boroda. Well, that's fine—and just common sense!"

"Not about that, either. I mean about your other—business proposition. If—if you are *sure*—still sure—about that, I—I accept it."

He did not understand for an instant. Then he did.

"What!" he shouted. "What are you sayin'? You don't mean—?"

"Yes, I do. If you are still willing to marry me, I—I am willing, too."

"Mary! Mary Brewster! . . . But wait—wait! You say you're willing—just willin'."

Her gaze lifted from the tablecloth. She looked him straight in the face.

"What must I say?" she asked, with a little laugh. "That I am glad, proud, happy? Will that satisfy you, David? I hope so, because it is all true."

They were sitting together upon the davenport, the

portrait of great-grandfather Brewster glowering above them. If the soul of that salt-seasoned old Tory could be supposed to occasionally look through the painted eyes on the canvas it was no wonder he glowered—just then. They had talked of many things, past, present and future. Just now they were speaking of the recent past.

"Yes," confessed Mary, "I might have said yes if you had asked me sooner, if you had asked me in a respectable way, I mean. But perhaps I shouldn't—I am not sure. I have always liked you, you know; and I realize now that it was a lot more than liking. I love you, David Cummings. . . . No, wait! And always I relied upon you, and imposed my troubles on you—"

"No, no," hastily. "There wasn't any imposition about it. Good heavens, no!"

"I always considered you the very best man I knew and my surest friend. I have called you my sheet anchor ever so many times. That is exactly what you have been. . . . And always will be, won't you?"

"You bet!" with a contented chuckle.

"Yes. But I am not sure that I quite realized how good and unselfish and generous you were—"

"Sshh! Sshh! You make me feel wicked talkin' that way."

"I didn't realize all of it until your grandfather talked to me that afternoon in his room. He made me see how wonderful you were and how—how picayune and unworthy I was. Before that I had been—not much, I hope, but I'm afraid a little—vain of—of I don't know exactly what. He pointed out to me that I had nothing at all to be proud of and you had everything."

David shook his head. "The poor old Skipper was a

pretty sick man," he said, regretfully. "I don't suppose he was really what you might call responsible for what he did say."

"Indeed he was! Well, he made me see you as you were. Yes, and I think he made me understand a little of how I had come to feel toward you. Oh, Dave, if you hadn't been so absurd! If you hadn't—but there! how could any one accept a proposal of marriage labeled a business proposition?"

"Here! You aren't sorry already, are you?"

"Don't be silly. . . . What are you thinking of? Why do you look so—so frightened?"

"Eh? Did I look scared? Well, you can hardly blame me. It just came across me, for the fiftieth time or so—that I, Dave Cummings, was goin' to marry a Brewster. A Brewster, by George!"

"Hush! You make me ashamed. Captain Barnabas told me that being proud of what your father and grandfather had done or were was being stuck-up over a second-hand nothing—that is what he called it. And he was right. If ever you catch me boasting of my family you must remind me of—of Ben. That will be sufficient, I think. . . . There! Now we are not to mention family names again—ever."

David Cummings passed his fingers through his hair.

"Well, if we don't," he declared, with conviction, "we'll be the only ones. The rest of Wapatomac won't mention anything else, for one while."

Azure's impatience could scarcely be held in until the breakfast table was laid next morning. Then, as her mistress took her seat, it broke forth.

"Mary," she pleaded, with clasped hands; "Mary, you *must* tell me; I can't wait another minute. Are you goin' to let Dave Cummings get you that bookkeepin' place in his bank? . . . Oh, you are? *Ain't* you?"

Mary shook her head.

"No, Azure," she said. "I am not."

"You're not! Oh, my land of glory! Then. . . . Oh, what *are* you goin' to do, for mercy sakes?"

Mary unfolded her napkin.

"I am going to marry him," she said calmly. "Azure, will you pour the coffee, please?"

(1)

THE END

THE BEST OF RECENT FICTION

THE BEST OF RECENT FICTION

Brass. Charles G. Norris.
Bread. Charles G. Norris.
Breaking Point, The. Mary Roberts Rinehart.
Bright Shawl, The. Joseph Hergesheimer.
Bring Me His Ears. Clarence E. Mulford.
Broad Highway, The. Jeffery Farnol.
Broken Waters. Frank L. Packard.
Bronze Hand, The. Carolyn Wells.
Brood of the Witch Queen. Sax Rohmer.
Brown Study, The. Grace S. Richmond.
Buck Peters, Ranchman. Clarence E. Mulford.
Bush Rancher, The. Harold Bindloss.
Buster, The. William Patterson White.
Butterfly. Kathleen Norris.

Cabbages and Kings. O. Henry.
Callahans and the Murphys. Kathleen Norris.
Calling of Dan Matthews. Harold Bell Wright.
Cape Cod Stories. Joseph C. Lincoln.
Cap'n Dan's Daughter. Joseph C. Lincoln.
Cap'n Eri. Joseph C. Lincoln.
Cap'n Warren's Wards. Joseph C. Lincoln.
Cardigan. Robert W. Chambers.
Carnac's Folly. Sir Gilbert Parker.
Case and the Girl, The. Randall Parrish.
Case Book of Sherlock Holmes, The. A. Conan Doyle.
Cat's Eye, The. R. Austin Freeman.
Celestial City, The. Baroness Orczy.
Certain People of Importance. Kathleen Norris.
Cherry Square. Grace S. Richmond.
Child of the North. Ridgwell Cullum.
Child of the Wild. Edison Marshall.
Club of Masks, The. Allen Upward.
Cinema Murder, The. E. Phillips Oppenheim.
Clouded Pearl, The. Berta Ruck.
Clue of the New Pin, The. Edgar Wallace.
Coming of Cassidy, The. Clarence E. Mulford.
Coming of Cosgrove, The. Laurie Y. Erskine.
Comrades of Peril. Randall Parrish.
Conflict. Clarence Budington Kelland.
Conquest of Canaan, The. Booth Tarkington.
Constant Nymph, The. Margaret Kennedy.
Contraband. Clarence Budington Kelland.
Corsican Justice. J. G. Sarasin.
Cottonwood Gulch. Clarence E. Mulford.
Court of Inquiry, A. Grace S. Richmond.

THE BEST OF RECENT FICTION

Feast of the Lanterns, The. Louise Jordan Miln.
Feathers Left Around. Carolyn Wells.
Fire Brain. Max Brand.
Fire Tongue. Sax Rohmer.
Flaming Jewel, The. Robert W. Chambers.
Flowing Gold. Rex Beach.
Forbidden Door, The. Herman Landon.
Forbidden Trail, The. Honore Willsie.
Four Horsemen of the Apocalypse, The. Vicente Blasco Ibanez.
Four Million, The. O. Henry.
Foursquare. Grace S. Richmond.
Four Stragglers, The. Frank L. Packard.
Fourteenth Key, The. Carolyn Wells.
From Now On. Frank L. Packard.
Further Adventures of Jimmie Dale, The. Frank L. Packard
Furthest Fury, The. Carolyn Wells.

Gabriel Samara, Peacemaker. E. Phillips Oppenheim.
Galusha the Magnificent. Joseph C. Lincoln.
Gaspards of Pine Croft. Ralph Connor.
Gift of the Desert. Randall Parrish.
Glitter. Katharine Brush.
God's Country and the Woman. James Oliver Curwood.
Going Some. Rex Beach.
Gold Girl, The. James B. Hendryx.
Golden Beast, The. E. Phillips Oppenheim.
Golden Ladder, The. Major Rupert Hughes.
Golden Road, The. L. M. Montgomery.
Golden Scorpion, The. Sax Rohmer.
Goose Woman, The. Rex Beach.
Greater Love Hath No Man. Frank L. Packard.
Great Impersonation, The. E. Phillips Oppenheim.
Great Moment, The. Elinor Glyn.
Great Prince Shan, The. E. Phillips Oppenheim.
Green Archer, The. Edgar Wallace.
Green Dolphin, The. Sara Ware Bassett.
Green Eyes of Bast, The. Sax Rohmer.
Green Goddess, The. Louise Jordan Miln.
Green Timber. Harold Bindloss.
Grey Face. Sax Rohmer.
Gun Brand, The. James B. Hendryx.
Gun Gospel. W. D. Hoffman.

Hairy Arm, The. Edgar Wallace.
Hand of Fu-Manchu, The. Sax Rohmer.

THE BEST OF RECENT FICTION